THE BELL CURVE

KEITHA SMITH

Other books by Keitha Smith

Maybury Place

The Tender Conflict

The Journey

Non-fiction work :

Mothering Heights
by Keitha Smith & Susan Brereton

PUBLISHED BY JUDSON PRESS

THE BELL CURVE

The Bell Curve

Copyright © 2014 by Keitha Smith

First Printed : September 2014

Published by : Blue Sky Creative Ltd

Book layout and cover designed by Paul Smith

All characters in this book are fictitious. Any resemblance to actual persons, living or dead, is purely coincidental.

A catalogue record for this book is available from the National Library of New Zealand.

ISBN : 978-0-473-29429-8

For Paul, Lauren and Alex
who support me through
all my "Margaret" moments.

CHAPTER ONE

The arrivals area at Auckland International Airport heaved with disembarked passengers. Hundreds of people from the seven planes that had arrived within the past thirty minutes jostled with one another as they searched for a trolley then for their bags. Some battled for space to simply stand, others battled with small and tired children. Some long-haul passengers battled just to stay awake after having endured a trip from the other side of the world.

Just such a passenger was Sarah Bell. Her joy at being home and back on solid ground had begun to be eclipsed by a desire just to lie down and have a nice little nap. The flight from London to Singapore had been a test of endurance, the second flight from Singapore to Sydney a chore, and the last flight across the Tasman an assault on her fortitude.

Sarah's wait by the carousel for her three pieces of luggage felt interminable. Just when she started to lose hope that her bags had in fact the same transition across the face of the planet, they finally appeared. She heaved them onto her uncooperative trolley and made her way over to wait for the next available immigration officer.

As she stood there something happened. Nerves appeared. Her elation at being home evaporated. In its place came thoughts that had never before crossed her mind. Would her family be happy to see her? What if she got home and found it wasn't home any more? What if coming home turned out to be some sort of gigantic mistake?

Her turn finally came. The immigration officer looked fiercely at Sarah's passport, then equally fiercely at her face, then back to her passport again. Sarah swallowed. Hopefully she looked just as she did in her photo despite thirty six hours trapped in a flying tin can: long black hair, blue eyes, a face with a warm countenance even though smiling for passport pictures had become strictly forbidden.

He looked up and unexpectedly smiled. "You've been away a while, haven't you?" he said.

"Eighteen months," she said, returning his smile as best she could. "Somehow it suddenly seems much longer."

"Been in London, have you?"

Sarah nodded.

"My daughter's there at the moment," he said. "Probably having a whale of a time and up to all sorts of no good. I bet your family are looking forward to seeing you."

Sarah swallowed again. "I hope so."

Sensing her disquiet, the immigration man smiled again. "I'm sure they are," he said kindly, as he handed over her passport. "Good luck, then. Welcome home."

"Thanks."

Giving her trolley an extra push to get it going in the right direction, Sarah made her way through customs, having nothing to declare except a stomach full of butterflies. She made her way down the short corridor to the arrivals hall to be confronted with a sea of expectant faces. She paused, her way barred by a group of Samoans welcoming home what looked to be a long lost relative, thus giving her the opportunity to scan the faces all around her.

At last she saw them. They were watching her, waiting for her to spot them. When their eyes met, their faces lit up with welcoming smiles. They waved. Sarah smiled and waved back and her butterflies flew away.

From a small distance Sarah observed them, still trapped where she was by the protracted greetings of the family in front of her. As she looked at her family she could see that some things had changed, and others had not. The most noticeable change was in her brother, who had shot up in height and wasn't the Todd she had said good-bye to eighteen months before. He was rapidly gaining in height on their mother. Although his face had yet to obtain maturity, Sarah could see that he was growing up nonetheless.

Beside him stood her mother. Sarah noticed at once that she had lost weight. Quite a bit of weight. It made her mother's face seem drawn. She wore a troubling expression that Sarah could not read. Although her mother smiled, Sarah felt as though something prevented that smile from reaching her eyes. Sarah wondered what was up.

Behind them stood Sarah's father. He seemed completely the same, his open face beaming with a warm smile, his hair blown by the wind, sticking out every which way. Big, solid, dependable dad.

Finally, the family in front of her realized they were blocking the way for more than just Sarah. The crowd parted to let people through. Sarah gave the trolley another firm shove and made her way forward.

Her father came striding up and enveloped her in one of his famous bear hugs. His hands, rough from years of using tiling grout, grazed her arms.

"You're home," he said, as though that made everything all right with the world.

"Hi Dad," Sarah said.

When her mother embraced her, Sarah could feel how thin she'd become. She wore an old dress - one that her mother reserved for special occasions - but it hung far more limply on her frame than in the past.

"Welcome back," Margaret said.

"Thanks, Mum."

Sarah turned to Todd. She said, "I pictured ruffling your hair like I used to. I don't suppose you'd put up with that any more, would you?"

He grinned. "Doubt it," he said, but he gave her a brief hug anyway.

"No school today? Or did you get let out early?"

"Study leave," Todd said. "Exams start Monday."

Dad indicated her trolley. "Is this all your gear?"

Sarah nodded.

"I thought you'd have accumulated lots more stuff than this," Margaret said.

"There didn't seem much point. I knew I'd only have to lug it home." Looking at Todd, she said, "Don't worry. I still managed to fit in presents."

Todd grinned again. "I knew you wouldn't let me down."

Jim said, "The car's out this way."

"Watch that trolley. It's got a mind of its own. By the way, where's Nan?"

Margaret looked away on the pretext of watching the traffic as they negotiated the car park. "She's at home. We thought there wouldn't be enough room for all of us and your stuff in the car."

"She's looking forward to seeing you, though," Jim said.

"She'll be waiting for us?"

"I expect so," Margaret said.

"Unless she's gone next door to visit her boyfriend," Jim said with a smile.

As they arrived at the car and started loading the luggage in the boot a confused Sarah said, "Nan's got a boyfriend?"

Todd sniggered. "Yeah," he said. "Mr. Alexander."

"Who's he?"

Margaret said, "His name's Michael Alexander. He's our new next-door neighbor. Well, almost new. He's lived there about twelve months now."

"What happened to the Aldridges?" Sarah asked, buckling herself in the back seat beside Todd.

"They moved to Australia about a year ago," Margaret said. "Retired on the Sunshine Coast. Didn't I write to tell you?"

"No."

From the front seat Margaret waved a lofty hand. "Oh well," she said, "things have been rather busy. I expect there's a whole range of stuff I forgot to mention."

Sarah, having seen her mother and observed the change, thought perhaps that comment might be something of an understatement.

"By the way," Margaret continued, "Joanna's sorry she couldn't come and meet you either. With Connor being so little it was just too difficult. He wants to be fed every five minutes from what she said. I'm afraid the airline was rather remiss in scheduling its flights. The timing was all wrong for Joanna."

Sarah smiled to herself, thinking how typical of her sister that sounded.

"I hardly expected to see her. I knew she'd been busy with the children."

As her mother continued to give an update on people they knew, Sarah looked out the window. All the sights were so familiar: the sprawling suburbs, the dormant volcanoes on which Auckland sat perched, the sparkling waters of the harbor. As she listened to her mother any lingering doubt about her decision evaporated away. In fact, sitting there with her father steering the car through the traffic, with her mother burbling on and her young brother squirming beside her in the back seat, part of Sarah felt she'd never been away.

And when, at last, her father pulled the car into Victoria Road, and then into the driveway beside the familiar white house with its smart grey roof, Sarah found that - for now at least - she did indeed feel like she was home. Now all she had to do was see where else this journey home would take her.

Sarah experienced a certain sense of *déjà vu* when she woke the following morning to find herself back in her old bedroom, back in her own bed. The trappings of her room were a poignant reminder of things from her childhood. Most memories good, a few bad. Some were probably distorted by childhood misconceptions. Everything seemed very small and unreal. And yet, when she thought about it, maybe it was the whole eighteen months she'd just been away that might not have been real. Perhaps it had merely been a dream and, like all the best dreams, had now concluded.

Looking around her at the faded purple walls - she remembered her father swearing as he painted them - at shelves crammed with dusty ornaments, dolls, books and treasures, it struck Sarah just how juvenile the room had remained. Why had she not noticed that before? Maybe, before, her surroundings had not mattered. They were simply the unimportant backdrops to her life. Well home she might be, but these trappings of youth were not something she needed any more. She might not have the slightest clue about what the future had in store for her but Sarah knew unequivocally that this room, and the things in it, would play no major part.

Sarah had a fair idea it was quite late, that she'd slept and slept her jet lag away. Now, though, she felt refreshed. Throwing back the covers, Sarah rummaged in her suitcase and found her toilet bag and took herself off to the bathroom. Once refreshed and dressed she made her way downstairs to see how the land lay.

She found her mother in the kitchen, her hands in a sink full of dirty dishes, muttering to herself and looking frustrated. Of Todd or Nan there was no sign.

"Hi Mum," Sarah said.

"Morning, lazy bones," Margaret replied. "I'd begun to think you were going to sleep the whole day."

Sarah smiled. "Almost. Dad's mowing the lawn, I hear."

Margaret sighed. "He wanted to do it before you came home but he's been flat tack with this large tiling job he's got on. He kept going on about wanting to get everything spick and span, but did he get around to most things he said he would? Of course not. So he had a bee in his bonnet about getting the lawn done this morning even though I said it would probably wake you up and that you wouldn't thank him for it."

"I don't think anything would have woken me today before I was ready."

"Hmm. Even Todd managed to get up before you. I'm beginning to think wonders will never cease to amaze."

"Where is he?"

"Gone to see Tom and Gerry. He slunk off about half an hour ago."

"Is Todd still friends with those two? How are they?"

"Fine. Growing. You'll see for yourself sooner or later I expect. Do you want breakfast?"

"Since it's eleven o'clock breakfast seems a bit unnecessary. Maybe I'll just have some coffee. Save myself for lunch."

Her mother straightened, lifting her hands out of the sink to draw off her marigold gloves. She slung them down on the bench.

"Don't get too excited about it. There'll only be sandwiches."

"I don't care. You don't have to spoil me. I'm used to making do."

Margaret gave Sarah a penetrating look, as though trying to discern every nutritionally poor meal Sarah might have consumed during the past year and a half. Sarah waited for some comment. In the end Margaret merely pursed her lips and said, "Joanna called."

"Oh?"

"She wanted to know if you had made it home safely. It seems she and Brett have to come over this way this afternoon so they thought they might pop in and say hello. Of course I could tell she was hinting at being invited so in the end I suggested they come for afternoon tea."

"Great. Will they have the children with them?"

Margaret nodded. "I think Joanna hopes Connor will sleep in the car."

"What about Isabella?"

"Oh she's past sleeping. She's three and a half now," her mother said, as though this would explain the mystery of childhood sleeping patterns.

"Thanks for inviting them, Mum. Do you want me to do anything toward it? Afternoon tea, I mean."

"No, no. There are some biscuits in the pantry. They'll do. But I have got a lot to get through today," she said, indicating the kitchen table which positively groaned under the weight of paperwork.

"Anything I can help with?"

Her mother looked irritated. "It would all take too long to explain. Besides, you've only just got home. You'd hardly want to launch into a whole pile of work."

"I don't mind."

"Don't be silly. Mind you, there is one thing you could do for me. You couldn't go and check on Mum for me? I haven't had a chance so far today."

"Sure. I'll go and have that cup of coffee with Nan then. I'll leave you to it."

After making her way across the back yard and waving cheerily to her father just as he trundled the mower around to do the front lawn, Sarah came to the little door at the side of the garage that led into the flat. Here her grandmother had lived since selling the family home after the death of Sarah's grandfather, Jack, five years ago. She knocked.

"Oh my dear," Pearl enthused, when she saw Sarah standing at the door. "What a treat to see you."

"Hi, Nan," Sarah said, putting her arms around her grandmother.

She pulled back slightly to look at her grandmother better, looking as she had done at everyone for signs of change. Yesterday, with all the bustle and confusion of getting home, of finding presents and settling in, she hadn't really had a chance to study her grandmother. Now she saw little outward sign of change. Pearl Hamilton still had the same serenity she had always had, the same wrinkled face portraying more wisdom than old age; the same grey hair neatly curled and styled, the archetypal picture of grandmother-hood.

Perhaps, though, beyond the veneer, there were alterations. Her beautiful blue eyes had lost a little of their sparkle. There seemed to be an air of edginess about her grandmother, and Pearl's movements were less free than they once had been. Still, for the grand old age of almost eighty, things could certainly be a lot worse.

"Sorry I didn't get much of a chance to talk to you yesterday," Sarah said. "Things were pretty crazy, weren't they?"

"Well, well, never mind, dear. You're home now, aren't you? And how lovely of you to come to see me this morning. I thought you would have had far more important things to do than come and see your old Nan."

"Nothing that can't wait. Sorry you couldn't come out to the airport yesterday."

A strange look flitted across Pearl's features, but she said, "It doesn't matter. Water under the bridge. Besides, I did have a nice cup of tea with Michael from next door."

"Yes, Mum said you'd made friends with the new neighbor."

With the old sparkle gleaming in her eye, Pearl said, "He's a lovely man. Now, speaking of cups of tea, do you want one?"

"Have you any coffee?"

Peering into one of the small cupboards in the kitchen, Pearl said, "I think there might be some in here somewhere. I'm afraid I don't drink it. These days I get precious little sleep as it is without filling myself up on caffeine. Ah, here it is. It's only instant I'm afraid. None of all these newfangled blends and brews.”

“Not to worry,”

Sarah watched her grandmother set to work in the little kitchenette. While she waited she idly picked up an old photo in a heavy frame that sat on one of the high shelves, a shot of her aunt Sheila, her mother and her mother’s twin brother, David, aged about six or seven, all dressed in outmoded swimwear. Sarah replaced the frame and wondered if she should ask any more questions about this Mr. Alexander from next door or whether such enquiries would be considered an invasion of privacy. It still seemed astounding to think of her grandmother interested in another man. From what Sarah knew, her grandmother had loved Jack Hamilton so entirely it seemed inconceivable that someone would ever come along who could ever hold a candle to him. Sarah could only conclude he must be a very special man indeed.

With the tea and coffee made, the pair sat down in the little lounge area to drink it.

Sarah said, “How are Uncle Ernest and Uncle Charles?”

Her grandmother laughed. Her brothers had always been the source of great amusement to her, even though Ernest was five years younger than her, and Charles ten.

“They’re both very well. Ernest has recently moved to a retirement village. Lambton Park, it’s called. Probably a dire place, but he seems to like it.”

“You haven’t been?”

Pearl shook her head. “It’s hard to get out these days. I don’t enjoy the bus like I used to. Your mother is pretty busy these days.”

“So I noticed.”

“Hmm. Anyway, like I said, he thinks the place is wonderful, but mostly because of a friendship he’s struck up with one of the other inmates. Rosa’s her name. She’s Spanish, apparently. Can you believe it?”

Sarah could not. Uncle Ernest had always seemed to her an intense, driven man, not given to the folly of romance. His own marriage to Aunt Priscilla had by all accounts been conducted with the rigidity of a transport schedule until she had taken Bus 316 to the afterlife. It seemed incredible to think of Uncle Ernest being in love. But love, it seemed, was in the air.

“And Uncle Charles?”

“Dear boy. He’s very well. Still in his same old house. He seems to manage fine on his own. Mind you, with Mary having been dead fifteen years, he’s had plenty of time to get used to it.”

“And there’s no one on the horizon he’s interested in?”

"Not that I know of. Not that either of my brothers tell me everything about their lives. Perhaps I'll always be the interfering big sister in their eyes. No, I think Charles is quite content with his life, pottering about the house, seeing friends, making those little model boats. Nothing strenuous. He'll never change from being the contented little boy he always was."

"And you, Nan? How are you, really?"

"I can't complain too much. I do still miss my old house and my friends, such that are left. With old age we all seem to have dispersed, one way or another."

Sarah sighed with compassion. "Don't you see your old friends much?"

"Well, it's like I said. It's hard to get out much any more. Like a lot of women of my generation, we either never learnt to drive or simply find the traffic these days too terrifying. Of course when I still lived at home I was forever bumping into people I knew, but not around here. It's a different area completely."

"But you must get out, though?"

"Oh, yes," Pearl said lightly, as though trying to cover up the fact that she'd said too much. "Your mother takes me out fairly regularly if she can spare the time. And those brothers of mine tend to call in if they're passing."

Sarah thought it sounded pretty narrow. She didn't like to think of her grandmother cooped up for days on end in this rabbit hutch with no one to keep her company. She knew first hand how lonely it could be to walk down a road and not see a soul you knew. In London, if it hadn't been for the comforting and ever present company of Cassie, she might have discovered the true meaning of isolation and loneliness.

"Mum must come to see you every day, though," Sarah said.

Pearl looked away. "She tries to, but some days it's difficult for her. There seem to be so many demands on her time these days."

Sarah pictured the piles of paperwork on the kitchen table, papers that looked circulated around rather than dealt with. "So I gathered," she said.

"At least I'm comfortable here," Pearl said. "Better here than some dreary rest home."

"It's not the same as it once was, though, is it?"

"Well, that's one thing about life, isn't it? Nothing ever stays the same. Just look at all the technological advancements that have been made in my generation alone. It's incredible. And of course old age, like all things, means change or adaptation. At least I haven't entirely lost my independence." She put her teacup down with a rattle, and offered the plate of biscuits to Sarah again. "But that's enough about me," she said. "What about you? I pictured it still being quite some time before you returned to us."

Sarah gave a nonchalant shrug. "I'd had my fill," she said, hoping she sounded convincing. She thought of her failed romance with Jeremy but quickly pushed the images from her mind. "But Cassie hadn't, which is why I came home alone. She still wants to see more of the sights we had on our list when we went across. She told me off for coming home before I'd seen Scotland but I have no regrets. Scotland's been there a long time. I suspect it will still be there if I ever travel north again."

Pearl nodded, apparently satisfied by the brief explanation. "Tell me all about what you're thinking of doing now you're home."

Sarah declined another biscuit. "I suppose my first priority is to find a job. I tended to spend most of what I earned in the U.K. on travel and sight-seeing, so I haven't exactly come home with a nest egg. I've a small amount to tide me over, maybe enough to put a deposit on a car, but not much else."

"Of course, dear. You'll look for something in the landscape design field again?"

Sarah nodded. "I do enjoy it. In fact I loved the job I had in London. I learnt a lot. I might have even taught them a thing or two as well."

"But you didn't want to stay?"

Now it was Sarah's turn to look away. "No," she said softly. "In my heart of hearts I knew the time had come to return home."

"And now that you're here, at home with your family, do you think this is where you'll stay?"

"Honestly? No. I'll stay for a while, of course. I'd feel bad if I moved out right away. But sooner or later I'll have to find my own place."

"Indeed. Independence is a very important thing. More important than you realize until you don't have it any more."

Sarah couldn't help wondering if she referred to Sarah or to herself but said nothing. She got the impression her grandmother had said all she was likely to say on that subject for the time being.

"I thought I'd just take things one day at a time," Sarah said.

"Very wise. After all, none of us know what's around the corner, do we?"

Sarah laughed, trying to lighten the mood. "Well, I know one thing that's around the corner," she said, "and that's Joanna. She and Brett and the children are coming by this afternoon to inspect me at two thirty. Mum said to tell you to come over. After all, they'll want to see you, too."

"All right," Pearl said, lifting her chin imperceptibly. "I will."

When Joanna arrived with her family she swept inside in the same dramatic way she'd been doing for her entire life. Her every movement seemed designed for the benefit of some unseen audience. She kissed her mother with a flourish. Judging from the brief look of surprise that flitted across Margaret's features, Sarah could only suppose such an action to be less about filial tenderness and more about a show of one-upmanship. Joanna had always been fiercely competitive, especially where Sarah was concerned. Sarah saw no reason for things to have changed substantively in eighteen months of separation.

Brett trailed behind her, carrying Connor in a car seat. Connor wailed plaintively for attention but at present was being roundly ignored by both his parents. His little face was suffused with scarlet as though he had been demanding assistance for some time. Isabella further aggravated his agonies. She stood beside her father and regularly dug her fingers into her new brother's cheeks. Whether she was trying to placate or provoke him, Sarah could not tell. Both the children, she noted, were clothed in the latest designer gear, dressed to the nines in the smartest outfits imaginable.

Brett held the car seat capsule as though it was a great imposition. His expression clearly indicated his antipathy for crying babies, perhaps even for children in general. He made no attempt to distract or discipline Isabella from her current course of action. He remained as he had always seemed to Sarah, a man not impressed with the inconveniences of life. His proud face bore a look of disdain, his clothes were immaculate, his teeth perfect, not a blond hair on his head out of place.

"I thought we were never going to get here," Joanna gushed. "I'm sure Beethoven had less trouble composing his ninth symphony than I've had getting these two ready to go out. Now then, where's Sarah? Ah, there you are," she said, as though she was barely able to distinguish her sister from the wallpaper.

She gave Sarah the slightest hug and a pretend kiss on the cheek. "Welcome home. So, let's look at you. You haven't put on a bit of weight while you were away have you? And you seem a little pale and drawn. Perhaps it's just as well you've come home now, to get a bit of sun."

Sarah laughed, refusing to be needled. "Hello, Joanna. You're looking just the same, I see."

In fact apart from the fact that her sister had maybe added a pound or two over the course of her last pregnancy, she did indeed look and act the same. Her hair, the same mousey color as that of their mother, had a permanent look of lacquer about it, as though someone had once styled and set it with some immutable bonding substance that now refused to change. Her expression travelled the gamut from haughty to petulant and back again in record time. She was the only one of the wider immediate family not to have inherited the blue eyes that came from her grandmother's side of the family. She had instead the brown eyes of Jim Bell, eyes that in Joanna's case took in and assessed absolutely everything only to find most things wanting.

"I do try," she preened. "Of course now that I've had children it's murder to keep one's figure in shape. You don't know how lucky you are not to have gone down that road, Sarah."

Margaret said, "Speaking of children, perhaps we should get these two youngsters out of the doorway. Let's all go through to the lounge. The rest of the family's waiting for us in there. What's wrong with Connor?"

"Lord only knows," Joanna said airily. "He seems to wail at the slightest thing."

"Hi, Sarah," Brett said, as they made their way to the lounge.

"Hi. How are you?"

"Oh, everything's on the up and up," he replied.

When they entered the lounge there was another round of false greetings as Joanna hugged and kissed her father and Todd and Pearl. Todd wiped his cheek with the back of his hand in case he had been accidentally contaminated by lipstick.

No one made much attempt to greet Brett, especially Pearl who'd never been able to disguise the fact that she did not particularly like Joanna's choice of life partner. Brett's interest lay in three things: in money, in status, and in himself. Since such an ethos was an antithesis of much of what had driven Pearl and her generation she found him difficult to like. To her he would always be little more than a jumped up car sales man, even if the cars were the top of the range.

Margaret, not able to bear it a moment longer, took the car seat off Brett and released little Connor from his cocoon. As soon as she lifted him out and took him in her arms he ceased wailing and began to look about him with interest. Sarah could see him trying to make sense of a world he could not yet see clearly.

"What a little faker," Joanna said, settling herself on the sofa furthest away from him. "You've got no idea how demanding he is. I've been trying to get him into some sort of established routine, four hourly bottles and regular sleeps, but do you think he'll have a bar of it?"

Margaret said, "He seems quite windy to me. Maybe he's in a bit of discomfort."

Joanna made a face. "Maybe all he wants to do is torment his poor mother." She turned to Sarah and said, "Of course I wouldn't be able to explain the rigors of it all to you, being that the world of motherhood is so foreign to you. I don't suppose you had much contact with children at all, swanning about in London like an international jet-setter."

Sarah thought about the bleak, cold London she had just left behind, of her poky flat and the long hours she had worked with Pete and April, and wondered just where Joanna had got her notions from. But then, Joanna had eschewed any ideas of going overseas. She had met Brett through her job, eyed him up as a catch with potential. The rest was history. She had certainly enjoyed lauding all the hype and excitement of a wedding over Sarah at the time. She'd paraded it all as the only course of action for any sensible person.

"You know us jet-setters," Sarah said. "If we do bother having children at all, it's usually only as a status symbol."

Joanna scowled.

Jim, trying to avoid being bruised by Isabella who had begun to use him as a trampoline, said, "How's business, Brett?"

Brett, unaware of everyone's disinterest said, "Actually, things are booming. The way the economy is going at the moment, everyone who's anyone wants to update their car. Of course for some people it's a sound investment, for others it's a way of reducing their tax liability, and for others it's all a matter of public perception. After all, the right car is just as important as the right job and the right house."

"Is it?" Pearl asked faintly.

Brett ignored her.

Wincing over another vicious blow from his energetic granddaughter, Jim said, "I wasn't aware of the economy doing that well. If you ask most people I know, things are the same as they have been for the last six months, and that's tight."

"You have to understand how these things work," Brett said in his most patronizing tone, speaking to his father-in-law as though he were a small child. "Wealth is always generated in an inverse pattern. The big companies, corporations and businessmen make the money. They then have more money to spend on wages and expenses, and eventually the small man on the street begins to feel the benefits. They call it the 'trickle down effect'."

"Trickle's right," Jim said, putting Isabella off his knee and onto the couch beside him. She immediately stood up and started using that like a trampoline as well.

"When's afternoon tea?" Todd asked.

"Soon," said Margaret. "I thought Sarah and Joanna would like the opportunity to catch up with each other first."

Joanna and Sarah looked at each other across the gulf of their lifestyles and Jim made imploring faces at Margaret.

"Oh, all right," she conceded, cross with having her plan thwarted. She handed the baby to his reluctant father.

As Margaret left the room, Pearl stood up abruptly. Sarah could tell she had had quite enough of Joanna and Brett, clearly appalled that neither of them had the good sense to discipline their daughter, who practically bounced off the walls.

"Perhaps," she said, "Isabella might like to come out to the garden with me?"

"Yeah," yelled Isabella. "I want to. I want to."

Joanna said, "All right, then. Off you go."

Todd said, "I'm coming too."

As soon as they were out of the room Todd found some excuse not to go out to the garden after all. Torn between the choice of staying in a room full of grown ups or going out to the garden with his elderly grandmother and hyperactive niece, the musty confines of his messy bedroom and play station would win hands down every time.

"Well then, dear," Pearl said, as she opened the back door and shepherded Isabella outside, "where shall we sit?"

"I don't know," Isabella replied.

"What about over here on the park bench, under this nice tree?"

"All right."

"You'll have to try to sit nicely. Your great grandmother's an old lady now and I can't cope with too much excitement. Besides, you're nearly four now, aren't you? That's plenty old enough for sitting still."

Isabella looked at Pearl with awe. "Is it?" she asked. "Is it really?"

"Of course. You just think. You're at kindergarten and you're a big sister now. You have to be at least a bit grown up to be a big sister."

"Really?"

"Really."

"All right," Isabella said, hoisting herself up on the park bench.

She sat there in her beautiful pink dress, her delicate pink shoes with silver buckles dangling in the air, her hair tied up with ribbons in bunches on either side of her head. Her little face frowned with concentration as she tried her best to sit nicely.

"Perfect," Pearl told her with a smile. "Very clever. Now, tell me, what's it like to go to kindergarten?"

"I like it. It's fun."

"Really? What makes it fun?"

"Lots of things. There's a cool house in the corner with little beds and dolls and a kitchen and dress ups and bags and books and toys and prams."

"Goodness. All that in one corner?"

Isabella nodded gravely.

"What else?"

Isabella thought about it. "You can do painting and stuff."

"Stuff?"

"Oh, you know. Play dough. Making things."

"And do you do that?"

"Not really. I like the dolls."

"Perhaps the dolls remind you of Connor. How do you like being a big sister?"

Isabella screwed up her little nose. "I don't know."

"No? Surely you must have some idea. What do you think of your little brother?"

"He's a bit yucky. He cries too much, and sometimes he makes the most awful smells. Pooh! It's very gusting."

"Disgusting? He's only a baby. He'll soon grow and learn."

"He's not much fun," Isabella said. "I try to talk to him but he doesn't really listen. I want him to play with me, otherwise maybe he should go back."

"Go back where?"

Isabella began swinging her feet back and forth.

"Back to the cabbage patch. Daddy said that's where he came from."

"Hmm. I'm not sure Daddy really explained that too well. You see, Connor can't go back. He's part of your family now, just like I'm a part of your family."

Isabella looked up at Pearl. "Are you part of my family?"

"Of course I am, dear. I'm your mother's grandmother, just like Gran is your grandmother."

"Gosh. You must be pretty old."

Pearl laughed. "Yes pretty old, although it isn't really very polite to say so."

"Oh."

"But since you are my very special and only great granddaughter, I think I can make an exception for you and let you in on a little secret. In one month's time, on Christmas Day, I'm going to be eighty years old."

Isabella's mouth went like an O. She might not have any idea of just how old that was, but the look on her face indicated her awe.

"And," said Pearl, "I'm having a party. You and Mummy and Daddy and Connor will probably come too."

"On Christmas Day?"

"Yes. All the family's being invited."

"Even me?"

"Even you."

Isabella looked momentarily downcast. "What about Santa?"

"He would have come and gone by then. Besides, he'll be too busy to come."

In a small voice she said, "Does Connor really have to be 'vited as well?"

"Yes, dear. He's family too, remember?"

Isabella sagged even further. "Nan?" she said at last.

"What is it, dear?"

Her face fell. "I wet my pants."

Pearl stifled a sigh. "Don't worry," she replied. "It happens to me all the time."

For Sarah, Monday morning arrived unheralded. Although she had no compulsion to get up early, she realized, upon waking, her jetlag had disappeared. Not only that, she felt quite energetic.

Since it was early, Sarah decided to take a walk. She set off for the little block of shops about twenty brisk minutes' walk away. She would maybe buy some milk and a newspaper, see how things had changed in her absence.

Stepping outside, she found the morning still cool. The air resonated with the distant sound of traffic as commuters made their way to work. She turned left out of the driveway, passed the house next door - home of the hitherto unseen Mr. Alexander. She noticed with interest that he had been busy. He'd evidently been trying to improve the property which had been somewhat neglected by the Aldridges in latter years. She could see his Subaru parked in the driveway.

At the end of Victoria Road she turned left again onto the main road. There were plenty of people about - the odd kid in school uniform, women in business suits trotting to the bus stop with their high heels clicking as they walked. The occasional jogger dashed past. She kept an eye out for the ever-present danger of being run over by some businessman reversing carelessly out of his driveway to join the rush hour crush.

Sarah looked about her with interest. She absorbed all the sights, sounds and smells almost in the same way she had observed some of the sights of Europe. It seemed wonderful to be back, to see all the different styles of houses as she walked by, to peer into people's gardens and see plants and flowers she had not seen for quite some time. Above all, it felt good to be back where she felt she belonged.

Sarah found the shops all just as they were when she left. Although the man in the little dairy wasn't familiar, he smiled jovially as she handed over her money for the milk and paper. She had no idea if they actually needed either milk or a paper but it made her feel as though she was at least making some small contribution, and more importantly, some effort.

Returning home, she found that both Mr. Alexander's car and her father's van had disappeared. It intrigued her to wonder where someone of Mr. Alexander's advanced years would feel the need to go so early. Letting herself in through the kitchen door, Sarah found her mother anchored at the kitchen table with vast mounds of paperwork in front of her.

"Morning Mum," she said.

Her mother swiveled in her chair to greet Sarah.

"I thought I heard you get up. I just assumed you'd gone back to bed."

"I fancied a bit of a constitutional. I think it must have been some sort of delayed reaction to being cooped up on the plane for so long. I see Dad's gone."

"Yes. He thinks he's about to be asked to start a sizeable new job any day now. They keep fobbing him off with excuses about when they actually want him to start so I think he figures he'll need be ready to go at a moment's notice. These days people expect not only service with a smile, but a prompt, quick, cheap, high quality job as well. If you aren't prepared to come to the party with all of these demands they simply go somewhere else."

"That's tough. He has been doing all right, though, hasn't he?"

"Enough to keep food on the table, pay the mortgage installment, and fork over the remainder to the tax man."

"Oh, well," Sarah said with a smile, "at least you've got the trickle down effect to look forward to."

Margaret made a disparaging sound. "What a load of rubbish," she said. "It wouldn't surprise me if he'd learnt that at some damned fool seminar. He's always going to them."

"That wouldn't surprise me either. One of those on how to get rich, or how to get richer than rich, I suppose."

"Ironically, the only people that get rich after attending those sorts of seminars are the people who run them. They may as well say, 'Come in sucker' as far as I'm concerned."

Sarah shrugged. "Each to their own, I guess. Anyway, I bought some milk and a newspaper. Thought I'd make some inroads into helping the local economy."

"You needn't have, although goodness knows, extra milk always comes in handy around this place. Between Todd and your father, they practically eat us out of house and home."

"Todd always was a bit of a locust, as I recall. Want a cup of tea?"

"Yes, please. As for Todd, believe me, he hasn't improved," her mother said. "We don't normally get the paper, though, so you didn't really need to buy one. Nobody has time to read it."

"I thought I might start looking for a job," Sarah said. "Scour the 'Situations Vacant' for anything interesting."

"But you've only just got home," Margaret said, her expression one of surprise.

"I have to start paying my way."

"Nonsense. What's the hurry? Why not wait until after Christmas? This time of year's not that great for looking for work anyway. People often don't start hiring until after New Year."

"What savings I brought home aren't going to last long, especially if I want to buy a car. If I'm not earning I'm hardly going to be able to pay board, am I?"

Margaret looked displeased. "You can keep your money. Your father and I are just happy to have you home again."

Sarah sat down to wait for the kettle to boil. Todd, still clad in his pajamas, burst into the room, his face suffused with panic.

"Mum, have you seen my school uniform shorts?"

Margaret shrugged. "Aren't they in your wardrobe?"

"I'd hardly be asking you if they were."

"What about in the washing basket?"

"Nup."

"Did you put them in to be washed? If you put them where they're supposed to go, I do at least try to get things washed and ironed."

Todd muttered something incomprehensible and left the room.

After he departed Sarah made the tea and sat down with her mother to enjoy it. Her mother, she noticed, kept making small sighing noises as she picked up various pieces of paper, frustrated noises as she picked up others. Rather than disturb her, Sarah picked up the newspaper and started reading.

Moments later Todd burst back in the room. His eyes were wild. He thrust out his grey school shorts, which were badly creased and had clearly been rolled up into a ball and carelessly shoved somewhere for the duration of the weekend.

"Look," he said. "How am I supposed to wear these?"

"I guess you're going to have to put one leg in one hole and one leg in the other," Margaret said.

"But they're not clean."

"And whose fault is that? Just exactly where were they?"

Todd looked away and muttered something that sounded like, "Under my bed."

"What were they doing there?" his mother asked. "Growing mushrooms? Taking part in some terrifying science experiment?"

"I don't know. Saturday was all a blur what with having to go and get Sarah from the airport."

Sarah looked up at him over the top of her newspaper. "Don't try to blame me," she said.

Todd sent her a resentful look then swung his attention back to his mother. "But what am I supposed to do?"

"In an ideal world you'd wear your other pair of shorts, but since you managed to miraculously lose those - without, I might add, any decent explanation - it's all a bit of a dilemma, isn't it? It's time, my boy, that you started taking better care of your things."

"That still doesn't help me know what to do with my shorts, does it?"

"The best I can suggest is that you iron them. At least that way they won't look entirely unwashed. Then, after school, we can put them through the wash so you'll be right for tomorrow."

"But I've got an exam today," he wailed, his voice going up a notch or two, "and I can't find my social studies notes."

"You told me you were all prepared for your exams," Margaret said, her frustration clearly growing. "What else have you been doing with your time if you haven't been studying? All those sessions you've had with Tom and Gerry must have accomplished something."

Todd reddened. "We've been looking at other stuff," he said. "Math and science."

"Great. So are you trying to tell me you aren't at all prepared for this exam today?"

Todd merely kicked the table leg and looked at the ground.

"Right," said Sarah, feeling she had to do something before things got out of hand, "Give me those shorts and I'll iron them. You go and have another look for your social studies book."

Todd thrust out the shorts and said with a cheeky smile, "Thanks." He bolted from the room before his mother had a chance to do anything.

"You're too soft," Margaret said. "He'll never learn."

Sarah, unperturbed, smiled and said, "What are sisters for?"

Pearl watched out of the window. She saw Ernest's little blue Daihatsu swing into the driveway so that when he knocked commandingly on the door - in the way that usually frightened the living daylights out of Pearl - she was ready and waiting.

It was nearly lunchtime. Pearl had been ostensibly watching out for Sarah who had taken to popping over at least some time during the day. Ernest had clearly already been out and about, all dressed in his best suit.

"Another bloody funeral," he said as he came into the room.

"Oh, dear," Pearl said. "Anyone I know?"

"Doubt it. It was an old work colleague, a fellow surveyor. We qualified around about the same time. The sort of chap I was always crossing paths with over the years. Hadn't seen him in a while, though. The wife said he'd got cancer a couple of years ago. He just went on a slow gradual decline as the thing ate him up."

Pearl shivered. "Don't," she said, thinking of Jack and of his rather swifter decline to the same illness.

"Sorry old girl," Ernest said. "It's just that I seem to go to one of these bunfights every five minutes lately. It's starting to get me down."

"Do you want a cup of tea, then?"

"God no. I feel like I'm swimming with the stuff. People were downing it by the gallon at the wake. You haven't got anything stronger, have you?"

Pearl looked sharply at Ernest. "It's a bit early, isn't it?"

"Oh, get off your high horse will you, and just answer the question."

"The answer is no. I'm surprised you'd even ask."

Ernest laughed sharply. "What? Worried you'll turn into some sort of widowed soak? I'd have thought you'd need a tipple now and again to cheer you up, living in a dog-box like this."

"You know very well I've never particularly liked alcohol. And even if I did, it wouldn't seem appropriate to me to have strong liquor with young children around."

"What young children?"

"Well, there's Todd."

"That young scamp. Isn't he practically a teenager?"

"All the more reason to keep temptation out of his way."

"I still don't understand why you want to live here," Ernest said, glancing disparagingly around.

Pearl suppressed a smile. The whole of his life her brother had been determined to have the last word, even risking the odd hiding or two from their own father in days long gone by. There he was, seventy-five years of age, a successful career, one marriage and two children behind him, a solid citizen in more ways than one. But underneath it all he remained the small, stubborn opinionated brother she'd always known.

She said, "What else am I supposed to do? You know there wasn't any way I could stay at home any longer. The property was too big to manage on my own."

"Yes, but technically speaking you weren't on your own. Or at least you shouldn't have been. Three strapping children you've had, and none of them particularly far away, yet none of them were prepared to move a muscle to help you keep your independence."

"They are all busy," Pearl said. "Busy with lives of their own."

"Oh they are, are they?" Ernest asked. "Let's recap a little, shall we, about how busy they are. Since his divorce, David's on his own with very few commitments. And as for Sheila, well that husband of hers, John, he's always trying to tell you how well off he is. Surely either one of them could have helped mow the lawns and do a bit of maintenance around the place. The least Sheila and John could have done was offer you a room in their whacking great house. Instead the best Margaret could offer you was this bread bin to live in."

"It seems infinitely preferable to living in some old folks' mausoleum like you do."

"What would you know about it?" Ernest said. "I can't even get you to come for a visit."

"It would depress me."

"Rubbish. They say there are none so blind as them that will not see. Still, I wish you would come if only to meet Rosa. She really wants to meet you. Charles has met her."

"How is Charles?"

"Haven't you seen him? He's panicking about having to sit the test to renew his driver's license."

"I haven't seen him for about two weeks. I wondered what he was up to."

"Yes, well, he's wasting his time there, but that's another story. Stop changing the subject. We were talking about you coming to Lambton Park to meet Rosa."

"Were we?"

"You know we were. God, why do you always have to be so bloody minded? Now, when are you coming to meet her?"

"Can't you bring her here?"

"What? To this place? You must be joking. Besides, truth be told Rosa doesn't like going out too much."

"Why not?"

"I don't think she can see the point. Why leave when everything you could ever want is right there at your finger tips?"

"So I'm expected to go there, am I?"

"Bloody hell, don't make it sound like that. The way I see it, at least that way you could kill two birds with one stone - you could meet Rosa and look at Lambton Park."

Pearl sighed. "I can't see why it's so important to you."

Ernest said defensively, "Well, it is important. It's important to me, and," and he added, again looking around with disdain at Pearl's accommodation, "important to you too, if only you'd see it. So, are you coming or not?"

Refusing to be railroaded Pearl sniffed, and said, "I'll think about it."

On Friday afternoon, when Sarah had been home nearly a week, she found herself home alone for the first time. Her mother had taken Nan to see Auntie Sheila, her father was still at work, and Todd had muttered something mysterious that morning about doing more study after school and being late home. Margaret had wondered out loud whether he had been shocked into activity by his social studies exam earlier in the week. He'd come home afterward looking very downcast.

On the odd rare day in England when Sarah had nothing special planned there always seemed to be a thousand and one things to do. Housework was always fairly high on the list, as were grocery shopping and bill paying, and any number of other mundane tasks. But, if a person couldn't be bothered with such evils, there were always places to go and things to see.

Back home, firmly off the tourist trail, it barely even occurred to Sarah that she could get out and about and see some of the local sights. She'd huddled at home all week, and had yet to make much effort to reconnect with the friends she'd left behind. Cassie had often been the driving force behind their social life, ensuring there was quite literally never a dull moment. For the time being Sarah felt a bit bereft of her company and not inclined to go out of her way to be sociable.

So she'd spent the week pottering about, having tea with her grandmother, looking through her old cupboards and drawers, unpacking, sorting out paperwork and bank accounts, flicking through the local paper and scanning the columns for jobs and a new car.

Having found in amongst her old belongings a pile of crumpled correspondence, she sat now with coffee at the ready, in the lounge, half lying like a cat in a pool of sunlight, looking through it all as she decided what to toss away. It seemed a bit odd to be back at home and yet not have the family with her, even though she'd made the decision to remain behind. There had been nothing really stopping her from going with her mother and grandmother to Auntie Sheila's. Now she felt a little guilty for staying behind. She felt aware of the house and the little sounds it made, of the noises drifting in on the breeze from outside. She felt as though she was waiting, waiting for someone to return and for the house to reassume its identity.

She got quite a shock when, at quarter past four, there came a knock at the door. This would be the first visitor to call since Sarah had returned. When she opened the door she found herself looking at someone she had never seen before. He was young, maybe thirty, with light brown hair, tall and of average build. He had a thin but handsome face. His green eyes mirrored his smile.

"Hi," he said, his voice deep and friendly.

Sarah looked at him closer. She knew she did not know him and yet somehow she thought she should. She scanned him for clues. He carried nothing, had no briefcase. The jeans and white shirt he wore bore no emblems or logos and yet he stood there looking at her as though she should know who he was.

"Hi," she replied.

"You must be Sarah," he said, as though he thoroughly approved.

"Yes," she replied. She gave him a quizzical look. "And you?"

"Me? Oh, yes, sorry. Of course. I'm your new neighbor. I'm Michael Alexander."

Sarah looked at him for a moment or two. Before she could stop herself, said with surprise, "You're Nan's boyfriend?"

CHAPTER TWO

On the way home in the car Margaret had to force herself to concentrate on the road, to channel all of her energy and anger into steering the car safely back to Victoria Road without either upsetting her mother or having a crash. It was no mean feat.

Of course being mad at Sheila was nothing new. For her entire life Sheila had been making Margaret's blood boil with her self-centered, unfeeling approach to life. As long as Sheila Seymour's life bloomed then that was all that mattered. No thought for anybody else and what they might be going through. No consideration. Practically no manners either, in the sort of way that defined caring society. Only a kind of showy attempt at sophistication designed to disguise Sheila's desire for number one.

Pearl, sitting beside Margaret on the journey home, said nothing. Her mother had made a point over all the years never to openly discuss the faults of her children among the other siblings. Margaret supposed she had to admire her mother for never taking sides or deliberately stirring up dissension between Sheila, David and herself. But there were times when she wished her mother would be a little less circumspect and simply come out with the hard truth. Which, in Margaret's opinion, showed Sheila as a self-absorbed cow and David as one of life's wastrels who needed to wake up to himself before he turned into a lecher.

Instead, her mother sat staring out the window as the suburbs passed by. John and Sheila had a house twenty minutes' drive from the Bells, in the most exclusive part of town they could afford. It was just the sort of snobbery Margaret had come to expect from that pair.

By the time Margaret pulled into the driveway tension coiled in her like spring. She counted down the seconds until she could be alone and rant and rave a bit. Then - once she'd got that out of her system - she could get on with making the dinner, doing the dishes, putting on washing, folding and ironing yesterday's pile of laundered clothes, making a shopping list in preparation for going to the store tomorrow, chip away a bit more at Jim's accounts and, if luck favored her, crawl into bed sometime this side of midnight.

Pearl took herself off to the flat with a little smile and not a lot else. Margaret let herself in through the kitchen door, tossed her handbag down with satisfying aggression, drew breath to let out a sound equivalent to a scream, when she realized Sarah hovered in the kitchen.

"Hi Mum," Sarah said.

Margaret looked at her daughter momentarily as though she might be a ghost. She's got so used Sarah being away that she struggled to adjust to the fact that she'd returned. But this was no apparition. In fact, with potato peeler in hand and dinner preparations underway, Margaret thought angel would be a much more fitting description. She let out her held breath. The tension started to ease at the unexpected sight of someone lending a helping hand.

"Hi," Margaret replied.

"How did the visit with Aunt Sheila go?"

Margaret's vision clouded again at the mention of her sister. "Excruciating."

Sarah sent her mother a direct look. "Why?"

"Oh, all the same old reasons. Nothing's changed, you know. Sheila is still very firmly Sheila."

"Still, Nan would have appreciated you taking her over."

"Not so you could tell. And as for Sheila, why that lazy fat cow can't drag herself over here occasionally, I don't know."

"Mum!"

"Well, it's true," Margaret said defensively. "She is lazy, and she's getting fatter by the day with all those lunches and morning teas and restaurant meals that she keeps going out to. And yet she won't stir herself to come across town to see her own mother. No, it's left to me to put myself out and take Mum over, and all for what? An ill made cup of tea, some packet biscuits, and an hour and a half of solid boasting about the wonderful life Sheila's living."

"It can't be that bad, surely."

"Want to bet? This visit we heard all about how they'd been invited out to some five-hundred-dollar-a-plate dinner where some foreign dignitary bored the pants off everyone with his after dinner speech. Then we heard about and saw the new outfit she'd bought to go in - some tent like affair to disguise her rolls of fat. Then we heard about how none of her jewelry matched the outfit so we had to ooh and gaa over some pendant she'd bought from someone who's supposedly handmade jewelry for royalty. Sickening is the word that springs to mind."

"I suppose I should have come too," Sarah said. "That might have given us all something else to talk about."

"You don't see Sheila rushing over to welcome you home do you? Why should you put yourself out for her?"

Sarah shrugged and said, "I don't know why I didn't feel like going. I guess I should have made the effort."

"To give her her due, Sheila did ask after you," Margaret conceded, "but to be honest, I think all you would have added was another audience member to hear all that boasting."

"Were the boys there? Reuben and Jason?"

"Don't even get me started on those cousins of yours," Margaret said. "Both of those boys need a good hiding if you ask me. They're turning out to be as spoilt and indulged as Sheila. Mark my words, there's trouble brewing there."

"I'd still like to see them some time," Sarah said.

"Yes, well, seeing is believing," Margaret drew herself up as if to shake the thought of the whole jolly lot of them away. "Anyway, how did you get on?"

Sarah smiled a lopsided smile. "Interesting," she said.

"Oh? How so?"

"We had a visitor while you were gone."

"Did we now? Who, pray tell?"

"Our new neighbor. Mr. Alexander. The man I thought to be about ninety nine not out, not to mention Nan's boyfriend of some description."

"Oh," Margaret said, before bursting into gales of laughter.

"You swines," Sarah said. "How could you?"

Margaret tried to stop smiling and said, "It wasn't intentional. It just sort of happened. You assumed and we just sort of let you go on assuming. That aside, I must say he's a lovely young man. And he has been very good to Mum. He gives her things to read that he thinks she'll find interesting then takes the time to discuss what she thinks afterward. The boyfriend bit has just become a something of a family joke."

"A family joke that I knew nothing about, and which I blurted out to him before I could stop myself."

"Oh, dear," Margaret said with a smile. "How did he take that?"

"Pretty well, considering. He laughed, and said he was flattered. He must have thought me to be some sort of idiot."

"I'm sure he didn't. He's much too nice for that."

"Nice or not, I felt a real fool. As I stood there looking at him I couldn't even remember why I'd thought he was older."

"Probably because Todd called him Mr. Alexander. These days anyone called mister is bound to be pushing eighty."

"Except if a person happens to be a school teacher," said Sarah. "Or more specifically Todd's school teacher."

"If you want to get really specific, he's Todd's English teacher. Todd's got someone else as a form teacher. Anyway, I wouldn't give the matter another thought. Like I say, he's too nice to be bothered about something like that. Anyway, what did he want?"

"He was looking for Nan. She's got something of his he needs back. He thought she might be here."

"Right. You'd better go and tell her. I'll carry on with dinner. It'll give me something to do while I wait for Todd and your father to come home so I can tell them all about what happened. I reckon we could all do with a good laugh."

Sarah paused on the threshold before letting herself out the kitchen door. "Thanks Mum," she said heavily. "It's nice to know you can rely on your family."

Perhaps, Sarah thought later, their family was destined to trouble between sisters. Sarah didn't have to look further than the mirror to find someone who didn't exactly see eye to eye with her sister. Her own mother and Aunt Sheila barely ever got on. Having two brothers had spared Nan. But rumor had it that her mother - the estimable Lillian Ferguson - had hated both her sisters with a passion.

But maybe things didn't have to be so arbitrary. Maybe effort and understanding could overcome any divide. After all, these were supposed to be enlightened times. People were encouraged to be more open with one another and share their feelings thus reducing confusion, misunderstanding and the harboring of grudges. And maybe that effort had to be made by Sarah, since Joanna - not renowned for acts of charity - could hardly be relied upon to make the first move.

With these sentiments in mind, Sarah headed for the phone the following morning.

"Hi, Jo," Sarah said brightly, when her sister answered.

"Sarah," Joanna said heavily, "I wish you wouldn't call me that. You know very well my name is Joanna."

Off to a great start, Sarah thought to herself. She felt the groundswell of sisterly affection within her tarnish somewhat.

"Sorry," she said. "How are you?"

"How do you think? I've had barely enough beauty sleep to suffice. Connor has been grumbling for three days solid, Isabella flooded the bathroom this morning, and Brett, of course, is at the car yard. We aren't all so lucky as you are to be able to sit around doing sweet Fanny Adams."

"Oh. I didn't realize Brett still had to work on Saturdays. I thought by now he'd have some junior sales rep to fill in."

"Hardly. Saturdays can be one of the best days. When one is on commission, one has to make the most of all opportunities. You cannot simply leave things in the hands of some junior lackey. Really, I would have thought you'd have learnt a thing or two while you were overseas. Still, I suppose it's hardly surprising since your interests have always run along the lines of manure and compost."

Sarah suppressed the thought that Joanna knew a thing or two about manure herself. Instead she said, "I wondered what you were doing today. I thought we might be able to catch up."

"I don't know about that," Joanna said. "I've got shopping to do. Then some of my friends with small children are going to meet up in the afternoon at one of those indoor adventure playgrounds, to let the older children burn off a bit of excess energy while we have coffee and catch up."

"What will you do with Connor?"

"He'll come too, of course. After being awake for a few hours in the night it wouldn't surprise me if he slept the whole afternoon away."

"Oh," Sarah said again. "Well, what about later, then? After Brett gets home?"

Joanna sighed, as though the very act of speaking was too much for her to be troubled with.

"I suppose you could come for dinner if you insist on inviting yourself."

"Great," Sarah said before Joanna had the chance to change her mind.

"Don't go to any trouble, will you? And why don't I bring dessert?"

"I think you'd better. I won't have time to make anything, you know. And after all, you have got all day."

"Right then," Sarah said. "I'll come about five thirty, shall I? You never know, if I'm in a good mood, I might even help you bath the children or cook the dinner or something."

Sarah found Margaret at her familiar place in the kitchen quietly cursing over the bank statements. Looking up as Sarah came in, her mother said, "I really don't know where it all goes, but it goes all right. It seems to me that your father has only just been paid for a swag of jobs he's done but by the time we pay the business bills, put money aside for tax and pay him a wage, there just doesn't seem to be any left.

"Then with the money your dad gets as a wage we have to pay the mortgage, put yet more money away for tax, pay yet more bills, shop for food and other ancillaries and dole out a ration to Todd, there's nothing left there either. We're like the proverbial mouse in the wheel, going round and around and getting nowhere."

"I have already offered to pay board," Sarah said. "You should let me make some contribution toward expenses."

"What expenses? A bit of food three times a day and some hot water for a shower? Don't be silly. You keep your money."

Sarah went to insist but the kitchen door burst open and in came Todd, followed closely by Tom and Gerry. Sarah was intrigued to see them again. Tom and Gerry - or more precisely Thomasina and Gerald Redstone - had always been something of a fascination for Sarah. Perhaps it was the twin factor, that strange partnership of life each had with the other. Perhaps it was simply what they were like, black haired, round faced, sloe eyed, always looking out from under their matching fringes with an intensity that could at times be most disconcerting. Sarah didn't really know.

Eighteen months had wrought a few changes. Tom and Gerry had shot up quite considerably. But where Tom had become coltish, with the beginning of feminine curves starting to appear, Gerry had grown awkward. It seemed as though he and his body had lost cohesion with one another. He'd had to get glasses too which made him look, Sarah thought ruefully, rather nerdy. Neither of them had lost their manner. Upon entering the room both sets of dark eyes fixed themselves on Sarah as they assessed her every bit as intensely as she did them.

"Hello, you two," Sarah said with a smile. "Nice to see you again."

Thomasina smiled shyly, while Gerald's eyes darted nervously about. He had a furtive look that suggested he had other things to do and other places to be. Meanwhile Todd seemed to be squirming on the spot, as though he had been caught doing something he ought not.

"Where did you three spring from?" Margaret asked.

"I bumped into these two on my way back from the dairy," Todd said.

"And what were you doing going to the dairy at this time of day?" his mother asked. "As if you don't eat enough as it is. There really shouldn't be any need for you to go wasting your money on sweets and junk."

"Oh, Mum," Todd said heavily. "Give it a rest, will you?"

"No, I will not," Margaret said angrily. "You might think you're old enough to do what you want when you want, but believe me you are not. I'm still responsible for you and for your diet, whether you like it or not."

Todd stared at his mother mutinously, clearly incensed. He looked mortified at getting a dressing down in front of his friends. Tom and Gerry took it all in much the same way they took in everything: with detached observation and little or no comment.

"You won't have to worry about what I eat for the rest of the day," Todd said. "Tom and Gerry have invited me to go to their house for lunch and a swim in their pool. There's also a barbecue on this evening. I'm allowed to stay."

"Really?" Margaret said, "And I assume the Redstones know all about all of this casual inviting, do they?"

Gerry shifted uncomfortably, but Tom said, "Yes, Mrs. Bell. It's fine with them. There are other people coming too, so one more won't make any difference."

"It might when they see how much Todd eats," Margaret said.

But since Sarah knew the type of parties Augustus and Hermione Redstone liked to throw - with everything coming together simply yet with sophistication – Margaret didn't have strong grounds for protest.

"So, can I go?" Todd asked.

"All right," Margaret conceded. "Although I'd like to point out that you'll be missing out on a very fine roast dinner here."

"That's a shame," Todd said, his voice bereft of all sincerity. "Better go and get my swimming gear," he added.

He left the room with Tom and Gerry trailing in his wake.

Margaret looked at Sarah with bewilderment. "You never know what that boy will be up to next," she said.

"Or me, I'm afraid."

"Why you?"

"Joanna's invited me to her house for dinner tonight," Sarah confessed. "Sorry. I had no idea about the roast dinner."

"Oh, Sarah! I bought it specially. A nice leg of lamb. I thought it would be a treat for us all, a pleasant family meal. It can hardly be that with half the family missing. Now what am I supposed to do with it?"

"Sorry. If I'd realized I wouldn't have made other arrangements," Sarah said again. "As for the lamb, it won't go off, will it? Couldn't we have it tomorrow? In fact, we could have the traditional Sunday lunch. Nan could come, and we'll make sure Todd is here. I'll help cook it."

For a few moments Sarah's mother looked determined to cling on to her anger but then she rolled her eyes and softened.

"All right, then," she said, "but I'll hold you to that, you know. I don't want to end up doing the lot myself."

On his way back from choir practice at church, Charles called in to see his sister.

"I'm beginning to think it might be time to pack it in," Charles told Pearl. "I mean, I enjoy the singing on a Sunday morning, and don't mind putting in time for practice. It's just that I'm getting tired of the relentless pursuit by certain older women in the group."

"Ah, I see. All the merry widows chasing after the merry widower, is it?"

"Not all. Just one in particular. And even then, one wouldn't be so bad if there didn't seem to be some sort of conspiracy going on. Every time I turn around the wretched woman is there. And some of these so-called chance meetings have definitely not been engineered by her alone."

"She's getting help?"

"I'm starting to think even the vicar is in league with her," Charles said gravely.

"Really? So, the age-old art of matchmaking isn't dead?"

"Most certainly not."

"But they've got the wrong match?" Pearl asked.

"It's not that. The woman concerned isn't particularly objectionable. It's just that I don't want to be matched. I feel no need to pair up with anyone ever again." Charles sent her a penetrating look. "I'm sure I don't need to explain such sentiments to you, Pearl, of all people."

"Quite right," she replied. "I couldn't imagine there ever being anyone I'd want to spend the rest of my life with. Not after Jack. On the other hand, not everyone feels the same way. Just look at our brother."

"Ernest? I never thought he had the romantic in him but after seeing him and Rosa together I'm beginning to change my mind. She certainly has worked some kind of magic in his life."

"Incredible. She must be quite a woman."

"She seemed so to me. Did Ernest tell you that she's Spanish?"

"Yes. She sounds very exotic. I can't imagine how she ended up living at Lambton Park alongside Ernest by the way he described her."

"Oh, there's some story there," Charles said. "She married an Italian, but between the Spanish civil war and World War Two, I think they moved here for a bit of peace. But knowing what New Zealand was like fifty or sixty years ago, I can't imagine that was an easy alternative either."

"I don't suppose it was. People were suspicious back then about everything, weren't they? I suppose it can't have been easy at all."

"You should meet her, you know."

"I know."

"Lambton Park really isn't as dire as you might think," Charles said.

"No? Well, as I said to Ernest, I'll think about it. I don't see you rushing to move out of your own home yourself, so you're a fine one to preach."

"I never suggested you move in. I merely think it might mean a lot to Ernest if you go and see him, see where he lives and meet Rosa."

"We'll see. Meantime, apart from being chased by the merry widow, what else have you been doing with yourself? Ernest said something about a driving test?"

"With turning seventy in January I have to re-sit my driver's license test so I've been busy swotting up on the road code. I know it's still a couple of months away but to be honest the old memory isn't up to scratch any more. Things take a lot longer to sink in."

"Sounds ghastly. Let me know if you need any help. I can test you if you want."

Charles smiled. "Thanks. I might just take you up on that. I must say, seventy seems to have come around very fast."

"You try eighty," Pearl said, returning his smile.

He laughed. "Yes, a fine old age. You mustn't be able to believe it."

"I don't know. In some ways I can. I only just said to Sarah that it's incredible how far things have come technologically in my lifetime. From that point of view it doesn't seem so inconceivable that eight decades could have passed. In fact it's surprising more time hasn't gone by. But when I look back at how quickly those eighty years have gone I realize how fast time really does fly by."

Charles said, "You know what I find odd? It's remembering people so long gone that barely a soul even knows about them. So few people know they once lived and breathed. These were people with hopes and dreams and aspirations, with families and memories, who once had things they valued. It seems a little frightening that people could pass away like that, never to be recalled."

"You're starting to sound a bit like Ernest. He was here the other day, quite maudlin with having to go to so many funerals recently. But that's life, I guess. You're born, you grow. You have ambitions, some of which get fulfilled and some of which don't. If you're lucky, you're happy and have a family, but then life diminishes. The next generation take your place, and then the generation after that."

"Heavens. How gloomy."

"Not really. At least it doesn't have to be. The trick is trying to stay happy once the ambitions have gone or are fulfilled."

"And you, Pearl? Are you happy and fulfilled?"

Pearl studied her shoes for a few moments then said, "I'm all right. Probably better off than some and happier than the rest. Who can really say?"

"I thought I'd find you in here," Sarah said to her father, who lurked in the back of the garage tinkering with some wood and his tools. "What are you up to?"

"I decided I might try to make a doll's house for Isabella for Christmas," he said, waving a piece of paper at Sarah, with a rough sketch and dimensions on it.

"That's nice. I'm sure she'll love it."

"That remains to be seen. Joanna has no doubt put it into the wee girl's head that the only acceptable house for dolls is one of those enormous plastic jobs you can buy in posh toy shops that cost an arm and a leg. I can but try."

"I wish I could tell you that nothing could be further from the truth but I fear you may be right," Sarah said. "Just seeing the way she had the children dressed made me realize that only the best is good enough. But I defy anyone to turn their nose up at something made with the love of a grandfather for his granddaughter. At the end of the day that counts for more than any rubbishy plastic house."

Jim laughed. "Very noble sentiments, but perhaps a little misplaced. The truth is, if we had the spare cash I'd probably just go and buy one of those rubbishy plastic houses and be done with it. I've only just started but already the project is giving me a headache." He tossed the sketch onto the workbench. "However, there are certain advantages to working out in the garage so I'm prepared to persist for now."

Sarah's eyes narrowed. "Ah yes, I see," she said slowly. "In that case, you might like to stay out here a bit longer. I'm afraid Todd and I have upset the apple cart."

Jim's eyebrows shot up. "Oh? What's happened this time?"

"Mum had a roast dinner planned but Todd's gone off to Tom and Gerry's and I wangled an invitation to go to Joanna's for dinner."

Jim looked even more surprised. "Did you now? I hope you realize what an honor that is. Your mother and I practically never get invited. Strictly high days and holidays. They're always too busy entertaining other important personages to bother with the likes of mother and father."

Sarah grinned. "I sort of invited myself."

Jim chuckled. "Good for you."

"I suspect it'll prove to be a bad decision in the end but I thought I'd give it a go. Meanwhile, I had no idea about Mum and her leg of lamb."

"She'll calm down. There's always tomorrow."

"That's what I said. We're going to have Sunday lunch instead."

"That'll be a treat. I can't think how many years it is since we've had one of those. Life's too busy these days."

"So it appears. Mum seems permanently snowed under."

"Apparently so. Anyway, don't worry too much about having upset your mother. She'll get over it."

"I'm just not used to having to walk on eggshells around her. It doesn't seem to take much to get her flustered."

"You can say that again."

"And what is it she's so busy with all the time? I can't bear to see her so under pressure."

Jim picked up a hammer and a nail and drove the nail into a piece of wood with considerable force. "Don't ask me," he said. "It's just the same old stuff. Nothing more and nothing less. It's just that her capacity for coping with it seems to have diminished."

"She does seem, well, different. Is she all right?"

"Don't ask me," her father said again, driving in another nail with a ferocious bang. "Like you, nothing I do ever pleases anyway, including trying to ask what's wrong."

"I'm sorry Dad."

Jim waved a lofty hand. "Don't worry about it," he said. "It's just a phase. It'll all blow over, sooner or later." He straightened, tossed his hammer aside and said, "Now, if you can spare me some time, I'd like you to come and take a look at my rose bushes. Something's up with them and I suddenly realize you're just the person who might know what I should do with them."

Sarah grinned. "Rose bushes? Right. Rose bushes I can do. It's people I'm not so sure about."

Jim smiled back. "That makes two of us."

After having parked Margaret's car - which Margaret had begrudgingly relinquished so that Sarah could get herself across town and further remove herself from the specter of the leg of lamb - Sarah climbed out and tried to get organized. Standing on the threshold of Joanna and Brett's home she realized she faced a dilemma. Nothing major, but a dilemma nonetheless. Laden as she was with wine, dessert, an offering of flowers and the keys to her mother's car, Sarah wondered how she was supposed to knock on the door without dropping the whole jolly lot.

The sensible solution would be to use the doorbell but since Sarah was already running late she wondered about the wisdom of such an action. Would the noise wake one or other of the children who may already be tucked up in bed? It certainly wouldn't do to get the evening off to a bad start by putting her foot in it.

The thought of feet gave Sarah the idea of kicking the door instead of knocking. Although the sound of foot on wood sounded rather more petulant than Sarah would have liked, it did the trick. Within moments Brett appeared to usher her in.

"Hello," Sarah said with her most friendly smile fixed in place.

"Hello, Sarah. We wondered when you'd show up."

"Yes, sorry. I thought I'd be here miles before now. The day somehow ran away with me."

"Really?" Brett said, as he showed her in to the living room. "How intriguing. I don't suppose you've had a lot of call for time management techniques since you arrived home."

"Not a lot, no," Sarah replied as she deposited the dessert and flowers on the coffee table and herself on the couch. "I suppose you couldn't live without them?"

"Definitely not. I went to a great seminar at the beginning of winter that has totally transformed my life in terms of productivity. I should dig out the workbook for you. I think you'd benefit greatly from it. Most people don't realize just how much money goes down the drain in real terms due to time wasting and inefficiency."

"I don't suppose they do," Sarah said. She resisted the urge to ask whether even time in the bathroom could be rigidly controlled by time management so as not to waste a single precious second. After all, Brett would probably take her seriously and tell her far more information than she wanted to know. Instead she said, "Where's Jo?"

Brett frowned. "Joanna is putting Isabella to bed. She'll be down shortly."

"Oh. I really am late, aren't I?"

"Yes, you are," a voice said from the doorway. Sarah turned to see Joanna standing there looking like a displeased school ma'am.

"Sorry," Sarah said, wincing sheepishly. "The thing is, I went into town to buy some stuff to make dessert, ran into an old friend, ended up having coffee with her. By the time I got home I had to rush to make dessert and get over here."

Joanna looked less than impressed. "I thought you were going to be here for bath time. You said you would help."

"I guess I really have no idea when bath time is," Sarah admitted.

"Half past four, Sarah. Half past four. And the time now?"

Sarah shrugged. "Six-ish."

"Try half past six. You're only two hours late. I hope you realize how disappointed Isabella was that her Auntie Sarah couldn't even be bothered to show up to see her."

Sarah sighed. "Look, Jo, I'm truly sorry. I just didn't realize."

"No, I'm sure you didn't. That hardly makes it right, though, does it?"

"Maybe I could go up and see Isabella now? Read her a story maybe?"

"I don't think so. She's hard enough to settle as it is without you making it worse. Hannibal had less trouble crossing the Alps than we have getting Isabella to go to bed at night. And even the fact that Connor is asleep is nothing short of miraculous."

"I'll just have to make it up to her next time."

"I'd think you better had," Joanna said, her expression sour.

"Maybe we should have a drink," Brett interjected. "Perhaps we could go through to the dining room?"

"That would be lovely," Sarah said, thinking to herself that she'd much rather just get back in her mother's car and drive straight home. "But I'm happy enough to help out in the kitchen?"

"There's another thing you're too late for. It's all done already."

"I got home a bit early," Brett confided, as if that magically explained how dinner had managed to ready itself.

"Not that you should have had to," Joanna said, not yet prepared to soften.

But by the time they had eaten the salmon starter, and a glass or two of wine had been consumed, Joanna finally found a way of getting off her high horse long enough to be civil.

"The house is looking lovely," Sarah said, when the conversation about Brett's potential customers for that day had been exhausted. It was a compliment Sarah did not find difficult to make. The house - a two-storied modern townhouse - was a two hundred and seventy square meter paradise of rooms that flowed one to the other with elegant ease. From the polished wooden floors, to the interesting window features and excellent indoor-outdoor flow, all set off with tasteful furniture and furnishings, there wasn't much to dislike. Sarah hated to think how much it must have set them back, but then no expense could be spared where real estate was concerned.

"We like it," Joanna said, as she cleared the plates away and went into the kitchen to get the main course.

"It suits our purposes for the moment," Brett said. "And of course with any appreciating asset in the right location, we figure we're making money hand over fist as we speak. By the time we're ready to upgrade, I think we'll have netted a tidy profit."

"Great," Sarah managed.

"You'll have to seriously consider buying some property yourself, Sarah," Brett advised.

"I can't imagine what with."

"What? Didn't you make the most of the Sterling exchange rate by saving up while in England? You were working, weren't you?"

"And travelling, and paying out money for food and accommodation and expenses, all of which are quite considerable in London."

"But still," Brett said incredulously. "You can't have come home with nothing?"

"Not nothing," Sarah replied evenly. "Apart from anything else I've got some great memories of places I've seen and things I've experienced. You can't put a price on things like that."

"You can't live in it and make money from it either," Brett said. "It does rather seem a pity you couldn't have heard another seminar I went to last year, about the importance of fiscal responsibility from the moment a person starts earning an income. I only wish I'd been fortunate to have attended it when I first left school. When I think of the resources I needlessly squandered due to mere frivolity, it sends shivers down my spine."

Not as many shivers as all this talk of capitalism is sending down mine, Sarah thought to herself.

"Well," she said, "life is a learning curve, there's no doubt about that."

Joanna brought out steaming plates of fettuccine, salad and garlic bread and sat herself down.

"And now that you are home," she said to Sarah, "just what is it that you are planning to do? You won't stay and sponge off Mum and Dad, I hope."

"Not in the long term. Mum seems to be very insistent about me staying until at least after Christmas. Dad, for reasons of his own, would be happy for me to stay even longer."

"What reasons?"

Sarah twirled the fettuccine around her fork. "Did you know they weren't getting on too well?"

"Rubbish. They seem just the same as ever. No better and no worse."

"Admittedly they've never been the most romantic couple in the world but it's different this time. Mum's different. Surely you must have noticed."

"I'd noticed Mum had lost a bit of weight. I don't read anything into that."

"And you hadn't noticed how busy she is, how everything is in a mess and that she can't seem to get organized to save herself?"

"I'm sure you're exaggerating. And don't forget, she's got Nan to worry about too, now."

"She's so busy she doesn't have much time for Nan," Sarah said.

Brett said, "Maybe it's that time of life. My mother went practically psychotic for a while there."

"I don't know how anyone could have told the difference," Joanna said to him. "Besides, you've really got no idea what you're talking about."

Brett looked sulky. "Can't a man have an opinion these days?"

"Not if it's a load of twaddle he can't," Joanna told him. "And if you want my opinion Sarah's making a mountain out of a molehill about Mum as well."

"I hope you're right," Sarah said, even though in her heart she knew something was definitely amiss with their mother.

Joanna went to reply when Isabella appeared in the doorway, teddy in hand, her blonde hair blurred around her head like a smudged halo.

"What are you doing out of bed young lady?" Joanna demanded.

Isabella immediately burst into tears and said, "I've wet the bed."

And then, not to be outdone, the unmistakable sound of Connor crying at the top of his lungs came drifting down the stairs.

Joanna stood up sharply and looked at Sarah. "Time to make yourself useful. After all, you did seem sorry not to have seen your niece."

Sarah couldn't help thinking that, in her wildest dreams, she'd never imagined coming home to be quite like this. She had to stop herself from saying, with a dramatic sigh, "What next?"

CHAPTER THREE

Sarah's desire to help cook the Sunday lunch rapidly vanished overnight. She couldn't help feeling it had something to do with baking that dessert yesterday, a supreme culinary masterpiece that never got touched on account of Isabella and Connor. Connor had persisted in being unsettled for at least as long as Sarah remained at her sister's house. Isabella, upon seeing the opportunity to avoid the privations of bed, had tenaciously played up until her exhausted parents capitulated and allowed her stay up to see her Auntie Sarah.

It hadn't taken Sarah long to realize the extent of Isabella's tenacity. In the end the only sensible thing to do appeared to be to leave. Neither Brett nor Joanna made any attempt to dissuade her from this course of action. And so by nine thirty Sarah had arrived back at Victoria Road.

Now yesterday's dishes lurked in the sink, a fetid reminder of hasty effort spent with little reward gained. It served as a guilty reminder that she had not had time to clean up before she left. She'd abandoned her responsibility in favor of not being any later. Her mother, in silent protest, had left everything pretty much as it had been the day before.

Sarah donned her mother's bright yellow gloves and set about rectifying her neglect. There wasn't sight or sound of the rest of the family. Earlier she had heard them all clanking about in a lackadaisical Sunday way, toilets flushing, cups of tea being made, the distant sound of the television. Without interruption, she made short work of the dishes and left them to drain. She then turned her attention to the controversial leg of lamb.

She turned on the oven and had begun to prepare the meat when her mother came in. Margaret cast an eye around the kitchen bench and dish rack full of dishes with a "Just as well" expression on her face. She said, "Looks like you beat me to it."

Sarah smiled. "Everything's under control."

"Not before time."

"Sorry about that. I know full well that I could have tidied everything up when I got back last night but somehow, after the rigors of wet beds and Isabella, I'm afraid I couldn't face it."

"What? Children or the dishes?"

"Both. The advantage of dishes over children is at least you get them momentarily under control. With children it appears to be a case of one thing after another."

"Tell me about it," Margaret said, as Todd burst into the room.

"Mum?" he said. "Can I have ten dollars?"

"No. Why?"

"I need to buy some stuff for school."

"What stuff? School's nearly over for the year. What could you possibly need?"

"Things. You know. Stationery and stuff."

Margaret frowned. "No, I don't know. Perhaps if you give me a list I could hunt around and get what you need on sale."

Todd sagged. "Forget it then," he said. After eyeing up Margaret's copious piles of lists he stalked wordlessly from the room.

"What do you suppose that was all about?" Margaret asked.

"Beats me," Sarah replied as she negotiated the leg of lamb on its tray into the hot oven. "He obviously wants the money for something."

"Obviously. But what?"

Sarah shrugged as she closed the oven door. "I don't know. What can you buy with ten dollars?"

Margaret frowned again. "Cigarettes. That's what you can buy with ten dollars."

Sarah said, "I think they're much more expensive than that these days. You don't really think he's taken up smoking, do you?"

"I don't know. All I do know is that something's up. Todd might think he's got your dad and me exactly where he wants us but the truth is I can still read him like a book. There's something suspicious going on but I just don't know what it is yet."

"Really? I thought he seemed fine. Still hanging around with Tom and Gerry doing the same dumb stuff they've always done."

"Todd would like you to think that but I'm not so sure."

Sarah pulled the potatoes out from the bottom of the pantry. "How many of these do you think we'll need?"

"Let's see. There'll be the four of us and Mum, so that makes five. That is unless we ask someone else."

"Like who?"

"I was thinking we could ask Michael."

"Michael Alexander? From next door?"

"Yes," Margaret said, looking directly at Sarah, daring her to argue. "Why not?"

"Because he's Todd's teacher. No thirteen-year old wants to have Sunday lunch with their teacher."

"Todd won't mind. He's been here for a meal before."

"Has he?"

"Yes. Any other objections?"

"Only the one where we don't invite him because he thinks I'm an idiot."

"Don't be silly. I told you he wouldn't have thought anything of the kind. Besides, it would please Mum. She thinks the world of him. As for those potatoes, there's plenty of time to think about those. Why don't you pop over and ask him if he's free?"

"Me? Why me?"

"I'm too busy, Todd's too unreliable and your father is up to his eyeballs in Isabella's doll's house, that's why."

Sarah made a face. "Do I have to?"

Margaret looked at her impatiently. "Yes, you do. Now stop acting like you're the one who's thirteen and get your backside over there."

The property next door at Number Eighteen was the chalk to the Bells' cheese. Where the Bells' house was a two storied substantial home with shingles and smart grey tiled roof, the one next door was a turn of the century villa, weather boarded with a corrugated iron roof and a veranda running around the front half of the house. The posts that held up the roof over the veranda were adorned with intricate lace fretwork, the roof trimmed with graceful finials. The windows, smaller than that of its neighbor, contained some fine leaded latticework.

The generous front garden had been on a slow decline for many lamentable years but the house itself - which the Aldridges had painted a startling sky blue - had been considerably smartened up with a new coat of paint. A rich cream had replaced the blue. The roof, once grey, was now a handsome shade of russet. In relief, the feature work had been painted a forest green. Over all, the house's new clothes gave it a much more dapper appearance. Whatever else might be said about Michael Alexander, Sarah had to concede he'd done a good job selecting the paint colors.

Sarah walked up the front path with some trepidation, torn between averting her gaze from the painful sight of the garden and avoiding looking directly at the house. To her annoyance she found herself suddenly concerned about her appearance. She felt her hair experimentally in the hope that not too much of it had escape the large clip by which she had it pinned up. She secretly hoped Michael wasn't home but with his car parked in the driveway Sarah thought such a prospect to be quite slim. In fact, barely ten seconds seemed to have passed when he opened the door in response to her knock.

"Hi," she said dubiously.

Michael smiled. "Hi."

Sarah stood there with the obstinacy of a mule, unable to bring herself to return his smile. She waited for him to make some teasing comment about her having come to torment him further. Instead, as though sensing her discomfort he said, "Nice of you to come over. To what do I owe the honor?"

Sarah attempted a small smile. In spite of herself she couldn't help warming to him. In truth she found his face rather compelling. It was a face with interest, with strong cheekbones, a distinctly European nose and a tapered jaw line. It was a kind face, framed by unruly brown hair that had a habit of sticking up in all manner of interesting directions. But for Sarah, the most compelling feature of all had to be his green eyes with which he regarded her with a quiet intelligence. The very thought that she had remembered them so well made her frown. More fiercely than she intended, she said, "I'm here to issue an invitation."

"Oh? That sounds serious. Perhaps you had better come in."

Sarah hesitated for a split second. A good bit of her wanted to refuse but in the end she decided she didn't want him to think her churlish as well as idiotic.

"Thanks."

She followed Michael down the central hall and into the lounge at the rear. As they walked down the hall Sarah couldn't resist taking a peek through the opened doors. She saw a couple of bedrooms, a bathroom, a room crammed with junk. In another room, which looked very much like a study, hundreds of books had been temporarily stacked on wooden shelves held up by concrete blocks. An air of everything somehow being a work in progress permeated, as though Michael had only lived in the house for as long as Sarah had been back home herself.

"Sorry about the mess," he said as he led her into the lounge. Sarah felt as though he had read her mind. She turned her attention to the lounge. It was a surprisingly spacious room considering how much smaller the house looked than the Bells. The right hand side was dominated by large floor to ceiling French doors that opened out onto another veranda not visible from the road. Off this some steps led down to the back garden. In the room itself, Michael had positioned a couple of worn couches to good advantage. Handy coffee tables were strewn with a myriad of items, reminiscent of the Bells' kitchen. There were one or two good pieces of art on the walls, and the almost mandatory bookcase filled with a good deal of weighty tomes. Toward the back of the lounge another doorway opened out onto what Sarah assumed to be the kitchen.

Michael began casually plumping cushions as if to further emphasize his apology. While he did this Sarah drifted over to look out of the open French doors, seeing a paved area outside which might have made a charming courtyard had it not been for the absence of anything resembling a garden. Instead, a riot of weeds choked most of the visibly viable plants, a testament to years of neglect.

"Don't look out there," Michael cautioned. "It's enough to make the average gardener shudder, let alone someone with your training and abilities."

Sarah turned to look at him, intrigued by the fact that he knew what she did. Still, she supposed he and her grandmother would have to talk about something. No doubt her name had come up when Sarah had announced she would be returning home.

"Yes, it's pretty bad. You're not a gardener yourself, then?"

"Sadly not. That's not to say I don't appreciate a good garden as much as the next man. But, I am realistic. Good gardens take time and that's something I don't have in unlimited quantities. Not to mention the money needed as well. Besides, having had a sneak peek at the house, you'll see just how much work there is to do inside before I even venture outside. I'm afraid mowing the lawn is about my limit at this stage."

"Never mind," Sarah said.

"No. Now, you mentioned something about an invitation?"

"Yes. Sorry. We're cooking the good old traditional Sunday lunch next door. Nan's coming, and even Todd's forcing himself to be there. Since there's plenty, Mum wondered whether you'd like to come and join us."

"Your mother did, did she? How very neighborly. Considering all I've got here is some stale bread and a few slices of indifferent cheese, the offer of Sunday lunch has considerable appeal." He smiled. "I accept."

Sarah found herself smiling back. "Great."

"Do you have to rush away or can I tempt you with a closer inspection of the hideousness of my garden?"

Sarah made a face. "Oh, go on then," she said. "How awful can it really be?"

"Pretty awful I'd say. About the equivalent of me being confronted with a dog-eared, ill composed essay at the end of weeks of intensive and inspiring tuition on the part of yours truly."

"That bad, huh?"

Michael nodded. "Come and see for yourself."

As the hands of the clock edged toward midday, Margaret's temper edged toward boiling point. Sure, Sarah might have started preparing the vegetables before she set off, but where was she? Why had she not returned to help as promised? But no, instead it had been left to good old muggins Margaret to organize the vegetables into the oven and keep an eye on things.

And what about dessert? Nobody had given a thought to having something sweet to offer afterward. It was unthinkable to invite guests and then give them half measures. So Margaret had abandoned the bank reconciliation - which was driving her around the bend anyway - in favor of making dessert.

However, nothing had gone right. She'd dropped the flour. It had fallen like snow, coating more surfaces than Margaret thought possible. She'd needed to separate some eggs, but went through three before she managed to get one that didn't run yolk into white. There wasn't enough butter so she'd had to make do with a bit of dubious looking margarine. And then the vegetables needing constant monitoring. So much for having help. It seemed just her luck not to have been endowed with that enviable culinary ability such as she'd seen Tom and Gerry's parents display.

Things reached crisis point when the pastry refused to co-operate. Every time she rolled it the shape became further from the circle she'd been trying to create. Then, when she tried to pick it up, the whole thing tore through the middle. Margaret picked up the pastry and crushed it angrily into a ball. Just as Margaret went to forcibly strike the ball with the rolling pin Jim came strolling in, looking casual, calm and nauseatingly relaxed.

Seeing Margaret poised with the rolling pin in mid air, he gave her a very odd look. "What on earth are you doing?"

Through gritted teeth Margaret said, "I'm having tea with the Queen of England. What does it look like?"

"It looks," he said firmly, "as though it might be time for me to call the men in the white coats."

"Don't be ridiculous," Margaret replied, relenting. She started to roll the pastry again.

"Ridiculous? You call me ridiculous? Just which one of us was about to cause grievous bodily harm to a ball of dough?"

Margaret continued vigorously rolling, not bothering to comment.

"What's all this in aid of anyway?"

"Sunday lunch. I did tell you about Sunday lunch, if you'd only bother listening."

"As it happens I did listen. My understanding was that you and Sarah were going to cook up this contentious leg of lamb you were complaining about yesterday. So, my questions would be, where's Sarah, and what on earth does pastry have to do with a leg of lamb?"

"I sent Sarah next door to ask Michael if he'd like to join us."

"Did you now? What possessed you to do that?"

Margaret raised her chin. "I thought it might be nice. Mum's coming too and I thought she might like to see him."

"Well, don't get me wrong, I like Michael as much as the next bloke, but doesn't that make more work? Can't Pearl see the guy whenever she wants?" Jim's eyes narrowed. "Or is this your way of getting rid of some of your guilt over the fact that you yourself don't spend enough time with her?"

"I don't feel guilty," Margaret said quickly. "It's hardly my fault if there's more to do than time allows."

"You still haven't actually told me what you're doing there."

"I'm making a dessert. Or at least I would be if things didn't keep going wrong."

"What for?"

"I would have thought that was obvious. After the main meal, you consume it. At least that's how I thought dessert worked."

"Ha ha. What I meant was, why are you making one? Why do we have to have one at all? If it's really necessary, couldn't we have had some ice cream, or sent Sarah to the store to buy something to warm up?"

Margaret scowled. "You never appreciate the effort I make, do you? It's always pick, pick, pick."

"My dear wife, it's not that. Of course I appreciate what you do. What I don't understand is why you persist on choosing the hard way of doing things. You bring all this fuss and panic on yourself. Why make a roast in the first place? Why invite extras? Why send your help away next door? And why upon why put yourself to all the extra trouble of making a second course?"

Margaret sniffed. "You can't invite guests without doing a proper job."

"Why?"

"It wouldn't be right."

"Then don't invite the guests. It's as simple as that."

Margaret could feel her temper rising to new heights at such annoying male logic when the kitchen door opened. In walked Sarah, followed directly by Michael.

Sarah held a bunch of mint she found somewhere in Michael's garden. Margaret found her anger evaporating at the sight of her daughter smiling and suddenly looking so obviously less constrained for the first time since returning from England. She looked happy and carefree in a way that Margaret had not even noticed had been missing from Sarah's former countenance. It made Margaret look at Michael with a renewed sense of interest. Suddenly she no longer regretted the effort she'd made on behalf of today's occasion.

"Sorry we're late," Sarah said. "We got talking about Michael's garden. Time sort of evaporated. Look what I found. Now we can have some mint sauce."

In the end things got organized with very little extra effort on Margaret's part. Hot on the heels of Sarah and Michael arriving, Todd magically appeared with Pearl, both of whom were prevailed upon by Sarah to set the table in the dining room. Jim got directed toward clearing some bench space so there would be room for him to carve the meat when the time came, and to opening a bottle of white wine he'd found lurking in the back of the pantry.

"It might have been there since last Christmas," Margaret said dubiously as she kept a weather eye on the progress of the roast potatoes, kumera and pumpkin.

"Isn't age supposed to do wonders for wine?" Jim replied, fishing around in the cutlery drawer for the bottle opener.

"That's red wine," Margaret said.

Sarah said, "It doesn't matter. One bottle between five of us won't go far anyway."

"I'd be surprised if Mum has any. She doesn't usually enjoy alcohol."

Jim went off to ask her and Sarah returned her attention to rescuing the dessert. Margaret had been happy to pass the whole thing over to someone else, while Michael - not in the slightest bit perturbed at finding himself sucked in to a melee of people all jostling and jockeying for position in the kitchen - happily consented to follow Sarah's instructions for making mint sauce, followed by stirring the gravy. He looked quite at home amongst the Bells, as though long accustomed to partaking in such family routines with them.

In the dining room Pearl enjoyed telling Todd what to do. He seemed uncharacteristically happy to oblige, making Sarah wonder whether their father had recently had some sort of quiet word with him. Todd and Pearl folded out the extra leaves on the rarely used dining table, set six places and discussed where everyone should sit.

When all the food was ready it got transported into the dining room in an odd collection of serving dishes so that everyone could help themselves, "According," Pearl said, "to their degrees of greediness."

Todd made a production of telling everyone where they were to sit. Margaret and Jim were seated at opposite ends of the table, flanked on one side by Pearl and Todd, and on the other by Michael and Sarah.

Sarah, sitting down beside Michael, smiled at him shyly. Earlier, and once she'd managed to get over her prior embarrassment, she had been surprised to find just how much she enjoyed talking to him. Michael had made no mention of their first meeting. Since he hadn't, Sarah gladly followed his lead.

When everyone had helped themselves and were about to start, Jim tapped his wine glass gently with his knife.

"Attention, attention," he said with a smile. "Seeing us all sitting here like this brings to my mind that a toast might be in order. After all it is a while since we all sat down to a meal like this, and even longer since Sarah was here with us too. So, I thought I might propose a toast to Sarah, which is probably as close as we'll get to a proper official welcome home."

Everyone smiled at Sarah except Todd, who made a face like he wanted to be sick. By choice it seemed he would rather not partake in something quite so sentimental, but in the end even he was spared. Before Jim could say any more the sound of the chiming doorbell filled the air.

Jim frowned. "Who the hell could that be right now?" he asked, before setting down his glass to go and find out.

He returned moments later with Margaret's brother David. He strode into the dining room in his brother-in-law's wake as though he owned the place, swaggering with confidence as though for him to call in was a regular occurrence. In truth it was more like three months since any of them had seen him.

"Hello, hello, what have we here? All the family together? What's the occasion?" He then spied Sarah. "Ah," he said with a broad grin, "the wanderer returns."

He came over to see her, necessitating Sarah to stand up and receive the hug he so evidently wanted to bestow upon her.

"Welcome home, niece of mine," he said dramatically. "Let me look at you."

He held Sarah at arms length examining her with theatrical flair, his eyes flitting all over her. Sarah felt a little like a possum in the headlights of an oncoming car but his scrutiny gave her the opportunity to do the same in return. Sarah found a few changes in her absence. David Hamilton had never been a tall man, but his lack of stature had begun to become more pronounced by the expansion of his girth, something he had clearly been working on of late. The waistband of his rather loud trousers positively groaned. The very least Sarah could say about such trousers were that they matched his equally loud shirt, which Uncle David wore unbuttoned almost down to his navel, revealing a lavish gold medallion and rather more chest hair than was comfortable to view.

There could be no doubting the hirsuteness of his chest but for some time he'd had a decreasing amount of hair on his head. When Sarah looked at him she realized he had chosen to disguise this deficiency with a thick toupee which he wore at an almost jaunty angle. Sarah was thankful when he pronounced, "I think you're looking exceptionally well," and released her so that she could smother the laughter she felt brewing within her.

"Mother!" he said, going around to the other side of the table to kiss

Pearl's cheek, before doing the same to his sister. He then realized no one was eating, so he said, "Dig in, dig in. Don't stand on ceremony on my account. Everything will be getting cold."

Jim grumbled something unintelligible from his end of the table and immediately began to eat. The others soon followed suit, except Margaret.

"Have you had lunch?" she asked, her tone full of fearful expectation.

"Now you come to mention it, no I haven't."

"I'm sure there'll be plenty if you want to join us," she said flatly.

"Great. Don't mind if I do. Shall I get a chair?"

Before Sarah knew it Uncle David had grabbed himself a chair from the kitchen table and had begun to elbow his way between her and Michael. Margaret hastily found him a plate, place mat and some utensils, and poured him out the remnants of the wine.

"Should have brought a bottle," he said with regret. "If only I'd known."

"It wasn't a formal lunch," Margaret lied. "More of an impromptu thing."

"Ah, yes, I see. But not quite so impromptu as to have invited a guest?" He turned to Michael. "I don't believe we've met. I'm David Hamilton."

"Michael Alexander," Michael said, taking and shaking the hand David offered.

"And you are?"

"The neighbor. Your mother and I have struck up a friendship over a mutual love of literature."

David's eyebrows shot up. "Have you now? I see. I'd guessed you must be Sarah's boyfriend."

Michael laughed. "No, no. Just a new acquaintance."

Sarah did not know what to make of this comment. Of course he wasn't her boyfriend, but he didn't have to make the prospect sound so very unlikely, did he? In the end Sarah concluded perhaps she'd be better off not asking herself that question. After all, what did it matter to her? As nice as he seemed, Sarah definitely wasn't in the market for a romance with anyone. After her last foray into the realms of love, she wondered whether it would be anywhere she ever wanted to go again.

Uncle David, burnt many times in love, wasn't so reticent.

"I should have brought Petunia," he said.

"Thank God you didn't," Jim murmured, but David did not hear.

"Who on earth is Petunia?" Pearl asked.

"My girlfriend," David replied. "Met her six weeks ago at a party at the yacht club. Wonderful girl. She's got aspirations to be a model."

"David!" Margaret chastised. "Aren't all women with aspirations to be models about twelve years old?"

David laughed, not in the slightest bit perturbed. "Perhaps I should have said 'mature model'. I've never had to resort to cradle snatching, I'll have you know."

Margaret's eyes narrowed. "How mature?"

Unabashed, David said, "I'm not saying there isn't any sort of age difference. You and I, Margaret, are getting to the stage where we've practically got an age difference with anyone under fifty. But at least I can safely say Petunia is more than half as old as I am."

"Bloody hell," Jim said under his breath. He said, "What happened to that other woman? Linley? Lindsay? Linda? Something like that."

David's face fell. "Belinda. I'm afraid it didn't work out." His sadness was momentary. And since nobody knew Belinda any better than they'd known any of David's other myriad girlfriends there wasn't much to be said by anyone else either. There had only been a sense that perhaps Belinda had been a bit more special than some of the others. "Not to worry, though. After all, on account of the fact that I was just the weeniest bit depressed about the departure of Belinda, a mate invited me to this shindig at the yacht club, and lo and behold, there was Petunia. You see, it just goes to prove that every cloud has a silver lining."

"Plenty more fish in the sea, eh?" Jim said.

David, either not hearing or choosing to ignore the sarcasm in Jim's voice, smiled broadly and said, "Yes indeed, and some mighty tasty ones too, I might add."

"David!" Margaret chastised, sending him meaningful nods in Todd's direction, trying to remind him to be a bit more circumspect around the younger member of the family. For his part Todd looked utterly horrified at the prospect of anyone of Uncle David's advanced years and dubious charms having a girlfriend. His lips curled disdainfully. He looked as though he'd been put off eating altogether.

As the meal progressed David continued to update the family on his latest exploits, most of which involved the hitherto unseen Petunia. The more David talked, the less everyone else could think of to say. Sarah wondered what Michael made of them all. The odd glance she managed to catch of him - when Uncle David leaned forward to impress upon them all some point he was trying to make - he seemed to be taking everything in his stride. She wondered if he was just being polite, longing for release in the same way the rest of them were. Sarah could see her father struggling to maintain his equilibrium. He and David had never had much in common.

The leftovers were just being passed around and dishes cleared away in preparation for dessert when the doorbell rang for a second time.

"Ah," Jim said knowingly. "I think that will be my silver lining."

A lull in the David-dominated conversation ensued as all ears strained to hear whom the new arrivals might be. They could hear Jim being uncharacteristically jolly as he made and laughed at his own jokes. Whoever had arrived had voices practically inaudible to the human ear. It wasn't until Jim returned to the dining room with the guests that the rest of the household even realized someone had actually stayed.

Behind him trailed Tom and Gerry, both casting their gaze around from under their matching fringes, eyes searching and taking in absolutely everything. Gerry blinked myopically, as though he had walked into a room filled with light too bright for his eyes. Sarah couldn't help wondering if he'd worn his clothes to bed last night. Even his glasses seemed off centre, as though he'd fallen asleep with them on his face, that with lying on his side they'd been pressed askew. Then, when he'd woken up in the morning he'd simply forgotten to adjust them.

Tom, on the other hand, seemed to have taken considerable care with her appearance. She wore her hair scraped up away from her face. Sarah thought she could detect faint traces of make-up while her short skirt and crop top were clearly designed to draw attention to her emergent curves. She saw Todd readily enough but her eyes soon spied another person at the dinner table, Mr. Alexander. Once apprised of his presence she continued to regard him stealthily from under her fringe.

Margaret returned with dessert and nearly fell over the twins as she entered the room.

"Hello, you two," she said with surprise. "What are you doing here?"

Dragging her gaze away from Mr. Alexander, Tom said, "We came to find out what Todd's doing."

"Quite clearly he's having lunch," Margaret said. "Which is not over yet. We've still to have dessert," she added, depositing the lemon meringue pie onto the table.

Todd looked at the pie, up at his friends, then longingly back at the pie again.

"I won't be a minute," he said.

Margaret frowned. "I suppose you'll want some too," she said.

Tom and Gerry both nodded.

Margaret sighed. "I'll go and get some extra bowls. Perhaps somebody could help find two more chairs as well."

Jim stood up and elbowed Todd. "Come and help."

Todd reluctantly slid off his chair. Gerry continued to lurk in the corner, not quite knowing what to do with himself. Tom, however, moved faster than greased lightning and quickly made herself at home in Margaret's chair.

"Hi, Mr. Alexander," she cooed.

"Hello, Thomasina. How are you?"

"Fine thanks. You can call me Tom, you know."

"Tom. Right."

"I didn't know you'd be here," she said.

He tried a small smile. "I didn't know either."

David turned to Sarah. "They're twins," he said, as though the discovery of other twins in the world besides Margaret and himself was something of a revelation.

"They are indeed," Sarah replied.

"How curious."

"In what way?"

"Oh," David said, waving a vague hand, "just in the fact that there seems to be a certain irony to Todd ending up with friends who are twins when his mother is one. And not just twins, but boy and girl twins."

Sarah followed his gaze as he looked carefully at Tom. She wondered what was going through his head and hoped it was nothing untoward. Meanwhile she couldn't help noticing Tom doing her damnedest to hold Michael's attention. He in turn attempted to maintain a professional distance.

Sarah said, "Todd's been friends with Tom and Gerry since, oh, probably since he was about seven."

"Really? All that time? And I never knew."

"Why would you?"

David shrugged. "I suppose I'd have expected Margaret to mentioned it. Then again, I suppose the twin thing never really meant that much to her."

Sarah was surprised. "And it did to you?"

"Maybe. I suppose because it's not that common. It's always been something a bit special to me. It makes me feel less alone somehow."

"Some people might think it would just make you feel less unique."

David smiled. "Ah, yes, but we are unique aren't we? I mean we're not the same sex, and we don't look alike, so it's not quite the same as for identical twins. Even then, I'm sure they have a clear idea of who's who. It's just other people who can't tell them apart or don't make the effort to try."

Margaret came bustling back in the room with bowls and spoons, formed her lips into a thin line of disapproval and sat down at the spare seat that had been slotted in between Pearl and Todd. Gerry had wedged his chair between Todd and Jim's. He was busy telling Todd about some old episodes of *Star Trek* he'd recently seen on DVD. Sarah noticed Todd didn't look particularly interested.

Dessert was dished up. David said no more about his thoughts on being a twin. It surprised Sarah that it mattered to him as much as it did. Not because his actions indicated otherwise, but because she had never attributed that degree of sentiment to a man she'd always thought of as largely superficial.

A strange silence fell over the group. Uncle David seemed inhibited by the presence of the twins and had lapsed into an almost moody silence. Pearl had attempted to talk to Tom but her monosyllabic replies and eyelash fluttering at Michael made for poor conversation. Jim looked like he'd rather be out in the garage. Margaret seemed miffed at the fact that she'd had her place at the table usurped and that her Sunday lunch had been hijacked by extras. Todd looked faintly embarrassed by the whole proceedings. Sarah wasn't sure this had more to do with the twins being on display in front of his family, or indeed the other way around. Sarah knew there'd been times as a teenager when she'd wished she could lock her family away and save herself from embarrassment.

When the lemon meringue pie was nothing more than a few crumbs in the bottom of the pie dish, Margaret gruffly suggested coffee. Pearl, David and Jim accepted the offer. Todd signaled to Tom that it was time to go but she strenuously ignored him. Margaret went to ask Michael whether he would like coffee when Sarah felt the need to intervene on his behalf. She discovered her embarrassment about her family had perhaps survived into adulthood after all. She felt she had to do something to rescue him.

"I wouldn't mind taking another look at your garden, Michael," she said loudly. "After all, if I'm to make some landscape design suggestions, I'll need to see it again."

If Michael felt any surprise by her comment he did not show it. "Great," he said. "Right now I need all the help I can get."

They beat a hasty retreat. Once they were out in the sunshine and away from the family their pace slowed as they strolled next door.

"Thanks for the rescue," Michael said. "I can't remember the last time I needed saving quite as badly as that."

Sarah smiled. "I'm just sorry my family are so awful."

"Oh, it wasn't your family that came to mind," Michael replied. "It was Thomasina Redstone. Unfortunately, every so often, one of the girls at school develops something of a crush on me. This year it's Thomasina."

Sarah glanced at him. She remembered her own school days and never recalled having the remotest crush on any of her teachers. But then none of her teachers had been even vaguely attractive, whereas the same certainly could not be said of Michael. Sarah swallowed.

"That must be tricky to deal with," she said.

"At times it's more than tricky, it's downright dangerous. These days a male teacher only has to look sideways at a pupil and they're up before a disciplinary committee. And I'm not necessarily talking about female pupils either." He led the way up the front steps, inserted the key in the lock and gave the door a hefty push. "And they wonder why males are being put off the teaching profession."

"I thought the pay situation put men off," said Sarah, following him back down the hall. She could not believe she'd returned here so soon when only this morning she hadn't wanted to come at all.

"Well, there is that. No doubt I could make a lot more if I'd decided to be a doctor, a dentist, a lawyer or an accountant."

"But you didn't want to do any of those things?"

"No."

Coming into the lounge, he said, "I think I could do with some coffee, after all. Want to join me?"

Sarah nodded and followed him into the kitchen. She watched him work swiftly, putting on water to boil, getting out the plunger and coffee grounds, fossicking in cupboards for mugs, finding milk and sugar. He seemed a man clearly at home in his kitchen. Looking at the way he had everything ar-ranged, the utensils hanging on the wall, the spice rack and the glimpses she got of the contents of his pantry suggested he enjoyed cooking. Strangely, this thought pleased her. She couldn't help thinking of Jeremy, and his allergy to anything domestic. "I make it a rule to never, never, do anything I could pay someone else to do," Jeremy had once said.

Stifling a sigh, she said, "So, did you always want to be a teacher?"

He shook his head. "Never. And between you and me, I still don't."

"Really? Then why do it?"

"Because I love the written word, have an affinity with teenagers, and I need an income."

Sarah frowned. "You make it sound a bit desperate."

"Oh, it's not so bad. The hours are long, there's a lot of preparation and marking to do in the evenings, and you are expected to get involved in a certain amount of extracurricular activities. And believe me, the extra in extracurricular doesn't mean extra in the pay packet either. It's all for love."

"So what would you rather be doing?"

"Ah, well, now we come down to it." He poured the water into the plunger, instantly releasing the smell of brewing coffee.

"Aren't you going to tell me, then?"

He laughed. "Oh, all right. The fact of the matter is, I don't mention it much because as yet there's nothing much to tell. What I really want to do is write books. Novels, in fact. Thrillers, crime, that sort of thing."

"Really? Somehow I can see you doing that."

"Yes, well, doing is the problem. Work is so busy that it's hard to find time. And," he said, looking around him with a disparaging gaze, "it's not as if there aren't plenty of other things to be done, is there? Did you mean it, by the way, about my garden? Or did you just say that to help me get out of there?"

Sarah shrugged. "Up to you really. Until I find a job I haven't got a lot on. If you wanted me to, I could give it some thought, come up with some suggestions. We'd have to talk a bit more about it so I could get a feel for what you want."

"What I want?" he echoed. "It would be fabulous. I'd worship the ground you walked on. Let's go and sit on the back steps and you can look at the mess all you like."

Sarah could feel herself going red at the thought of him worshipping the ground she walked on but in spite of herself, a bit of her reveled in the sentiment. She would definitely need to give that part of herself a serious talking to later. Meanwhile, she followed Michael through the lounge, holding his coffee while he opened the French doors. She sat down on the opposite side of the steps and leaned against the sun-warmed balustrade.

For a while they sat in silence, enjoying the afternoon sun and the tranquility. At length, Sarah said, "I still feel I need to apologize for my family."

Michael looked surprised. "Why? They seemed very familyish to me. What else was I to expect?"

"Not walking in on some sort of battle out of World War Three between Mum and Dad. Not having to be subjected to Uncle David."

"Everybody disagrees with one another at some stage," he replied casually. "I bet there's not a couple around married for as long as that who don't fight on occasions."

Sarah wanted to tell him that of late it seemed more than just on occasions, that her mother appeared to find her father intensely irritating at times, but she did not want to be disloyal by blabbing the family secrets to a relative stranger.

"You're probably right," she said. "However, nothing can really excuse Uncle David. I'm beginning to think he's beyond redemption."

Michael looked at Sarah, his expression one of contemplation. "I couldn't help thinking that beneath his veneer of bravado, he wasn't a particularly happy man."

"He has had his fair share of sadness, I will admit. His daughter, my cousin Brenda, got killed in a car accident by a drunk driver about six years ago. After that his marriage to Aunt Irene disintegrated. Brenda was their only child - which they'd both always been sad enough about anyway - so that when she died there didn't seem to be anything left to keep them together. Maybe the marriage was over before that anyway. Aunt Irene pretty much lived vicariously through Brenda and the accident devastated her. In the end she moved to Australia to try to put some distance between herself and the constant reminders.

"As for Uncle David, I think he started to look for some comfort, but in all the wrong places and with all the wrong people. I think his flirting and all the endless women has become a bad habit that distracts him from the fact that he's still hurting."

"Grief certainly does strange things to people. I often wonder if in fact it doesn't just exaggerate traits that were perhaps already there."

"You sound as though you speak from experience."

Michael frowned, the first time she had seen him looking anything nearing troubled. "You're right. Sadly, my own brother, Bruce, died about six years ago too. Ironically also a drinking related fatality, only he was the one who'd been doing the drinking."

"I'm sorry," Sarah said sadly. Considering this, she said, "You don't think..."

"What? That it could have been the same accident? No, if there was anything to be thankful for, the only person Bruce killed was himself. He was a barrister, you see, and had been out celebrating the fact that he'd won some landmark case. Unfortunately, he celebrated rather more than his body could tolerate. On his way home in his very flash BMW, he drove straight into a tree. Killed instantly."

"I'm sorry," Sarah said again, wishing she could think of something more profound and helpful to say.

He shrugged. "There's nothing anyone can do about it now, least of all you and me. Bruce always lived his life with a degree of infallibility, but in truth, like all of us, he had his weaknesses."

"What about your parents? I don't suppose you'd ever get over something like that, would you? Nobody expects to outlive their own child."

"I guess not. However, I think they honestly believed Bruce to be about as super human as he did himself. Even now, six years later, I still don't think they believe he's gone, let alone have a clue as to how to come to terms with it. They've got a whole room in the house, Bruce's old bedroom done up like some sort of shrine to his memory, with all the memorabilia one might associate with a successful life."

"Really? How does that make you feel?"

He shrugged again. He drained the dregs of his coffee, making a face at the bitterness. "I don't know. My thoughts and feelings about my parents aren't exactly clear-cut."

Sarah thought about her own parents. "Whose are?"

Michael smiled briefly. "Yes, well, at least you aren't competing with the ghost of your dead brother for their affections, are you?" Seeing the look on her face, he said, "You think I'm being a bit harsh?"

Sarah regarded him closely. "I couldn't say. I mean, I don't really know anything about it. Do you still see them, if things are that bad?"

"Sometimes. Not much." He brushed a spot off his jeans. "It's another thing I don't often talk much about. It all seems a bit too much like a plot out of a bad American television movie. You know the kind I mean. Elder brother, successful, handsome, charming and the apple of his parents' eye has his life tragically cut short, leaving poor grieving parents with the other son - the one who has no driving ambition, who's not wildly successful, and in comparison to his brother, seems a little short on charm. Can you wonder that I don't see them much?"

"But what are you talking about? You're successful, aren't you? And you've got ambition. And I don't want to give you a big head or anything, but you seem pretty charming to me."

"Do I?"

Sarah said, "Just ask Tom. She thinks you're fantastic."

Michael sighed. "I don't want to sound petulant, but the thing is, all of that stuff just doesn't cut the mustard with Ma and Pa."

"Why not?"

"I'm afraid school teaching is considered too demeaning and not nearly successful enough. Ambition should consist of wanting to win landmark lawsuits, or making a million dollars by the time you're thirty. At the very least it should involve finding a cure for cancer. Wanting to write books is a waste of time and not worthy of an Alexander."

Sarah sat there looking at Michael for a while. Everything he said, he'd said lightly enough, but it wasn't difficult to hear the hurt in his voice. She wondered how his parents could let their grief blind them to the attributes of their remaining son.

"I'm sorry," she said again.

He grinned lopsidedly. "I was afraid you would be. That's precisely why I don't talk about it."

Yet talk he had, and to her. Later, after he had quickly steered the conversation onto the topic of his garden, after she had excused herself on the pretext of going home to help clear up, she had to wonder why he had chosen to confide in her. However, she couldn't help feeling pleased that he had.

CHAPTER FOUR

The Monday morning scramble to get out of the door could not have been described as dignified. From the calm oasis of her bed Sarah could hear more shouting than could surely be necessary, mostly from her mother. However, in her mother's defence, her shouting seemed to stem from a lot of provocation from both Todd and her father. Both intermittently yelled through the house for directions on where to find the usual complement of lost items, baffled queries as to why the toothpaste had run out and whether breakfast was ready yet.

Hearing the irritation in her mother's voice reach new heights, Sarah decided the time had come to get out of bed. Maybe she could help. Failing that, maybe, at the very least, her presence might calm muddied waters.

She threw on her robe and headed for the stairs when the telephone began to ring. She heard the unmistakable exclamation of Margaret saying, "For God's sake! What now?"

Sarah scooped up the phone as she reached the one on the hall table. "Hello?"

"Sarah? It's Auntie Sheila here."

"Auntie Sheila! How nice to hear from you."

"Yes, darling. Welcome home. Sorry you couldn't come over last week. It would have been lovely to see you. Margaret, Mum and I had a lovely little tête-à-tête. I'm sure you would have enjoyed it, too."

Sarah felt her eyebrows rise at a description of events so different from her own mother's. Instead said, "Yes, sorry about that. But I'm home for good now. I'm sure there'll be other times."

"Indeed, indeed. I feel awful not to have seen you when you've been home...how long is it?"

"Ten days today. Barely enough time for my feet to have touched the ground."

"Of course. And I'm sure you must have so much to do."

"Quite a bit more than I pictured. On top of which, I'm supposed to be looking for a job."

"Oh. Any luck so far?"

"I'm only *supposed* to be looking," Sarah said with a laugh. "I didn't actually say I *was* looking." She glimpsed herself in the mirror and attempted to smooth her tousled hair. "I have seen one or two ads for positions that I might apply for but my C.V. needs a bit of work first. We'll see. Mum seems keen for me to have a bit of a break until after Christmas. In a way my life does sort of feel on hold until after that."

"In that case we'll be able to catch up I'm sure."

"I might even come this week with Mum and Nan," Sarah suggested.

"Ah, yes, well, perhaps not this week. You see, that's the reason I'm calling. I'm not going to be able to do this week. But that's not to say I wouldn't like to see you soon. But now that it's December the round of Christmas events kick off. Our calendar is looking very full. Perhaps, though, you'd like to come for dinner some time?"

"That would be wonderful," Sarah said, thinking to herself she'd be sure to check with her mother first and definitely not offer to bring anything more than wine.

"Now, let's see. Looking here on the calendar, almost every night next week is full, and there are some penciled-in dates for the week after. No, it's no good. That's getting too far away, isn't it? Wait! What about this Friday? Could you come this Friday?"

"I'm pretty sure that will be okay. I'll double check with Mum just in case there's something on that I don't know about. Other than that, yes, I'd love to come."

"Great. Will you come on your own? There's no one special you'd like to bring?"

Unbidden, a picture of Michael popped into Sarah's head.

"No," she said firmly. "It'll just be me. Anyway, I'll get Mum. You can tell her about the change of plan for this week."

Because no way in the world would Sarah be the one to break the news.

Sarah walked into the kitchen.

"Morning," she said. "Phone for you. It's Auntie Sheila."

Margaret pursed her lips. "I'll take it in here," she said getting up from the table to get the cordless kitchen phone.

"Sheila?"

"Hello, Margaret."

"You're out of bed early."

"Well it's all busy, busy. You know what it's like at this time of year."

Margaret clenched her teeth. How busy could Sheila possibly be when she had a cleaner, could call up a caterer if she couldn't be bothered cooking? She knew Sheila sent a good deal of their washing out to some service who washed and ironed it and brought it back like the elves had done it all.

"What can I do for you Sheila?"

"Well, um, it's about this afternoon. Er, things have got a bit confused here. I've had to change things around a bit. Jason neglected to tell me about some end of year performance his band is giving in a concert at school tomorrow afternoon, which means my usual Tuesday hair appointment has had to be moved to Thursday morning. However Thursday morning I was supposed to meet some friends for coffee to discuss plans for the upcoming charity Christmas ball I'm helping organize. And since I'm such a vital member of the organizing committee, we've rescheduled for Friday morning.

"Friday morning I was supposed to have a dress fitting for said ball, and the only other time I can do that is Wednesday afternoon. Wednesday afternoon I was supposed to be meeting John at the lawyers to sign some papers so when I called him to see about changing the time he said he's had a cancellation this afternoon. But that, of course, is when you and Mum are supposed to be coming.

Margaret said nothing while she digested all of this, then said, "I see."

"So, as you can probably appreciate, there's just no way I can juggle anything else. Something has to give. The thing is, Jason lives for his music. It wouldn't be right if neither of us could be there even though the event will probably give me an atrocious headache. And of course John's too busy to go instead of me, especially since he's had to rearrange his day today to fit in the lawyer visit."

Margaret could feel her blood beginning to boil.

"Margaret?"

"What? What do you want me to say? Oh, yes Sheila, fine Sheila, three bags full Sheila. Not bloody likely. What about your mother Sheila? You make absolutely no effort to be involved in her life, leave everything up to me, and then drop us both like a hot potato the minute something better comes along. And I'm supposed to be happy about this?"

"That's a bit harsh considering it's only a few days since I saw you anyway," Sheila said. "And of course I am involved with Mum."

"Are you? How? How many times have you run Mum to the shops, or taken her to the doctor, or made sure she's all right in the last six months?"

"I do other things," Sheila said defensively. "It's not as if I'm on hand like you are."

"And why is that?"

"Well, you did offer to have her."

"Only because neither you nor David lifted a finger."

"Margaret," Sheila said firmly, "I'm not going to discuss this with you any more. Things were decided for the best. If it's not working out for you, if you're finding it too much, then you must deal with it. There's no sense in shouting at me just because you're not coping. We all make our own destiny in life and mine is to be involved in worthwhile events and support my husband in his busy and demanding career. I'm sorry if my change of plans has upset you but that's just the way it is. But I'm tired of the fact that you're always unhappy. If you want to be that way, fine, go right ahead, but I won't let you drag me down with you."

With that, Sheila put down the receiver leaving Margaret fuming on the other end.

"So you see," Margaret said, shifting uncomfortably from leg to leg, "I'm afraid there's nothing to be done about it."

Pearl's silence stretched on.

"It's all quite unavoidable," Margaret added, wishing she could crush something. Why she should have to justify Sheila's behavior she didn't know. Certainly if it wasn't for the fact that Sheila had hung up on her, Margaret would have insisted Sheila call their mother herself and explain why she was too busy to see her.

But no, Sheila had to make things even more difficult by ranting at her and then dramatically putting down the phone. If Margaret had not been so mad about that she would have called Sheila back and told her in no uncertain terms that she was not going to be the bearer of bad tidings to their mother. Sheila could jolly well do her dirty work herself.

Pearl let out a thin sigh. "Yes, I suppose it can't be helped. And I suppose too, that we should be giving credit to Sheila for making time for her boy."

Margaret knew what she would like to give Sheila, but it certainly wasn't credit.

"Yes, well, God knows, it's not before time," Margaret said heavily.

Pearl looked directly at Margaret, making Margaret feel about five years old again. Pearl said, "Perhaps we could do something else this afternoon? Go for a drive? Go to the shops? Take a little stroll?"

"The thing is," Margaret said, "I have got quite a lot on my plate this afternoon. Perhaps we could do something later in the week? Once I've cleared the decks a bit?"

Pearl examined her fingernails.

"They say it might rain later anyway," Margaret said lamely.

"Oh, in that case," Pearl said, her tone far from philosophical, "maybe it's just as well."

As Margaret made her way back into the house to get on with her busy life Pearl sat despondently on the couch, re-examining her fingernails. She had begun to feel very small, as though with the passing of the days her bodily frame kept on being somehow reduced. She wondered whether, if things went on at their current pace, people would soon cease to notice her at all. It felt as though she had begun to not count for anything any more, that she was taking up a place on a planet where there wasn't any room for her, as though she no longer had anything of value to contribute. It made her feel withered inside, a bloom once bright now diminished and well past its best. The only thing left required someone coming along with a giant pair of secateurs and all evidence of her could be erased.

Certainly her family did not seem to need her. Sheila fitted her in as she did any other item on her agenda: something that could be rearranged, and if need be, ultimately dropped from the schedule altogether. Margaret seemed to be in the grip of some madness and was quite unreachable, and although Pearl was worried about her, there didn't seem to be anything tangible she could actually do about the situation. Margaret had erected some sort of walls about her behind which Pearl was not permitted.

As for David, well, she did not like to think about David. She cringed as she thought about him strutting around like a peacock on Sunday, preening in his vulgar clothes and that ridiculous wig he'd decided to wear. All those women, all that shallow endeavor. Underneath it all unhappiness slowly ate him up. Well, seemed to be eating all the sensible parts of him, anyway.

It saddened her that none of her children were filled with joy. Sheila's happiness had a vague quality to it. In Pearl's opinion she crammed her life with vacuous things that served only to paper over the cracks. Sheila and John thought wealth bought them happiness but Pearl wasn't so sure. If that wealth and position should ever be challenged, or even taken away completely, would what remained stand the test of time?

Then there were her grandchildren. Joanna, who could be a child of Sheila rather than of Margaret, had fallen into exactly the same trap of seeing money as the be-all and end-all of life. She appeared to consider herself above things like spending time with any of her family any more than strictly necessary. Jason and Reuben she never saw from one year's end to the next, a fact that did not ultimately make Pearl feel too sorry. They were overindulged and had little thought for anyone other than themselves.

Todd, who had always been a bit of a handful, had at least always been respectful. But even that respect had undergone some sort of erosion as some unseen influence crept into his life. Pearl hoped that it turned out to be no more than teenage petulance. But with his own mother not happy and his father increasingly silent in response, things hung in the balance at a time when he could do with all the stability - and discipline - he could stand.

Sarah was a breath of fresh air who blew in now and again. But she had her own life to lead and Pearl felt she could not expect more from her than she already gave. Before long she would move away into a flat with some other young people, get a job, and come by even less. It was the way of the world.

Then there was Michael. He'd also been something of a diversion but he was busy, and not a relative anyway. On Sunday he had not been as attentive as before. The reason for this was more than obvious to Pearl. And while the loss of attention to another wasn't something she begrudged, it did make her feel a little sad.

She was in danger of sinking further into the doldrums when a sharp knock came at the door. Ernest beamed on the threshold.

"Morning, morning," he said brightly.

"Hello, Ernest," Pearl said, accepting his perfunctory kiss on the cheek. "Come in."

"Don't mind if I do. How are you this morning?"

"Well enough," Pearl replied, indicating he should take a seat.

"You don't look it," he said as he collapsed heavily down. "You look like death warmed up. What's wrong with you?"

Pearl sighed. "Just feeling a bit sorry for myself."

"God, really? You took your time about it. I've been feeling sorry for you for ages."

Pearl smiled. "Have you? Thanks."

"Pearl, my old girl, you've got to get out of here."

"Not that old chestnut again."

"Oh, I don't mean permanently. I've given up on trying to convince you of the merits of looking for new digs. No, no, I mean now, today. What have you got planned anyway?"

"I've got some sheets and a nightie I need to wash."

His eyes narrowed. "Not that damned incontinence again? Why don't you go and see someone about it?"

Pearl could feel herself reddening, but said, "You don't know what you're talking about."

"Don't I? What else have you got on your agenda?"

"Nothing. Sheila's had to cancel this afternoon, and Margaret's too busy to do anything else."

"Great. That means you'll have no excuse."

"Excuse for what?"

"For coming with me to meet Rosa. And," he said, holding up his hand, "this time I won't take no for an answer."

Really, Pearl thought, there wasn't any excuse. She couldn't think of one single thing to prevent her from going.

"All right," she said. "I'll come."

Having secured her agreement Ernest wasted no time in bundling Pearl into his car. He allowed her only time enough to put her washing into the machine, to put a bit of face powder on and to brush her hair. He folded her into the car like a treasured object into a box then slammed the door firmly behind her. She wondered if he sensed she might all of a sudden make a run for it.

He looked heartily pleased with himself when he hopped into the car beside her and sent her a grin that reminded Pearl of their younger days. Ernest would always get that look right before he did something that got him his own way. The very thought of it made Pearl smile in return. To her surprise, she found herself looking forward to getting out for a change of scene.

She'd wanted to go and tell Margaret where she was off to but Ernest would concede to no further delay.

"She probably won't notice you're gone anyway," he said.

When Pearl went to defend her daughter she stopped, realizing Ernest was probably right.

The drive took only ten minutes and meandered through two neighboring suburbs. These days, houses seemed to stretch as far as the eye could see. Pearl couldn't help thinking that even Jack would be shocked by the rapidity of progress over the last couple of years. In fact, in some ways, coming this direction felt like visiting another town completely.

Lambton Park itself was situated at the end of a cul-de-sac street, where a sweeping driveway led up to the complex. This lay on land Pearl recalled as once being covered in strawberry fields. She remembered coming out here to pick strawberries with her mother one summer. Charles had come out in hives from eating too many. Her mother had spent hours boiling the strawberries up to make jam and the house had been filled with a hot, sweet aroma.

"I didn't realize this was where Lambton Park was," Pearl told him.

"You would have if you'd accepted my earlier invitation to come," Ernest chastised.

Pearl said nothing. Instead she looked out of the window. It was hard to believe that here there had once been row upon row of strawberries planted in mounts of soil and surrounded by yellow straw that let off a grassy smell in the warm sunshine. In her mind's eye she could still see the rickety shed presided over by Mrs. Holmes, her starched apron stretching precariously around her large girth as she carefully monitored the weighing scales as people came to pay for their pickings. The fields had been dotted with people working industriously, sheltering under conical hats to keep the summer sun off their faces. Now, though, no traces of this remained.

In its place had been built a complex the likes of which Pearl had never seen. Lambton Park was comprised of three types of accommodation - individual units built of sturdy brick, smart tile roofs and low maintenance aluminum joinery, each with their own little gardens; two wings of terraced houses which were somewhat smaller; and a residential wing for those needing more intensive care. The complex sported a swimming pool, tennis courts, a little shop, a dining room if you didn't want to self cater, a library, an infirmary and a common room.

Everything had been neatly laid out, generously landscaped and prodigiously cared for. Whoever had been responsible for landscaping had brought in a small collection of enormous date palms whose presence gave the village a tropical feel.

As Ernest drove slowly down the main drive he waved now and again to people he knew. Pearl's mind boggled over the fact that somewhere so modern and friendly-looking could exist for the elderly. Rather than being repulsed by it - as she thought she would - she felt charmed. Not that she could imagine herself living in a place like this. Nevertheless, she could see now why Ernest found the prospect of living here more than a little tolerable.

Steering the car off the main driveway, Ernest negotiated his way down one of the many access ways that flowed like tributaries off the main avenue. He stopped moments later on a parking space outside a squat little house surrounded by a neat but utilitarian garden.

"Home sweet home," he said. "Out you get."

"This is your unit?" Pearl asked as she climbed from the car.

"Sure is. Two bedrooms, a bathroom, kitchen and lounge. Imagine, four separate rooms. It'll seem like a palace compared to what you're used to."

Pearl frowned. "You can cut those remarks out for a start, unless you want to take me straight back home."

"Right-o, right-o, calm down. Just joking. Come inside and see for yourself."

Upon entering the house Pearl had to concede that it was very nice. It was light and airy, the kitchen had plenty of room to work in, the layout compact yet making the most of the space. It was all very tastefully decorated.

"So, you actually own this house, do you?"

"I do," he said, "although under certain provisos. In the event of my death - or my decision to move elsewhere - my contract states that I have to sell the house through a particular agency so that the owners of Lambton Park ensure the new owners fit the criteria."

"Criteria?"

"You know. Old, of sufficient health and mental capacity for independent living, able to pay for the other expenses. That sort of thing."

"What expenses?"

"We all have to pay a body corporate fee for insurance, rates contributions, landscape and communal building maintenance and toward the salary of the twenty four hour medical clinic staff."

"Is that much?"

Ernest shrugged. "It's not too bad actually. Because there are so many residents the shared cost brings the price down somewhat. Since we don't pay rates as such, it doesn't work out that much more expensive than ordinary rates plus usual home maintenance costs. And you have to take into consideration the fact that everything is organized for you. No dealing with grubby tradesmen and unreliable staff."

Pearl said, "It's very nice."

"I knew you'd like it," Ernest boasted.

"And Rosa? Where does she live?"

"About three units that way," he said, pointing out the window. "Come on and I'll show you."

Having had more of an objection to coming to Lambton Park than she had of meeting Rosa, Pearl realized her prejudice for one had numbed her curiosity about the other. She did not know much about Rosa, or even much about what to expect. She briefly considered the idea of asking Ernest for more information but in the end decided she would just wait and see for herself.

Ernest started out from the house very intrepidly, having the posture of a man confident of where he was going and the welcome he would receive when he arrived. Pearl trailed after him down a cobbled path that threaded its way across a manicured lawn, passed two other houses identical to Ernest's own, whereupon reaching the third house he swung off the path toward the front door.

Although Rosa's house was the image of all those around it, hers differed in one contrasting respect. Where all the surrounding houses had neat, almost municipal gardens around them, Rosa's was filled with a riot of color. Instead of the usual rose and daisy and ornamental shrub, there were Canterbury Bells and snapdragons and viscaria and cosmos and linum, a riot of crimson and pink and red and yellow, as though someone had waved a magic wand and created a rainbow with a wave of their hand.

"Rosa does the garden herself, you know," Ernest said proudly, as though knowing Rosa gave him some vicarious honor.

"Sarah would appreciate this," Pearl said. "It must take a lot of hard work."

"She potters," Ernest said mysteriously, before turning to knock on the door.

Moments later, the door was thrown open and there was Rosa. Pearl had to look twice at her to make sure she was real. For Rosa resembled something that you might find in a European music box, a tiny woman, ballerina-like, with fine features, and exquisite skin which looked as though it might be painted on. She had long grey hair woven into some sort of complex style. Her tawny eyes sparkled as she looked out of the doorway.

Her clothes were exotic too. It seemed as though she'd been swathed rather than dressed, with layers of interesting fabrics in a profusion of colors which Pearl would never have considered combining. On Rosa it looked as natural as the plumage on an exotic bird. And when she spoke, her accent was rich and unmistakably foreign, with a glamour that antipodean accents could never manage.

"Ernest," she said with a huge smile, her face lighting up in delight. The way she said his name made even solid old Ernest seem larger than life. Pearl could not help but look with semi-bulging eyes as Ernest kissed Rosa on each cheek with a flourish almost as if he had spent his whole life dramatically kissing foreign women.

Seeing Pearl, Rosa smiled a little shyly and looked back at Ernest. "Don't tell me this is your sister? Have you at last managed to persuade her to come to visit?"

Ernest nodded.

"Oh," Rosa exclaimed, turning her attention back to Pearl, "what an honor! I cannot tell you how delighted I am that you should come to visit. Come in, come in. Long have I desired to meet you. I had begun to fear it would never happen."

"Thank you," Pearl managed. "It's nice to meet you too."

They followed Rosa into the living room, which, like her garden, seemed very sumptuous. Rich fabrics were combined with precious objects and distinctly European furniture. Pearl felt that by walking over the threshold she had been transported somewhere else entirely. Rosa beckoned for Pearl to make herself comfortable on the sofa. Pearl moved a spectacularly embroidered cushion as she sat down, pausing momentarily to admire it.

"Rosa made those," Ernest said, indicating the set of unbelievably ornate cushions.

Pearl looked at Rosa. "Did you?" she asked.

Rosa looked bashful.

"They're wonderful," Pearl said, feeling very impressed.

Rosa waved a dainty hand. "When I grew up, many women in my town could make this sort of thing. Later I trained as a seamstress. At one time I made a respectable living out of my work."

"I'm not surprised. Did Ernest tell you I made hats in my younger day? They were nothing like this, though. Do you still make anything?"

Rosa laughed. "My old eyesight is not what it once was but I still enjoy embroidery. I do a little, now and again, and will occasionally make a cushion for someone who asks for one."

"I suppose you have your children lining up to have you make things?"

Frowning ever so briefly, Rosa said, "Alas, I do not see quite as much of my bambinos as I would like. Patricia and Marcus are both very busy people. You know children. They have lives of their own."

"Yes," said Pearl. "They certainly do."

"You would like some tea, perhaps? I would also make you coffee if you prefer, but I do not think you would like it the way I make it."

"God no," Ernest said. "Fearful black stuff. Like watery potting mix."

Pearl sent a reproachful look Ernest's way. He remained completely oblivious. Turning to Rosa she said, "Tea would be lovely. I don't usually drink coffee at the best of times."

"Would you like to come into the kitchen and talk with me while I make it?"

"I'd love to," Pearl said.

Ernest stayed in the lounge to read the paper while Pearl and Rosa went into the kitchen.

"I almost feel I should be apologizing for my brother," Pearl said.

Rosa laughed again, a sound like a piece of music. "You do not need to do that. Your brother and I have been friends for some small time now. I think I understand him rather well. He has a very good heart even though at times he can be, how do you say, a little gruff?"

Pearl smiled. "That sums him up exactly. How long have you lived here at Lambton Park?"

"Longer than Ernest. I have been here three years, since not long after it opened."

"And you like it?"

"Oh yes. Before, on my own, I was very lonely and yet not quite ready to be bundled away into some place where I did not retain my independence. Independence is very important, no?"

"Yes, I should say so."

"Well, here, I have the best of both worlds. I still look after myself, yet there is help at hand if I need it, and plenty of company if I wish."

"I always picture these places as being full of busybodies," Pearl said.

With a wry smile, Rosa said, "Oh, I think there is always some of that wherever you are. The trick is avoiding it. So, I have made a little intimate circle of friends and am content. I have found in this world that there are always the critics but I pay them very little attention. Which, at the end of the day, is no more than they deserve."

Pearl smiled. "That sounds like a healthy attitude."

"Sometimes it has been more like survival skills. When my husband, Marco, and I decided to come to live in New Zealand, we experienced very big culture shock. I do not think the men and women of this country knew what to make of a Spanish woman and an Italian man, with the war still fresh in their minds. In truth we did not know what to make of them either, so different was their lifestyle and way of thinking from our own.

"But we found a place for ourselves, with the purpose of finding a better way of life for our children. And indeed they have become very successful. Having moved away from their roots, they have integrated so well into New Zealand life that you would never know that once, they came from somewhere else."

"That sounds very tough. Remembering those days, we probably were a suspicious, parochial lot."

Rosa nodded, but her eyes sparkled as she poured the hot water into her ornate teapot with a flourish. "Indeed," she said. "But I have found a sense of humor helps enormously. Marco and I did laugh at some things we found here."

"I suppose it was either that, or cry."

"The hardships we experienced here were nothing in comparison to what we had already endured. Perspective is also a fine companion, no?"

Ernest called from the lounge, "What are you two doing in there? You've had enough time to plant an entire tea plantation, grow the bushes and harvest the leaves."

"You must have patience," Rosa called back, "or you will be next complaining your tea is too weak." To Pearl she said, "Men are such babies, are they not? No patience whatsoever."

"I don't know how you put up with him," Pearl said with a grin.

Afterward, Pearl could scarcely remember enjoying a morning as much as she had with Rosa. She was such an interesting conversationalist, and she took such delight in almost every topic of conversation they covered. She had read widely, seemed interested in Pearl's opinion on a wide range of subjects, could see the funny side of just about anything and brought out a whole different side of Ernest than Pearl had ever seen. Rosa seemed to be able to see past people's exterior and know what lay beneath the surface.

Returning to her little flat seemed like a very great anticlimax. Pearl realized she was sorry that she had not been to meet Rosa earlier. They had all agreed that Pearl should return again soon for them to talk some more. Rosa wanted to show Pearl her collection of old photographs, which, from the few Pearl had seen, looked very interesting.

"Alas," Rosa had said, "there never seems enough time in the day for all the good things it might contain."

A long time had passed since Pearl had thought that way. Her days were often filled with emptiness. Although she read a good deal, did the odd crossword, and even, desperately, watched the odd television program, it hardly seemed worth mentioning beside the interests Rosa had. What with stitching, gardening, reading and entertaining people, no wonder Rosa never had much time to leave Lambton Park. During Pearl's time there three women called in to say hello and to find out what Rosa was doing. All three had seemed a little deflated to find their Spanish friend already busy, as though they had been deprived of light and laughter.

Maybe, Pearl thought, it was more about attitude than it was about anything else. Maybe the secret of life was simply to enjoy it to the full. Yet such an attitude seemed a rare gift. Pearl knew from her own journey through life that such people were few and far between. How lucky of Ernest to have found himself such a friend.

When Ernest returned to Lambton Park after dropping Pearl home he headed straight back to Rosa's.

"That went well, I thought," Ernest said.

"Indeed. I must say, Ernest, your skills with description do need a little work. Pearl wasn't at all as you had led me to believe."

"Why not?"

"You told me, did you not, that she was interfering and not very interesting? This is not true. I found her very interesting and she did not seem the type to interfere at all. No, no. On the contrary, she is a very *contained* person, who does not give her opinion lightly."

"You should try being her younger brother. To me, it seems as though she's spent her entire life bossing me around."

Rosa laughed. "This is the prerogative of the big sister, no? Besides, it would not surprise me to learn it is indeed you who are the bossy one."

"Me?" Ernest's face was a picture of innocence. "I've never bossed anyone around in my entire life."

She laughed again. "Of course you have not. Do you think she really will come back again?"

"Oh, I'd say so. She was very chirpy when I dropped her off. Given her a new lease on life, this visit."

"Good. From what you tell me, her circumstances are such where a little cheering up would not go amiss."

"She's lonely, of course. What else could you expect?"

Rosa's eyes narrowed a little as she thought about this. "No," she said at length, "I do not think that lonely is altogether the right word to use. I think it is something else."

"Like what? Of course she's lonely."

"My dear Ernest, there are some people who can live in the midst of scores of people and still be lonely. With Pearl, though, I think there is some other thing which stops her being truly happy."

"Oh, you do, do you? Well, then, clever clogs, tell me what it is."

Rosa sent him a rye smile. "You are very impatient today. But since you ask me, I think it has to do with *need*. I think Pearl misses being needed. She does not really need or want for her life to be overflowing with people, but what she does want is to be needed. For we elderly people, this is very difficult, is it not, to find a place where we are needed? I think if she could find somewhere where people needed her this unhappiness that you speak of would disappear altogether, no?"

Ernest shrugged. "Don't ask me," he said. He reached over and took her hand, his face serious. "All I really know is that I need you."

CHAPTER FIVE

If Sarah had been a different sort of person she might have felt uncomfortable about pulling up in the sweeping driveway of her aunt's house on Friday night in her mother's slightly battered station wagon. The only other vehicles of such dubious distinction to darken the doorstep probably belonged to the cleaner or the gardener or the laundry service. Even then Sarah would not be surprised if someone told her that Sheila's husband forbade them from using the driveway at all.

But Sarah was not a different kind of person. Since masses of wealth had never held any great appeal for her she refused to be impressed to the point of cowering. She drove confidently up to the house without a second thought about whether her mother's car might leak a little black patch of oil onto the spotless surface of the red brick cobbled driveway. As it was, having the car at all had become a bone of contention, one Sarah would rather spend as little time as possible dwelling on.

"I fail to see," her mother had said, "why I should lend you my car so you can go to see that useless, overweight waste of space."

Sarah had been appalled, but her mother showed no sign of repentance. Sarah had finally said, "So, will you or will you not lend me your car, or do I have to ask Dad if I can use his van full of dusty floor tiles?"

For a minute this seemed exactly what Margaret would suggest. In the end she'd capitulated. After all she'd said more than once that Sarah only had to ask if she wanted the car. Besides, it wasn't even as if Margaret needed it herself.

Sarah climbed out of the car and looked up at the house. She had not visited for nearly two years. In spite of her dispassionate opinion about money she could not deny it was a handsome house indeed. It sprawled itself across the large site, a behemoth of architectural magnificence, whose rich facade and lush gardens spelt out the fiscal situation of its inhabitants like a grand neon sign. It had multiple levels and interesting nooks and crannies - like facets of an ornately hewn diamond - triple garages and a parking pad for the boat during winter. To the left of the house lay a deep in-ground swimming pool whose aqua waters glistened faintly in the mid evening sunlight.

Sarah knew who had designed the garden - a man known in the industry as something of a snob - but Sarah had to concede that he knew his stuff and had created a lush, affluent looking garden that did justice to a house such as this. From the driveway a wide path led up the gentle slope toward the front door. Sarah, making her way up the path, clutched an extremely inferior bottle of white wine and wondered what the evening would bring. She pressed the door buzzer, and waited.

From somewhere within the bowels of the house she could hear music emanating. Since she had been unable to hear any internal chime of the doorbell she could not be sure the thing even worked. She went to give the buzzer a second press when the door was wrenched opened revealing a flustered looking Sheila.

Sarah smiled brightly at her aunt hoping her face did not betray the shock she felt on seeing how right her mother had been in her assertion. However unkindly expressed, it could not be denied that Sheila had put on weight. She had always been fairly sturdy, having inherited Grandpa Jack's more muscular frame, but this sturdiness had now solidified into something more substantial, particularly around the bust area. To be fair Sheila did her best to disguise her girth beneath a smart navy trouser suit. This buttoned down the front with large silver buttons that, Sarah noticed, curiously matched her earrings. The fabric dropped in a sheer fall over the mounds of her ample bosom and in doing so cleverly disguised the true nature of her shape.

"Sarah!" her aunt exclaimed. "How lovely to see you."

Sarah kissed her aunt. "Hi, Auntie Sheila."

"Now, we'll have less of this 'auntie' business. Goodness, you're quite the young woman these days. I think we can safely dispense with the formalities. Come in, won't you? Sorry I kept you waiting on the doorstep so long. I had my head in the oven." She leaned conspiratorially toward Sarah as she shepherded her through the door. "In truth I wondered if one of the boys might hear the door and come and see you in, but they live in their own worlds you know."

"Never mind," Sarah said, handing over the bottle of wine.

As she followed her aunt down the hallway toward the stairs that lead to one of the upper levels of bedrooms the noise of the music got louder and more recognizable as that of an ill-played electric guitar.

Sheila rolled her eyes. "That's Jason," she said. "He's in a band at school, takes it all extremely seriously and deafens us with hours of practice. It's all quite unintelligible stuff. I went to one of their school concerts just this week. I'm afraid diabolical would be generous terminology."

Sarah laughed. "I remember our school bands and they were pretty dire too. Still, from small acorns can grow large oak trees."

"Yes, that ultimately block your view, take away your sunlight and in fall shed their leaves so as to clog up all your drains."

Sarah grinned. "That's the end of my garden metaphors."

Sheila smiled back. "Oh, I can't take the credit," she said, waving an airy hand. "I heard someone else say it once. Come into the kitchen while I check on the progress of dinner."

As they entered the kitchen Sarah said, "So, what form is Jason in? I seem to have lost track of the years."

"He's in Form Six, only they don't call it that any more."

"Don't they?"

"No. It's Year Twelve now."

"I can't keep up."

"You aren't the only one," Sheila said heavily.

"What school's he at?"

"Riverleigh College."

"That's co-ed?"

"All boys. Sometimes I wonder if that's a good thing or not. But the school has a very good academic reputation and he's meeting the sorts of boys who will probably go on to be movers and shakers of some kind or another. Anyway, from Reuben's perspective it hasn't done him any harm. Since he's made the transition to university he's had girls swarming all over him. Not that he minds. Quite the reverse in fact. He's got the makings of a real Casanova."

"Really? What's he studying?"

"He's doing a degree in Business Studies, with some property papers as a major, I think. Not having been to university myself, I don't really understand the finer points of how degrees work. His ambition appears to involve being better qualified than his father so he can hopefully earn more money. We'll have to see, won't we? Wine?"

"Yes, please. I hope that stuff I bought isn't too awful."

"I've got some in the fridge anyway," Sheila said, whisking Sarah's bottle quickly out of sight.

"And what about Jason? Does he know what direction he wants to take yet?"

Sheila poured out the wine with a flourish and said, "Not yet. Of course, in his pea brain I'm sure he pictures himself being famous, a lead guitarist in some sensational rock band. We're hoping reality sets in at some point next year as he'll have to make some proper decisions about university degrees and the like."

"You think he'll go, then?"

Peering myopically into the oven, Sheila said, "John won't have it any other way. Back in our day you could get away without qualifications of practically any sort whatsoever. Look at John. A self-made man with barely a qualification to his name except School Certificate. Now, though, things are different. Well-qualified people are highly sought after. Those less qualified have to have the killer instinct in order to succeed. I don't think John sees that killer instinct in either of the boys."

"Who's a killer?" a voice said from the doorway.

They turned to see Reuben leaning casually on the doorframe, rhythmically tapping a cordless phone on his thigh. He had the black hair of his father and the blue eyes of his mother. In Sarah's absence he had developed into a handsome young man who clearly knew this fact very well. He'd evidently been trying to enhance what nature had given him by working out and sported a burgeoning set of muscles as a result.

Sarah smiled widely at him. "Hi, Reuben."

Reuben smiled a quirky smile in return, weighing up whether more was required of him than a mere hello. In the end he said, "Hi, cous. Back from England, then?"

"Yep."

"How was it?"

"Great. I had a wonderful time."

"What did you come back for then?"

"Reuben!" his mother chastised. "That's hardly polite."

"I only wondered why, if she was having such a wonderful time, she'd decided to come home."

"Fair enough," Sarah said. "No offence taken. To be honest, I came home because there's only so much wonderful you can stand before it all somehow stops being wonderful."

"Heh? Come again?"

Sarah smiled at him, thinking that, in spite of his hip clothes, his hip haircut and his hip attitude he really had no idea at all. Was it possible she too had once been so naive?

"It's like when you go to party. At first you really enjoy it but after a while you're looking around at your mates saying, 'I've had enough of this,' and before you know it, you're somewhere else. I figure the trick is to leave before you start resenting the fact that you're there at all."

"So you came home while the going was good?"

"Precisely."

Reuben shook his head skeptically. "I'll take your word for it."

He strolled nonchalantly over to his mother and handed her the phone.

"I wondered when I was ever going to get that back," she said. To Sarah she said, "I don't think I've seen this phone for about a week. He spends endless hours on it talking to this girl and that girl."

Reuben reddened in spite of himself. "Give it a rest, Mum."

As he went to leave the room Sheila stopped him in his tracks. "And where do you think you're going?"

He shrugged. "I'm going to get ready to go out."

"Not until after dinner you're not."

Reuben sent a resentful look Sarah's way. "Of course not," he said. "I'm meeting Mandy at eight o'clock."

With that he left the room, leaving Sheila shaking her head in despair. "He's twenty, now, did you know? Supposedly out of his teens. Heaven help us, I can't imagine he'll ever be ready to leave home."

Sheila continued talking until John arrived home, mostly about her busy life. Between conversations she supervised the cooking of dinner. Although she tried to make it look as though she was making everything from scratch, Sarah couldn't help but notice the caterer's boxes and packaging surreptitiously concealed here and there.

Eventually the sound of an engine outside made Sarah look out of the window. From her vantage point in the designer kitchen she could see John pull into the driveway in his sleek black BMW, which, according to Brett, he'd bought just two months ago. He paused as he waited for the automatic garage doors to glide up, glancing as he waited with intolerance at Margaret's station wagon.

Moments later he entered the kitchen and put his smart black leather briefcase down on the breakfast bar.

"Hello all," he said, making no move to kiss Sheila or make any other affectionate gesture. "The traffic was hell tonight. If you hadn't made me leave early I probably wouldn't have made it home for hours."

"That's nice, dear," Sheila said. "I've told you before, it does you good to finish early now and again."

"Well, I've brought work home, so don't think I'll be sitting around all evening, nattering. How are you Sarah?"

Sarah had forgotten John's manner, his directness, how he lived his life like every moment had to count for something. There could be no time wasting, no pussyfooting around and no sentimental claptrap. Even sport - golf and sailing - were things you did as a means to an end, even if the end only was winning. If the killer instinct had somehow bypassed Reuben, and the as yet unseen Jason who remained upstairs murdering his guitar, it was definitely alive and well in John Seymour.

"Fine thanks," Sarah said, feeling as though she could have said she was feeling tired or sick or even hormonal and John would have taken the same amount of notice as he did now.

"Great," he said. "What's for dinner?"

"Chicken," Sheila said. Leaning Sarah's way she added, "It's his favorite."

"Good, sensible, nutritious meal," John said firmly. He patted his waist-line. "Keeps you trim. Not too much fat and not too much red meat." He looked at his wife and said to Sarah, "Some of us could do with a bit more chicken and a bit less fat."

Sarah didn't know where to look. Sheila hid any feelings she might be experiencing with a cheery smile, giving Sarah the distinct impression that she hid a great deal of her emotions in precisely the same way.

"Dinner's about twenty minutes away if you want to make a start on your work," she said, as though he hadn't made any comment about her weight whatsoever.

"I will," he said, grabbing his briefcase and striding from the room.

"Men," Sheila said, with a shake of her head. "Hopeless, aren't they?"

Jason appeared just as things were being dished up. A wiry boy, he reminded Sarah of one of those bendy people you could buy from the toy shops when she'd been younger, someone you could mold into whatever shape you wanted and simply leave them there. He had the same black hair and blue eyes as his brother, but with the disadvantage of fewer years, his features were less defined. He held himself awkwardly, as though hours of leaning over his guitar had given him a stoop.

"Is dinner ready?" he asked blandly.

"Obviously not quite," his mother said patiently, "but by the time you go and get your brother and your father, I think you'll find it will be."

He made a face. "Do I have to?"

"Yes. And say hello to Sarah will you?"

"Hello, Sarah," he said like an automaton, before stalking out of the room.

"See what I mean?" Sheila said. "About men? They're like some sort of odd domesticated animals, always on the verge of turning wild again."

Sarah said, "It's much the same in our house I'm afraid. Todd gets worse by the day, and I think Dad's past being concerned about making an effort."

"Yes," Sheila said with a sigh. "It's always left to women to keep up appearances, isn't it?"

Eventually they all assembled in the dining room that Sheila had clearly spent quite a bit of time dressing for the occasion. There wasn't a thing out of place, from the sparkling cutlery, to the fresh centerpiece of flowers, to the finely laundered linen. For the most part, the three men took absolutely no interest in all this industry whatsoever, focused as they were firmly on the food. Sarah took the time to acknowledge Sheila's hard work even though it was largely wasted, and received a warm smile for her trouble.

Jason came to the table with the Road Code. It occupied his attention when he wasn't playing guitar or pretending to do his homework.

"I'm hoping to sit my Learner's License in two weeks," he said when questioned about why he had brought it to the table. "You can't expect me to know it all by then if I don't study."

"You haven't even booked the test," John said. "Mind your manners and put the damned thing away."

In the middle of the meal Reuben got called away twice to the telephone, both with calls from girls. The first one he appeared to cut short in favor of eating. The second one clearly pleased him no end. He returned to the table looking very smug.

The only thing that interested Reuben particularly about Sarah's time away was the London pubs and clubs scene and, inevitably, what the girls were like.

"I don't know," Sarah said. "I wasn't really looking."

After he had eaten sufficient of his chicken to loosen his tongue, John began to tell Sarah about his latest business venture. He had secured some land in an old part of town that would soon undergo something of a Renaissance. He was full of enthusiasm for a project that stood to make him yet more money, sadly, Sarah thought, at the expense of demolishing some buildings that had about them a dilapidated charm and could instead be restored to their former glory. Sarah couldn't help thinking that Michael would be upset if he knew. The way he talked about his house in Victoria Road, Sarah knew he had an appreciation for things of historical architectural significance.

At one point, when Sheila went to reach for more potatoes, John said pointedly, "I don't think you need those, do you?" and then went merrily on expounding on the virtues of the site he had found as though he hadn't said anything untoward at all. Sarah couldn't help but feel very sorry for her aunt.

After the meal, the males dispersed. John, as promised, went straight back to his study. Reuben was now miraculously meeting someone called Chloe, and all mention of Mandy was gone. Jason went back to his room clutching his Road Code and muttering about the injustices of life. Sarah couldn't help but be pleased to see the back of all three of them.

She helped a vaguely embarrassed Sheila to carry the detritus of the meal into the kitchen but when Sarah made no comment about the conduct of her family, Sheila relaxed a little and began talking as though they'd all been on their best behavior.

Then, suddenly, as though she had finally realized Sarah was there, Sheila said, "I haven't even asked what you've been doing with yourself."

Sarah could have pointed out that, technically speaking, she still hadn't asked, but instead said, "To be honest, I've just been cruising along this week. I tidied up my C.V. and have posted away two job applications. I caught up with a couple of old friends for coffee, and I did some preliminary work on a garden design for Mum and Dad's neighbor."

"Oh, he's the one Mum's befriended, isn't he?"

Sarah nodded.

"Mum speaks very highly of him. But then, I suppose when you're old, you're just grateful anyone takes any notice of you. I hope he isn't after her for her money."

"I didn't know Nan had any," Sarah said lightly, although inside she was appalled Sheila could think Michael might have an ulterior motive.

"Not much, I wouldn't think, but you never know, do you?"

"I think I can safely assure you that Michael is not a fortune hunter."

Sheila seemed vaguely disappointed. "Oh? Well, I suppose you'd know. Of course, I do feel the weeniest bit guilty about not being able to have Mum to live here. It's just that our lives are so busy, and the boys are awfully noisy, and if John goes away on business I do like to be available to go with him. It would be like having a pet. It just isn't fair to buy a cat or a dog if you can't take care of them properly. It's not as if you can put an old lady into a cattery or kennels if you need to go away, is it?"

Sarah busied herself with the dishes in the sink to save herself replying.

"And," Sheila continued, dropping her voice, "my nerves are not what they once were. Just between you and me, the doctor has prescribed some of that Prozac stuff. Don't let on to John, will you? He doesn't believe in medication. But then, he wouldn't, would he? He's never had a sick day in his life."

"I'm sorry to hear that," Sarah said.

Sheila waved her hand dismissively. "Naturally, everything would have been so much simpler if Mum hadn't been so opposed to the idea of a rest home, although I still don't really see what the objection is. Being waited on hand and foot, twenty-four hour company, someone to bring you hot cocoa at bedtime. It's paradise."

"You know how much she values her independence."

"Yes, but all these protestations, it's selfish really. I bet she didn't give a thought to how the rest of us might feel."

Sarah said, "Maybe, at her stage of life, she thought she'd earned the right to choose."

"Huh. How many of us can really say we have choice about anything much?"

By the look on her aunt's face there seemed little point debating the issue, even though Sarah privately thought that there were always choices to be made about how you lived your life, however minor. It clearly suited Sheila to abdicate all responsibility and blame others for their shortcomings, all without recognizing she might have some admissions of her own to make.

"And as for David and your mother, well, what can I say? David seems to live his life in an appalling manner and think of no one but himself – or whichever bit of skirt he's currently after - and your mother just seems to want everyone to be as unhappy as she is."

Sarah could not deny her mother's unhappiness but she did not think her mother would appreciate being discussed behind her back. Sheila took Sarah's reticence as a sign she had lost interest in the conversation, and instead asked baldly, "Tell me, what have you heard about liposuction?"

Looking unhappily at the calendar, Margaret stared at the date willing it to change. Saturday the 8th of December. How could it be one week into December already? How could it be only seventeen days to Christmas? How, Margaret wondered, was she to get everything done that needed doing by then?

She looked with a growing sense of panic at yet another list she had made. It said: make Christmas cake, write Christmas cards, (buy Christmas cards - 4 x packets of ten), buy mixed fruit, order Christmas tree, find decorations, decide menu for Christmas meal, write invitations for Mum's birthday, pick up dry cleaning, make Christmas present shopping list, pick up Mum's repeat prescription from chemist, prepare Jim's invoices for November, make shopping list for next week, peg out washing. Margaret bit her lip to stop herself from crying. Where on earth would she find time to do all of those things, let alone the two-dozen other things that hadn't even occurred to her yet? She looked at the list again through eyes filled with tears, not even sure where she should start. She couldn't imagine how things had managed to get away on her so badly.

In the end she managed to pull herself together sufficiently to decide what to do first. It had to be shopping. She could get a number of things off her list simply by going shopping. Knowing full well that the shops would be crowded, the car parks clogged and the irritations many and plentiful could not be a deterrent. Besides, the cupboards were beginning to look woefully empty. It would not be long before the males in the house started complaining long and loud about the distinct lack of food on offer.

Margaret wondered to herself if there wasn't a strong case for cancelling Christmas. It turned everyone into maniacs and was more trouble than it was worth. In their case it wasn't as if there was any need to keep up a pretence for the children. Todd seemed to have known all along that Santa was a fraud, only playing along with the charade because it was worth his while.

But then, even if Christmas was cancelled, it would still be her mother's eightieth birthday. There could be no escaping the fact that there must be some sort of celebration and that out of the three offspring, Margaret was the only one reliable enough to actually do something about it. As usual, everything got left to good old Margaret.

She peered in the pantry to decide what else needed adding to her shopping list when Sarah came into the kitchen.

"Morning, Mum."

"Hi. How are you?"

"Fine. Thanks for the use of your car last night."

Feeling the need to make amends for being so churlish the night before, Margaret asked, "Did you have a nice time?"

Sarah filled up the kettle and plugged it in. "Yes, thanks."

"What did you talk about?"

"Oh, lots of things. Uncle John is full of enthusiasm for his next project, Reuben is girl mad, and Jason's studying for his Learner's License."

"God help us. Let's hope he fails."

Sarah grinned. "I don't think he's even got his test booked yet. You'll be safe for a while."

"Good. How about Sheila?"

"She seemed fine. She certainly lives in a social whirl. I don't think I could stand it."

"Huh. I don't know. I think I could get quite used to someone doing all my housework and swanning around playing ladies. What did she cook?"

Sarah glanced away. "Chicken. It's Uncle John's favorite. Do you want tea?"

Margaret looked at the clock. "No. I need to get to the shops. What else did you talk about?"

"I don't know. The boys, education, what I've been doing, liposuction."

Margaret's head shot up. "Liposuction? Don't tell me Sheila's thinking of having liposuction? That would be her. She's too bloody lazy to even be bothered losing all that blubber she's put on. No, it's far easier just to have someone suck it out with a vacuum cleaner. If that doesn't take the cake, I don't know what does."

"Some of her friends were talking about it. It got her thinking. She never actually said she wanted to have it done herself."

"Why else would she be talking about it? God, she's got more money than sense. I don't suppose she mentioned Christmas?"

"Only in as much as most of their upcoming social functions are Christmas celebrations."

Margaret made a scornful noise. "Typical. I bet she hasn't even given a thought to what we might be doing, especially when it comes to celebrating Mum's birthday. No, she's probably quite happy to get involved organizing things where people are going to inflate her ego by telling her what a good job she's done. But when it comes to helping her own sister to do something for her own mother, she's nowhere to be seen."

"Maybe she doesn't know what needs doing," Sarah suggested.

"Maybe she should open her big fat mouth and ask."

"I'm happy to help," Sarah said. "I've already said I would."

Margaret sighed. She appreciated her daughter's willingness to help, but it seemed all wrong to her. Sarah should be enjoying herself, spending time settling back down, not being burdened with tasks which rightly someone else should do. Not when Sheila and David weren't doing anything.

"We'll see," she said. "Meanwhile, I'd better hit the track before the morning completely disappears."

Margaret ripped the shopping list out of the notepad and slipped it into her wallet. As she straightened things out and put items she thought she might need into her handbag, Todd came bursting into the room.

He looked briefly at Sarah then eyed his mother's handbag with suspicion. "Where are you off to?"

"Town. I've got errands to run and I need to go to the store. Why?"

"Can I come?"

"What? To the store?"

"Nah. Just to town."

"What for?"

Todd cast his eyes around as if searching for a reason. His face lit up with an idea. "I'm supposed to be meeting Tom and Gerry," he said. "We're going Christmas shopping."

"This is the first I've heard of it. Why aren't you going in to town with them?"

"They're going somewhere else first. They will've left already."

Margaret looked at him sharply but his face was a picture of innocence.

"It'll save me getting the bus," he said.

"All right then," she conceded. "Are you ready?"

Todd looked down at his clothes, assessing whether he could get away with them or not. "I'll be two minutes," he said, tearing out of the room.

Margaret shook her head with despair. "Boys," she said to Sarah. "They really are hopeless."

Sarah smiled. "You should try living with Cassie. Then you'd know the true meaning of chaos."

Margaret said, "I think I'll go and get in the car. Tell Todd to come straight out will you? Don't let him get distracted on the way."

Margaret was half way to the kitchen door when the front door bell chimed.

Sarah said, "I'll get it."

Margaret felt sorely tempted to just go and get in the car anyway. Although there'd been enough delay, she thought she'd better hold off five seconds and wait to see who'd arrived, just in case. Her heart sank when moments later she heard the distinctive voices of Joanna and Brett and high pitched squeal of an excited Isabella. Margaret closed her eyes in despair, took a deep breath and put her handbag away.

Sarah led the troops into the kitchen.

"Look who's here," Sarah said.

"Look indeed," Margaret replied.

"Gran!" Isabella cried, catapulting herself at Margaret.

Margaret bent down to hug her granddaughter, catching a gust of the simple smell of baby shampoo. "How are you?"

"Great," Isabella said, her face lit up with a smile. "I'm going to a party."

"Are you really?"

Isabella nodded solemnly. "It's a fairy party," she confided. "I've got my wings in the car."

"Gosh. They'll go nicely with that pink dress you're wearing, won't they?"

Isabella nodded again. "Where's Granddad?"

Margaret said, "I'm sorry honey, he's not here. He's busy with work at the moment."

"Oh."

Margaret straightened. "Hello, Joanna. Brett."

Joanna regarded her mother coolly. "Hello," she said, her voice grudging.

Brett tried a lopsided smile but said nothing. Judging from Joanna's expression it was clearly more than his life was worth. He shifted awkwardly on his feet, bearing the weight of Connor in his car seat.

"I'm surprised you're not at work," Sarah said, filling the ensuing silence.

Brett said, "We've started a new roster. We're all to have one weekend in five off. I'm up first."

Margaret continued to look assessingly at Joanna who had clearly got her dander up about something, but Joanna carefully avoided all eye contact.

Todd came into the room like an explosion. "Ready," he said. Then, realizing his elder sister had arrived, he looked at Margaret for confirmation. "Aren't we going now?"

Joanna's gaze swung around and at last she met Margaret's eye. "You're going out?"

Margaret nodded. "We're off to town."

"That's just wonderful," Joanna said heavily. "First I call and you don't call me back. Now I come around and you're about to go out."

Sarah said to Isabella, "I'd love to see your fairy wings. Would you show them to me?"

Isabella nodded with enthusiasm and took Sarah's hand. They quickly disappeared out of the kitchen with Todd hard on their heels.

"What is this all about?" Margaret asked. "Me forgetting to call you back?"

"It seems to me," Joanna said haughtily, "that you are forever forgetting about me."

"I hardly think that's true."

"Isn't it? I'm always the one calling you. You never make time for the children or me. Some of my friends from coffee group have mothers who do everything. They help at home, bring around meals, they look after the children, they take them places and buy them things."

"Maybe those mothers have nothing better to do with their time."

"And you do?"

Margaret could feel the outrage building within her. "Of course I do. Don't be so insulting. All I do is work, work, work. What do you think I'm doing with my time? Lying about eating chocolates like your Aunt Sheila?"

"You're certainly not investing a lot of time in your grandchildren,"

Joanna accused.

"That's because I have other responsibilities. Helping your father with his business, looking after your grandmother, running this house, cooking meals for everyone here, not to mention washing and ironing and a million other damned things."

"Get Sarah to help. She's got nothing better to do with her time."

"She's looking for a job and trying to get herself re-established."

"Bully for her. She should try looking after a toddler and a newborn. Moses probably had less trouble leaving Egypt and parting the Red Sea than I have trying to manage with those two."

"Technically," Brett said, "I think it was God who parted the Red Sea."

Joanna glared at him. "Trust you to suddenly become a biblical scholar. You're no help either."

"I know it can be difficult," Margaret said with as much patience as she could muster. "After all, I have been there myself. Three times in fact. But being a parent to Isabella and Connor is your job, not mine. I'm sorry you feel I haven't helped enough but my plate is very full at the moment. Don't forget I've also got Christmas to prepare for. I've got a thousand and one things to do if I'm going to put on this birthday lunch for Mum on Christmas Day."

"Lunch? What lunch?"

"What do you mean, what lunch? Only the one I've been talking about for some time now. The one where I attempt to get the whole family together to celebrate not only Christmas, but Mum's birthday as well."

"You never said anything to me about it being at lunch time. We've already said we'll go to Brett's parents for Christmas lunch."

Margaret stared at her daughter. "Well, you'll just have to tell them otherwise, won't you?"

Joanna's expression was like hard steel. "Why should I? Why do I always have to put myself out for other people? Nobody pays me a second thought. Did you think to ask what might suit me? Don't I deserve a bit of consideration? Just who is it in the family with the new-born?"

"You're a fine one to talk," Margaret snapped. "When did you last give thought to anyone other than yourself? When, for that matter, did anyone give any thought to me? But I did think of others, and particularly of the older members of the family, not in the least your grandmother. I want her, and Ernest, and Charles to be able to enjoy the day and not feel like they might miss something because they can no longer stay up past cocoa time. And that goes for Connor and Isabella too. If we have lunch, you'll be home in the evening to put them to bed and your routine won't be thrown out too much."

"What about Brett's parents?"

"I don't know. Is either of them turning eighty? Meet them for breakfast, do something on Christmas Eve, see them Christmas night. Surely there's some solution."

Joanna glared at her mother. "And this is your final word on the subject?"

Margaret raised her chin. "It is, yes. If it doesn't suit you, then I'm sorry, but that's the way it is."

Joanna looked at Brett and said, "Come on then, we're going."

CHAPTER SIX

In the wake of Joanna's dramatic departure Margaret resumed her original plan and had Todd in the car and underway just after eleven o'clock. Margaret did not look at the clock. Nor, for that matter, did she look at the speedometer that would have shown her driving nearly twenty kilometers above the legal speed limit. If it wasn't for the fact that she noticed Todd's grip on the front seat beside her - his knuckles white from holding on - she might have remained oblivious to her folly.

She glanced down at the speedometer and realized she had let her anger get the better of her. She eased off the gas pedal and at the same time heard Todd ease a deep breath out of his lungs as he relaxed with relief.

"Sorry," she said.

"God, Mum. You need to take a chill pill."

"Yes, well, that's easier said than done, isn't it?"

"Don't know why. You just have to stop getting so stressed out."

"Oh, I do, do I? And then who do you think would cook the meals and run around after you and your father?"

Todd shrugged elaborately.

"No. Exactly. It wouldn't be either of you, that much I can tell you."

Todd wound his window down a fraction. Their rate of travel had decreased even further the closer they got to town. They slowed to a crawl as Margaret joined a line of traffic.

"What was Joanna all moody about, anyway?" asked Todd.

Margaret sighed. "She's another one in life who wants everything her own way. She's put out because I plan to have Christmas lunch to celebrate Mum's birthday. It doesn't suit what she's already arranged."

"I don't see what the big deal is anyway. It's only Christmas."

"It's not 'only' Christmas and that's the whole point. The very fact that

Mum will be eighty on the day makes it otherwise."

"But we don't usually make a fuss of Nan on her birthday," Todd pointed out. "I don't remember us doing anything when she turned seventy or seventy five."

"You were only three when she turned seventy so you'd hardly remember, would you? Things were different then, anyway. Dad was still alive for one thing."

"But he'd died by the time she got to seventy five, hadn't he?"

Margaret nodded. "Just. Mum certainly wasn't in any mood to celebrate. Like I say, things were different then, just as things are different now. At eighty you've got a lot more life behind you than you have in front of you. The fact that her brothers are both still alive makes it all the more special. It would be wrong to let the occasion pass without some sort of celebration, even if I am a bit too busy to arrange things properly."

Margaret had to press furiously on her horn as another driver tried to line jump and had to resort to squeezing in front of her when he ran out of road. Instead of giving an apologetic wave he glared at her and made a rude gesture.

"That's the problem with people today," she said angrily. "Nobody's got any consideration for anyone else."

The sun beat strongly down and the temperature in the car began to rise. Margaret could feel herself becoming more agitated. Todd lapsed into silence, bored of being sympathetic toward his mother's histrionics. Eventually Margaret negotiated her way into the store car park. After circling four times she managed to find a spot on the outer reaches of the parking area. It lay so far away from the store entrance she may as well have parked her car on the outer reaches of space.

"I don't know how long I'll be," Margaret said, looking at her long list. "I've got a few places to go before I even start in the store. Do you want to rendezvous later and see how we're going?"

"Nah," said Todd. "I'll get the bus home."

"Or get a ride with Tom and Gerry?"

Todd's expression was momentarily blank. "Yeah. Right. I suppose I could."

He swung the passenger door open with considerable force, narrowly catching it before it went careening into the car parked next door.

Margaret clambered out, hampered by the fact that the straps of her bag caught around the hand brake.

"Wait!" she called.

Todd turned impatiently.

"Are you sure you've got everything you need? You will be home for dinner, won't you?"

"Course. I'm not a little kid any more, Mum."

With that he turned on his heel and stalked away leaving Margaret standing there with her long list and her despair. As she watched him retreat she wondered to herself what he was really up to.

It was, Pearl decided, something akin to living life in the stalls of the theatre. On stage all manner of things were happening but although you were there, sitting quietly in the dark, you were not required to participate. You were simply there as a member of the audience, a nameless face in a sea of other nameless faces.

This morning there had been a flurry of activity on stage. She'd heard Jim's van door go as early as half past seven, then heard him fossicking about in the garage next door for something he'd misplaced. She'd heard him make some sort of muffled oath following a crash. Pearl felt sure he'd probably dropped something on his foot. Minutes later he'd started the van up. It coughed unenthusiastically but eventually came to life.

Later, after Pearl was up and dressed, breakfasted and had changed the sheets on her bed, she heard another car pull into the driveway. Peering out, she saw that Joanna had arrived with her family. This cheered Pearl up no end. Hopefully it wouldn't be long before someone got dispatched to bring her over. She could then spend a little bit of time on stage. Not necessarily in the limelight. No, not that. She'd be content enough just to have a bit part.

Time passed. Pearl had seen Sarah come outside with Isabella but rather than coming her way, they had gone to the car. Pearl watched as Sarah retrieved from the back seat a set of fairy wings which Isabella duly donned, before fluttering around looking impossibly sweet. Then, mysteriously, Joanna came out of the house, bundled the children hastily into the car and gestured impatiently to Brett. The entire situation seemed beyond his comprehension but he co-operated nonetheless. Without so much as a by-your-leave they were gone, no thought to Pearl given at all.

After that, Pearl thought there was probably a pretty good chance someone would come and see her, particularly Margaret. However minutes later, after the hasty departure of Joanna, Margaret had departed too. She'd got in the car in a high dudgeon. Todd slipped wordlessly into the passenger seat before Margaret reversed angrily out of the driveway.

No one had remembered. Pearl had hoped that someone would remember, that perhaps in an uncharacteristically unselfish act Joanna had come to cheer Pearl up on a day when she always felt down. December the 8th. Her and Jack's wedding anniversary. Since his death it had been a day full of bitter-sweet memories. Sweet were the recollections of a life spent together, bitter the thought that more than five years had gone since his passing.

But then people on stage never really took any notice of the audience, did they?

The problem with mothers, Todd concluded, lay in their inability to draw the line. It was always questions, questions, questions. Then, when you went to the trouble of giving them an answer, they never seemed satisfied. They wanted to know and understand every little detail of your life then criticize you for every little failing. It seemed incomprehensible to them that he or his friends might want to live their lives in the opposite way from tight-arsed adults. What did it matter if you had a messy bedroom or went out without saying where you were going or couldn't be bothered studying because school was crap anyway? Uncle John had scraped through school by the skin of his teeth, left at the first opportunity, and had gone on to make megabucks. He seemed to make money by the truckload. It sure wasn't because of some poxy piece of paper people called a qualification.

Then, to make matters worse, Todd seemed to have found himself stuck with a mother whose recent behavior reminded him of some demented mouse going around and around inside a wheel until it drove itself completely crazy. Thirteen wasn't too young to know neurotic when he saw it. It was downright embarrassing. The only thing worse than having a neurotic mother was listening to all her crazed ravings. Who the hell cared about Christmas anyway? Who gave a stuff whether Joanna and her ridiculous husband and unappealing children came or not? As far as Todd was concerned they could all stay away. The only potential benefit appeared to be the fact he could possibly be in for a few hefty presents as some form of guilt offering. Something had to make up for having to live permanently in a lunatic asylum.

What got him more than anything else - and there was quite a lot that

got at Todd just at the moment - was that, as adults, the whole bloody lot
of them could make up their own minds about what they wanted to do and
when they wanted to do it. Todd craved to be able to do just that, to be his
own person, to do his own thing, to follow his own rules instead of someone
else's. In fact, from where Todd stood no rules at all would be a damned good
start. Yet in spite of the freedom they had, the power of choice, most adults
seemed shackled by what they chose to do, rather than released. It seemed a
complete waste.

From the store Todd trailed along Fraser Street, heading for the mall.
The further down the street he got, the more congested the footpaths became. At Atkinson Square competing buskers on opposite sites of the central
area deafened everyone in a small radius. Those sitting in the sun - trying to
enjoy a moments respite from the madding crowd - sat with pained expressions on their faces.

Todd cut across the square, angling his gaze away from the buskers in
case they indicated he should give them some money. He'd only pay them
if it meant they'd stop. On the far side of the square he took the shortcut
along Waterhouse Road, threaded his way through Seddon Street and arrived at the back entrance to the mall. Here, then, he hoped to meet up
with his friends.

Sarah had just finished tidying the kitchen and was about to go and see
what chaos lay upstairs when the doorbell rang. It was, she decided, getting
more like Piccadilly Circus every day. On the threshold she found Tom and
Gerry, looking out at her with bland expressions from their sloe eyes.
"Is Todd home?" Tom asked.
"No. I thought he was supposed to be meeting you two in town."
Tom and Gerry looked at each other.
"In town?" said Tom. "We're not going to town."
"Oh," Sarah said, her mind working overtime. "I must have got the
wrong end of the stick. Will I get him to call you when he gets back?"
Tom looked put out. "I suppose you should," she said heavily, wasting
no time in backing off from the front door. Gerry, without taking his eyes
off Sarah, followed suit. He came and went in the same manner, without so
much as a word.
Sarah was also speechless. She wondered what Todd was up to.

The mall was even more crowded than the footpaths outside. The management of the mall had evidently decided to try to get everyone into the Christmas spirit by completely overdoing the decorations. A huge tree took up the atrium area in which Todd stood, forcing shoppers to circumnavigate its girth and thereby necessitating them to jostle one another. From every vertical surface hung wreaths and tinsel streamers. Large red bells hung incongruously overhead looking as though they might at any moment drop on some unsuspecting shopper's head.

In the middle of the mall the fakest Santa's grotto Todd had ever seen had been erected. There frustrated parents lined with their unhappy children for the dubious honor of meeting Mr. Claus himself. Todd couldn't help laughing out loud when he saw the man they'd hired to play the part. By the look of his red cheeks and bulbous nose he spent the rest of the year getting hammered at the local bowling club.

Todd navigated his way around prams and old people leaning on walking sticks, passed people weighed down with shopping and around the invariable couple standing right in the middle of the thoroughfare arguing about where to go next. On the far side of the mall lay the food court. Here Todd hoped to find who he was looking for.

He paused on the outer perimeter of the food court and scanned the tables. There, on the far side by McDonald's, sat the group he sought. He swallowed hard, thought for a moment or two then sauntered over.

"Hi," he said to the group as he neared.

Five faces looked up, faces which belonged to the coolest kids in his year at school. Justin, who could surf; Daniel, who knew all sorts of things about money; Amber, rumored to be a girl for a good time with a figure to match; Dominic, expert on illegal substances; and Beth who was by far the most beautiful girl Todd had ever seen. In Todd's book this meant she did not have to be famous for anything else.

A silence ensued as all five regarded him, collectively weighing him up to see whether he was acceptable to talk to or not.

Daniel said, "Hi, Todd. What are you doing here?"

"Escaping home and the olds," Todd replied with as much swagger as he could muster.

"Where are geek boy and moron girl?" Amber asked sarcastically.

Todd shrugged indifferently. "Don't know. Don't care."

"I thought the three of you were buddy, buddy," Amber said, looking around at the others and making a face. They all laughed, except Beth who watched Todd with a fixed gaze as she wrapped her red lips around the straw of her drink.

Todd said, "Just because you've grown up with people doesn't mean you have to stay friends. You could say we're moving in different directions these days."

"Really?" Justin said, his gaze assessing.

Todd nodded. He really meant it. He was sick to death of Tom and Gerry and of the fact that people always assumed they would be together. Tom could think of nothing other than Mr. Alexander. She'd become a pain, wanting to know this and that about him as though Todd sat in his bedroom with binoculars trained on his teacher's house. Todd didn't mind Mr. Alexander. He could be cool and seemed sympathetic to what most of the students in their class were thinking and feeling, but Todd did not want the Spanish Inquisition about the guy every time Todd saw Tom.

And then there was Gerry. His obsession with the very outdated *Star Trek* had grown to exceptionally annoying proportions. He did not want to spend time with someone who said things like, "Beam me up, Scotty," and, "Make it so," who talked about replicating some rations when what he really wanted was snacks from the kitchen, or tetryon pulses and astrometrics laboratories, when he needed to go to the bathroom for a dump.

"Well then," Justin said, "you may as well pull up a chair."

Sarah stood on the threshold of Todd's bedroom, marveling at the mess, when the doorbell rang again. She'd been contemplating the idea of tidying up a bit but instead ran downstairs, taking the steps in bounds, before reaching the door rather breathlessly.

Opening the door, she found Michael standing there. He grinned when he saw her.

"Hi," he said. "I was hoping you'd be home."

Sarah smiled back. "Yes, here I am. At the moment it seems the safest and most peaceful place to be. Everyone else is out."

"Oh?"

She paused for one moment, then said, "If you've got time for coffee I'll tell you all about it."

Sarah watched him hesitate. "I shouldn't really. I've got so much school-work to do. Marking exams, grading assignments, finishing off the dregs of my reports. We've only got three days of term left so the pressure's really on."

"Sounds ghastly."

"It is and it isn't. However, maybe a fortifying coffee might hold me in good stead. I can't be long though."

"Come in."

They walked down the hall to the kitchen and Sarah filled the kettle.

"I've just been over to see your grandmother," Michael said. "I was look-ing through my book collection for some references and came across a book of sonnets I thought she might like. They're a bit too soppy for my taste so it will be interesting to see what she makes of them."

"You're very good to take the time."

"It's easy. I like her. Good, old fashioned, straightforward common sense combined with an interest in life and literature. I suppose she's a bit like the grandmother I never had."

"You don't see your grandparents much either?"

"They're all long gone. My parents are a bit older so it means you don't have that same connection and sense of family. Speaking of which, you were saying about your family?"

"All I can say is, you're lucky to have missed the fireworks. Mum, who at the best of times seems to live on her nerves, seemed very stressed this morn-ing. Lots of sighing and frowning and recriminations. Then Joanna turned up, obviously in a snitch about something. I don't quite know entirely what, but she was most put out. To coin one of Joanna's own sayings, Alexander Fleming had an easier time inventing penicillin than anyone has of placating Joanna when she's in a mood like that."

Michael laughed sympathetically. "Sounds like a recipe for disaster."

Sarah handed over his coffee. "That's putting it mildly. It just seems unfortunate that Christmas is so close. The very thought of having to have this party for Nan is tipping Mum over the edge. The last thing she needs is for Joanna to stir up trouble."

"Families, eh? Can't live with 'em, can't divorce 'em."

Sarah smiled. "Well, except in America. You can do pretty much any-thing like that in America."

"True. Anyway, the reason why I called around was to see if you want-ed to go out tomorrow afternoon. By the time I wade my way through the workload I've got on at the moment I probably won't be free before then. But I thought that by that stage at least a bit of leisure would be in order."

Sarah sipped her coffee while she gathered her thoughts. "What did you have in mind?"

"I don't know. We could go and have coffee? But then, maybe you'd rather steer clear of the shops? It's a busy time of year."

"Yes. Can't say I'm too fussed on shops at this time of year."

"Me either. Philosophically, I wonder, if you've seen one shopping centre, have you seen the mall?"

Sarah laughed. "Corny joke."

"I know. I apologize. I can only put it down to end of year stress. What about the beach? If the weather holds we could drive over and take a bit of a stroll?"

"That sounds nice. I'd like that."

"Great," he said with a broad grin. "It's a date."

Margaret's first port of call had been to the pharmacy by the Square. There she had been left to stand at the counter for a full ten minutes before someone got around to paying her any attention. When she had asked for the prescription in the name of Hamilton there'd been a further delay of five minutes as not one but three sales assistants looked through the pile of prepared prescriptions waiting to be collected. All to no avail. At length someone recalled the fact that the item for Mrs. Hamilton was on back order and wouldn't probably be in until Wednesday or Thursday at the earliest. All Margaret could say was that she was jolly glad it wasn't a case of life or death and that she would appreciate it if someone could call her the moment the item arrived.

She wouldn't hold her breath.

At the stationery shop Margaret thought she'd have a look at their Christmas card selection (pitiful), invitations for the party (non-existent), and ideas for presents for one or two members of the family (uninspiring). She got so sick of having to make way for people to squeeze past her that in the end she decided she'd be better off on the teeming streets.

Margaret then made her way to the dry cleaners and had fished around in her pocket for the yellow ticket she'd been given last week. Handing it over, the elongated woman behind the counter had peered at the docket through her half rimmed spectacles that she wore on a silver chain around her neck. Making a funny clicking noise in the back of her throat, the woman turned wordlessly on her heel and walked imperiously away only to return empty handed.

"What, precisely, was this item?" the woman asked, her tone haughty.

"There were two of them. Both jackets. One a man's black jacket, the other a navy blazer."

In fact one was Todd's school blazer that Margaret had found in his room looking as though it had been trampled over by a herd of wildebeests. The black jacket belonged to Jim and had not been worn practically since the Beatles first came on the scene. It was simply an added extra to take advantage of the two for one deal Margaret had seen advertised.

"I'm afraid," the woman said, "that these items have not yet been returned from our offsite depot."

"Which is where?" Margaret asked.

"I'm not at liberty to say," the woman replied, as though Margaret had just asked for the secret underground location of an armaments arsenal.

"Well, what are you at liberty to tell me?"

"Simply that there must have been some sort of delay. Perhaps your items required extra cleaning?" The woman suggested this in such a tone as to absolve herself from any blame. "Monday," she added. "Try again on Monday."

By this stage Margaret had wasted over half an hour of her precious time and achieved precisely nothing. She was hot and footsore and tired of the crowds. She'd be better off, she realized, if she just went to the store, got want she wanted and headed home.

Since her entire shopping expedition thus far had been a catastrophe Margaret supposed she shouldn't have been too surprised by the fact that the store proved to be equally disastrous. For starters Margaret had lost her carefully compiled shopping list. This forced her to wander along the store aisles in a daze. To make matters worse, some bright spark had decided to reorganize the entire shop since last she'd been. She struggled to find anything she recalled as having needed.

In spite of the fact that the store was cool, Margaret could still feel her blouse sticking unattractively to her body. The waistband of her skirt kept skewing sideways so that she had to periodically whiz it back. The aisles were as clogged with people as the footpaths outside had been. She also seemed to have had the misfortune of entering the store at the same time as an elderly couple who took up the entire aisle and who seemed as confused about what they wanted as Margaret.

She'd just managed to pass them, feeling optimistic that she was about to make some headway when a young boy, pushing his mother's trolley as though he was on the race track at Le Mans, ran it into the back of Margaret's heel. Pain shot through her foot and it took all Margaret's strength not cry out loud. Since his mother failed to notice her son's carelessness, the boy simply made a face and continued merrily on his way.

Margaret's blood began to boil. For the umpteenth time today she could feel tears welling in her eyes. Then, to add insult to injury, she felt a tap on her shoulder.

Margaret turned, ready to give the tapper a piece of her mind.

"Margaret?" the woman asked. "It is Margaret Bell, isn't it?"

Margaret nodded, looking at the woman. She tried to recall if she knew her, and if so, where from, and her name. She was about Margaret's age, perhaps a little younger, but infinitely cooler. Smart dress, nice make-up, elegant all over. Margaret couldn't help noticing the woman's carefully sculpted nails. You didn't get nails like that washing the dishes and cleaning the toilets.

"It's Cynthia Reed," the woman supplied. "Our girls were at school together. Victoria and Bronwyn?"

Memory crystallized. "Of course. I'm sorry. How are you?"

"Fine. It's you I'm concerned about. How's your foot?"

Margaret looked down. Just above the shoe line a red welt had begun to appear. It hurt like hell. The only thing that hurt more was having an acquaintance scrutinize her leg that had seen better days and needed shaving.

"Nasty," said Cynthia. "I saw that lout run into you."

"Par for the course these days," Margaret said stoically. In reality she'd love to line the boy up and run a trolley into him. She felt she couldn't exactly say so.

"It's been a long time," Cynthia said, looking away from the offending leg. "How are things?"

"Oh, you know," Margaret replied. "Busy, busy."

"Yes, I do know. Haven't the years flown by?"

Margaret nodded.

"But then, life moves on, doesn't it?" Cynthia said sagely. "Those school days for the girls seem like a distant memory now. Of course they've long since flown the coop. I, too, moved onto other things."

"Oh?"

Cynthia laughed with self-deprecation. "I eventually went back to the workforce, part time at first, but now I run my own business."

"Really?" Margaret managed. "Doing what?"

"Personnel consulting. I find people jobs. Imagine that?"

Margaret tried to imagine but failed. "It sounds very interesting."

"Long hours," Cynthia confided. "Plenty of competition out there. How about you?"

"I'm still at home," Margaret admitted. "You knew I'd had a third?"

Cynthia frowned briefly. "Of course. I'd forgotten all about that. A boy, wasn't it?"

"Todd."

"And he'd be, what, eighteen, now?"

Margaret stifled a sigh. "In his dreams. No, he's thirteen, fourteen next March."

"Goodness me, that must be a bit of a handful. I must say I was relieved beyond measure when both of my girls grew out of their teens and went their own merry way."

After a small silence Margaret asked, "They're well, are they?"

"A box of birds, both of them. Victoria is a partner in a prestigious city law firm. Thrives on all that wheeling and dealing. I'm thrilled to sometimes be able to help recruit new staff for them. I'd never pictured us having anything other than a mother-daughter relationship, but being associated in business has given things a new dynamic. I think," Cynthia said, lowering her tone, "that she's found a whole new respect for her mother dearest."

Margaret, thinking of Joanna's wet weather face this morning said, "How nice for you. Is she married?"

"Alas no. I think men are sometimes a bit intimidated by her success. But to be honest she's so busy with work it doesn't seem to bother her one iota."

"And Bronwyn?"

"Now *she's* married. To a diplomat, no less. They're on an overseas posting at the moment, although I can't say where. With the world having been turned upside down with all this mad terrorism, one can't be too careful."

Margaret nodded. Everyone, it seemed, was on high alert. Even the dry cleaner.

"They haven't any children, then?"

"Heavens no! Thank goodness. I really do feel far too young to be a grandmother." Catching sight of something Margaret must have inadvertently betrayed on her face she added, "Not that there's anything wrong, *per se*, with being a grandparent. I suppose both of your two are married by now? As I recall, both were quite attractive in their own way."

Margaret smiled thinly. "Joanna's married, with two children, a girl and a boy. She has a lovely house over in Westglade."

"Westglade? Well. And what does her husband do?"

"He's a car salesman. European cars."

Cynthia nodded slowly, digesting this information. "And Sarah?"

"She went into landscape design and has recently returned from London."

"And she's living?"

"Back at home for now. She isn't married and since she's only just got back it seemed more practical for her to come home until she sorts herself out."

"So you have got a house full. I suppose your marriage is still going strong?"

Margaret thought of Jim. Could she really describe their marriage as still going strong? It was more like a shirt that had lost its starch. Still wearable, around the house, but not something you'd consider donning to go out.

"We're still together, yes."

Cynthia said, "My husband and I divorced three years ago."

"I'm sorry."

She laughed. "Don't be. I'm *much* better off without him." Cynthia straightened and looked around, realizing they were causing an obstruction. "Anyway, lovely seeing you. I guess we'd better get out of everyone's way. Give me a call if you ever think of returning to the workforce."

Margaret said, "I'm not sure I'd be good for anything these days. I've never even worked a computer."

Cynthia waved her sculpted nails. "Never underestimate yourself. Besides, we give career advice too." She dove into her refined handbag. "Here. Take my card. You never know what's around the corner."

As it happened, Margaret could probably have taken a pretty good guess at what was around the corner. More shoppers, more trolleys, more delays. In the end she felt she'd done a pretty good job at remembering what she'd originally put on her list, grabbing one or two extras here and there to be on the safe side.

That was until she got to the check out. When the pimply-faced check-out operator had finished laboriously swiping her items one by absolute one, Margaret simply could not believe the total owed. She wondered if the shop's rearrangement of goods had been some sort of conspiracy to disguise the fact that the store chain had put up the price of every single thing it sold.

"Good God," Margaret said out loud. "That much?"

The woman in line behind her nodded sagely and said, "It is almost Christmas, you know. They always put the prices up."

So Margaret had begrudgingly written out her check, being relieved beyond measure by the fact that they had an overdraft facility. Then the pimply youth had the gall to look suspiciously at both Margaret and her check. And even though she produced the store's own check identification card he felt compelled by some mysterious force to call over the supervisor for additional verification.

The supervisor, who probably wasn't that much older than her pimply underling, had hair the color of ketchup. She wore a petulant expression that indicated she felt herself above store work really. She looked at Margaret's check then at her identification then at Margaret herself, before saying, "You'll have to sign again."

"What?"

"You need to sign the check again. On the back."

"Why?"

"Your signature doesn't match."

"Of course it does," Margaret snapped.

The ketchup-haired girl regarded Margaret with a surly expression, but said nothing. The woman behind her in the line coughed politely.

"Oh, very well. Give me the damned pen," Margaret said. She signed with precision, keeping her eyes firmly on the paper, handing it over with a stab.

The supervisor rechecked the signature. "Fine," she said to the pimply youth, before stalking off.

"I suppose an apology would be too much to hope for," Margaret said to him.

He looked at her as though she might possibly be from another planet. Nowhere in his vast years of experience had he ever heard of such a concept.

"No," Margaret said. "I thought not."

The woman behind her said, "There's nothing like a store nazi to make your day, is there?"

Margaret couldn't agree more.

While Sarah made herself a sandwich she remembered again about her grandmother. She had thought about going to see her earlier, before all the trouble blew up, and before she thought she ought to at least try to tidy things in the house up a bit, and before Michael had come to see her. His visit, however, had left her quite preoccupied.

She decided to make a couple of extra sandwiches, dug out some chocolate biscuits, then headed down the driveway. As she rounded the corner of the garage she could see her grandmother sitting on her sofa, hands clasped in her lap, her expression dreamlike. She sat, Sarah thought, in the same way a person might when expecting a bus, simply waiting with the utmost patience for time to pass.

Sarah knocked softly on the door. It seemed to take a moment or two for the sound to register with Pearl, but once she saw who it was her face lit up.

"Sarah! My darling. How are you?"

Sarah smiled warmly and hugged her grandmother. "Fine. Have you eaten? I've brought over some sandwiches."

"Lovely, dear. Come and sit down. Do you want a cup of tea?"

"Not especially. I had coffee with Michael earlier."

"Dear boy. He came to see me too, you know."

"So he said. He mentioned something about a book of sonnets."

Pearl sat back down on the sofa, and patted the little old leather bound book. "Here they are. I've only looked at a couple."

"Plenty of time. Sorry I haven't come over sooner. It's been a bit of a madhouse today."

Pearl frowned. "So I noticed. Is everything all right?"

"That depends on what you call all right. Joanna is mad because she's not getting her own way, Mum is mad because nothing ever goes her way, Todd is slowly turning his room into a rubbish dump and Dad's run off his feet with this big job."

"Oh dear. Your father's never been particularly resilient where hard work's concerned. I hope he's managing. As for Joanna, well, they say a leopard never changes its spots. I'm afraid I don't need to tell you how important she finds it to always get her own way. I wonder if it's a lesson she'll ever learn."

Sarah shrugged.

Pearl said, "In Todd's case, though, a bit of mess is of less importance than what's going on in his mind I would have thought."

"Yes, well, I think both his mind and his room are of the same kind. Both are certainly receptacles for garbage, that's for sure."

Pearl shook her head. "It seems a great pity that your mother is too busy to see what's going on right under her very nose."

Sarah took a thoughtful bite out of her sandwich. "That'd be way too much for her to cope with at the moment. Anyway," she said, "I haven't even asked how you are today."

Pearl sighed. "A little melancholy. It would have been your Grandpa Jack and my wedding anniversary today."

"Really? Of course. December the eighth. Sorry, I didn't even realize."

"Never mind, dear. It's thoughtful of you to call anyway, and bring lunch."

"But still. It's a special day."

"Yes. Or at least it *used* to be. Mind you, I still have my memories."

Sarah smiled gently. "You miss him a lot, don't you?"

"Of course. We always were such great friends. Apart from being husband and wife, I suppose it's companionship that in the end you miss most. You know, being with someone who knows all about you, including your faults and foibles, and who loves you anyway."

Sarah felt her heart contract with compassion. She wished she could think of something profound to say that might lessen her grandmother's pain, but there did not seem to be the words. Glancing at the little book of sonnets Sarah wondered if even the great William Shakespeare himself could've quite come up with the right thing to say.

Instead she said, "Remind me again how the two of you met."

Pearl laughed. "Oh, you don't want to hear all that."

"Of course I do. It's very interesting."

Pearl smiled coyly. "Oh, all right, although it's hard to know where to start. It was all such a long time ago. You know, of course, that I was a milliner by trade. We made hats in a stuffy upstairs room over a textile warehouse. I didn't enjoy it much but it seemed good to be doing something with my hands. The thought of office work, of taking dictation and being chased around the boss's desk, never held much appeal for me."

"No wonder, put like that," Sarah said. "Bosses aren't allowed to do that sort of thing any more."

"Quite right too. Anyway, I got invited to a twenty-first birthday party of a friend. Edwina Johnson was her name. I knew her from school, although we never ran in the same circles. We weren't even the same age. I was a little younger, perhaps by as much as two years. Nevertheless, we kept bumping into each other. She came from a moneyed family but for some reason her parents had chosen to send her to the local school rather than the private one twenty minutes away by bus. Money always meant a distinction of some sort, just as it does today. To give Edwina her due she always was very nice, not snobbish or trying to laud it over other people.

"Since we kept seeing each other she asked me if I wanted to go to her party. It was at their house by the beach. She'd planned a garden party. I can still picture it all now: a marquee, buffet lunch, elegant sitting around in the sun, games on the beach if you could be bothered. The war had not quite started so it was still very grand."

"It sounds very glamorous."

"It was. Well, to me anyway. Of course the fact that it was on during the day and in the height of summer meant only one thing. I had to wear a hat. So I decided to make one of my own." Pearl laughed again. "It was a ridiculous thing, with a big floppy brim. I thought I ought to shade my face.

"Jack was there, at the party. He was a friend of one of Edwina's dashing brothers. Since he'd known the family for years it was natural for him to be invited. Not that he came from a wealthy family, that much I'm sure you know. I think he knew the brothers through sport, most likely cricket. Jack was always very keen on cricket.

"Anyway, Jack said afterward that he came to the party, looked across the lawn, saw me standing there with my mad hat, and thought to himself he simply had to meet someone prepared to wear something so outlandish. So he found Edwina, made her introduce us and the rest, as they say, is history."

"It sounds very romantic."

Pearl smiled. "It was. We just clicked, straight away. Like something out of a movie."

Sarah smiled back. "I hope I meet someone like that," she said.

"Well, don't let me color the past by making everything sound completely rosy. We might have clicked, and been the best of friends, but even in a situation like that you still have to work at a marriage. I worry that these days people see the happy ending as being the moment they fall in love. In reality that's just the beginning. The happy ending only comes when you learn how to love and respect your spouse to the point where you can take whatever life throws at you."

Sarah couldn't help thinking about Jeremy. "I suppose it can be a bit like falling in love with a dream instead of with reality."

"I suppose you might be right. Maybe the problem with people today is that when they wake up from their dream and discover they're living in a nightmare, they haven't the faintest clue what went wrong or what to do about it."

"I think some of them work out what to do about it pretty quickly," Sarah commented. "They get divorced."

"Hmm. Anyway, do you want to know the moral of my story?"

Sarah grinned. "What?"

With a twinkle in her eye, Pearl said, "If you want to meet a great man, make yourself a great big hat."

On the drive home Margaret couldn't help ruminating over the misfortune of bumping into Cynthia Reed. It seemed a cruel twist of fate to encounter someone like that while feeling so out of sorts with the world. Wearing less than glamorous clothes. Being caught with hairy legs. Feeling sweaty and malodorous. Being disorientated and disorganized. Confronting someone who, as a peer, should have been in many respects just like Margaret herself.

In truth, she struggled to identify any similarities between the two of them whatsoever. Cynthia was well heeled, well dressed, well groomed and well off. Margaret was, well, frumpy, frazzled and frustrated. No comparison at all. It made Margaret wonder where it had all gone wrong.

The more she thought about it the more Margaret realized she knew precisely where it had all gone wrong, and maybe why it continued to go wrong to this very day. Everything had been pretty settled and organized until one thing had happened, one tiny little thing that had grown within her until the day he was born. Todd.

When Margaret discovered she was pregnant the girls were already in their teens, starting to become usefully self sufficient, on the cusp of lives of their own. The instant Margaret's worst fears were realized, life changed irrevocably. Suddenly, a gulf opened up between herself and her friends, a gulf that only widened once Todd actually arrived. Suddenly Margaret, who had become used to a fair degree of freedom, found her life turned upside down by a difficult pregnancy, then by a new and difficult infant.

The endless round of feeding, changing, sleeps and washing drove a wedge between Margaret and the life she had known. She could no longer do the things she had once done. No tennis. No cozy chats with friends. No shopping trips just for the sake of it. No time to herself.

Of course, to be fair, Margaret did love Todd, even if now and again he seemed completely unlovable. She would not have been without him. No, of course not. But, if she was honest, she could also imagine life without him, perhaps even a little too readily. In such a life she too would be like Cynthia Reed, having a successful career, being a needed and wanted member of society. She'd look attractive, be free to do as she pleased, not shackled by commitments and responsibilities. Not divorced, necessarily, but certainly with a much more dynamic relationship than the one she currently had.

Margaret sighed as she turned the car into Victoria Road. It was very difficult not to feel resentful. The temptation to consider an alternative to life at that moment overwhelmed her. How could she not compare what she had to what she imagined could otherwise be? But the end result was resentment, plain and simple. And Margaret was wise enough to know that resentment could be a dangerous bedfellow. If she wasn't careful life could quickly get a whole lot worse.

Pulling into the drive, Margaret sat for some moments in the car just thinking. Then into her thoughts intruded the image of her very expensive grocery items defrosting with unseemly haste in the boot of the car. So Margaret left behind her ruminations and stepped out of the car and back into the real world.

The trunk of the car groaned with plastic bags, and Margaret knew she would have to get a move-on before things spoiled. She opened the kitchen door, returned to the car, and grabbed two handfuls of bags and lifted them with as much strength as she could muster. The weight of them tugged on her upper arms. The bags - full of heavy tins and packets - banged uncomfortably on her legs as she tried to walk with speed into the house.

By the fourth such trip Margaret had started to get extremely hot and agitated, a feeling fuelled all the more by the fact that she could hear the distant chatter of the television. She recognized the strains of a cricket commentator trying to make the slowest game in the world appealing to his viewers. That Jim could be sitting having a lovely rest while Margaret's arms strained and her heart pounded made Margaret's blood boil all the more.

On the fifth and final trip, disaster struck. One of the store bags, inappropriately packed by the pimply youth, split open, the contents catapulting onto the floor. Two liters of milk in a plastic bottle exploded as it hit the floor, flooding everywhere, and into the middle of this a glass jar filled with maraschino cherries - a Christmas gift for Uncle Charles - shattered into a million pieces on the hardness of the tiles. Into the sea of white bled the syrupy red liquid, fused together with fragments of razor-sharp glass.

"Bloody hell," Margaret screamed. "What else could possibly go wrong today?"

Jim appeared in the doorway. "What in God's name have you done?" he asked angrily. He looked down. "Oh hell. What a mess."

Margaret, standing there still clutching the other store bags she had brought in, looked down to see the red and white mess rising like the tide around her shoes. It floated past her and started to creep into the pile of bags she'd already deposited on the floor.

"Oh my God," she wailed, promptly bursting into tears. She felt physically unable to stand and the rest of the plastic bags slipped from her sweaty hands and landed in the sea of syrup.

"For goodness sake," Jim said irritably. "Pull yourself together. There's no point in crying over spilt milk."

Margaret looked over at him, barely able to distinguish his features through her tears. How could he not know that she couldn't really give a damn about the spilt milk? That what she really cried over was the sheer frustration of her life? Metaphorically, she was the spilt milk, useless now, spread thin, and rapidly spoiling. It was all too much. Margaret could not for the life of her pull herself together. Instead she stood like an island in the sea, sobbing and sobbing as though at life's end.

Margaret heard rather than saw her husband move. He took two steps closer and in the thinnest voice she had ever heard him use, said, "What is wrong with you? Blubbering like a fool. I'm sick and tired of your endless whinging and whining, as though everything in life is out to get you. I don't know what is wrong with you, Margaret, but God knows I've tried to find out. I've put up with you turning all of our lives into one giant ball of stress, with you not being able to cope with the smallest thing, with you withdrawing from me into wherever it is that you've gone.

"I don't know what you've done with the Margaret I know and love but it seems to me that she's gone. All that's left is some tragic shell that screams like a banshee at the drop of a hat and who has the emotional warmth of a cast off shoe. Well, I've had enough, do you hear me? Enough. Somehow you got yourself into this mess, and by God you're going to have to get yourself out of it."

Then, beneath the sound of her own sobbing, Margaret realized all had fallen silent. Her husband had gone.

CHAPTER SEVEN

The garden centre buzzed with activity by the time Sarah arrived at ten o'clock the following morning. With Christmas looming shoppers were already out in force - tracking down what little bargains were to be had at this time of the year - pausing to wonder whether Aunt Sophia would like a climbing rose, or if great Aunt Milly might read more into it than they intended if they bought her a Venus Flytrap. Of course for other shoppers a trip to the garden centre was a form of self-defence. They'd been forced into tidying up their gardens before hordes of relatives descended for a day of festive merriment, followed by a round or two of criticizing the hosts and their horticultural abilities. Others still were simply there because they were die-hard garden fanatics and the garden centre proved the ideal and indeed only place to be on a sunny Sunday morning.

Sarah, hot after having walked twenty-five minutes to get there, hung about in the cool fernery area until she felt her internal temperature drop sufficiently for concentration. Being surrounded by tranquil plants gave her a chance to regain a sense of equilibrium. Smelling the peaty aroma of the soil and listening to the tinkling of the water feature was like a salve to the soul.

Ostensibly she'd come on a research mission but just to be away from Victoria Road was reason enough to have walked so far. The atmosphere was so thick just now you could cut it with a knife. This morning there'd been no sign of anyone other than Todd. As far as Sarah knew her mother had not yet got out of bed. Her father had not even been in it. He had not come home last night, an unprecedented act on his part. Sarah didn't really know who to feel sorriest for in the whole mess.

On the one hand she knew full well that her mother was not the easiest person to live with right now. From her point of view life was just one giant uphill battle. When Sarah had come back from her grandmother's yesterday it had been to find her mother on her hands and knees in the kitchen, clearing up the remnants of the latest disaster. While her face bore the hallmarks of tears her expression wasn't one of sadness but one of anger. She attacked the floor like a woman possessed, muttering about injustice and a listing off a truly astounding litany of frustrations. Everything in Margaret Bell's life appeared to have gone wrong all at once, as though someone or something was out to get her.

On the other hand, her father was under pressure himself. He'd clearly used up every ounce of compassion he had left for her mother. He was worn out with her cheerlessness, worn out from being shut out, tired of being overworked and under appreciated. Although she could not entirely make sense of her mother's account of what had transpired, Sarah couldn't blame him for wanting some breathing space. She only hoped that was all it was. Breathing space. She certainly did not like to think of her parents' marriage being in more serious trouble.

As for Todd, he had come skulking into the kitchen like a spy on a reconnaissance mission. Sarah thought he could probably skulk for the country, the way he'd made such an art form out of it. He'd rummaged in the pantry and come forth with a pile of biscuits that he clearly intended to eat in place of breakfast. Sarah confined herself to giving him the, "What would Mum say?" look. She could not bring herself to say the words.

"How are you?" she'd asked.

"Fine," Todd mumbled around a mouthful of biscuits.

"How was town yesterday? Get any shopping done?"

Todd looked wary. "A bit. Mostly just looked around."

Sarah had examined him closely as she'd casually asked, "And what about Tom and Gerry? You met up with them all right?"

Todd glanced away. "Course."

"Did they buy much?"

He studied the remaining pile of biscuits, obviously trying to decide on just how inventive to be. "One or two things."

"That's good," she'd said. Todd had looked directly at her then, as though he had heard something in her voice. Sarah knew full well it was guilt he was really hearing, coming through loud and clear. Innocently she added, "I'm glad you saw them. I wondered if you'd manage to find each other with the shops being so busy."

Todd looked away again. She could tell he'd wished he'd thought to say that in the first place.

Keeping up with the innocent tone she asked, "And what are you going to do today?"

Todd picked at some invisible food particle stuck in his tooth. He shrugged. "Dunno. I might take a walk? Maybe see Tom and Gerry?"

Or maybe not.

"Don't you think you ought to do something to help out around the house before you go out? It might go a long way toward making Mum feel better."

Todd had made a face. "Nothing ever makes her feel better."

"Still, what with one thing and another, now might be as good a time as any to make an effort."

He rolled his eyes. "Yeah, yeah."

"You could make a start on your room," she'd suggested. Giving him a knowing look, she said, "After all, it would be nice for you to do something in return for Mum giving you a lift to town yesterday. So that you could meet Tom and Gerry."

Todd's eyes had narrowed almost imperceptibly as he tried to discern whether the game was up. He'd looked at her long and hard and in the end decided discretion to be the better part of valor.

"All right," he'd conceded.

Sarah nearly fainted with surprise. It had been like a minor miracle to see Todd slink back off to his lair and even more miraculous to see him industriously tidying just moments before she'd left the house. Now though, she imagined he'd probably either abandoned his endeavors or he'd crawled back under the duvet.

Sarah turned her attention to matters at hand. She might have come to the garden centre as a means of escape but she had come for other things too. One motive was to browse around and look at what was in stock at the moment and eye up any new varieties of plants, and to familiarize herself with what was currently available. If either firm she'd applied to join gave her an interview she did not wish to appear out of touch with current trends. One could not assume that gardening, and in particular plants, never changed. In fact they changed all the time.

Her main reason for coming, however, was to start making some cost estimates for how much Michael might have to spend if he went ahead with her landscape design. She'd almost finished it, but until she had a look around Sarah could not give him an accurate costing. She wanted to be able to give him alternatives to several plants that might be a bit more expensive. Not that she would actually recommend he buy plants from a garden centre of this type. There were nurseries out in the country where you could buy the same plants for half the price. But at the moment Sarah had no transport to get out there, and short of waking up her mother this morning to ask her if she could borrow the car, this place would have to do. Sarah would sooner wake a sleeping dragon.

Sarah withdrew the design she had formulated from her pocket and set to work. Her plan was to plant out the garden in keeping with the style of the house. Not exactly an English country garden but of that ilk. She'd gone for a mix of styles and with a combination of flowering and non-flowering plants so that there would always be a little color in the garden, even in the middle of winter. She envisioned it as a place you would enter and immediately be relaxed, but where color, sight and smell would interest the senses.

She would combine small plants such as viola, foamflower, forget-me-not, phlox, marsh marigolds and white aquilegia with larger shrubs of pit-tosporums, *palmatum dissectum*, dwarf rhododendrons and perhaps even a cabbage tree for contrast. She envisaged little ferns creeping around feature stones, wisteria winding its way around the back of a seated area, and delicate violets sheltering in the lee of a small grove of herbs. And if she had to be really honest what she could not help picturing was she and Michael sitting out there, talking together about nothing in particular and admiring the view.

She had thought long and hard about him since yesterday. In fact coming here this morning was, as much as anything else, supposed to have taken her mind off thinking about him any more. Only now did she realize she'd been foolish to think that she could separate the landscape design from the owner of the land.

One thing kept going through her head more than any other. She kept recalling his words. "It's a date," he had said. A date? Had he meant it, or was he just speaking figuratively? After all they had made a plan, to go at a particular time, on a particular date. People did that all the time. Sarah herself had made "dates" with people in the past with whom she had no romantic interest whatsoever. So what about this case? Had she been reading more into it all than he intended? Was it just a harmless, throwaway comment? What if it wasn't? What if he had meant it in a romantic sense?

Sarah didn't know whether to be pleased or panicked by such a possibil-ity. She thought of Jeremy, and could feel her face frowning. All that upset seemed so recent. She did not like to think of risking it all again so soon. And yet...

Sarah stood staring at a display of hebes, her mind far away. She felt her breath catch.

"Hold on my heart," she whispered to herself. "Hold on."

Sarah knew her grandmother's advice had been to get herself a great big hat. Sarah's advice to herself was much more simple. Safety in numbers. And when she got home, she knew exactly what she was going to do.

Sarah did not go straight home in the end. By the time she had finished looking around the garden centre and had walked the twenty-five minutes back to Victoria Road her mind had become filled with resolve. She walked directly past Number Twenty and straight to Michael's house. She marched up to knock on the front door before she changed her mind.

He opened the door almost sleepily and smiled lazily when he saw her.

"Oh," Sarah said. "I didn't wake you did I?"

He glanced over his shoulder at the hall clock, which read eleven fifteen.

"I should think not," he replied. "I call this more my 'sleep with my eyes open' look. I've ploughed my way through so much paperwork this weekend I'm wondering why I didn't opt for a career as a public servant. Actually," he added, "I am a public servant. However, I now know exactly why I didn't choose life as a pen pusher. I would have been exceptionally bad at it."

Sarah managed a small smile. "So will you still be able to make it this afternoon?"

Michael nodded. "Everything seems pretty on track for me to be able to get away. You?"

"Yes, fine. I feel a bit bad for disturbing you but there was something I wanted to check."

"Oh?"

"I wondered how you'd feel about me bringing along an extra this afternoon?"

"An extra?"

"I was thinking of inviting Nan."

Michael regarded her closely. "Pearl?"

Sarah nodded. "She's at a bit of a low ebb at the moment. Yesterday would have been her wedding anniversary and she was understandably feeling sad about it. I got to thinking that a trip out might do her the world of good. A bit of sea air, a change of scene and a chance to stretch her legs. I know she might slow us down a bit since she can't walk too far or too fast, but it might work wonders in the 'cheering her up' department."

"Of course," he said without hesitation. "Sounds like a great idea."

Sarah tried to read his expression to tell whether he meant it or not, but he remained sincere. Perhaps, like her, he was a bit relieved.

"Good. Thanks. About what time?"

"Two o'clock?"

"Fine. I'll leave you to it."

Michael made a face of mock horror. "Thanks very much."

The beach at Rosemont was a perfect crescent of white sand which ran for half a kilometer, and which was currently littered with an assortment of bodies in various states of undress. Mercifully, the local council had banned complete nudity. The beachfront was lined with a green necklace of pohutukawa trees, whose distinctive red flowers were beginning to appear just in time for Christmas. Shielded behind these trees an eclectic conglomeration of houses had sprung up, some massive and palatial, others humble and happily shabby. All had one thing in common, namely that of being in demand. Even the humblest old cottage these days fetched outrageous prices should one happen to come on the market.

Michael struggled to find a car park within a comfortable vicinity of the beach, but in the end their search was rewarded by securing a handy spot as someone else pulled out. Sarah had tucked Pearl into the front seat beside Michael so that she could enjoy the view and the legroom. Once they had parked, Sarah got out quickly to help her grandmother to her feet.

As Pearl straightened she paused to look at the view, lifting up her head to see from out beneath her trademark sun hat.

"Oh," she said. "Isn't it beautiful? It's positively years since I last came here. Just look at the color of the water."

Michael came around the car to join them. "It's like a tray of sapphires," he said.

Pearl looked at him with interest. "Yes. How clever you are. Just like a tray of sapphires."

"Come on, Nan," Sarah said. "Let's walk."

They made their way through the car park and onto the sand. The afternoon sun beat down warm and strong, relieved by a small breeze. The air was filled with the sound of happiness. Of children laughing, adults talking, seagulls calling to one another, and of the sound of the sea as the waves lapped gently onto the foreshore. There was the smell of the beach too. Of damp sand and salt water, of the sea breeze and of sunscreen lotion.

Sarah tucked her arm through her grandmother's to steady her as she found her beach legs. Michael flanked Pearl on the other side. The soft dry sand gave way under their steps. Families and groups sheltered out of the strength of the sun under umbrellas and small sun canopies. They made their way down onto the firmer sand, compacted by the receding tide, to avoid the obstacle course and to make walking easier.

"Well," said Pearl at length, "this is very pleasant. I only hope I'm not holding you two young things up."

Sarah said, "I told you before, Nan. We want you to come."

"Besides," said Michael. "There isn't any rush."

Pearl smiled under such reassurance. "I used to come here a lot as a child, you know. We all did. Our whole family. Ernest and Charles and I used to have running races to see who could be first to touch that cliff at the end of the beach. Ernest figured that since I was a girl he'd be able to outrun me, no problem, and that Charles, being five years younger, would never be able to keep up. In truth we beat him more times than he'd ever care to admit."

Sarah grinned. The idea of Ernest running anywhere these days seemed as remote as the days Pearl now recalled.

"Was it a long way to come?"

"Not very. Our house was about twenty minutes' walk inland, on the other side of the Rosemont shops. Mum used to pack us all off in the morning to play, and then she and Dad would come along at lunchtime and bring the picnic. In those days no one had concerns about children being off on their own. We could all swim and there was barely any traffic. I don't remember being lectured on the perils of stranger danger either, although goodness knows, the world's never been short of lunatics."

Michael asked, "How old would you have been then?"

Pearl considered this. "Fifteen, maybe? That would have made Ernest ten and Charles five. Before that just Ernest and I would go off together. Charles was too young. And if Ernest was here no doubt he'd say Charles was a mummy's boy. But at that age, who isn't?"

"I'm not sure Todd was," Sarah commented.

"I'm not sure I was, either," said Michael.

Pearl laughed. "Well, then. That proves me wrong." She laughed again.

"And then, later, I used to come with Jack. You remember me telling you yesterday, Sarah, about my friend Edwina, and her twenty-first birthday, where I met Jack? Well, just along here, perhaps half way down the beach, was right where they lived. The very spot of the party."

"Here at Rosemont?" Sarah asked.

Pearl nodded. "I wonder who owns the house today?"

Sarah shrugged wistfully.

Michael said, "Well, whoever owns it has a great spot. Forget Westglade. If I had a bit of money I'd much rather live here."

Sarah glanced over at him and he smiled at her.

"Not," he said, "that I particularly need or want a bit of money."

"Quite right," said Pearl.

"Even owning property is a double edged sword," Michael said. "It's a bit like an albatross. Those birds, soaring through the sky, are the most incredible sight. What a wingspan. But if you had to wear one around your neck? I've read *The Rhyme of the Ancient Mariner*, and it's not a good look."

They all laughed.

They heard the sound of someone calling out and paused to see who shouted. The voice came from a thin, elderly woman who approached them with as much speed as her aged body could manage.

"Pearl?" she cried. "Is that you Pearl?"

Pearl screwed her eyes up to try to see clearer.

"Edwina? Is that Edwina Johnson?"

The two friends made a little dash toward one another and embraced with laughter.

"We were just talking about you!" Pearl said. "However did you recognize me? It's years since we last met."

Edwina smiled. "I think," she said, "it was that hat."

Edwina and Pearl opted for quiet conversation under the shade of a tree, leaving Michael and Sarah free to stroll off on their own. So much for Sarah's plan of safety in numbers. However, rather than feeling concerned Sarah instead felt rather glad.

They walked for a while without talking, before Sarah felt she had to say something.

"I can't believe how good the weather has been since I got back," she said.

"I don't think you're alone. It's years since anyone can remember things being as settled as this so early. Usually it's wind and lashings of rain at regular intervals right up to Christmas with only the odd glorious day to give you hope that summer will eventually arrive."

"We certainly can't complain about that today. In fact, if anything, it's almost hotter than I like it to be."

"Don't let anyone hear you say that," Michael said with a grin. "We're supposed to be grateful for good weather, remember?"

"Of course."

"So you wouldn't necessarily class yourself as a summer person?"

Sarah shook her head. "Not especially."

"What's your favorite season, then?"

Sarah tilted her head as she considered this. "The in-between seasons, I'd say. I don't like too much heat, but then I don't like too much cold. On balance I'd probably say spring is my favorite, even over autumn, although I love the autumn colors. What about you?"

"Oh, I'm with you. Spring all the way. There's something hopeful about spring. New life bursting forth. Better weather. More things to look forward to."

"I keep thinking about my friend Cassie, back in England, shivering in the midst of winter and having a miserable time."

Michael glanced at her. "Do you think she'll be having a miserable time?"

Sarah laughed. "Not knowing Cassie. She's probably having the time of her life."

"You're missing her, though?"

Sarah nodded. "She's great fun. In some ways it seems strange to be home without her. But then I feel being home is the right thing, especially at the moment. I couldn't imagine myself being away from home for a second Christmas."

"And what are you hoping Santa will bring you?"

"I don't know. What about you?"

Michael frowned a little. "Ironically, while all you wanted for Christmas was to come home, all I want is to not have to go home for mine."

"To see your parents?"

He nodded. "I don't feel in the mood to go home to see them and sit around in their mausoleum of a house, pretending to play happy families. It's always false. Every year seems to make it just that little bit more so."

"But they'll expect you?"

"I suppose so. You're kind of duty bound to put in some sort of appearance, aren't you?"

Sarah fell silent. "I'm not sure what kind of Christmas we'll end up having either if it makes you feel any better."

Michael managed a small smile. "It doesn't, but thanks for the sentiment. Things haven't improved, I take it?"

"If anything they've taken a turn for the worse. Dad didn't even come home last night after he and Mum had some sort of bust up. I'd been over at Nan's so I don't really know what transpired. Mum seemed very angry."

"I'm sure they'll get over it. Underneath it all they seem to have a solid relationship."

"I don't know," Sarah said slowly. "It's like Mum's become a different person."

"Oh?"

"Everything gets her down. Nothing makes her happy any more."

"Maybe she needs a holiday."

"Maybe. She and Dad haven't been away for quite some time. Trouble is, at the moment, Dad's busy with this big job and Mum's in a furor over Christmas and Nan's party, it's not exactly an ideal time to slip away. Besides, I think if you asked Mum she'd say she needs more than a holiday. I think what she really wants is to get away from everything, perhaps even including Dad."

"It would be up to them, anyway. You could hardly force them to go."

"No. The thing is - and I must say I feel a bit bad for thinking this - Mum isn't that busy. Sure she does Dad's accounts and runs the house, but neither of those things are particularly onerous. Then there's Todd. Although he does need looking after, he's also no longer a baby.

"I keep wondering if my being home has increased the workload but if anything I help more than I hinder. And then there's Nan. The way Mum acts, it's as though she's developed some sort of allergy to her own mother."

Michael fell silent for a moment as he thought about what she'd said. "Okay, then, let me ask you this. Do you think a person can be overwhelmed by the mere thought of something?"

"I don't know. I suppose so. It would depend on what they were thinking about."

"I guess it's a bit like the little boy who hears a faint creak under his bed and suddenly pictures a monster lurking, ready to pounce. He can imagine the green hand creeping slowly up from the darkness coming to get him. Just the very thought is enough to send a chill of fear to his very core. He holds his breath, straining to hear more. His heart pounds, his eyes widen as he tries to see through the dark but the rest of him is paralyzed with fear."

Sarah gave him a wry smile. "You sound as though you're speaking from experience."

Michael grinned. "Oh yes. Believe me, I still won't sleep with the wardrobe doors open. I've got a terrible aversion to cupboard monsters."

Sarah glanced at him, not sure if he was entirely joking. "But how does that relate to Mum?"

"It's like you said before. She might be busy, but she's not that busy. I just wonder if she's simply overwhelmed with the thought of all there is to do, so overwhelmed she's sort of paralyzed with not knowing where to start. It's like being in a maze and not knowing how to find your way out."

"And Nan?"

"If Margaret isn't coping with even the ordinary things, maybe having the added responsibility of looking after her mother is simply the straw that breaks the camel's back. Not," he said, "that I'm implying your mother is a camel."

"Of course not."

"Maybe the corporate thought of all that responsibility is more stressful than the individual responsibilities themselves. The mind can be a powerful thing. It also strikes me that she might have lost sight of herself. Perhaps she's spent so many years caring for others, being weighed down by responsibility, she doesn't know who she is anymore."

Sarah looked at Michael thoughtfully. "You mean as though she's trapped?"

"Precisely. Like a caged bird. Maybe she looks out through the bars of the cage and wishes she was free, but knows full well that even if she did break free, she wouldn't know where to go or what to do any more."

Sarah considered this. "You might be right. Anyway, I suppose in answer to your earlier question, if I had to say what I wanted for Christmas from good old Santa, it would be that things would improve on the home front. Right now it seems hard to see how, but that's what I'd like."

"Talking of Santa reminds me of a joke I heard once," Michael said.

"What joke?"

"What three things do Santa and Satan have in common?"

Sarah shrugged. "I don't know. What?"

Michael smiled. "Both wear red, both have exactly the same letters in their name, and both are interested in whether you've been naughty or nice."

"Really? I'd never thought of that before. How bizarre."

He smiled again. "Isn't it?"

She had waited all day for him to come to her to make reconciling overtures. Never before had she stayed closeted so long. It had damn near killed her to remain within the confines of the bedroom. But she strove to make a point, and she could hardly do that if she ended up to her elbows in dishes or sifting through endless pieces of paper, could she?

She wondered where he was and what he was doing. She wondered whether or not he thought of her. Perhaps he could not find the words he needed to apologize for so cruelly abandoning her yesterday. She still could not believe he hadn't come home last night. He, like most men, had his pride. Margaret could see that it might take him a bit of time to come to terms with swallowing that pride.

But the day had worn on. Sarah had gone out, come back then gone off again. Todd had loitered uncharacteristically in his room for most of the morning before disappearing with stealth. Now, mid afternoon, the house had fallen quiet and Margaret had grown tired of waiting. It seemed clear Jim wasn't coming. If she wanted things to be all right again it looked like she would have to be the one to make it so. She found, strangely, that much of her anger had gone. In its place had come fear, fear that somehow something might have been ruined beyond repair.

Margaret put her head out of the bedroom door and strained to listen. If Jim had come home he might be watching the cricket on television again. But no. Silence reigned. As Margaret walked tentatively along the hall she looked first into Joanna's old room - where everything sat with pristine prissiness - then into Sarah's, which, with her return had been transformed by her presence. Everything sat in orderly fashion - her clothes, her cosmetics, her papers, the few keepsakes she had brought back. It all looked very temporary. Margaret had to remind herself again of her good fortune in having her daughter back, albeit briefly.

Margaret braced herself as she reached Todd's room by the top of the stairs. Her eyes widened with shock at being able to see the floor. The bed had been neatly made and everything organized into some semblance of order. She wondered whether Todd might be ailing for something.

She descended down the stairs slowly, almost as though intruding into an area that did not belong to her. And funnily enough, that's exactly how she did feel - as though she had become someone else, that she no longer belonged here in this house or even in her own body. It felt like some sort of strange amnesia. She had woken up to find herself living someone else's life, someone whom she did not particularly like.

At the bottom of the stairs Margaret paused. A sound came to her, the sound of wood being sawn. Instantly Margaret knew where to find Jim. He'd be in the garage working on the doll's house.

She stood for a while trying to decide, but in the end the waiting got the better of her. She let herself out the back door, averting her gaze momentarily until her eyes adjusted to the brilliance of the sunlight. Then she walked across the lawn toward the garage. The mossy grass cushioned her bare feet as she walked.

On the threshold she hesitated one last time, tempted to turn back, but in that instant, Jim looked up. He froze and stood regarding her without expression.

"Hello," she said.

"Hi."

She made a gesture toward the doll's house. "How's it coming on?"

He straightened. "Pretty well. At this rate I will get it finished."

"Good."

Jim continued to watch her.

"Have you got time for a break?"

He shrugged. "S'pose."

She looked over her shoulder at the park bench. "Perhaps we could sit?"

Jim hesitated. Margaret's fear increased. She made a small appealing gesture and he capitulated.

Margaret sat on the edge of the bench and waited for Jim to join her. When he did he left ample space between them. He sat hunched forward with his elbows resting on his knees. He studied the calluses on his hands and studiously avoided her gaze.

"Where were you last night?"

"I slept in my van."

"I was worried."

"Were you?" Jim did not sound convinced.

Margaret sighed. "I thought we should talk," she said.

"Did you? What good will that do?"

"I don't know, but it can't do any harm, surely."

"I wouldn't be so sure. I've tried and tried to talk to you lately. I'm not entirely sure any more will make a blind bit of difference. If anything, it might make things worse."

"For me or for you?"

"For me. I'm fed up of trying."

"So are you saying you want out?"

Jim looked at her then, a penetrating stare. "Divorce?"

Margaret swallowed. In a voice barely above a whisper she said, "Yes."

Jim rubbed his brow as though trying to soothe a headache. "Is that what you want, Margaret?"

"Do you?"

"Of course not. Don't be ridiculous. Just because we're going through a rough patch doesn't mean we should throw it all way. Unless that's what you want?"

She shook her head. She could feel the tears coming, felt one small one escape and run down her face.

"Well then," said Jim, "just what is it that you do want, Margaret? Because, by God, you're making the whole family completely miserable at the moment."

"I know," Margaret whispered. "I just don't seem to be able to help it. Everything is too much."

"And what, exactly, is everything? The kids, the house, your mother, my accounts?"

"And Christmas. Don't forget Christmas."

"How could I?"

"Everything I touch just seems to go wrong. I waste so much time because even the smallest things go awry. I seem to be drowning under everything."

Jim regarded her thoughtfully. "Maybe you need to make some changes. I don't know. Maybe you need to decide what direction you want your life to take from here on in. Start working toward it. You could take up some of your old hobbies. You could go out and get some sort of part time job. Anything, really, that gets you out from these four walls occasionally."

"But I've already got a part time job. Your accounts."

"We could find someone else to do them."

"We can't really afford to pay someone else to do them."

"Why not? It would be a deductible business expense, wouldn't it? Or come to that, I'll learn. It couldn't be that hard, could it?"

Margaret's face filled with skepticism. "You'll do them?"

"Why not? If it meant you were happier and could get out and do something you enjoyed, I'd be prepared to give it a go."

"But what about Todd?"

"Todd? Apart from holidays he's at school from nine till three thirty, then not home until about four. That should be plenty of time to study or get some part time job."

"You're forgetting about Nan. Who would take care of her?"

"My dear Margaret," Jim said, "she's pretty capable of taking care of herself. Besides, I think you'll find you haven't actually been spending that much time with her of late anyway."

Margaret looked quickly away. "Don't remind me. I find facing her so difficult. She looks at me like I've failed."

"Don't be silly. She's concerned for you."

Margaret buried her head in her hands. "I just can't cope with her and there's no reason why. Like you said yourself, she's very independent. But just having her around makes me feel, well, obligated. And that in turn makes me feel guilty. I shouldn't feel that way, should I?"

"Ordinarily, no. But you seem to have made it your mission in life to live for everyone but yourself. I think if you changed that you might find you'd feel different about other things as well. As for Christmas, I think you need to make a point of asking for help. Sarah's volunteered. Take her up on her offer."

"She's doing enough already."

"Well, ask Sheila. Promise me you'll call her up and ask her for help. If you're waiting for her to put her hand up, she never will."

Margaret considered this. "All right," she conceded.

"And while you're at it, promise me something else, will you?"

"What?"

"That you'll start putting aside some time to think about the future. About what you want to do. Not me, not Todd, not Sarah, not Pearl, or any of your other relations. Just you."

Margaret managed a small smile. "All right. I will."

Todd walked along the footpath, dragging his feet despondently. With only three days left before school finished he should, by rights, have been over the moon. But there lay half the problem: there were only three days left until the end of term. Three days for Todd to be able to set the tone for the entire summer. Succeed and his world could expand in infinite ways. Fail and the walls of his already limited life would all but close in on him.

After yesterday Todd had imagined the future to be little more than a foregone conclusion. His newfound friends would quickly embrace him as one of their own and include him in all manner of interesting escapades. But today Todd had fallen at the first hurdle.

It had been Justin who had casually mentioned the plan for Sunday.

"Are we all still on for swimming tomorrow?" he'd asked.

Everyone had been in agreement.

"Great. What time will we meet?"

"Eleven thirty?" Amber suggested.

"All right," said Justin.

"I'm organized with the supplies," Dominic said cryptically.

Everyone exchanged knowing looks and laughed. Then, almost as if they had suddenly remembered he was there, Daniel said, "You should come, Todd."

"If you aren't too busy with your other friends that is," smirked Amber.

"Where are you going?"

"Baker Point Pools. Do you know it?"

Todd nodded. It was further than he could easily walk but there were some things in life that were worthy of sacrifice. The chance of seeing Beth in a bikini ranked very high on such a list. Todd thought he'd be prepared to walk a decidedly long way indeed to see that.

And in the end Todd had walked the whole way with expectation driving him on. That, and the fact that he was running horribly late. Once again fate and his family had intervened. All this crap with his parents fighting for a start. Todd had little doubt that the fault lay with his mother somewhere.

In truth, the situation scared him a little. He wondered if perhaps his mother wasn't becoming a little unhinged. As much as they cramped his style Todd did not want to think about the possibility, however remote, of his family disintegrating. The thought of his mother being ignominiously dragged off by men in white coats made him shudder.

What had really spoiled it for him in the end wasn't all that domestic drama but his own sister. Todd had always liked to comfort himself that he had at least one decent sibling. Now he wasn't so sure. How did Sarah know he hadn't met Tom and Gerry? He felt she could see straight through him with those Ferguson blue eyes. Had she known? Or had she only been guessing? Either way, she'd had him cornered. He'd felt he had little choice but to go along with her suggestion of tidying his room.

As it turned out he hadn't really noticed what a state his room had become. He'd become the master of the quick clean-up job, hastily shoving things here and there to give the overall impression of cleanliness. But such short cuts had finally caught up with him - today of all days - since there no longer remained any room to surreptitiously shove a single extra thing.

So by the time Todd had done enough justice to the room to warrant being allowed out, he'd been running so late that by the time he reached Baker Point the clock had eased past twelve.

At the turnstile Todd parted with a chunk of his pocket money but with Beth in mind, he regarded it as a sound investment. Entering the pool grounds Todd's eyes were momentarily blinded with the sun reflecting off the aquamarine pool. The strong smell of chlorine and sunscreen assailed his nostrils. He glanced around, trying to locate the group. There were people everywhere. People on the plastic loungers, people on the grass verges, people slightly removed and taking shelter from the sweltering sun beneath a group of trees. The water seethed with a mass of people. A steady stream of humanity lined up one by one to throw themselves, lemming-like, off the diving board.

Todd debated whether to get changed or find the group. In the end, with so many heads bobbing in the pool, he decided on scouting around first. Otherwise he had nowhere to leave his stuff.

During the first five minutes of his search Todd remained optimistic. After all, the place was packed. But by the time ten, and then fifteen minutes passed with no sign of a single one of them, Todd's spirits took a battering. His mind whirled with possibilities. Maybe they'd decided to call it off and no one could find his number to call and let him know? Maybe no one remembered he had been invited in the first place? Perhaps, on getting here, they'd decided the place was simply too crowded and they'd opted to go somewhere else? But where would that be? Perhaps - and this was the hardest thought of all - perhaps they'd never had any intention of going at all. They could have set the whole thing up to guarantee Todd a long walk for nothing.

After half an hour Todd gave up and set out for the arduous walk home. He could not even be bothered having a swim to get his money's worth. The occasion had been spoiled. To make matters worse he inwardly lamented the loss of seeing that bikini.

He then returned to the troubling thought of only having three days left. It wasn't long. And how would he handle seeing the group tomorrow anyway? He just did not know.

Todd's thoughts consumed him so much that he did not notice a car pull up beside him until the passenger yelled out his name. Hope rose inside him. But when he looked up it wasn't Justin and his friends, but his cousin Jason.

"Todd," he said again. "What on earth are you doing out this way?"

Todd shrugged. "I've been to the pools."

The driver leaned over. It was Reuben. "At Baker Point? Bloody hell. Don't tell me you walked all the way from your place to Baker Point?"

Todd nodded. He felt perilously close to tears.

"Mate," Reuben said. "I hope it was worth it. Hop in."

Todd wrenched open the back door and slid in.

"Whose car's this?" he asked.

Reuben grinned over his shoulder. "It's mine. All mine."

Todd's eyebrows rose. "You bought it yourself?"

"Nah," said Jason. "The olds bought it for him."

Todd shook his head with disbelief. Never in a million years would either of his parents buy a car for him, especially not one this nice.

"Where are you going?" Reuben asked. "Do you want us to take you home?"

Todd shrugged again. "Where are you two going?"

Jason and Reuben looked at each other and grinned largely.

Jason said, "Reuben's going to give me a driving lesson."

"I thought you had to have your Learner's License first?"

"So? Who's going to know?"

"Awesome."

"Want to come along? We thought after the lesson, we might buy a few beers and go and hang out at the beach."

Todd's mind boggled. At least he would have something to tell the group when he saw them tomorrow. Maybe all wasn't lost.

Todd grinned back. "Epic," he said.

When they reached the end of the beach they walked over and touched the sandstone cliffs that were etched with the signature of the moving tides.

"We made it," Michael said.

They paused for a moment and stood there looking not at the cliffs but at each other. Sarah surveyed his face, finding it interesting and expressive. She could not help but feel a compulsion to look at him. He seemed to be scrutinizing her with his searching green eyes, perhaps trying to divine her thoughts.

The intensity of his gaze made Sarah remember her earlier resolve. She laughed quickly to hide her feelings, and turned away.

"We ought to be heading back," she said. "Nan will be wondering where we've got to."

"All right," he conceded, but by the expression on his face Sarah feared he realized she was running away.

Sarah felt a change of gears on their conversation was required. She said, "So what are you going to do with your summer holidays? Go away?"

He shook his head. "I wasn't planning on it. Not this year. I thought I'd stick around and try to break the back of my novel. If I can make some serious inroads into it hopefully that will be enough to sustain me through term time when opportunities to write are few and far between."

"Have you actually started?"

"Sort of. The plot and characters are developed. I've started the beginning about ten times but it's not perfect yet. I realize what I really need to do is just thrash out what I've got then flesh it out later. No doubt there'll be plenty of editing to do before I'm through. However you can't edit what you haven't written. That's where I have to start."

"I couldn't imagine knowing where to start."

"Sometimes I don't either. I think you've got to take the bull by the horns and just go for it. Then, if I start to suffer any writer's block, there's always the house to work on. I should try to at least get one more room started and finished this holidays."

"Which reminds me," Sarah said, "I should be ready to give you your garden design in a day or so. I went to the garden centre today and reckon I've got everything I need to pull it all together."

"Did you? Thanks for that. I hope you aren't going to too much trouble."

Sarah studied her feet as they sank into the soft wet sand. "I don't mind at all."

"I'm looking forward to seeing what you've come up with."

"I hope you won't be disappointed."

"Hardly. I guess I'll be adding gardening to that list of tasks, then, won't I?"

Sarah smiled. "Poor you. You'll have to make it like school. Draw up a timetable. Write from nine in the morning, until noon. Lunch, followed by two hours decorating. Afternoon snack, then one hour's gardening. Prepare dinner. Back into the writing."

"God. That sounds horrible. What a slave driver you are. Mind you, you're probably right. If I don't plan my days one will run into the next. Before I know it, it'll be time to go back to school again."

"I remember when I was young the long summer break practically used to drag. Now, after having been off work for a couple of weeks, I wonder how I stood it, hanging about so long with nothing much to do except play with Joanna."

"Have you started looking for a job yet?"

Sarah nodded. "I've applied for two. I'm hoping to hear this week whether either of them will offer me an interview."

"Maybe they both will. Did you consider that?"

She shrugged. "That would be good."

"Maybe both of them will offer you a job as well."

"I wouldn't presume to count my proverbial chickens. We'll just have to see. If neither of those come to pass I'm sure something else will come along."

"And you definitely want to work for someone else? You haven't considered setting up your own business?"

"Not really. I'm not sure I could stand the whole marketing side of things. I love what I do, but to get out there and push my own barrow - if you'll pardon the pun - isn't what I envisage myself doing. Then there's the fact that I need a regular income. Ideally I'd like to go flatting again soon. But until I have a wage coming in I won't be able to afford it."

"You could always board. It's usually a bit cheaper than flatting."

"True. However, I don't really want to end up living in someone's damp basement just for the sake of moving out of home."

"I've thought about maybe getting a boarder," Michael said.

Sarah's heart lurched. "Oh?"

He nodded. "I've never really done anything about it, though."

"I suppose you'd have to complete some more renovations first."

"Yes, I suppose you're right. The other thing that puts me off is ending up with someone intrusive. Ideally, when I'm not working, I like to use the time for writing. You never know whether a boarder would be tolerant of being left to their own devices night after night with only the television for company. I'd hate to feel obligated to make conversation."

"It sounds as though you've made up your mind."

Michael looked at her thoughtfully. "Actually," he said, "there are a great deal of things I'm still making my mind up about."

"I still can't believe it's you," Pearl said to Edwina. "It must be at least fifteen years since we last saw each other."

Edwina nodded. "As I recall, that would have been at the funeral of one of my brothers. Perhaps Peter?"

"Yes, I think so. Are they both gone?"

"Sadly yes. Rupert died quite soon after." She paused, looking thoughtful. "I was sorry to hear about Jack."

"Thank you. He's been gone more than five years now."

"Really? My, how time flies. I still regret not making it to his funeral. Circumstances were rather against me at the time."

"Never mind. It's all water under the bridge now. Tell me, you aren't still living at your parents' old house, are you?"

Edwina laughed. "Oh no. That got sold forty years or more ago. It's probably had umpteen dozen owners by now."

"It's odd, you know, but I was only just talking about you yesterday. To my granddaughter, Sarah, who you just met."

"Really? What a coincidence. What made you think of me?"

"We were talking about your twenty first birthday party. Do you remember it?"

Wistfully, Edwina said, "I've never forgotten it."

"Neither have I. It was the day Jack and I met."

"I remember."

"What a fortuitous day," Pearl said. When Edwina said nothing, Pearl said, "You never got married did you?"

Edwina shook her head.

Pearl was curious. "I can't imagine you weren't asked," she said.

Edwina smiled wryly. "Oh, I had my offers, believe me."

"But none of them were the right one?"

"No. There was someone, once, a friend of one of my brothers, but he married someone else. I'm afraid that after that no one else could quite take his place. I missed my chance and it seemed better to stay single than to shackle myself to someone I didn't truly love."

Pearl felt compassion well within her. After having had a lifetime of happiness with someone it seemed such a shame for her friend to have missed out on a similar experience.

Edwina laughed shortly. "Now don't go feeling all sorry for me," she said, as though reading Pearl's mind. "I've had some happy times and probably done all sorts of things the average married lady of my generation didn't do. I've seen much of the world, have met scores of interesting people. I've never been tied down, nor have I felt deprived in any way."

"That's good," Pearl said. "I think it would be awful to have lived a life you subsequently regretted."

"Oh, I think there are always things every person regrets. Life is full of opportunities. We don't really ever take advantage of them all."

Pearl nodded. "Do you still live around here?"

"Why, yes. I've always loved it here. But Rupert inherited my parents' house and when he decided to sell it he offered to buy me a little cottage instead, out of the proceeds. I think," Edwina confided, "that he felt a bit guilty because my father was such a stickler for the old traditions. In my father's eyes it would have been unthinkable to leave any girl substantial property, whether she was married or not. I think Rupert thought the small amount my father did leave me to be quite unacceptable, especially considering my spinsterly state.

"I could have refused his offer, of course. In fact a bit of me was sorely tempted to tell him what he could do with his charity. But one must be practical, and at the end of the day it seemed a fine solution. I could stay in Rosemont, and he got to ease his conscience. A beautiful partnership, don't you think?"

"And you're still there? In this cottage?"

"No. Eventually it became too much for me to manage. It required a lot of maintenance, more than I could afford. It needed a complete renovation, inside and out. By then, property prices had escalated so I sold and used the capital to buy myself an apartment in the Rosemont Village retirement complex. Do you know it?"

Pearl shook her head. "I've only just become acquainted with the place my brother lives in."

"Where's that?"

"Lambton Park."

"Miles away. I've never been. What's it like?"

"Very modern. Very nice. Much different from the mausoleum I had pictured." Pearl looked momentarily stricken. "Not that I mean to infer that there's anything wrong with where you live."

Edwina laughed. "Fear not. No offence taken. In fact, I really like where I am. It's quite a little community. There are even one or two souls such as myself who have lived their entire lives in Rosemont. We have much in common."

"And there's no gossip, and people saying snide things behind your back?"

Edwina looked at Pearl with surprise. "Hardly. Or if there is, I certainly don't know about it. What makes you think that?"

Pearl looked guilty. "It's what I've always pictured."

Edwina lifted one eyebrow. "Really? Well. Ah, I see your granddaughter and her young man returning. What a lovely couple they make."

Pearl watched as Sarah and Michael neared. Indeed, they looked entirely suited. She only wondered whether they realized it too.

CHAPTER EIGHT

Monday passed without Margaret fulfilling her promise to Jim. She had meant to call Sheila and have it out with her, really she had. But every time she went to lift the receiver something happened. Mostly, Margaret decided, pride had happened.

In truth she did not want to lower herself and grovel. Begging had never been in Margaret's nature, especially in regards to Sheila. In Margaret's opinion Sheila had always had life too easy - had always had too high an opinion of herself - without Margaret adding to her sister's good fortune by playing second fiddle.

However, she had made a promise. Come hell or high water she meant to keep that promise. About now the only person Margaret would vaguely consider begging was Jim. She did not want him to leave her. She'd realized in those wasted hours on Sunday, that she very much did not want Jim to leave her. Their marriage might be a starch-less shirt but it had meaning nonetheless. His anger, his, well, antipathy in her hour of need, had made the very existence of that shirt to be tenuous at best. Fear had crept into Margaret's heart. She might have lost her way, her self-esteem and even her marbles, but she did not want to lose Jim on top of all that. She needed him. It was as simple as that.

So when Tuesday morning came Margaret's resolve hardened. She needed to fulfill her promise almost as much as she needed help. As she picked up the phone she said to herself, over and over, think of Jim, think of Jim, think of Jim. Hastily, Margaret dialed the number.

The phone rang again and again. It was only nine a.m. Surely Sheila would not have gone out already? Margaret always got the impression years had passed since Sheila had seen daylight this side of ten o'clock.

Eventually, a gravely post-pubescent voice answered the phone, lackluster in his enthusiasm for the day.

"Hello?"

"Reuben?"

"It's Jason."

"Jason?" Margaret said with alarm. Since when did he sound so old? "It's Auntie Margaret here."

Silence.

"Is your mother about?"

More silence. Margaret could almost see him shrugging through the telephone.

"Hold on," he said.

He ground the receiver into some hard surface on his end of the phone leaving Margaret hanging. Margaret hated to think how much the fees were to send Jason to Riverleigh College but if his manners were anything to go by, Sheila and John definitely weren't getting their money's worth.

"Hello?" came the voice of her sister.

"Sheila? It's Margaret."

There was a small but telling pause. "Hello."

"How are you?"

"Fine." Reluctantly, she added, "You?"

"Not too bad. Pretty busy."

"Aren't we all?" Sheila said quickly, and Margaret knew the game was up. Sheila could most definitely tell Margaret had called because she wanted something. These days, they spoke on a needs basis only.

"I wondered," Margaret said, reminding herself, think of Jim, think of Jim, "whether you'd be able to lend me a hand organizing Christmas?"

"What?"

"Christmas. Mum's birthday. I need some help getting things organized." In an appeal to her vanity, Margaret added, "You're good at that sort of thing."

Another telling pause. "Oh Margaret, I don't know. Perhaps if you'd asked me a while ago."

"What? Are you saying you won't help me?"

"No, no. Not won't. Can't. It's a physical impossibility."

"But why?"

"I'm snowed under. Apart from all my social commitments to events I'm already helping organize, I simply couldn't find the time. The amount of functions we've been invited to this year is, well, almost embarrassing. As it is I've been wondering how I'll manage seeing Mum between now and Christmas. There's barely a minute to spare."

"She's your mother, too," Margaret said. "Haven't you got a duty to help me?"

"Duty?" Sheila laughed. "Yes, well, I suppose I would have if she was solely my responsibility. However, I think you've made it fairly obvious over the recent past that it's a shared responsibility."

"Well then, do your share."

"I would," Sheila said condescendingly, "if you'd made it clear three months ago that my help would be required. I simply can't shed my existing commitments at the drop of a hat because you've suddenly decided you can't manage."

"And that's your final word on the subject?"

"In a manner of speaking. I certainly won't waste my breath suggesting you ask David to help. All I can suggest is that you organize caterers or some-thing, if it all really is beyond your capabilities. Although God knows, you'll never get anyone decent at such short notice."

"Caterers?" Sheila must be joking. Margaret and Jim could never afford that.

"I'd recommend mine," she continued, "but for the fact that I know she's already booked solid. These sort of things have to be planned months in advance, Margaret, if you expect them to be done properly."

Margaret stared at the phone, panic welling up inside her.

"By the way," Sheila said, "Jason mentioned that he and Reuben saw Todd on Sunday. They picked him up out Baker Point way and took him to the beach. He seemed an awfully long way from home. What was he doing out there?"

Margaret's mind went blank. How could she confess to Sheila that she had absolutely no idea what she was talking about? As far as Margaret knew, Todd had been with Tom and Gerry. He said he'd been with Tom and Gerry. No mention had been made of either Jason or Reuben, or Baker Point for that matter.

Clutching at straws, she said, "He went to the pools. With some friends. I didn't realize he'd bumped into his cousins."

"That's what Jason said. He reckoned he and Todd and Reuben had a right old laugh. It's nice," Sheila said heavily, "that at least some of the family get on."

Nice? Later, Margaret couldn't help thinking it wasn't nice at all. What on earth would a twenty-year old young man and a sixteen-year-old youth possibly have in common with a thirteen-year-old boy? Enough to have had, what did Sheila say, a right old laugh? Margaret, momentarily distracted from all thought of Christmas, aimed to make it her business to find out.

That night, after dinner, Margaret, Jim and Sarah sat around the dinner table talking. Todd had mysteriously vanished as only he could when the vaguest suggestion existed that someone might ask him to wash the dishes or clear the table. That, and the fact that he was still smarting over the interrogation Margaret had given him when he'd got home from school.

Inevitably, Jim brought up the subject of Sheila. The night before he'd said nothing. Margaret had waited in guilty silence but he'd been tired after a hard day at work and wanted nothing more than to watch the news in a state of stupefaction before disappearing out into the garage.

"It was no go, I'm afraid," Margaret said.

"What? She won't help you at all?"

Margaret shook her head.

"Why not?"

"Some such nonsense about having to work on her double chin."

"Eh?"

Margaret laughed shortly, but there was little humor in the sound. "She's got functions coming out her ears. She's afraid she can't spare the time. She's going to steadily eat her way to Christmas, leave all the hard work to me, then come here and eat some more."

Jim stared at his wife as he processed this. The look on his face suggested his unease, in case this latest turn of events might upset Margaret's fragile equilibrium.

"Why don't you let me help, Mum?" Sarah said. "I'd love to. It would be fun. And besides, it's not as if I don't have the time."

"I still can't help feeling as though I'd be robbing you of that time," Margaret said again.

"To be honest any more time to myself might just send me round the bend. I'm not used to it. In fact, I'd go as far as to say that I'm no good at it any more."

"Are you sure?"

Sarah smiled. "Just look on it as a once in a lifetime opportunity to milk me for all I'm worth. Pretty soon the job offers will be flowing in and I'll be beating off gainful employers with sticks."

Margaret laughed. "All right, then. You win."

"Good," Sarah said. "And the first thing we're going to do is have a strategy session. Tomorrow morning. Nine o'clock sharp."

Margaret almost sagged with relief. Jim smiled broadly.

"There's lots to be done," Margaret warned.

"I don't care. If it frees you up to get on with other things, then I'll be delighted."

Margaret cringed at the thought of those other things. "Shopping," she said. "I haven't started the shopping. Even the jar of cherries I bought for Uncle Charles got smashed."

"Cherries?" said Jim. "What does Charles want with cherries?"

"He likes them," Margaret said.

"God. Why can't he make do with a packet of shortbread like an ordinary old person? If you ask me, you need some help with the shopping too."

"Are you offering?"

Jim wavered. Shopping lay way out of his usual league.

"All right," he said firmly. "When will we go?"

"What about tomorrow night?" Sarah suggested.

"Wednesday night? No one will be open."

Sarah laughed. "How is it that both of you can sit in front of the television and never see what's right under your noses? Haven't you seen the mall advertising that they're open until ten o'clock every night until Christmas?"

Jim quailed. "The mall? God help us. Still, needs must I suppose."

"You don't have to," Margaret said to him in a tone that suggested that he dare not pull out.

He waved a dismissive hand.

"What about Todd?" Margaret asked. "I'm not sure I entirely trust that boy as far as I can throw him at the moment."

Sarah said, "That's easy. I'll keep an eye on him."

"Are you sure? He's such a handful. I'm not sure he isn't worse than Isabella."

Jim said to Margaret, "She did get him to tidy his room."

Sarah laughed. "Piece of cake," she said.

After the dishes were done Margaret hunkered down over the kitchen table to work on the accounts, promising to leave all thoughts of Christmas to one side until she and Sarah could strategize. Jim opted for the garage, claiming he could hear Isabella's unfinished doll's house calling to him. Todd lurked in his room, for once not hogging the lounge and, subsequently, the remote control. Sarah figured he'd probably decided he stood less chance of a further ear bashing if he remained out of sight and out of mind.

Sarah flicked idly through the selection of channels. There were two programs on that she'd already seen in London, an American comedy of the plot-full-of-holes variety and a documentary about a couple who decided to give up urban life and head for the hills. They were a strangely unappealing pair and Sarah couldn't help feeling there was probably one or two people around relieved by their departure.

When the phone rang, Sarah gladly abandoned her post to answer it.

"Sarah?" came a familiar voice.

Sarah felt a jolt of surprise. "Michael! How are you?"

"Good. Tired. One more day to go, and a half-day at that. I think I'm looking forward to the end of term more than the students."

Sarah grinned. "Poor you."

"Yes, indeed." He paused. "I'm glad I got you," he said.

"Oh?"

"Yes. I wondered if you wanted to come with me to our end of year Christmas bash? It's nothing fancy this year. Last year we went to a posh hotel and half the staff came down with food poisoning for their seventy-dollar-a-head contribution. This year we're having a barbecue at one of the teacher's homes. It seemed safer. And cheaper."

"Must be a big home."

"It is, by all accounts. They live in Baker Point. Stunning sea views and all that malarkey. And just in case you're thinking teachers obviously get paid more than you thought, her husband is an accountant. A high powered one."

"Right then."

"So, do you want to come with me? Although I very much doubt I'll be the only one there without a partner, I thought it might be fun if you could come."

Partner? Sarah swallowed. She moved from her spot in the hall back into the lounge. With her free hand she pushed the door closed and turned off the television before sinking down onto the couch.

"When is it?"

"Tomorrow night. Short notice I know. You can blame that on me for being a bit slow on the uptake."

"Oh."

"Problem?"

"Yes."

"Can't come? Don't want to come?"

"Can't. The thing is, we've had something of a minor miracle happen here since I last saw you."

"That sounds intriguing."

"Somewhat. While we were at the beach on Sunday, Mum and Dad obviously had a chance to talk. When I got home Mum was practically serene. We've had two days of calmness like I haven't seen since I arrived home. I've persuaded Mum to let me help organize Christmas and even Dad is making an effort. He's taking her shopping tomorrow night."

It was Michael's turn to say, "Oh," although he sounded rather baffled.

"The thing is," Sarah said again, "I agreed to stay home and look after Todd. He's in the Dog Box. With capital letters."

"Really?"

"Really. Caught having an Unauthorised Outing. And," she added, "I suspect it isn't the first time, although I've not said anything yet."

"Right. So. Cinderella gets to miss the ball and stay home with the Ugly Duckling."

"Something like that. It's the first sign I've seen since I got home of Mum and Dad making an effort with one another instead of all those empty conversations, or worse, no conversation at all. I'd feel terrible if I turned into the reason they wouldn't go. I'm sorry. Otherwise I would've come."

"Not to worry," he said, sounding very unconcerned. "Just a thought."

Yes, Sarah mused, just a thought. A thought about her. And if she was Cinderella, just who was he?

Sarah decided to circumvent any excuses her mother might have of actually sitting down to make Christmas plans by getting up early, tidying the kitchen, throwing on some washing and making space on the kitchen table for them to work.

Sarah needn't have bothered. Her mother needed no such persuading.

Her complete relief at having finally secured some help that she didn't feel guilty about accepting meant she was rearing to go. Once Todd had been dispatched to school with strict instructions to come directly home at lunchtime - when the final half-day of term ended - they got straight down to business.

"Right then. Where to start?" Margaret wondered.

"I thought about that," Sarah said. "I thought we should make a list of everything we can think of that needs doing, then decide from there who should do what."

"Great." Margaret sounded dubious. Her lack of success with lists had begun to take on legendary proportions.

"I'll do it," Sarah said firmly, reaching for the paper and pen she'd prepared earlier. She wrote in a firm hand "Christmas Party" at the top of the sheet, underlining it several times.

"Actually," Margaret said, "I did already start a list of sorts."

She got up from the table to look through several piles of paper for it. Sarah despaired. Naturally, even after a few minutes of scrabbling, Margaret could not find the list.

"Let's start again," Sarah suggested. "A fresh approach."

"All right."

"Now, then, there's food and drink."

"And a cake. We'll need a cake."

"Of course. We'll also need enough crockery and cutlery and glasses."

"Yes. There are spares lying around somewhere in the house, although God knows where."

"What else?"

"Decorations? What about seating? Where shall we eat? I'm not sure Ernest and Charles and Mum will quite be up to eating off their knees. And then there's the other end of the spectrum - Isabella and Connor. If they're coming."

Sarah wrote down "Seating".

"Perhaps we need to work on the guest list," Sarah suggested. "Decide how many people are actually likely to be here. That way we'll be able to work out how best to accommodate them."

Margaret nodded slowly. "I suppose we'll have to. I'd put it off. The prospect of having to cater for all those people frightened me half to death."

Sarah turned the page of her pad and wrote another heading entitled "Guests."

"So, who have we got?"

"Well, there's the four of us. You, me, your father and Todd."

Sarah scribbled. "And Nan. We can hardly miss the guest of honor off the list, can we?"

"Of course not."

"And what about Joanna, and Brett, and Isabella, and Connor?"

Margaret looked across at Sarah. "She reckons they're not coming."

"So she says. But then how many times in your life have you known Joanna to say that sort of thing and then calm down. She's just miffed because she isn't the centre of attention."

"I don't know," Margaret said. "She was pretty angry."

Sarah shrugged. "Leave her to me."

Margaret's eyes narrowed. "Are you sure? I don't want to make things worse between the two of you."

"Don't worry, Mum."

"If you're sure. Who else?"

"There's Uncle Ernest and Uncle Charles."

"Definitely."

Sarah said, "I think we ought to include Ernest's friend Rosa on the list too. Nan says they're very friendly. I think Nan really likes her as well."

"She might be busy with family of her own, though."

"Maybe. There's no harm in asking, is there? One more won't make any difference either way."

"I suppose not."

"Next is Uncle David, Auntie Sheila and Uncle John and the boys. Anyone else?"

"I don't know. How many do we have so far?"

Sarah counted. "Seventeen."

"That many? Yikes."

"There are one or two others as well."

"Like who?"

"On Sunday we met an old friend of Nan's at the beach. She's called Edwina. She might have plans, being that it's Christmas, but you never know, she might be at a loose end. She's never been married."

"Do you think?"

Sarah nodded.

"I had sort of thought we'd just limit it to family. Being that it's Christmas I figured most other people would be busy with their own families."

"You're probably right. I do think we should ask Nan, though, if there's anyone else she wants to include. After all, it is her birthday."

Margaret flicked idly at one of her dog-eared fingernails. "I guess so."

"It would be worth asking."

"All right," said Margaret. "While we're inviting the world and his wife, I wondered too about asking Tom and Gerry if they wanted to pop in later in the afternoon. After the meal. It would give Todd some company."

"Could do. Like you say, they may be busy with family celebrations."

"Mum has a soft spot for them I think. Maybe they remind her of David and me in our younger days."

Sarah laughed. She seriously hoped not.

"There's another person I thought we should ask," Sarah said.

"Oh?"

"Yes. Michael. He's been such a good friend to Nan. I'm sure she'd love it if he came."

"Good idea, although once again I doubt he'll be available."

"You never know," Sarah said. "He isn't that close with his family."

"Really?" Margaret asked. "I didn't know that."

"They're older," Sarah explained, "and he had a brother who died. Michael said they've never got over his loss."

"I don't suppose you would," Margaret said. "No one ever expects to outlive their children. Will you ask him then?"

Sarah nodded. "I'm going to ask everyone over the next couple of days. We need to get numbers firmed up as soon as possible. That way we'll know where we are for catering purposes."

"Are you sure?"

"Of course. I've got the time."

Margaret looked enormously grateful.

Sarah said, "Before we go on to talk about the nitty-gritty of food and the like, I did have one other idea that's not on the list."

"Did you?"

"Yes. I thought we should put together a kind of collage about Nan's life. You know, old photos and memorabilia. We could put it on a board somewhere so that guests could have a look at it over the course of the day."

Margaret frowned. "That sounds like a lot of work."

"Not at all. I'd love to do it."

"You would?"

"I'd hardly volunteer if I wasn't keen."

Skepticism floated across Margaret's features. But when she'd clearly reconciled herself to the fact that she would not be required to help she conceded it was a good idea. It also made her realize something else.

"I suppose we'll have to have speeches of some sort. A cake cutting, a round of singing 'Happy Birthday', that sort of thing."

"Definitely," Sarah agreed.

"I couldn't," Margaret croaked. "Make a speech, I mean. And I don't think your father would be too thrilled about the idea either."

"There's Uncle David?"

Margaret shuddered. "He'd probably end up talking about his latest girlfriend. Pansy, or whatever she was called."

"Petunia."

"Sure. Petunia. I knew it was a flower."

"What about Uncle John?"

"He'd probably bore everyone about finance instead."

"Uncle Ernest?"

"Maybe. Although, knowing him, he'd more than likely regurgitate childhood stories featuring himself as the winner. Uncle Charles might be better."

Sarah said, "I think Uncle Charles would be perfect."

Uncle Charles, oblivious to that fact that plans were being made on his behalf, was busy writing a letter to his son. Peter had lived in America for ten years and during that time Charles had sat down every month to write a careful letter. He wrote in measured copperplate handwriting in an attempt to bridge the gulf between father and son. It was what Charles thought of as his "no pressure" letters, filled with innocuous happenings and throwaway anecdotes. None of them said most of the things Charles actually felt in his heart.

Like how he wished Peter would come home for a visit. Or his sorrow that Peter cared nothing for things outside his New York socialite scene. Or that Charles still felt extremely sorry that Peter had married such a shallow woman. Or how he would like Peter to occasionally get in touch with his sister, about whom Charles sporadically wrote. Not that Rosemary was much better. Her life outside London on some animal sanctuary was a million miles removed from home and even further removed from Peter's chic existence.

But Charles said none of those things, even though at times he had to steel his pen not to write them. He had learned that the only way to preserve contact at all was to tow the diplomatic line and bite his tongue. Or in this case, his pen. For this diplomacy Charles got rewarded with biannual telephone calls - ten or fifteen minutes of stilted conversation where Peter mumbled thanks for the letters and told Charles everything was much the "same". Not that that actually meant anything to Charles. He'd never been to America, had never been invited, so there was nothing for him to be able to compare this "sameness" to.

In contrast Rosemary never phoned, but she did write, probably every three months or so. On thick recycled paper that seemed to absorb her writing and make it very difficult to read. Mostly, it contained tales from the sanctuary, of rescued miniature ponies, distressed colonies of badgers and the plight of the lesser spotted something-or-other. Lately, there'd been mention of some fellow called Richard. Richard, who had a background in conservation and was as different as chalk from cheese than Rosemary's former husband, who, in Charles' opinion, had all the makings of a modern day pirate. He'd lacked only the wooden leg, parrot and eye patch.

As Charles finished writing a paragraph about the America's Cup yacht race, which he hoped Peter would find interesting, the phone rang. Charles picked it up in the hall.

"Hello?"

"Ernest here," Ernest boomed.

Charles couldn't help smiling. "How are you?"

"Box of birds. Yourself?"

"I'm very well."

"What are you doing?"

"Writing to Peter."

Ernest snorted with contempt. "What could you possibly have to say to that pansy?"

"Ernest. That's my son you're talking about."

"I know. Only joking. But even you must admit he's got himself a pretty easy wicket over there in the U. S of A. Fancy wife. Fancy house. Fancy car. Fancy job. Not like our lot here."

"At least he seems happy," Charles managed.

"Course. And why not? Hey, I wonder if he's got a fancy piece, to go along with all those other fancy things of his?" Ernest guffawed loudly.

"I should hope not," Charles said. What was it about his brother that always made him feel so po-faced?

"No. Probably not. He's always known which side his bread's buttered."

After a small silence Charles said, "Was there something you wanted?"

As a rule Ernest did not call up merely to pass the time of day.

"Well, actually, there was. I wondered what you were doing lunch-time-ish tomorrow."

Charles thought. There was a lunch on for some of the senior citizens at church, potluck, where the women went into a frenzy of baking in order to try to outdo each other. Often it could be quite a good time, and only held once a month. Suddenly he imagined a picture of Marjorie Wilson holding out her plate of butterfly cakes, smiling at him coquettishly. She the spider, he the fly.

"Nothing," he said firmly.

"Good. In fact, great. I wanted to talk to you about something. Wouldn't mind your advice."

That would be a turn-up for the books, Ernest actually wanting instead of giving advice.

"Right-o," Charles said. "Do you want to come for a sandwich?"

"Lord, no. I was thinking we could go to the pub. The Angler's Arms, or whatever that place is called on Waterhouse Road. Last time I went there it was still blessedly unmodernized."

A pub. Rather a far cry from a church hall luncheon.

"All right. What time?"

"Just before midday? Ten to? Better get in before all the workers slack off and come in for their liquid lunches."

"Okay," said Charles. "See you then."

When their mammoth planning session had finished, Sarah went out to the mailbox. While they were plotting and planning, Sarah had seen the postie edge along the road. She'd propped her 1950's issue bicycle on the fence, before rummaging around in her satchel for a wad of letters. The letters were then unceremoniously bundled through the slot on the mailbox, before the postie had used her regulation leg-of-lamb thighs to pedal to the next house. Sarah wondered whether there would be a letter for her from Cassie. Nearly three weeks home and not a word.

Now, though, that Sarah and her mother had talked their way through the finer points of the roast chicken or turkey versus the advantages of a bar-becue; had discussed the logistics of cooking enough potatoes for upwards of fifteen people; thrashed the issue of whether they could actually expect any of the guests to make a contribution in the way of food; and narrowed down what sort of cake they would have, Sarah felt free to get on with her allocated tasks.

First and foremost her job was to call the proposed guests. Starting with Joanna. It wasn't something Sarah thought she could easily do without the fortification of some fresh air. A trip to the mailbox seemed the logical choice.

Scanning the letters she saw three Christmas cards addressed to her parents in recognizable handwriting, four bills including one from the Inland Revenue, and two letters from the bank. At the bottom of the pile of letters was one addressed to Miss S. Bell. It was not, however, from Cassie.

Sarah tore it open.

Dear Miss Bell, she read, I am sorry to inform you that your recent application for the job of landscape designer has been unsuccessful. Thank you for your interest. Blah, blah, blah.

Sarah's spirits sunk. She hadn't even got to the interview stage. How very galling.

So much for her blithe boasts about the likelihood of her beating off new employers with sticks. She hoped it wasn't a sign of things to come.

"Oh it's you," Joanna said flatly.

"You were expecting someone else?"

"Three people actually. Including some sodding little tradesman who's supposed to've been here five hours ago to fix my dishwasher."

Sarah decided to try the sympathetic approach.

"What a nuisance. Has it been broken long?"

"Days. Weeks. It feels like years. However, I'm sure you haven't phoned up to commiserate with me about the state of my dishwasher. Make it quick, will you? I need to keep the line free in case that weasel is trying to call."

Did she mean the tradesman? Or was she talking about Brett? Sarah didn't dare ask.

"Right. Well, it's about Christmas."

"What about Christmas? I think I've made my position pretty clear."

"You don't really mean it, do you?"

"Don't I? I tell you, I'm sick to death of being taken for granted. Mum and Dad do it, the children are experts at it and Brett's getting better at it by the day." She broke off to yell at Isabella. "Don't climb on that," she shrieked. To Sarah she said, "What's it got to do with you, anyway?"

Sarah stifled a sigh. "I'm helping Mum organize everything."

"You would. God, you just can't help it, can you? You're only back from overseas five lousy minutes and you're already trying to get everyone eating out of your hand."

Clenching her teeth, Sarah said as evenly as she could, "This isn't about me, Joanna. In fact, when it boils down, it isn't about you, either. The point is, we're trying to do something special to celebrate Nan's eightieth birthday, and I'm trying to take a load off Mum's shoulders because she's had a bit of a rough time lately."

"I can't see why," Joanna said unsympathetically. She broke off, shouting, "I said get down." There was an almighty great crash in the background as something breakable hit the floor. "Bloody hell! Mum should try living here for a day and that would give her something to not cope about. Livingstone had less trouble tracing the source of the Nile than I have looking after these two. Look, I've got to go. There's pot plant from one end of the kitchen to the other no thanks to you, and Isabella's just peed right in the middle of it all. Bloody great."

"What about Christmas?" Sarah asked lamely.

"Christmas! As if I haven't got enough on my plate."

"Well, will you come?"

"I'll think about it," Joanna snapped, and promptly put the phone down.

Sarah, left staring at the receiver, could not help but part with a small smile. If Joanna said she'd think about it, chances are everything would be all right.

"Auntie Sheila? It's Sarah."

"Sarah! Darling. How nice to hear from you. Didn't we say we should have less of this 'auntie' business, though?"

Sarah said, "It's hard to break the habit of a lifetime. How are you?"

"Hectic. It's just one thing after the other at the moment. You're lucky to catch me at home. Yourself?"

"Very well. Busy too, as a matter of fact, although probably not quite as busy as you."

"Really? That sounds intriguing. Have you found a job yet?"

Thinking of her rejection letter, Sarah said, "No, I'm still working on that."

"Plenty of time," Sheila comforted. "So, if it isn't a job that's keeping you busy, what is, pray tell?"

"I'm helping Mum organize Christmas."

A small silence ensued. "Oh."

"It seemed the natural thing to do," Sarah told her. " After all, I have got the time whereas someone like yourself understandably has prior commitments."

Sheila rallied, buoyed up by the mention of something as important sounding as "prior commitments".

"That's very good of you," she said with gusto. "I suppose your mother told you I'm unable to lend a hand, much as I regret it."

"She did mention that. Never mind."

"So what can I do for you?"

"As a matter of fact, two things."

"Go on."

"First, I just need to confirm you'll definitely be here for Christmas lunch. We need to firm up the numbers for catering purposes."

Sheila was aghast. "You haven't managed to find a caterer at this late stage in the game, have you? If you have, I hope you got references."

"No. I'll come to that in a minute. I take it you're coming?"

Sheila sigh was palpable. "Yes. Or should I say, I'm working on it. We're invited to a champagne breakfast first thing with some close friends who have boys of similar age, so there's no problem persuading Reuben and Jason to go to that. I'm afraid there has been the weeniest bit of dissension in the ranks over lunch, however."

"Oh?"

"I'm afraid neither boy is thrilled with the prospect of spending time with a group of ageing relations, whether it's their grandmother's birthday or not."

"But surely they'll have to come," Sarah said with disbelief. "What else would they do?"

"No doubt there'll be something about a girl at the bottom of Reuben's reluctance. As for Jason, he'd probably be just as happy to spend his entire day in his room alternating between playing his guitar and learning the Road Code. He's got a date booked for his test at last. January the thirteenth."

"That's still a while a way."

"Yes. There's some sort of backlog. There's been a bit of a staff shortage at the local office."

"So, you and Uncle John are definite, but the boys are maybes," Sarah said.

"Something like that. But I know the birthday is important so I'll talk to John. I'll make him insist the boys come. In fact, better put us down for four. I'll start on the boys myself this afternoon before John and I go to the dinner we've been invited to with our bankers."

"Thanks, Auntie Sheila." In for a penny, and in for a pound she said, "I knew I could count on you."

"Don't mention it. Now, you said there was something else?"

"Yes. Like I said, we aren't getting caterers. We've decided to go for the traditional Christmas dinner over a barbecue since we don't want things to be too casual, and also because we'd probably never hear the end of it from Uncle Ernest if he doesn't get his standard meat and three veg.

"We thought perhaps we would do chicken instead of turkey. Several chickens, in fact. We can then use the oven in Nan's flat to cook the vegetables. Peas and beans can be done on the stovetop here. Then there's dessert. We thought we might order a couple of nice ones from that shop in town. A cheesecake, a gateau and maybe a chocolate log.

"We also thought we might ask them to make a birthday cake for Nan, with some fancy icing saying, 'Happy Eightieth' or something like that. I'm going to attempt to make the traditional Christmas pudding. Otherwise there'll be ice-cream, cream and probably custard."

Sheila said, "I suppose that all seems adequate."

"Hmm. I figure if we break it down between us, it won't be too much work, especially if we've ordered some things in. What I wondered was whether you'd be prepared to buy a couple of chickens, or some vegetables. Alternatively, there's always drink."

This caught Sheila off guard.

Sarah quickly said, "To be honest I know Mum would never ask you in a million years, but I knew you'd be keen to make some sort of contribution to the party. I just thought if I let you know what we need, you could consider how best to help."

"Of course," Sheila said magnanimously. "After all, if you can't spare your time, you can at least make some other contribution."

Sarah took a breath. "So what shall I tell Mum you'll be bringing?"

"Tell her we'll bring some alcohol. Beer, wine, perhaps even some champagne. What do you think?"

"I think," Sarah said, "that would be perfect."

No sooner had Sarah put the phone down than it began ringing beneath her palm. She hesitated before picking it up again.

"Hello?"

"Hello," said an unfamiliar masculine voice. "I wondered if there's a Sarah Bell there?"

"Speaking."

"Oh, hi. It's Rob Furness here from Furness and Smyth. We received an application from you recently for the position of landscape designer."

Sarah felt her stomach flip. Could this be more bad news on the job front?

"Yes, that's right," she managed.

"We were wondering if you would be able to come for an interview?"

Sarah had to stop herself from saying, "Really?" Instead she said, "That would be great."

"Good. Looking at our calendar here, it's, what, Wednesday today? Things are pretty chock-a-block until early next week. It seems every man and his dog wants garden work done before Christmas."

Sarah tried out a small laugh. "It's amazing what having a deadline does to people."

The unseen Mr. Furness laughed in return. "Too right," he said. "In fact the same applies to us. We've been thinking about taking on an additional designer for some time but you know how it is. You get so busy with the day to day stuff, the rest gets pushed to one side."

"Are you wanting someone for an immediate start?" Sarah asked tentatively, looking down at her pad with all the things she'd committed to do before Christmas.

"Chance would be a fine thing," Rob said. "No, we're looking to start the successful applicant in the New Year. Would that be a problem?"

"Oh no," Sarah replied.

"Good. Just to give you a bit of background, we're a bit of a one-stop-shop when it comes to gardens. I'm the resident designer and my partner, Greg Smyth, he provides the physical gardening labor. We do one, or the other, or both - whatever the client wants. We've already hired some extra assistance for Greg, so now it's my turn."

"It sounds very comprehensive."

"We can talk more about it when you come for your interview. Now, how would Tuesday suit? Say three thirty?"

"That," Sarah said, "would be perfect."

"Pearl?" Charles said into the phone.

"Hello, Charles."

"How are you?"

"Fine. Perhaps just a little tired. It's been so warm at nights that I'm not sleeping so well."

Charles laughed. "You wait. By Christmas it will be bucketing down and everyone will be moaning."

"I know. How are you?"

"Good, good. No complaints. I've just been writing to Peter."

"Dear boy. How is he?"

"Last time I heard he's fine. That was a while ago mind you."

"Oh well. Christmas will soon be here. He'll call then, won't he?"

"Most probably. Or I'll call him."

"And Rosemary? Have you heard from her?"

"Hmm. She's in love."

"What? Again? After swearing off men for life?"

"A temporary state of affairs at best," Charles said. "If you'll pardon the pun."

"So who is it this time?"

"He's called Richard. Picture someone tall and dark, with a shaggy beard, open sandals and socks, with an affinity for animals coupled with a love of natural yoghurt and fondness for organic wine."

"Please tell me you're joking," Pearl said.

Charles laughed. "Actually, I've no idea. It's just that from the few things Rosemary's written, that's exactly what I've pictured."

"Oh dear. Still, he sounds right up her alley. In fact, if it wasn't for the beard, they could be twins."

Charles laughed again. "Poor Rosemary. She's been a hopeless case since toddlerhood."

"Isn't it funny," said Pearl, "how some of the traits you observe in your children persist right through into adulthood?"

"I know," Charles said. "Same goes for siblings too."

"And just what are you implying?"

Charles said, "Actually, I was thinking about Ernest. He called me today, you know. In fact, that's one of the reasons I'm calling now."

"Oh?"

"Yes. I'm meeting him tomorrow for lunch. I thought I might pop in and see you on my way to town, if you were going to be home?"

"Of course."

"I'll be there about ten thirty, eleven o'clock? The thing is, I wondered if you'd mind testing me on my driving knowledge. I'll bring the Road Code and you can ask me questions. If you don't mind, that is?"

"Of course not."

"It'll just be for an hour. Until I meet Ernest. And catch this, he apparently wants my advice."

"Ernest? Surely not."

"That's what he said."

"Goodness. You have to wonder if he's entirely well."

"That," Charles said, "is what I thought."

It took Sarah a while to locate Uncle David's work telephone number. Margaret had been vague about where he even worked these days.

"He gave me a card of his a while ago," Margaret said. "It's some sort of sales position. Either that or product management. I can't remember."

"Do you know where you put his card?"

Margaret looked apologetic. "I can't remember that either. It's probably somewhere there on the kitchen bench."

Sarah looked at the piles of paper with something akin to desperation.

"By the way," she said to her mother, "I've got an interview for a job next week."

Margaret looked aghast. "I thought you were waiting until after Christmas?"

Sarah shook her head. "I did tell you I'd applied for two positions. One firm turned me down flat but the other have just offered me an interview."

Margaret attempted a watery smile. "Congratulations."

"It's only an interview."

"But still, that's a start."

"Yes. And you don't have to worry. They don't want anyone to start until the New Year."

Margaret had looked about as relieved as a person with a commuted death sentence.

Sarah had then set about hunting for the elusive business card which she unearthed between a postcard she'd sent home at the beginning of her trip, and a notice from Todd's school reminding parents to please pay immediately if they wanted their child to go on some school trip to the museum.

Dialing the number, Sarah ended up speaking to three different people before she was finally got connected to Uncle David. One of the three even sounded vague about whether they'd ever heard of David Hamilton. Someone in the background mumbled something before the person said, "Oh, *that* David."

When he came on the line at last Sarah told him who it was.

"Sarah! My goodness. You're the last person I thought of hearing from."

"How are you?"

"On top of the world. You?"

"Good thanks."

"All settled down, then?"

"Getting there."

"Excellent. How's that boyfriend of yours? Oh, that's right, he's a friend of Mother's, isn't he?"

"He's good," Sarah replied. "The thing is," she continued quickly, desperate to stem the tide of inanity, "I'm calling about Christmas, and about the party for Nan. I wanted to check you're coming?"

"What? Yes. Of course. I'm looking forward to it. It'll be nice to have somewhere substantial to go this year for a change."

"Great. We're planning on having Christmas lunch, then a bit of a presentation time for Nan. Does that suit?"

"Sure. Fine. Just one thing, though."

Sarah waited.

"I wondered," David said, "if I could bring along a guest?"

"Petunia?"

"Petunia? Oh, no no. That's all off. Cow. She turned out to have a right nasty streak."

Sarah couldn't help thinking it must have been a pretty wide nasty streak if even Uncle David had been able to discern it in the ten days since they'd last seen him. He'd waxed so lyrically about Petunia.

"Sorry about that, Uncle David."

"Not at all," he blustered. "Onward and upward, that's my motto. Especially upward."

He laughed at his own joke.

"Who is this person, then?" Sarah asked with as much patience as she could muster.

"Her name's Daphne. Wonderful woman. She's Australian, but we won't hold that against her, will we? She's a potter, come to live in New Zealand because she likes the clay."

Sarah wondered, after an acquaintance of surely less than ten days, how he could be so certain of her wonderfulness. Or how, for that matter, he could even consider bringing someone he barely knew himself along to his mother's eightieth birthday party.

"She'll be all alone," Uncle David said in a whimpering tone. "We couldn't have that, could we?"

Sarah buried a sigh. "I suppose not."

"Great," he said, perking up immediately. "We'll see you Christmas Day, then."

He promptly hung up, before Sarah had even had the chance to broach the subject of some sort of financial contribution. She scowled at the phone. He need not think he could get away with it that easily.

Mid afternoon the phone went again.

"Todd," Margaret yelled up the stairs, "it's for you."

Todd's ears pricked up. He put aside his Playstation and went out into the hall.

"I'll get it in your bedroom," he yelled back.

He could hear his mother muttering something about him having a cheek, but Todd wasn't concerned. If it was who he hoped, a bit of privacy wouldn't go amiss.

It was fair to say that the last three days had not entirely gone to plan. First there'd been the small problem of his cover for Sunday having been blown. Second, the group had remained elusive, like trying to locate the soap in the bath only to have it slip away from you. Granted he'd tried, but there'd always been something to thwart him.

For a start none of the five actually seemed to be attending any proper classes. Not that the teachers seemed particularly bothered. After a vague enquiry as to their whereabouts most seemed to give it up as a waste of time. Which it was. Todd had learned nothing this week. Nil. Zilch. Zero.

Next, every time Todd managed to spot the group heading his way Tom and Gerry showed up right at the same time, thus seriously damaging his credibility. They were like some weird kind of double shadow, if that was possible. And of course as soon as the group saw him with the twins they would point and smirk and head off on a completely different trajectory. At one point he'd even told Gerry to piss off but Gerry had grinned idiotically and remained both unmoved and unconcerned by Todd's anger.

Then, finally, today, Todd had managed to come across Daniel. They'd had a brief and, from Todd's point of view, fairly satisfying conversation during which they'd swapped phone numbers so they could keep in touch over the holidays. So it was with great expectation that Todd went to answer the phone, thinking that things were already looking up. He knew it wouldn't be Tom and Gerry. Todd had already lied to them about going out this afternoon.

"Hello?"

"Todd, it's Jason," his cousin said.

Todd was taken aback. He hadn't yet decided whether he should be mad at his cousins for blowing his cover.

"Hi," he said flatly.

"What are you doing?" Jason asked.

"Not much."

"Did you finish school today?"

"Yeah. At lunchtime. You?"

"Nah. I've been off for a couple of weeks. I've been hanging around all day doing nothing."

"Where's Reuben?"

"He's got some poxy part time job with Dad. He has to do it toward some uni paper he's taking next year. Plus Dad's paying him."

"That's lucky."

"Tell me about it. To make matters worse, Mum's been harping on at me about Christmas and about this lame party your Mum's having for Nan's birthday."

"You should try living here and being in the thick of it. Aren't you going to come?"

"Dunno. I might. It sounds as though there won't be a lot of choice in the matter."

Todd said sadly, "There's definitely none for me."

"Too bad. Hey, I was wondering if you want to meet me in town on Friday night?"

"What? Just you and me?"

"Kind of. Mum's going into town to meet some girlfriends so I can cadge a ride with her. I'll then hook up with her later for the trip home."

"I'm not sure I'll be allowed," Todd said. "Unfortunately Mum found out about my trip to Baker Point and going off with you guys. She wasn't very happy."

"That's Reuben's fault. Big idiot. He blabbed at dinner that night, even though I kept trying to kick him under the table. He's so used to being able to do what he wants, I think he's forgotten what it's like to not be able to breathe for adults. Was she pretty mad?"

"Yeah. Livid."

"That's only because you lied. Parents hate that. The trick is to make things seem like the truth, and to not give them reason to suspect. If I want anything from my mum the first thing I do is start pulling my weight a bit. Then I tell her as much of the truth as I can get away with and usually that works. Besides, if you tell her that my Mum will bring you home, she surely can't object?'

"I don't know. Maybe she hasn't had enough time to get over the last episode."

"Go on," Jason urged. "No harm in asking."

Todd considered this. But hanging out in town with his cousin sounded a damn sight more attractive than sitting at home. If what Jason said was true, at least he had one cousin he could rely on for a bit of discretion. And, if he followed Jason's advice and was economical with the truth, he could tell his mother that Auntie Sheila would be there the whole time. Which she would be. In town. Just not necessarily with Todd and Jason.

Todd discovered he was grinning. "I'll see what I can do," he said.

After dinner, Sarah had washed the dishes while Margaret had fussed about in preparation for going out. Jim had slunk off, presumably to psyche himself up for facing the shops. Todd sat ensconced in the lounge with the remote control. Uncharacteristically, he'd been very polite at dinner, and had even helped clear the table.

Her mother said, "Did you see what I did with those dry-cleaning tickets?"

"I saw them earlier today when I was looking for Uncle David's business card."

"Ah, yes, here they are. I figure I may as well not waste another trip into town without collecting the dry-cleaning now that they've managed to find my items."

"You haven't forgotten the chemist called about Nan's prescription, either?"

"No. And people say miracles never happen."

"Are you ready?" Jim asked, popping his head nervously around the kitchen door.

"Almost."

"Hurry up woman, or the shops will be shut."

"Coming, coming. Now where is that shopping list? Ah ha. Found it."

"Come on then," Jim said. "The sooner we get going, the sooner we'll be home."

"Don't rush on my account," Sarah said. "Make sure you stop and have a coffee or something."

"We will," Margaret said.

Simultaneously Jim said, "We won't.

Sarah grinned. "Get out of here you two. You're worse than Todd."

Margaret paused as she went to close the side door. She grinned at Sarah. "Thanks for this," she said. "I really appreciate it."

In the wake of their departure Sarah collapsed into a chair at the kitchen table. She pulled over her pad and started making some more notes about Christmas. She found, however, that her mind wasn't really on the job. She'd used the word perfect several times that day, but the truth fell a little short of perfection. Instead she kept finding herself thinking about Michael. Picturing him at the barbecue, a glass of wine in his hand, talking and laughing and generally having a great time. Without her. She realized she missed him and that she would love to have gone with him, even though the prospect of meeting his work mates was a little daunting.

Her resolve, it seemed, was slipping.

CHAPTER NINE

To stop herself thinking any more about what sort of time Michael might have had the night before - and indeed to stop herself from rushing straight over there as soon as she'd had breakfast - Sarah went to visit her grandmother.

She found Pearl in high spirits, making scones, as she prepared for a visit from Charles.

"I don't suppose he'll want to eat them," Pearl said with a little lopsided grin. "He's going to meet Ernest for lunch. Knowing Charles, he'll want to leave room. He never was one for excess. Ernest now, he'd eat the whole plateful and still go and have more for lunch."

Sarah smiled. "It's funny how different we all are."

"You can say that again. Anyway, I thought to myself I'd make the effort nonetheless, even though it will probably be largely wasted on Charles. I thought I could send some of the scones along with him for Ernest and Rosa."

"That's a lovely idea."

"Something about meeting Rosa did a lot of good for my soul. I've felt, ever since that day, that I'd like to reciprocate her kindness, but I couldn't quite make up my mind how I should go about it."

"You'll be seeing her again then, I gather?"

"I should say so. Ernest suggested we make a date for me to go over there again next week some time. You should meet her too, you know. You'd love her."

"Really?"

"Yes. She's such a little thing, but what she lacks in stature, she makes up for in personality. She's one of the most alive people I think I've ever met."

"She does sound special." Sarah paused before saying, "We thought that we would ask Ernest if he'd like to bring her along on Christmas Day."

"For my birthday? Oh, that would be wonderful." Pearl frowned momentarily. "I hope you're all not going to too much trouble. I don't want anything fancy."

Sarah laughed. "Don't you worry about it, Nan. Everything's in hand."

After they had talked about the plans for Christmas Day, Sarah excused herself on the pretext of letting her grandmother get ready for the arrival of her guest. In truth, just talking about what they were planning had been sufficient to make Sarah realize she couldn't really afford to waste too much time. There were still a lot of arrangements to make, including having another go at Uncle David about forking out some money.

Before going inside, Sarah took a detour to the mailbox, ostensibly to check for mail from Cassie, but in the back of her mind she knew that plain old curiosity was part of her motivation. She couldn't help glancing sideways as she walked down the length of the driveway. She soon realized Michael's car wasn't there. With a gulp she wondered if he'd even come home after the previous evening. Surely he must have. He probably had to go back into school to wind things up before his holiday began.

With nothing more to be seen in that direction, Sarah turned her attention to the mailbox. Sure enough, the postie had already been. A small wad of letters rested in the box. Pulling them out, Sarah gave each one a quick scan until she saw Uncle Charles pull up. Sarah waited while he parked his car and climbed out, realizing while she waited that the expected letter from Cassie had finally arrived.

"Hello, Uncle Charles," Sarah greeted as he approached.

"Young Sarah," he beamed. "How are you this fine morning?"

"Very well. You?"

He laughed. "As you say, very well. What are you up to?"

"I'm up to my eyeballs in plans for Christmas. Mum has mentioned to you about Christmas lunch?"

"She did say something a while back."

"It's all still on. The plan is to have lunch, then do something to celebrate Nan's birthday. The thing is, we were wondering if we could prevail upon you to make some sort of little speech."

Charles looked incredulous. "Me?"

Sarah smiled reassuringly at him. "Why not? You'd be great."

"I...I'm not sure I'd know what to say."

"Of course you would. I'm sure you'd have no problem coming up with some lovely things to say about Nan. Perhaps even propose a toast to her?"

"Oh, I...I suppose I could."

"Have a think about it. Let me know."

"Not Ernest?"

Sarah shook her head.

Charles nodded slowly, as though digesting this information.

"I do need to tell him about lunch, though," Sarah said, "to make sure he definitely knows it's on. We thought he might like to bring Rosa."

Charles smiled. "I'm sure he would. Do you want me to ask him? I'm seeing him this lunch time?"

"Would you? That would be great."

"No problem."

Sarah said gently, "You could bring someone, too, Uncle Charles, if you wanted."

A strange look flitted across his elderly features. "Ah, no," he said, "I really don't think so."

Sarah nodded. "I've just been to see Nan," she said. "She's really looking forward to seeing you."

"Good, good," he said. "Although whether she'll still think so after I've gone is a matter of some debate."

"Oh?"

He waved the Road Code at her. "Pearl's going to test me on my driving knowledge."

"Really? You ought to get together with Jason. He's studying for his test, too."

"Jason?"

"Auntie Sheila's youngest."

"Of course. Poor senile old fool," he said, patting his forehead. "When's his test?"

"Soon. Yours?"

"I haven't really looked into it," Charles said. "I'll be seventy in late January so I thought I'd better get a head start with brushing up on my knowledge. The poor old brain isn't what it used to be, but I'm not ready to hang up my driving hat yet."

"I wouldn't have thought you'd need to learn all that again," Sarah said, indicating the Road Code. "In fact, I thought they changed the rules a while ago, and that you don't have to re-sit your practical road test until more like eighty."

Charles's eyebrows shot up. "Really?"

"I don't know for sure." She gave a small self-deprecating laugh. "I'm not quite up to the stage of having to look into it. However, I definitely heard that only a practical test was involved and, like I said, that the age limit for re-sitting this test has been raised."

"But Ernest said..." Realization dawned. "Ernest," Charles said with a sigh. "If he's put me crook, I'm going to kill him."

Sarah watched him disappear off to her grandmother's, muttering under his breath about his brother. She couldn't help a little smile crossing her lips. The idea of Ernest being so mean was quite believable. The idea of Charles ever actually killing anyone was ludicrous.

The thing is, Cassie wrote, London is actually pretty dull without you. Why did you have to go home? There's no one to go shopping with, or sight-seeing with, or to the pub with. That Tony Adamson never used to flirt with me while you were around, but now that you're gone he's like a bee around the proverbial honey pot. I'm sorely tempted to buy some fly spray. He must think that now I'm on my lonesome, I'm fair game.

On the up side, I have got a new flatmate. I had to interview about fifty girls before I found someone remotely suitable, but no sooner did she move in, than she went away. The bonus is that I'm charging her twenty pounds more a week than you paid, and she's paying up! And no, before you ask, she's not some green fresh-off-the-plane Kiwi or Aussie, but a bona fide Brit. She's from Scotland of all places, and is down in London to do some cooking course. I said to her she'd be welcome to try out her recipes on me any time she liked. The kitchen might welcome a change from being merely a place to heat up meals from Sainsbury's.

Oh, I realize I haven't been very clear. When I say she went away, I don't mean for good. She's gone with some of her classmates to Paris, where they're studying some special kind of sauce making. Don't ask me the specifics. I mean, I thought all sauces came out of a packet or a bottle. Nobody ever told me you could actually make them yourself.

She's back next week, and then only for ten days or so before going home for Christmas. And catch this...she's asked me if I wanted to go to Scotland for Christmas! I told you we should go to Scotland and, voila, the opportunity presents itself. See. You should have stayed. Except for the fact that if you'd stayed I'd have never been invited on account of the fact that I wouldn't have needed a new flatmate in the first place. Life's complicated, isn't it? Oh, and her name's Morag, by the way, in case you were wondering. Morag McDonald. I'm sorely tempted to accept her invitation since the desire to see the rest of her family is getting the better of me. I want to know if they all wear kilts and speak so fast that I won't know what they're saying, and if they're all called Dougal and Angus and Hamish. I'm sure they must all drink scotch, so how could that be a bad thing?

Anyway, I'd better go. James and Linley have invited me out for a meal tonight and I still haven't made up my mind what I'm going to wear. I just wanted to let you know that life's not the same now you're gone, and that, whatever I end up doing for Christmas, it just won't be the same without you.

Sarah lay back on her bed, looked at the ceiling and grinned. What with invitations out, a new flatmate and someone flirting with her, it sounded like Cassie was having a ball. It made Sarah feel immensely relieved.

It took Charles fifteen minutes to find a park even remotely close to Waterhouse Road. It made him fondly nostalgic for the days of his youth when there wasn't anything worth going to town for anyway, when you went by bus instead of by car, and the word "mall" was associated only with England, conjuring up images of royalty, in their horse drawn carriages, being pulled elegantly toward Buckingham Palace.

It didn't help that Charles wasn't in a disposition particularly inclined to see his brother. In fact after finding out that Ernest had sent him on a wild goose chase of useless learning and concern about a test he'd now found out he definitely did not have to sit, he felt rather more inclined to give Ernest a black eye than the time of day. Sarah had been right. The rules had most definitely been changed and the specter of a road test now lay ten years further down the track. And he wouldn't have to relearn all those rules and regulations anyway. It made his blood boil just to think about it.

As it transpired, he was further delayed by the fact that The Angler's Arms was in fact now called The Galactic Vintner. Contrary to Ernest's assertions the place had indeed undergone a makeover and now resembled something futuristic and alien. Gone were the dark mahogany booths, the veil of smoke, little round tables with decades of watermarks on them and the threadbare carpet.

Instead a combination of chrome and silver and a rather lurid purple had been installed. The waitresses were dressed in a metallic fabric and wore strange headdresses with antenna poking incongruously up. The place was packed, mostly with thirty-somethings sipping wine and nibbling on lettuce leaves. Charles found Ernest squirming uncomfortably in the back corner.

"God," he said. "Look what they've done to the place."

Charles resisted a smile. "It's like something out of the eighties," he said lightly, as he slid onto the chair opposite his brother. He held his hands together for good measure, in case temptation should overcome him. "I think they call it 'retro'."

"A bloody travesty more like. Why can't the modern generation leave things well alone?"

Charles shrugged. "It's called progress," he said. "They're making it all the time. In all kinds of avenues. Even when it comes to renewing your driving license."

Ernest's eyebrows shot up at his. His mouth twisted with a combination of apology and amusement. "Ah, yes, sorry about that. I just couldn't resist. When you started talking about it, fussing like an old woman, I just couldn't help letting you stew."

"Thanks a lot."

"Just think how much more knowledgeable you are now."

Charles's eyes narrowed. "I could kill you, you know."

Ernest guffawed. "No you couldn't."

One of the alien waitresses approached. "Would you like to order?"

Charles noticed her antenna wobbled while she spoke. Her lipstick was the same lurid purple as the carpet.

"I don't suppose you do pies and pints, do you?" Ernest asked dubiously.

The waitress's eyes widened. "Oh, no," she said, horrified.

"No? I thought not. Come on Charles," Ernest said. "Let's get out of here."

In the end they found a relatively old fashioned cafeteria devoid of anyone under the age of about fifty. There they purchased mince pies and strong tea that came in utilitarian teapots with extra water so you could help yourself to more. There wasn't a glass of wine or an antenna or any purple in sight, apart from one old lady who'd evidently recently opted for a lilac rinse at the local beauty salon. There wasn't even one of those wretched coffee-making machines to make bilious gurglings as it frothed milk.

"That's better," said Ernest, tucking with gusto into his pie. He'd also selected a cream bun for good measure and had already given Pearl's scones a fond once-over.

Charles sipped his tea. "Now, you wanted to ask me something? You said something about needing advice?"

Ernest laughed, and wiped his mouth vigorously with a serviette. "No, no, my dear boy. Not advice. I've already made up my own mind about it, but I just wanted to tell you, see what you thought.

"About what?"

"About me asking Rosa to become my wife, that's what."

Charles put his teacup down rather more sharply than he intended.

"You're thinking of proposing?"

Ernest nodded.

"Goodness."

Ernest looked put out. "Well?" he demanded.

"Well, what?"

"Aren't you going to say something? Congratulate me?"

Charles smiled wryly. "Don't we need to wait for Rosa to accept before congratulations are due?"

A strange look flitted across Ernest's features. Charles perceived that lack of success wasn't something Ernest had considered.

"You don't think she'll have me?"

Charles thought about Rosa, thought too about Marjorie Wilson. With Marjorie, nothing could be misconstrued. Her interest could not be doubted. With Rosa, on the other hand, well, she had a self-sufficiency that transcended blatant interest.

Charles said, "To be honest, I don't know. I don't know Rosa well enough. However, if you're sure of your feelings and sure it's what you want, then by all means, ask her."

"I will," said Ernest huffily. His eyes narrowed. "You don't think it's a bad idea, do you?"

Charles smiled. "No. Of course not. Rosa's an amazing person. I'm sure she'd make you very happy."

"There's the small matter of her being Catholic. I can't abide all that popery."

Charles said, "I'm sure you'll work it out. These days it seems as though very few things are insurmountable."

"Good, good. Yes, capital. How's Pearl?"

"Actually, she seemed happier today. I think your trip out with her was a resounding success. She's also been out with Sarah and that young fellow from next-door and bumped into some old friend. They've been talking on the phone every day ever since. It seems to have done her the world of good."

"Still wish she'd move out of that dog kennel they've got her in."

"You can't make her," Charles said. "She'll move when she's good and ready. Besides, you never really do know what's around the corner, do you?" He lifted his teacup in a toast, smiled warmly at his brother, and said, "Well, anyway, good luck to you."

Friday evening, after having been free of school for an entire two and a half days, saw the twins turn up at the Bell house. Tom and Gerry, perhaps feeling assured of their welcome, came knocking at the kitchen door, rather than the front door. Sarah invited them somewhat pointlessly in to the kitchen.

Margaret looked up from a pile of papers consisting mostly of the last three days mail that she'd spread out in front of her on the kitchen table.

"Hello, Tom. Hello, Gerry," Margaret said.

"Hello, Mrs. Bell," Tom said.

Tom, it appeared, had dressed for the outing with some care. Margaret couldn't help frowning at the wisdom of letting a thirteen year old girl wear quite that much make up, or that short a skirt either, for that matter.

Gerry murmured something that might well have been a hello but no one without bionic hearing would know. Both twins stood their ground, staring out motionlessly from beneath their matching fringes. Margaret couldn't help hoping she and David had not been like this when they were younger. She sincerely hoped there wasn't a scrap of resemblance between the two of them whatsoever these days.

"Todd's not here," Margaret told them.

Twin expressions of disappointment flitted momentarily across their features.

"Oh," Tom said.

"No, sorry. He's gone into town with his aunt and his cousin," Margaret explained.

At least she hoped to God that was the case. Todd had been suspiciously well behaved, as well as uncharacteristically forthcoming about the proposed outing. Every objection Margaret made Todd had counteracted with something smooth and soothing, as though his mother was a fool to even argue the point. Sure he had done the wrong thing on his trip to Baker Point, he could see that now. It was foolish and thoughtless and immature he had told her. But things were different now. He had learnt his lesson. He knew the importance of honesty. Besides, what would be the harm of a trip out with relations, especially when his aunt would not only be there in town too, but would also deliver Todd safely home to the doorstep.

Margaret had almost wished she was on speaking terms with Sheila so she could have called her up to check the veracity of some of these claims. As it was it seemed hard enough to reconcile herself to having to welcome her sister into her home come Christmas Day, let alone calling her up to play detective. Sheila, she knew, would probably quickly turn the situation into something it wasn't, inferring Margaret's parenting skills were not up to par.

"He never told us," Tom said, clearly battling to keep accusation out of her tone.

"I don't suppose he had much of a chance," Margaret said. "Let's just say his shore leave was cancelled, and he had things to attend to here."

Gerry grinned. "No away missions for him, then."

Margaret looked confused.

Sarah slid down into the seat opposite Margaret, said, "It's a *Star Trek* reference."

"Ah. Yes, well in that case, you're right Gerry. No away missions for him."

Sarah said, "I'm glad you've come by."

Immediately, both twins retreated behind their uniformly bland expressions.

"You see," Sarah said, "we were wondering if you'd like to come along on Christmas afternoon, some time after lunch, to help us celebrate Nan's birthday. I'm sure Nan would love to see you. I know Todd would welcome the company."

Gerry's mouth moved like a fish's. Tom looked surprised.

"You'd have to check it out with your parents," Margaret said.

Both nodded vigorously.

"So would you like to come?" Sarah asked. "If you're allowed?"

More nodding. "Yes, please," Tom said.

"I didn't honestly think they'd be that keen," Sarah said after they had gone.

"You never know with people and Christmas. It's the sort of day that seems to bring out the best and the worst in people. Maybe they'll be longing to escape by the afternoon. Or maybe they just feel honored to be asked and included."

"Still. An eightieth birthday party. It's hardly a hip occasion, is it?"

"Especially," said Margaret with a rare smile, "if some of those 'hips' have been replaced."

"Ha ha."

Margaret looked at Sarah. "What are your plans for this evening?"

Sarah studied her fingernails. "More planning for Christmas, I suppose."

"You should have a break from it," Margaret said.

"Will you be taking a break from your paperwork?" Sarah countered.

Margaret looked abashed. "Maybe. When your father comes in from the garage we might watch a bit of television together."

"Good," said Sarah firmly.

"How is everything coming along anyway?"

"Pretty well. I've almost talked to everyone and they all seem to be coming. Uncle Charles phoned today to say he passed on the invitation to Uncle Ernest, and that we're to expect Uncle Ernest's call when he's asked Rosa about coming. Nan seemed delighted with the idea of asking her friend Edwina and was going to call her today. I've talked to Uncle David and Auntie Sheila, and now, even the twins."

"So only one person to go, then?"

Sarah nodded. She felt her heart skip a beat. She'd managed to avoid going next door all of yesterday and all of today. She did not know what was putting her off.

"Why don't you pop over now?" Margaret suggested. She swiveled in her chair and craned to look out of the window. "It looks like he's home."

Sarah shrugged. "I suppose I might as well. After all, I've finished his garden plan. I may as well kill two birds with one stone."

"Hi," she said when Michael opened the door. She couldn't quite work out whether she'd managed to rearrange her face into a smile or not. Truth be told she felt nervous. Giddily nervous.

He smiled warmly at her. "Hi yourself. Come in."

"I hope I'm not disturbing you."

"Don't be silly. Why do you always say that?"

"Do I?"

"Seems like it," he said as he led her into the lounge.

Sarah looked at him sheepishly. "Sorry." She waved the paper she held at him. "I finished your garden design."

"Great. I'm looking forward to seeing it. I'm also extremely pleased you had a reason to come over. I've been trying to think of a reason to come over and see you for two straight days. I couldn't come up with a thing. With an imagination like that I can hardly see me ever being able to write a book, can you?"

"Now you're the one being silly. You should have just come over. Or phoned. You don't have to have an excuse."

"Don't I? Good. Neither do you."

Sarah grinned. "How was the party?"

"Party? Oh, the end of year bash? Not bad, on the whole. Nobody got food poisoning that I know of. No embarrassing trysts in the broom closet. The food was okay. You should have seen the house, though. It was amazing."

"I'm sorry to have missed it."

"Yes, and I would have benefited from your company, too. Poor teachers. All they can ever talk about is teaching."

"I'm sure you're exaggerating."

He smiled. "Perhaps a little. How did your parents get on with their wild night on the town?"

Sarah rolled her eyes. "Poor Dad. He said he found the mall excruciating, and that he never wants to go again. Nevertheless, in spite of his protestations, I gather they did manage to not only cross a few things of one of Mum's interminable lists, they also managed to have a pretty good time. I think Dad's presence helped Mum from getting stressed out by the little things."

"That's good. I'm glad it was a worthy sacrifice."

She nodded. "I'm helping Mum out with Christmas too, so that's taking a bit of a weight off her shoulders. In fact, apart from the landscape design, the other reason for me coming over was to talk to you about Christmas."

"Oh? How so?"

"Well, you know it's Nan's eightieth birthday?"

Michael nodded. His green eyes watched her closely.

"And that we're having a bit of a combined Christmas lunch and birthday party?"

"Yes."

"We were wondering if you'd like to come and join us. I mean, I know you've got commitments with your own family, but, if you needed an alternative, you'd be very welcome. That is to say, you'd be welcome whatever the reason. For a start, I'm sure Nan would love it if you could come."

"Nan?"

"Of course. She's very fond of you. You've been so good to her."

Michael regarded her thoughtfully.

"You don't have to come if you don't want to," Sarah added in a small voice.

"Will I be the only non family member there?"

"No. Uncle Ernest is inviting his friend from Lambton Park. I think I told you about her. Her name's Rosa."

"Right."

"And Nan's inviting her friend who we met the other day at the beach."

"Edwina?"

"Yes. And Tom and Gerry might come along in the afternoon."

Michael rolled his eyes. "There's a reason to stay away."

Sarah laughed. "I'll protect you."

"Thanks. Anyone else?"

"Uncle David's newest girlfriend."

"Petunia?"

"No. Sadly he and she are no longer seeing eye to eye. You might say he's got himself a new flower."

"What? Already?"

Sarah nodded. "This one's called Daphne."

"Good God, I thought you were joking when you said he'd got himself a new flower. Who will be next? Daisy? Hyacinth? Pansy? Lily?"

"I know. Horrible isn't it? So do you think you could bear it? Would you like to come?"

"Of course I want to," he said. "I can't think of anywhere I'd rather be. I'm sorry to say it will give me the perfect excuse not to have Christmas lunch with my parents."

"Do you think they'll mind?"

Michael looked at her and sighed. "Probably not."

"You'll still see them, though?"

He nodded. "I'll most likely go around for my duty visit in the morning. They'll protest a bit about lunch but underneath it all they'll secretly be relieved. Now, what about this garden plan?"

They went outside into the forlorn courtyard. The sun had suddenly dipped, casting strange elongated shadows that would soon fade completely. Stillness hung in the air. It made the courtyard seem close and filled with echoes. Away from the street, screened from view from every other living soul, Sarah felt acutely aware of Michael's presence. She wondered if he felt it too. If she wasn't avoiding his gaze she felt sure she'd see him sending her darting little glances.

As a form of self-defence, she became business like. She unfurled her papers and began explaining in detail what she envisaged. Michael stayed mostly silent, but every so often asked a question to clarify a point or to try to better catch Sarah's vision. Michael, she noticed with peripheral vision, seemed equally businesslike. He seemed to do a lot of nodding.

At length, he said, "Well, this is great. Excellent in fact. I love the way you've kept the garden in character with the house but at the same time it all sounds quite easy care."

"It's a fallacy, you know," Sarah told him.

"The easy care garden?"

She nodded. "No matter how low maintenance you try to make it, there's always some work to be done. I've drawn up a costing, too."

Michael peered at the figures and nodded some more.

"Some of these ideas are interchangeable with others," Sarah explained. "You might not want to spend that much money all at once, or might not mind paying a little bit extra for some of the feature plants."

"Yes, money. It's the bane of our lives, isn't it? I went out yesterday, after I'd finished up my last few things at school, and bought some paint. I'm going to make a start on my study. Useless idea I know, but I sort of figure that in order to write my book I need to create a space to do it in. How are you at interior design?"

Sarah grimaced. "It's not really my thing. I'm much better with plants."

He looked at her directly. "You're very good with plants. I love this design. I really appreciate the time and trouble you went to, to put it all together. What I wish is that I could wave a magic wand and have it all done and complete, right this instant, so that I could show you just how much I like it."

Sarah laughed. "I'm afraid it'll take you a bit longer than that. It requires just a teeny bit more effort."

He smiled. "I don't mind really. It'll be worth it."

Sarah looked into his eyes. "I'll help you if you want."

"Would you? I'd love that."

"Maybe we could work on it bit by bit. I suppose it will depend on your budget."

"My budget," he said, "is highly suited to the concept of bit by bit. I hope you mean it when you say you'll help. I intend to hold you to it."

"I will," she replied. "It'll just depend on whether or not I get a job as to how much time I can spend on it."

"You've heard back from your applications?"

She nodded. "One rejection and one interview, booked next Tuesday afternoon."

"Congratulations," he said warmly. "Sorry about the rejection. Looking at this, they don't know what they're missing."

"The other job is by no means certain. But, on the bright side, they don't want anyone to start until the New Year. Which is just as well, as far as I'm concerned."

"Oh?"

"It's all this stuff that needs to be done between now and Christmas toward the party. As I said, I told Mum I'd help since the whole thing seemed to be getting the better of her. Only problem is I seem to have volunteered to do a lot of the things that are going to take time. On top of that Mum still really needs help to sort herself out, get more organized. Honestly, the hornet's nest of paper she's created for herself on the kitchen bench is enough to make even the sturdiest heart quail."

"And you're proposing to do what?"

Sarah shrugged. "I don't know. Help her get some sort of proper system going? No wonder she dithers. By the time she finds what she's looking for there's no time for anything else. I mean, I'm no organizational guru, but even I can see that if she put things into some semblance of order she'd save herself an awful lot of time. I suppose backpacking and travelling light helps you do more with less."

Michael made a face. "Maybe when you've finished sorting Margaret out you could come over and sort me out. Is there anything I can help you out with?"

"Now that you mention it, there is."

He looked surprised. Perhaps, Sarah reflected, he had not been expecting her to want assistance from him.

"Really? What?"

"I want to put together a sort of history of Nan's life for the party. You know, with photos and little anecdotes. I thought it might be quite nice for everyone to see what her life has been like."

"Sounds interesting," Michael said. "Why don't you come inside and I'll make some coffee. You can tell me more about it."

Todd slunk in at ten thirty p.m. His parents stood guard like sentries in the lounge. It seemed clear both would much rather be in bed, but had pretended to watch television for some time in the guise of waiting up. They busily went through the pretence of watching something that no one in their right mind could be interested in as Todd entered the room.

"Have a good time?" his father asked, barely taking his eyes off the screen.

"Yup," Todd replied.

"You're later than we expected," his mother said.

Todd shrugged. "We went for burgers and fries before coming back. After the shops closed, that was. Hungry work, shopping."

His father nodded in agreement but his mother bore holes in his face with her scrutiny. In truth, Auntie Sheila had still been finishing her meal at nine thirty. To fill in a bit of time Todd and Jason had joined a group of Jason's mates at a burger joint. They'd given Todd the once over but tolerated his presence fairly well. Todd, in turn, gave them the once over and discovered that perhaps Beth wasn't as pretty as he'd originally thought. The talk was smutty and in half an hour he'd learnt more than could be considered appropriate.

"How was Auntie Sheila?"

"She seemed to have a good time," Todd said lightly.

In fact she'd had a great time with her friends. Her only complaint was that she'd eaten too much and she'd had to undo the button on the waistband of her skirt before they commenced the drive home.

"Did you buy anything?" Margaret asked.

Prepared for this question, Todd said, "Not yet, but I've definitely worked out what I'm going to buy you for Christmas, Mum."

This made his mother smile.

"Think I might hit the hay," Todd said. He yawned lavishly. "I'm knackered."

So he took himself off to think about all the cool stuff he and Jason had done that evening and to dream about a girl called Suzette who had a chest that Beth could only aspire to.

At ten thirty five Sarah came home. She was on the doorstep of Michael's house, saying her good-byes, when Auntie Sheila's car had pulled up. Perhaps, if it wasn't for that, Sarah wondered if Michael might have kissed her. As it was, he'd jokingly offered to walk her home. Sarah had laughed and assured him of her safety. After all, she was the girl next door.

She found her parents heading for bed, their vigil of waiting for Todd finally over.

"Good night?" Margaret asked.

Sarah found she had to stop herself from saying, "Wonderful."

Saturday morning saw a break in the fine weather. Where last night the clear sky had enabled Sarah to see a thousand stars twinkling in the cosmos, today the sky was festooned with grey. People would all be bemoaning the fact that the weather always packed up come the weekend. Still, many would be comforted by the fact that, with ten days to Christmas, the shops would be open, come rain or shine.

The temperature remained high, high enough to preclude the likelihood of rain, in spite of what the forecasters said. Sarah couldn't have cared less. Her mind roiled with turmoil. She had enjoyed herself immensely the previous evening, when she and Michael had sat around talking. It had been all so easy. He was so easy *to* talk to. Of course, you could think to yourself, it was only talk, no harm in that. In reality, the more time she spent with Michael, the more she fell under his spell.

Trouble was, she'd been that way before, and look where that had got her. Not only that, she had signed herself up for further exposure this very morning. She and Michael had arranged to meet up for a visit to her grandmother. They'd figured, while talking about the history board last night, that they may as well get the truth straight from the horse's mouth, so to speak.

Pearl bustled about in the lounge as the hands of the clock neared ten fifteen. Ever since Sarah had called first thing, to ask her about the possibility of she and Michael coming over that morning, she, Pearl, had been in a state of anticipation. She always loved to see the both of them. In their separate ways they'd both been so good to her. How flattering to think they were going to go to so much trouble for her. And although she definitely did not want any fuss made of her at the party, she had to admit that a part of her would be disappointed if no one went to any effort at all.

Sarah hadn't been the only caller that morning. Charles, released from the pressure of revising, had phoned to say he'd be going with some of the other old people from his parish, on an outing to some water lily gardens. He'd called, he said, to let her know his whereabouts, just in case she wanted to get in touch with him. Pearl couldn't imagine why he would take the trouble to tell her that, but wished him well nonetheless.

Ernest had called, ostensibly to see how she fared, but behind his nonchalance she felt sure something else hung in the balance, perhaps even something else he wanted to tell her. When she tried gently questioning him to this effect he avoided answering directly. Pearl told him about Charles going to the water lily gardens for the day and that momentarily roused Ernest out of his complacency.

"Water lilies?" he'd bellowed. "Pansy would be a better word, wouldn't it? What does he want to go off to a place like that for? Next thing people will be calling him a fairy."

Pearl assured him that nothing of the sort would happen and changed the subject to Rosa. Pearl wondered if Ernest would be seeing her today.

"Might go over later this morning," he'd barked. "Got a few things to tidy up first."

"Send her my best wishes," Pearl had said. She'd gone on to tell Ernest about Sarah and Michael's plan for her birthday.

"Tell them," Ernest said, "that if they need any extra photos to come on over." And with that he'd hung up to get on with his day.

On reflection Pearl couldn't help thinking that both of her brothers were acting very oddly today. She hoped a day in the country for Charles, and some time with Rosa for Ernest, might go a long way toward diffusing their strangeness.

Pearl had no more time to think about it. The doorbell rang, and Sarah and Michael had arrived.

Before she knew it, Pearl had the photograph albums out and busily pointed things out to the two young people. Looking over the memories of her life on her trip down memory lane, Pearl had to concede that the lane had been both meandering and very pleasant.

"And look," Pearl said, turning another page of the ageing black background album, "there's your mother and David at the age of two. See their funny hats? I made those out of an old tablecloth. The material was all wrong, too floppy. They spent their entire summer peering out from underneath the front of them. Come to think of it, they used to look out from under those hats in much the same way as Tom and Gerry look out at you from under their fringes."

"What year was that?"

"Nineteen forty six or seven, I think. Just after the end of the war. Hence the use of the table cloth for fabric. Material was in very short supply, along with practically everything else. When I think of the things we used to make do with in those days, it seems incredible now. We didn't even have a camera, let alone film for it."

"So where did these photos come from?" Michael asked.

"I don't rightly recall," Pearl said. "Ernest had a camera so perhaps he took the pictures. We had another friend who came around sporadically and took photos too. He did it for a lot of people in exchange for things. With Jack in the building trade there were always odd jobs Bill wanted doing in exchange for pictures. People always speculated about where he got his film from, but as far as I know, nobody ever did find out."

Sarah raised her eyebrows. "The black market?"

Pearl laughed. "Probably. Either that or he did other favors in exchange for the film. Or, of course, he might have known some American soldiers stationed here. They always seemed to have everything at their fingertips."

"It seems so fascinating now, those war days," Sarah said, "for those of us who didn't have to live through it."

Michael laughed. "I think it's a familiar trait of humanity, to romanticize the past. Think about Roman times and you probably picture the empire, the excess and probably the Colosseum. Gladiators fighting, the crowds cheering, the heat, the excitement of the crowd, the Emperor waving regally to the crowd and doing his 'thumbs up' or 'thumbs down' over the fate of some poor soul. But I can guarantee you it wasn't very glamorous for ninety-five percent of the rest of the population. They probably struggled with poverty and disease and oppression, with the ever-present threat of being the one in the hot seat in the arena. Either that or being sent to some far-flung corner of the empire to commit acts of barbarism against equally oppressed foreigners. No thanks very much."

Pearl shivered. "Horrible."

"Yes," Michael said, "but no less so than some of the things that went on during the Second World War, I'm sure."

Pearl said, "Of course. But, as you say, the mind often glosses over the past, editing out the bad bits. That, and the fact that for many of us down here, the war was more removed. There were always rumors of attacks, but never any actual hits. Many of our young men died but on foreign soil and in ways that, thankfully, we could not imagine. No, war for us meant more the anticipation of the horrors of war, and with the privations and shortages that accompany such times. We were the lucky ones."

A silence fell as the trio thought about the past. Pearl idly turned a few more pages, going further back into history.

"You know," she said, "it's Ernest who's got all the old family photos. Ones of my parents and our childhood days. I gave him what little I had when I moved here because there simply wasn't any room. You should go to see him. He suggested that you do."

"Are you sure he wouldn't mind? Sarah asked.

"Oh no," Pearl assured her. "In fact I'm sure he'd be delighted to see you."

It was just as well, Ernest thought, that his unit had been fitted with a pure wool, textured, loop pile, tufted carpet with woven polypropylene backing and generous layers of underlay. It was a fact that he knew well from having studied in depth the specifications of his home in Lambton Park prior to purchase. His late wife's even later brother had had affiliations with the carpet industry and had expounded so much about the benefits of a good quality carpet that, when the time came for Ernest to consider a new house purchase, he felt almost as well qualified to make a sound judgment.

This morning that carpet quality was being severely tested. Indeed, the mileage he had covered as he paced up and down was such that a lesser carpet may well have been decimated by Ernest's level of agitation.

As he paced Ernest muttered. He had, he considered, plenty to mutter about. After all, it wasn't every day a man considered making a marriage proposal. He had to make sure he got it exactly right.

The first time around, with Priscilla, he hadn't taken too much trouble over the whole plighting of one's troth thing. Priscilla had made it abundantly clear in a thousand subtle ways that she would not only welcome his proposal with open arms, she was downright expecting it. She had been raised much better than to actually come out and say so but Ernest knew without a shadow of a doubt that his advances would be favorably met. He hadn't even turned a hair over asking Priscilla's father for permission. In the end the matter had been settled with so little trouble and expense on Ernest's part, he almost felt guilty. Almost. Guilt, after all, had never featured largely in Ernest Ferguson's repertoire of emotions.

Ernest had then gone on to conduct his marriage in much the same way as he had the proposal. He knew what he expected. Priscilla delivered more or less everything required of her, covering the gamut of everything from marital relations and the producing of children, through to domestic harmony and regular, if not somewhat doleful acquiescence. In essence, they had rarely ever had a cross word.

With Rosa, though, Ernest could not be so sure of his reception. They had made no declarations of love for one another and by some were not even perceived as a couple. Yet underneath this superficiality Ernest felt they had a deep affection for one another, and that they were ideally suited.

When Ernest had informed Charles of his intentions he had not even questioned the likelihood of the success of his proposal. In his mind he had it all figured out. He would ask Rosa to marry him, she would accept - seeing the arrangement as both eminently suitable and mutually beneficial - and by March or April of the following year the whole thing could be expeditiously wrapped up. He would persuade Rosa to sell her unit and move into his - which had by far a more pleasant aspect - and although she would protest at first, and be reluctant to bid adieu to her beautiful garden, Ernest would soon convince her of the merits of the move. He'd even give her license to create her garden magic in his own humble plot.

Talking to Charles had blown those thoughts completely out of the water. He'd gone from being superbly confident, through to bloody near having palpitations at the thought of being rejected. Charles had sown the seeds of doubt, and had wished Ernest good luck in the sort of way a person wishes luck to someone about to undertake surgery for a triple bypass. You hope it goes well for the poor blighter, but there's definitely some doubt in there about the likelihood of success.

Ernest had thought about the whole idea of proposing a lot overnight, had in fact been unable to sleep and unable to think about little else. There had been much to mull over. What would he say? What would Rosa say? Would she answer straight away or want a little time to think about it? How would he interpret such a request? If she said yes, would her agreement be straightforward? Would there be other things to consider that had not occurred to Ernest? If her answer was unthinkably no, would she give a reason? Would that reason make him feel better or worse? Would she laugh outright and tell him to come to his senses and stop being ridiculous? Would she let him down gently yet make him feel good about having asked, even though her answer had to be no? Ernest could not be sure.

Of course, bottom line, there was only one way to find out. And so, in the early hours of the morning, as the line between night and day became blurred in the predawn twilight, Ernest resolved that today would be the day. There seemed absolutely no sense in prolonging the agony. She'd either say yes, or she'd say no. His desire to ask remained unchanged.

He'd been momentarily thrown when the day turned out to be grey and rather depressing. In all his musings and imaginings about the day he had certainly not figured on banks of clouds and a sneaking wind. It seemed a rather ill omen.

At this point he'd commenced pacing. In an attempt to dispel his nerves, he'd decided on the importance of getting his speech right. While he thought, he walked. Backward and forward, backward and forward. Eventually, he had his speech down pat. Now, all that remained was to get himself appropriately kitted out for a visit of such magnitude.

Ernest could never recall agonizing once in his entire life over what to wear. After all, what the hell did it matter? However, suddenly, it seemed to matter very much indeed. In the end he settled on his favorite suit and a conservative tie. He could only hope that no one caught him on the way from his unit to Rosa's. He did not think he could cope with the third degree on why he'd dressed up.

He paused before leaving the house to admire himself in the mirror. He turned this way and that.

"Not bad," he said to himself.

Then he discovered a new problem. He felt a bit empty handed. He had neither ring nor flowers, and he did not relish the prospect of detouring to get either. Besides, neither would substantially alter the outcome. No woman in her right mind would accept a proposal purely on the basis of a bunch of flowers, although he felt pretty sure the sight of a sparkling ring had probably swayed one or two. He did not think Rosa was one of those.

He let himself out of his house, stopped momentarily to breathe in the air, in which he detected a growing level of humidity. He glanced at the leaden clouds and wondered about the likelihood of rain. He took in one large gasp of air and set off along the most inconspicuous route, stealing a flower for his buttonhole from a neighbor's garden on the way.

At Rosa's house everything looked tranquil. She'd opened up many of the windows. He could see her bedroom net curtains being sucked in and out gently by the breeze. Her garden looked as immaculate as ever. Thankfully there seemed no sign of anyone else around.

He paused at the door and knocked jauntily.

He waited.

No response.

"That's odd," he said to himself.

He knocked again, adding an extra jaunt.

He strained his ears listening for signs of activity. He then tried peering through the net curtains but they provided too much screening to see anything. He wondered if Rosa had popped out briefly but they were all well versed in the perils of poor security. Crime at Lambton Park, though rare, wasn't entirely unheard of. The unscrupulous were no respecters of age. Plenty of people of all descriptions came to visit relatives. A thief might easily penetrate the area undetected.

Ernest tried the door, but found it locked. Rosa had, however, given Ernest a spare key. After knocking for a third time he decided to use it.

"Rosa!" he shouted, as he let himself in.

He walked toward the lounge and as he neared the door he could see her, sitting upright in an armchair whose back was to the door, supported on one side by one of her exquisitely embroidered cushions.

"Rosa?"

She did not reply. Ernest figured she must be wearing one of those personal stereo things, the ones with headsets. He knew she owned one. She liked to lie in bed at night and listen to opera if she couldn't sleep.

He entered the room even further, advancing slowly so as not to startle her, little knowing that he who in for the shock. For, when he finally saw her face to face, he could scarcely believe what he beheld.

There was something about travelling by car that people took for granted, a casualness, Sarah thought, which enabled them to get into a vehicle whose potential to kill or maim was undisputed, without turning so much as a hair. She'd read once that more people had lost their lives in car accidents than in the entire wars of the twentieth century put together. In spite of this, people heedlessly hopped in and drove off.

It wasn't the safety factor of driving that occupied Sarah's mind, however. Sitting now, with Michael, driving to Lambton Park in his Subaru, it was more the feeling of intimacy that a confined space generated than the chance of them being involved in some traffic incident that got her thinking.

In some ways it was a feeling similar to hopping into a cupboard with someone and closing the door, but without the darkness. Not that Sarah had a lot of experience with communal cupboard dwelling. At her fourth form social at one of her classmate's house they'd played sardines and Sarah had ended up in a cupboard with Martin Sloane. He'd given prior instructions to his mates not to find them at all. She'd spent an uncomfortable twenty minutes with him breathing quite literally down her neck before Sarah twigged that no one was coming.

Today though, there'd been no such engineering of circumstances. After having talked with her grandmother and realizing Uncle Ernest could be of help - and that furthermore he'd be home - it seemed the logical thing to go over to see him straight away. After all, the clock was ticking. Christmas was only ten days away, which, considering all the other things that needed organizing, didn't leave much time to try to get the photo board done. At least if they were able to gather their resources today, there'd be less panic down the track.

Sarah hadn't bargained for the way she'd feel getting into the car with

Michael. It should have been the most natural thing in the world. Instead it had the effect of shrinking their surroundings to a rough couple of square meters and diminishing the outside world to mere scenery. And although Sarah tried to focus on that scenery she couldn't help being mightily aware of Michael sitting beside her, of his every little move as he drove the car. She couldn't help wondering what it would be like to be with him in the car as a matter of right, rather than in the capacity of someone for whom he was doing a favor.

Sarah cast around lamely in her mind, trying to think of something profound to say. Her own sense of inadequacy defeated her. In the end she settled on reiterating her thanks for his help with the project, adding, "I hope this is not putting you out too much."

"Not at all," he replied. "You've saved me from a fate worse than death - painting."

"Yes, but it isn't as if your time is limitless. You've only got the summer to get the painting done. And then there's your writing. What time you waste now by not painting will inevitably eat up your writing time later."

Michael looked unconcerned. "Not to worry. Anyway, after a year of full-on work a man needs a bit of time to unwind. You know what they say about all work and no play."

Sarah raised her eyebrows. "I'd scarcely call this playing. A visit to an old folks' home could hardly be classified as fun."

"I don't know. I'm having a good time. Besides, you evidently need a bit of help. For a start you don't call them old folks' homes these days. You call them retirement villages."

Sarah laughed. "So you think I'd be lost without you, trying to negotiate the finer points of rest home etiquette?"

He glanced over at her. "Yes," he said. "I think you probably would."

"Thanks," she retorted flatly.

"I suppose it does seem a bit strange to be interested in going to a retirement village but I must confess I am a little curious. I haven't met good old Uncle Ernest and I'm looking forward to meeting Rosa as well."

"Me too. The way Nan speaks about her, she must be something special."

"Well, prepare to find out. Here we are."

Michael slowed the car and turned in through the imposing front entrance way.

"No sentries to check our passports," he whispered. "No armed guards or barbed wire fences either."

Sarah grinned. "I think Nan expected that the first time she visited."

"I know. In fact, it's very nice. Wonder where we go? Pity Pearl was a bit vague about the precise location of Ernest's unit."

"Perhaps we should find somewhere to park and ask someone."

"Good idea."

Not far past the main entrance lay a larger building, clearly the administrative hub of the complex. Outside were a series of purpose built visitor car parks into which Michael negotiated the Subaru.

As they climbed out of the car, Sarah shivered. "Temperature's dropped," she said.

Michael looked up at the heavy clouds. "Definitely looks a bit ominous. Let's get a move on."

As they approached the administration building a man of about fifty came through the glass doors. He wore a shirt and tie and clearly looked as though he worked at Lambton Park.

"Excuse me," Sarah said.

The man halted in his tracks and peered at Sarah as though he had not previously been aware of her approach. He blinked a couple of times in an attempt to bring her into focus and drag his mind away from what had previously been occupying it.

"Yes?"

"I wondered if you could tell me where we could find Ernest Ferguson's unit?"

The man looked taken aback. He peered at Sarah more closely.

"I'm sorry," he said, "may I ask who you are?"

"Of course. My name's Sarah Bell. Ernest Ferguson is my great uncle." The man glanced sideways at Michael. Sarah said, "And this is my friend Michael Alexander."

"Right," said the man.

"Is the unit far?" Sarah asked. "Should we leave our car parked here and walk?"

"I think," said the man, "that you'd better come with me."

Without further explanation the man turned on his heel and strode off along a path that wound itself through the maze of units. Sarah and Michael looked briefly at one another. Michael shrugged, not knowing what to make of the reticent fellow. There seemed little choice but to do as they were bidden.

Alarm bells set off in Sarah's mind as they rounded a bend to see an ambulance parked outside one of the units. Its lights flashed hypnotically around and around. Sarah found herself hurrying to catch up with the man. She touched him on the arm and he turned around.

"Uncle Ernest?" Sarah questioned. "He's all right, isn't he?"

At that precise moment heavy droplets of water began to fall from the sky, randomly at first, with each drop hitting the ground with a plop, turning the concrete into a polka dot of damp. Seconds later, on a gust of wind, rain started falling in a torrent.

"You'd better come inside," the man said loudly.

He began running toward the unit with Sarah and Michael hard on his heels.

Inside, the trio stopped momentarily to brush the rain from their clothes and shake the damp out of their hair.

"Uncle Ernest?" Sarah asked again.

"He's through here," the man said, indicating Sarah proceed.

With her heart thumping, Sarah crossed the threshold into the lounge. Two ambulance officers obscured her view but when one of the burly men moved aside she was surprised to see Uncle Ernest sitting on the sofa, alive and well, with tears running down his cheeks. He seemed unaware of anything. He did not look up at the arrival of three more people.

She turned. "I don't understand," she said.

The man frowned. "I thought...Mr. Ferguson didn't call you?"

"No. Our visit today is more of a spur of the moment thing. What's happened? Why is Uncle Ernest so upset?"

"I'm afraid Mrs. Antonio has passed away."

"Who? I don't know who Mrs. Antonio is."

Then the second ambulance officer moved and then Sarah could see for herself. There, in an armchair, sat an old woman. She sat quite still and erect, as though frozen in time, as though all anyone had to do was come along and press a button - like releasing the pause button on a DVD - and she might just as easily get up from the chair and carry on with life. Only the waxy color of her skin truly betrayed her lifelessness. The woman, whoever she had been, had the most tranquil expression on her face. It appeared that whatever had caused her to make the transition from life to death had caused her no pain.

Sarah stepped forward and Uncle Ernest looked up. The tears continued to trickle silently down his leathery cheeks. He did, however, recognize Sarah.

"What am I going to do now?" he said. His voice came out softer than Sarah knew Uncle Ernest to be capable of. He looked up at her with eyes appealing for assistance. "How will I manage without her now that Rosa's dead?"

CHAPTER TEN

By Tuesday morning the inclement weather had yet to depart. The rain alternated between lashing down in heavy torrents, coming down almost horizontally on the wave of prevailing winds, or descending like a Scottish mist, swirling about in diaphanous eddies. A veil of damp covered every surface. People rushed about frenetically trying to complete their pre-Christmas business. After three solid days, Christmas cheer hung thinly in the air. Many people went around scowling and complaining about everything from lack of parking to not being able to get the washing dry.

It wasn't the weather, however, which made Todd Bell scowl and complain. In fact the weather featured as the least of his worries. Neither did he have any complaints about parking or wet washing. No, Todd's burden rested in the inequity suffered the world over by myriad thirteen year olds, namely lack of freedom and the inability to successfully get his own way a hundred percent of the time.

After stomping around in his room for an hour, getting more and more frustrated, Todd decided the time had come to have another go at getting around his mother. He found her, as usual, sitting at the kitchen table poring over endless pieces of paper.

He slid into a chair opposite and folded his arms mutinously.

His mother looked up. She regarded him with skepticism before returning her attention to her work.

Todd shuffled in his chair, and sighed heavily for effect. She looked up again. For a few moments they engaged in a staring contest, before his mother capitulated.

"What?" she said. "What now?"

"I don't want to go," he said.

"Todd, we've been through this already. I want you to go and that's that.

End of story. And there's no point in giving me the evil eye. I'm not going to change my mind."

"What's the point? Why should I have to go? I hate funerals. I never even met the old bird."

"Todd! Have some respect will you? I am fully aware that you never met Rosa. Neither did I. But she meant a great deal to Uncle Ernest and seemed to have meant a lot to your grandmother too. It's only right and proper that we should go along. Not only as a mark of respect, but also as support for the members of our family who are grieving."

"No one will notice whether I'm there or not."

"I'll notice."

"So?"

"There won't be anyone home this morning to look after you."

"So?" Todd said again. "I don't need a baby-sitter."

"Fourteen," his mother said to him. "You have to be fourteen to be left unsupervised."

"Yeah, well, that's only three months away. Why make a big deal about three stupid months?"

Margaret looked at him archly. "You needn't think things are going to change radically once you are fourteen anyway. While you're living under our roof you need to toe the line and follow the rules, no matter how old you are."

"Yeah, yeah," Todd muttered under his breath.

His mother frowned at him, giving Todd the look he knew meant he should start being wary.

Trying a different tack, he said, "Jason doesn't have to go."

Margaret's frown deepened. "Doesn't he now? And just how, precisely, do you know this?"

"I talked to him this morning. On the phone. He said his mother would never dream of asking him to go somewhere he strongly objected to going. He said that funerals at our age might give us a trauma."

"What next? I suppose Sheila would be dumb enough to fall for a line like that."

"It might be true. You wouldn't want me to end up in therapy as a result of suffering trauma."

"The only trauma you're likely to suffer from is feeling the back of my hand. You aren't too old to spank, you know."

Todd plastered his most outraged face across his features. "That's child abuse," he said. "These days, you could get reported for something like that."

"It wouldn't surprise me. The world has gone crazy, that's for sure."

Todd sighed. "Couldn't I stay home? Just this once? Like Jason?"

Margaret looked at him sharply. "You needn't think that rules that apply to Jason apply to you. For a start he's older. Secondly, his mother has always had a completely different way of looking at the world than I have, parenting included."

"He's not that much older. Only a couple of years."

"He's sixteen, Todd. Sixteen. There's a big difference between that and your age. Come to think of it, he's far too old to be suitable company for you anyway. I really think the pair of you should stick to friends your own age."

"But he's my cousin," Todd protested.

"Yes, he is," Margaret said, "but if spending time with him makes you uncooperative over things like this, then we might have to review the whole idea of you seeing him at all. I would be negligent in my duties as a parent if I didn't vet who you spent your time with, wouldn't I?"

Todd scowled.

"Wouldn't I?" Margaret questioned again.

"Yes, Mum," Todd said, reluctantly and under his breath.

"Good. That's what I like to hear. So, perhaps you'd be kind enough to go and get dressed now. Unless you'd like me to come and help you with what to wear?"

Todd looked scandalized. "No, thanks," he said rapidly, removing himself from the room with uncharacteristic haste.

If he had have looked back he would have seen his mother pause for a moment, jiggle her pen in her hand before allowing herself a secret, satisfied smile.

Sheila stood in front of the long mirror in her bedroom and turned from side to side, trying to get the best view of herself. She'd donned her favorite funeral dress, an expensive black number that, in theory, should add length to her frame and in consequence shed pounds before her very eyes. This did not seem to be entirely working.

No matter which way she turned there seemed no disguising the fact that she'd become overweight. In fact, there either was less dress than there had been since last time she wore it or there was more of Sheila to go around.

If Sheila attempted to be honest with herself, she knew the latter had to be more likely than the former.

Through the folds of the fabric Sheila squeezed her stomach experimentally with both hands. Things wobbled ominously. She released her grip, and turned ninety degrees. She used one hand to prod her left butt cheek and watched it do a terrifying impersonation of a jelly on a plate. And that was only one side of her backside.

Sheila clasped her hand over her mouth to stop herself from crying out. She stood staring at herself in the mirror, her eyes wide with realization. How, she asked herself, had things got this bad? And what on earth could she do about it?

John came sauntering out of the en suite bathroom, towel tied around his waist. His body, lean and toned from exercise, glistened from the shower. Although both of them had turned fifty last year, there were no prizes for guessing who had taken care of themselves and who hadn't.

Sheila quickly removed her hand from her mouth and smooth down the dress.

"Are you sure I can't get you to change your mind about the funeral?" she asked.

He looked up sharply. "I've told you already, I can't waste any more time today. In fact, if it wasn't for that session at the driving range with Douglas Heyes this morning, I'd already be hard at work at the office. I barely had time to spare for him but since he's one of my most important contacts, it would hardly be politic to give him a brush off when he asked me to hit a few balls with him, would it?"

"But I don't want to go on my own," Sheila said.

"I have to question why you're going at all. Did you know the woman? Did I? Was she part of our social scene? Did she ever put any business our way? Is there anything to be gained by going to the funeral? The answers: no, no, no, no, no. Five bloody good reasons not to waste our time, I would have thought."

"Margaret's going."

"Bully for her. She would. It's probably just the sort of thing she likes these days. She's about as exciting as a funeral procession herself."

"John!"

He looked up at her, daring her to disagree. Sheila felt her protest dying on her lips. Besides, John did have a point.

Instead she said, "Margaret told me Uncle Ernest is devastated and that

Mum is very upset, too. Margaret suggested we need to go to support them,
rather than for any personal attachment to the deceased."

"Let her. It's just the sort of thing you might expect from Margaret the
Martyr. At least she has her mournful expression down to a fine art."

"You definitely won't go then?"

He shook his head. "If you really feel obligated to go, take one of the
boys."

"They've gone," she said.

"What? Already? That must be the first time in living memory either of
those two layabouts have been up before the crack of nine."

"I'm not sure Reuben even made it home last night," Sheila confessed.

"And Jason?"

"He said something about not wanting to be traumatized, then something else about a sale of computer games before he took off."

"Well, then," John said. "It looks as though you're on your own. By the
way," he added as he straightened his tie, "that isn't what you're wearing,
is it?"

"I thought I might," Sheila said. "Why?"

"Nothing, I suppose. It's just that it does rather remind me of a Sumo
wrestler trying to squeeze himself into a bin liner."

And with that, he disappeared.

The telephone rang insistently until Margaret struggled from her chair
to answer it.

"Hello?"

"Margaret?"

"Hello, David."

"How are you?"

"Fine, I suppose. You?"

Yes, good, good. Bit of a late night last night." He whistled softly then
laughed. "That Daphne! Boy, has she got some staying power."

Margaret rolled her eyes. "Don't tell me any more."

"Don't worry," he said. "I won't."

Margaret said nothing. She suspected she knew precisely why David had
called, and wasn't about to make it easier for him.

"Er, Margaret," he said, "about this morning."

"What about this morning? I thought I gave you pretty clear instructions on the when and where when we spoke two days ago."

"Yes, yes, you did. No problem there. The thing is, though, it appears I might not be able to make it after all."

"Might not?"

"All right, then. Won't be able to make it. Is that better?"

"No, as a matter of fact, it's not."

"Oh, Maggie Moo, don't be like that."

"Don't call me that."

"What? Maggie Moo?"

"Yes. Now, what's your excuse? And this better be good."

David paused. Margaret felt sure she could hear squirming going on down the line.

"It's just that Daphne can't come with me."

"So? Come on your own."

"I would. It's just that I promised Daphne I'd help her out with something and I can't bunk off work twice in one day. The powers that be here aren't that keen on any kind of unnecessary deviation from the work schedule."

"How inconsiderate of them. Couldn't you put this thing you have to do for Daphne off until another day?"

"Tried that."

"Couldn't she come with you?"

"'Fraid not. It appears my darling Daphne has something of an allergy to funerals."

"What on earth are you talking about?"

"Bottom line? She hates them."

"David, nobody on earth likes funerals, except perhaps undertakers, although with a vested interest, I don't think you can really count them."

"Still," David said. "Seems senseless to upset the apple cart for someone we don't even know, wouldn't you say?"

"What I'd say is that I think that this family of ours is truly hopeless. One can only hope, when your turn comes, people are rather less apathetic, don't you think?"

Jim sauntered into the kitchen as Margaret replaced the phone onto its cradle. His hands were covered in grime, his hair full of sawdust.

"Jim! Look at the state of you. We need to be ready to leave for the chapel in twenty minutes."

Jim glanced absently at the clock.

"Plenty of time. Besides, I didn't want to completely waste the morning. Bad enough having to down tools for that length of time without at least achieving something."

"Not you too. Funeral apathy seems to be at an all time high today."

"Eh?"

"First Todd went on and on about not wanting to go. Then he told me neither Reuben or Jason are going. Following on from that, David called to say he won't be able to make it either. I'd say that rates at about a 'D' for family solidarity. I only hope I never need to seriously rely on anyone in this family."

"Don't be silly. Our going really is only a token gesture."

"No, it isn't. It's something more than that. It's our way of saying that we care, that we're there when it counts. Truth is, we all seem to care more about ourselves than we do about our kith and kin."

"You're overreacting. Besides, don't you think grief is a personal thing? Surely the way people express their sorrow is as diverse as people themselves?"

Margaret shook her head slowly. "I suppose next you'll be telling me you can't come either."

"No," he said. "I'll be there, although I did start to wonder about what I should wear."

Margaret took a step closer to him. She reached up and brushed some of the dust out of his hair.

"I suppose you've been out there in the garage upsetting Mum by making a lot of din working on that doll's house?"

He smiled. "I've nearly finished. I just needed to do some nice quiet sanding."

Margaret clenched her teeth. "She probably thought she'd woken up in the dentist's office."

"I was quiet as a mouse. Honest."

Margaret couldn't help smiling in return.

"You'd better go and get showered then. And as for what to wear, I've already got everything laid out for you. By the strangest of coincidences, I've just had your black jacket dry cleaned. You'll look as smart as the best of them."

Jim made a face. "Gee, thanks. Just what I always wanted."

Joanna waited an eternity for Brett to come to the phone. When he did come on the line he seemed none too pleased by the interruption.

"I thought I've told you before, just leave a message and I'll phone you back. I can't just drop everything the minute you call, especially if I'm showing clients a selection of vehicles."

"Sorry," Joanna said in a tone that implied she was anything but.

"What's so important, anyway? Is the house on fire? Has one of the children ingested a deadly poison? Are we about to be invaded by aliens?"

"Ha ha. You were supposed to have called me back about this morning, remember?"

"No."

"The funeral?"

"Bloody hell. Joanna. You don't seriously expect me to drop everything for a funeral, do you?"

Joanna was most put out. "You said you'd ask. You said you'd find out if they could spare you."

"Yes, but I didn't really mean it, did I? Look, I don't know how to make this plainer. Even if I could spare the time, which I can't, do you honestly think I'd make the effort for someone as distant from me as, say, some poor peasant in China?"

"It's not for Rosa. It's for Uncle Ernest."

"I doubt very much he'd trouble himself for us, had the shoe been on the other foot."

"But if you don't go, how can I? I can hardly manage both children on my own at a funeral."

"It's simple, Joanna. Don't go."

"Mum will give me the guilts."

"Your mother always gives you the guilts. You've never particularly minded before."

"I'm sure the saintly Sarah will be there."

"So? You've never given a tuppence for what she thinks, either. Joanna, I've got to go. Some people have just come into the show room and I've got to head them off at the pass before Evan McNeill nabs them first."

"Thanks," Joanna said into the disconnected tone. "Thanks a bloody million."

"Hi, Mum."

"Hello, Joanna. Were you about to leave?"

"Bit of a problem there I'm afraid."

Margaret stifled a sigh. "Oh?"

"I'm afraid I won't be able to make it. Brett just phoned to say that some very important clients have come in, asking specially for him, and he just can't get away."

"You could come anyway."

"With the two children? On my own? I don't think so."

"You'd manage, surely?"

"It would be easier for me to take up pole vaulting and win a gold medal at the next Olympic Games than look after those two horrors on my own in an environment where things are supposed to be suitably dignified. Do you seriously want to hear Connor wailing in the middle of the service or Isabella announcing she's wet her pants at the top of her lungs?"

Margaret paused. "I suppose not. Haven't you got Isabella sorted out yet with all that pants-wetting business?"

"The experts say she's going through a phase, one probably triggered by the birth of Connor. It's known as classic regressive behavior. Since the baby appears to get all the attention she's decided the best way for her to get some back is to do things that necessitate us intervening. Like wetting her pants. Or holding her breath until she turns blue. Or swinging from the chandelier. Or any of about fifty other strategies she's devised."

"Good grief. Can't you just give her a smack or something?"

"Mum! Don't you know you just can't do that any more?"

"So Todd tells me."

"Anyway, I am sorry, but that's that. Tell Uncle Ernest I send my sympathies, but honestly, I think everyone would prefer I stayed away."

"I suppose," Margaret conceded.

"Better go," Joanna said. "I can tell trouble's brewing."

Margaret hung the phone up with a frustrated sigh.

"Perhaps 'E' might be a more applicable rating," she said. "We really are the most hopeless family."

Sarah found her mother in the kitchen staring angrily at the telephone receiver.

"What's that naughty phone done now?" Sarah asked from the doorway.

Margaret looked up. "What?"

Sarah couldn't help smiling. "You look like you could murder the phone."

Margaret's lips quirked. She moved to replace the receiver. "Right now," she confessed, "I probably just about could. Better that than killing the person on the other end, I guess."

"Oh?"

Margaret shrugged. "I suppose there are some things in life that can't be helped. If David can't make it to the funeral, so be it. If Joanna can't make it to the funeral, so be it, too. I suppose at least I tried to get a decent amount of Ferguson representation together to support poor Uncle Ernest."

"That's the most important thing. That you tried."

"Shame it proved such a pointless waste of time. I just said to your father earlier that, on current form, I can't imagine the turnout to my own funeral will be high. In fact, Jim'll probably have to hire some of those professional mourners just to make a quorum crowd."

"Don't be silly. Besides, I think it's only committees that require quorums. I'm also pretty sure that while there are some people out there with no one to see them off, when the time comes, a long time from now, you won't be one of them. And, if it's any consolation I doubt Rosa will be one of those, either."

Margaret shrugged again. "I suppose so. Let's hope no one else calls up to say they can't make it. I feel like I've been answering the phone all morning. Look at me, I haven't even got dressed yet." She looked closer at Sarah. "On the other hand, look at you. You're all ready and looking very nice this morning. Is that a new dress?"

Sarah nodded. "I bought it yesterday when I went looking for an outfit for my job interview this afternoon. I must say, under the circumstances, it's pretty hard to generate too much enthusiasm for facing an interview. There's a bit of me that's quite tempted to phone up and cancel."

"You don't mean that?"

Sarah sighed. "Not really. I just never envisaged having to attend a funeral on the same day. I guess I should be grateful that it wasn't someone closer to us."

"True. Still, you don't have to go either," Margaret told her. "I know what I said, and as much as I'd like you to go, if it makes a difference to your performance this afternoon then it might be wiser not to."

"No," Sarah said quickly. "I'm definitely going. I need to."

"Oh?"

"I don't know. I'm not sure I can explain it but, somehow, being there and seeing her, you know, dead, was a really strange experience. I've never seen anyone dead before. And then seeing Uncle Ernest so upset - it felt like being shown a peek of someone else's private world. I can't define it in words. Michael said he felt exactly the same way. We both feel obligated to go, as though it wouldn't be right if we didn't turn up."

"So Michael's going?"

"Yes. In fact I thought I'd go with him. That way there'll be more room in your car for you, Dad, Todd and Nan."

"Are you sure?" Margaret asked. "We could all squeeze in. I wouldn't want you to feel excluded."

"I won't."

Margaret regarded Sarah. "You like him, don't you?"

Sarah held her mother's gaze. In a voice that seemed distant to her own ears, she simply said, "Yes."

Margaret nodded slowly as though mentally digesting this information. "And yet I sense in you a reluctance of a kind."

Sarah slid into one of the kitchen chairs, as though her legs could no longer bear the weight of her body. Margaret followed suit.

"I don't know. I don't think reluctance is the right word."

"No? Yet there's something about him that makes you hold back. Is it this business with him not getting on with his family? Do you wonder whether this indicates some deeper character flaw?"

"No, Mum. Of course not. I mean, I haven't met Mr. and Mrs. Alexander, so I suppose I can't entirely judge, but from what Michael says they haven't exactly made things easy for him."

"Well, what then?"

Sarah shrugged. "It's not him. It's me. Oh, don't misunderstand me. I like him. In fact, I like him a lot. But something happened while I was in England and it's fair to say it's made me more than a little wary about jumping in too soon."

Surprise registered on Margaret's features.

"What? What happened?"

Sarah tried to arrange her face into the most disinterested expression she could manage. "Not what. Who." Sarah readjusted her disinterested expression before saying, "His name was Jeremy Duncan. I met him through one of Cassie's innumerable admirers. He was typical Home Counties, young, good looking, well bred, from a wealthy family and completely charming.

"We started seeing each other. He lived in London and knew the city much better than I did. I'm afraid I got totally taken in by him. He literally was too good to be true. I suppose I should have twigged earlier than I did. He never made any attempt to introduce me to his friends outside of the original contact. And although he talked about his parents' home in the country, whenever the subject of visiting came up he would make excuses about why just then wasn't a good time to go. Once we even got as far as making a date. Then he cancelled at the last minute because of some pressing and entirely fictitious work commitment."

"And the truth?"

Sarah laughed shortly. "The usual. Another woman. Someone he'd known for years, whose family and breeding and share portfolio matched his own. They were engaged. It was expected. He said that in his own way he loved her, just as he also professed to love me. But there wasn't a way in hell he could break it off with her. In reality, I was just the convenience woman, someone to help idle away fallow hours while in the city. I wasn't supposed to care, to take the relationship as seriously as I did, blah, blah, blah. All the usual excuses to go along with that sort of scenario."

"Oh, Sarah. That's terrible. How did you find out?"

"Just as you might expect - completely by accident. We went out one night for a meal, a quaint little back street Italian restaurant. I presumed it to be just the sort of place we both enjoyed but in retrospect I feel sure it was the anonymity of the setting that appealed to Jeremy more than anything else.

"Of course, this particular time, that anonymity backfired. One of Jeremy's friends was up from the country, also enjoying a night out, and he clearly assumed I must be some sort of a work colleague. He came over to say hello and inadvertently blurted everything out, simply by what he asked and what he said. The conversation had shades of starting to watch a movie at the half way point and not understanding the plot. It wasn't until I looked over to see Jeremy squirming uncomfortably that it dawned on me he had another woman."

"Oh, dear. I am sorry. That must have been tremendously difficult."

Sarah laughed again. "Oh, I think dumping a plate of spaghetti marinara in his lap made me feel considerably better for about ten minutes. But I felt devastated. He'd seemed so wonderful, so kind, so caring, so fun. In truth he proved to be conniving, selfish, shallow and deceptive."

"And you worry that Michael might turn out to be the same?"

Sarah formed her lips into a straight line. "What do they say? Once bitten, twice shy?"

"But Michael's not like that, surely?"

"No, I really don't think so. I just don't want to rush it, that's all. I haven't met his friends or his parents or seen any of the wider circle of his life, and believe me, after what I went through, I truly think that stuff is important now."

"Sarah, why didn't you tell us about this? About Jeremy and what happened?"

"I suppose it all happened so fast, meeting him, going out, the whole romance. Maybe on a subconscious level I knew it was all too good to be true. Then, before I got around to telling you about it, it had ended."

Margaret looked thoughtful. "I wish I could have been there for you," she said. "I guess if I'm honest, I knew something was up with you when you came home. I was just too wrapped up in my own problems to do anything about it."

"But you are feeling better now?"

"A bit. I suppose I just realized what I'd be throwing away if I let myself get overwhelmed to the point where I lost your father. And with his help, and with yours too in a way, I'm starting to try to change the way I go about things, how I look at myself. I feel less panicky somehow. And if anything I think that what happened to Rosa serves as a reminder to people like us that life is very precious. I know she wasn't exactly young but she died so unexpectedly. It makes you realize that none of us know what's around the corner. It's a reminder to make the most of every day."

Sarah thumbed the corner of a pile of her mother's papers while she thought about this.

"I know," she said. "That's precisely what I've been thinking myself."

The venue for the funeral had turned out to be something of a surprise. Many had assumed, since Rosa had a Catholic background, that the service would be conducted under the pious and watchful eye of Rome. That discreet priests wearing uniformly sacrosanct faces as they administered the obsequies would conduct proceedings, ushering one of their own into Kingdom

Come. In fact Rosa had been extremely specific that this wasn't what she wanted. And although her reasons for this would ever after be undisclosed and very much her own, she had in contrast been very clear about what she did want.

Instead, the service would be held in a private chapel adjacent to one of the largest and most well tended cemeteries in the district. It was reached down a long cobbled driveway that wended its way through immaculately cared for gardens before forking off into a series of small car parks. These were screened from the chapel itself by solid hedges of fir.

People scurried from the car parks through the solidly pouring rain like an army of black ants moving with precise haste. They sheltered under a collection of suitably matching black umbrellas that bobbed up and down like a field of doleful anemones performing their own funeral lamentation.

As Sarah and Michael attempted to find a car park it seemed clear that there would be a fair turnout to see Rosa off. They ended up finding a vacant spot hidden beside a mini van bearing the logo of Lambton Park that had evidently been used to bus in those residents wanting to go but unable to transport themselves.

Michael had brought along an umbrella big enough for the two of them. It was a large green and white striped golf umbrella, the sight of which made him grimace.

"Sorry," he apologized. "It doesn't seem a very respectful color."

Sarah smiled. "As if it really matters. From what little I knew of her I doubt Rosa would have cared. As long as we don't get completely soaked, then I certainly don't mind."

Michael grinned. "You'll have to stand close."

"I don't mind that either," she said softly.

He leapt out of the car and struggled to get the umbrella up with lightning speed. The gap between the car and the van was narrow. In the end he had to move behind the car before he could manage to get the umbrella aloft. By the time he came around so that Sarah could get out and shelter directly under it he was laughing with the absurdity of the situation.

"It's pretty hard to be dignified when you're drenched," he said. "Quick, move in a bit. The rain seems to be coming straight in from that direction."

"It's like the sky is weeping over the loss of Rosa," Sarah said as they headed for the chapel.

"A precipitation elegy, perhaps," Michael suggested. "Or maybe the sky is making what they call a jeremiad."

"A what?"

"A jeremiad. It's a word to describe a long-winded complaint about a person's troubles."

"Really? How do you know that?"

"It was in a poem I read recently. I had to go and look it up. What I found most surprising - considering how good some people are at giving their own version of a jeremiad - it's a wonder we don't use the word all the time."

Sarah smiled. "I know exactly what you mean."

Once they got under the cover of the front awning Michael swept the umbrella aside. In the process of collapsing it he inadvertently showered himself with further droplets of rain. He shook his head despairing and valiantly tried to swallow a smile.

"I think," he whispered, "I can feel a jeremiad coming on."

Sarah elbowed him discreetly, and tried to subdue her own smile. "Don't," she said. "Come on, let's go inside."

They found the rest of the family waiting for them. Todd stood by his parents' side as though about to be strapped into the electric chair. His face was a picture of sorrow, although for completely the wrong reason. Sarah noticed he'd decided to wear some of the components of his school uniform, although whether this was an enforced decision she did not know. Likewise, her father looked equally uncomfortable in his suit and tie. He kept re-adjusting his tie, fingering it resentfully as he struggled to get used to the restrictive feel.

Her mother, Sarah saw, wore an old funeral favorite in which she looked noticeably thin. She wore a matching look of anxiety on her face that seemed to give the impression that the entire responsibility for the successful outcome of the service lay exclusively with her. Beside her - and looking contrastingly rotund - stood Auntie Sheila. Her dress was elegant and obviously expensive but whoever had sold it to her should have been burdened with a guilty conscience for not talking her out of it. It did nothing to enhance her figure, or more precisely, Sarah thought, it did way too much to enhance her figure. As for Uncle John, he was conspicuous only by his absence.

To Sheila's left Uncle Charles hovered by his sister's side as though guarding a precious vessel. They were deep in conversation. Both of them had looked up and acknowledged Sarah and Michael with brief smiles. After that they kept their focus somewhere around shoe level. Nan's face looked strained, as though she had been doing a great deal of crying over the past couple of days. This realization made Sarah feel guilty. She'd had so much to do and think about in preparation for both Christmas and the afternoon's job interview, that she had not had time to see her grandmother.

"Where have you been?" Margaret hissed.

"We couldn't find a park," Sarah said.

"I know," Jim said. "We were the same. All the handy ones had already been taken."

"We'd better get inside quick," Margaret said, "before there are no seats left."

"Where's Uncle Ernest?"

"Already inside. Right down the front, surrounded by a bevy of supporters from Lambton Park. We couldn't get near him."

"Oh, well," Sarah said, as they made a move. "At least he's got people around him."

Margaret's mouth formed a straight line of disapproval.

"I told you we should have been here earlier," she whispered.

As they entered the chapel a suited gentleman with a face like a British bulldog handed out the order of service. He then directed the party to one of the last empty rows toward the back. They sidled in, trying to be respectfully quiet, Charles first, followed by Nan and Sheila, then Todd, Jim, Margaret, and lastly, Sarah and Michael.

They sat down and arranged themselves. Sarah looked down at the photograph of Rosa on the front of the service booklet. It portrayed an animated looking Rosa who smiled full into the lens of the camera, her expression one of secret delight, as though she knew the answer to living a happy life. The sight of it made tears prick at Sarah's eyes. She looked up quickly, blinking them back as she orientated herself and absorbed the surroundings in the chapel.

The interior of the chapel was a contrast of light and wood. The walls along the side of the building were punctuated with a series of thin floor to ceiling windows, narrow embrasures that gave little glimpses of the outside park and gardens. In between, the walls were timbered with some sort of rich, dark dignified wood. At the front, on a raised stage, and in front of a brick back wall, sat the casket. It had been festooned with a rich bouquet of flowers the likes of which Rosa had probably both enjoyed and grown during her lifetime. Around the bottom of the bier someone had carefully arranged a display of the beautiful cushions Sarah had not been able to help noticing in Rosa's lounge. She found her eyes misting over again and had to look away.

Her eyes went left, to the rostrum, the microphone waiting in mid air for the speaker to arrive, then right, to the enormous arrangement of flowers. Trumpets of white lilies triumphed over an assortment of lesser flowers, all also white. Their color contrasted sharply with the green of the foliage, and beyond that, the terracotta brick wall.

Moments passed in which the crowd settled and a sense of anticipation grew. Whispered conversations were stilled. Sarah, no longer knowing entirely where to look, focused on Michael's knee, then found herself absent-mindedly observing his hands. They looked caring, comforting and capable. The desire to put her hand into his was overwhelming.

Then, there came a rustle through the congregated mourners, like a wind through autumn leaves. Sarah looked up to see that a figure had appeared behind the microphone. He was a giant of a man, with massive shoulders, but when Sarah looked at him more carefully, his face was the epitome of sympathetic understanding. He very probably had stood in the same place so many times in his capacity as officiant that his face had learnt to reflect the attitude of his heart. He would have been in his late fifties, Sarah judged, his dark hair peppered with grey. A lifetime of lines hovered around his eyes.

"Welcome," he said, in a voice as richly timbered as the walls that surrounded them, "to the celebration service for the life of Rosa Maria Antonio."

He introduced himself, let everyone know the format for the day's service then went on to outline in summary the things he had learned about the life of Rosa. He referred to her late husband Marco, her two children, Marcus and Patricia, together with their respective children, some of whom could not be there in person. He mentioned Rosa's enjoyment of life, her great skill as a seamstress, her passion for gardening, her wisdom and patience and peace and above all her abiding love of people. He did not, however, make any specific reference to Uncle Ernest.

When he had finished his moving speech he asked Rosa's son, Marcus Antonio, to come forward and say a few words. Marcus came to the dais, a pugnacious man who looked directly at the gathered group with thinly veiled suspicion, as though he wondered who on earth they all were and what right they thought they had to be there.

"Thank you for coming," he said in an icy voice. He seemed as sincere as one greeting an old adversary. He began then to talk of his mother from carefully prepared notes that he produced from his flashy suit pocket with a flourish. He spoke dispassionately about Rosa, as someone might talk about a stranger of some renown whom you knew more by reputation than in person.

His anecdotes about his childhood lacked any kind of warmth. Although he'd obviously written one or two statements which he thought might provide the audience with some level of amusement, his frightening demeanor meant that no one dared so much as snigger. He reminded Sarah of the archetypal Italian mobster, albeit one with a New Zealand accent. From the little she knew of Rosa she could scarcely credit her having such a cold fish of an offspring. Everyone's relief when he sat down was palpable.

Following the ferocious Marcus came a sweet lady from Lambton Park who read an obscure poem in archaic language that Sarah found difficult to gain anything from. She wondered about Michael's opinion on the subject and would be sure to ask him later. In turn came a wizened old man who had been one of Rosa and Marco's first neighbors. He talked about how he had become friends with the couple, how they had both enriched his life and the life of his late wife. He spoke as one for whom the hours of time were rapidly running out, with an immense sadness for being one of the only people he knew left in the land of the living, a moving and simple speech which moistened the eye of many, including Sarah's.

The officiant then announced that Rosa had requested the singing of the aria "Ave Maria", during which people were invited to spend the time in quiet contemplation of her life. The woman who came to the front of the chapel to sing was in her mid fifties. She had dressed for the occasion just like a peacock, her rich attire contrasting with the brick background. She took a deep breath that in turn swelled her ample bosom, and from her mouth came the most amazing sound. Her voice contained such beauty and clarity that many were surprised she did not regularly grace the stages of opera houses throughout the world.

It was strange, Sarah found, considering the life of someone she had only met after death had claimed her. All she could do was to give thanks for the life of a person who so clearly had influenced the lives of others, especially those of Sarah's own family. The haunting beauty of the music brought fresh tears to Sarah's eyes. She found herself unable to stop them rolling, one after the other, down her cheeks and onto her lap. Margaret passed her a tissue from the right, and on the left Michael took her hand in his. Sarah looked over at him, and he smiled at her, a smile of such affection and reassurance that Sarah felt her heart melt within her. Through her tears, she smiled back.

The aria came to an end. The silence that followed was punctuated by the sound of sniffing and sniffling as the congregated mourners struggled for equilibrium. The officiant returned to the dais, and requested them all to stand for the saying of the Lord's Prayer, after which four identically suited men from the funeral directors' carried the casket from the chapel. From there, Marcus and Patricia and the respective members of their immediate families who had taken the trouble to attend would accompany Rosa to her final resting place, while the rest of the assembled crowd were directed into the adjacent reception room for the obligatory cup of tea and club sandwich.

"Lovely service," Uncle Charles said, when the Ferguson family gathered in a suitably remote corner of the reception room. The only person not with them was Uncle Ernest. Sarah remained as close to Michael as she could get. They'd held hands until separated in the rush for the door by the crowd. Sarah wished there was a legitimate reason for picking up where they'd left off.

"Lovely," Margaret agreed.

"That woman sure had a pair of lungs on her," Jim said.

Todd sniggered. "She had a big pair of something else, too."

"Todd!" Margaret remonstrated. "Please. Keep it seemly. This is a funeral, you know."

Todd shuffled uncomfortably and muttered something about not wanting to have come in the first place.

Uncle Ernest came striding over, his bulbous face filled with outrage.

"They wouldn't let me go," he said angrily.

"Where?" Charles asked.

"With them, to the graveside."

"Why?"

"They made a big point of saying it was for family only. Don't they realize I was practically part of her family? Of course not. And do you know why? Because none of them ever bothered to take the time to come and see their own mother and grandmother, that's why. It's despicable."

"I know it's hard," Charles said, "but you have to try to respect their wishes. Everyone handles these things differently. It wouldn't be right to interfere. Come and have a cup of tea."

As Uncle Charles led the outraged Uncle Ernest away for a cup of tea, Sarah stepped away from Michael and drew Nan over closer to her.

"How are you?" she asked.

Pearl attempted a small smile. "A bit flat, truth be told. I only ever met

Rosa once, but that meeting meant so much to me. She had a way about her, and she, well, I suppose you could say that she inspired me." Pearl looked up at Michael to include him in the conversation. "I guess you could say that I've not only been letting the grass grow under my feet, I've let the grass grow so high I've begun to be unable to see over the top of it."

Michael said, "I think we all feel like that, from time to time."

"What? You young things? I couldn't imagine that."

"Oh, I don't know. Youth is no barrier to getting into a rut. Being young doesn't automatically mean being intrepid."

"True. Likewise, nowhere is it written in stone that from a certain age you have to simply find a place to sit down and wait for death to arrive, does it?"

"I should hope not," Sarah said.

Pearl's small smile increased. "Of course it's not always that easy," she said. "The body slows up, things aren't what they once were, your mind isn't always as sharp. But within such limitations there's no reason to stop living life to the full."

"It's something we can all be mindful of," Sarah said.

"Too right," Pearl said. "I've found, you know, that life is about making adjustments. Things never stay the same, no matter how hard we try to rail against it. The trick is being able to find meaning in your circumstances, to find your place - a place with meaning and purpose. I remember before I had the twins, wondering to myself what life was all about. I felt like I had no focus. Then, when the twins were born I had more focus than I sometimes felt I could cope with. But of course they grew up, as did Sheila.

"I still remember the day Sheila went to school, the quietness of the house. I suddenly realized my purpose needed to change. I wasn't the mother of pre school children any longer. I needed to find a new meaning and direction for my life within that context. It happened again when they became teenagers, again when they left home, and most significantly, again when Jack died."

"You've managed to, though, haven't you?" Sarah said.

Pearl shook her head. "I don't know. I'm not sure I've managed it this time around. Jack's been gone more than five years. All I've really done is mark time. Meeting Rosa, talking with her and understanding some of what she went through as a younger person, made me see how her *attitude* to life had so much to do with the *outcome* of her life. I've begun to realize lately that, this time, I have not made that transition as I did when I was younger.

I have lost my meaning and purpose and it's time now to regain what I have lost. You don't think eighty is too old to be turning over a new leaf?"

"Definitely not," Sarah said.

"Good," Pearl said. "Now all we have to do is persuade your mother that she needs to turn a new leaf over as well."

Sarah thought that she herself was by no means exempt from this either. Her life had changed, merely by her decision to come home. And although she was attempting to resettle by doing things like looking for a job and slowly contacting old friends, in truth none of these things made a difference that truly mattered. Her emotional life and her heart were the areas she needed to change. She needed to try to find the courage to put the past hurts behind her, to take a risk and move very firmly on with her life. She wondered if, when it came to the crunch, whether she would be brave enough to do so.

CHAPTER ELEVEN

When, on the following Tuesday evening, Sarah had found her mother in the kitchen quietly having what could reasonably be called to a paddy, she quickly thought she'd had quite enough of her mother's histrionics. Margaret had busied herself by throwing her papers on the floor and jumping up and down on them, raving about the bloody tax man, idiotic suppliers and mean-spirited slow payers.

"What do they expect us to live on over Christmas?" she'd demanded. "Fresh air? I tell you, I'm sick and tired of excuses, excuses, excuses. And what about this party? How are we ever supposed to be ready?"

Sarah briefly wondered what had possessed her to come home to live at all. Right now she could be in England with Cassie, preparing for Christmas by being gently frozen before being ritually squashed on Oxford Street. But she took a deep breath, as though she was the mother with the recalcitrant child. She'd politely urged her mother to get a grip on herself, helped to tidy up the strewn papers and made a placating cup of tea. They'd then sat down in a much more rational fashion.

Sarah had said, "Things aren't quite as dire as you're portraying. There's still six more days until Christmas. Maybe someone will pay before then. As for the party, let's talk about it in the morning, when we're fresh. Things are in better shape than you imagine."

Margaret had looked dubious, but Sarah held her ground. They now sat, on the Wednesday morning, in the lounge. Sarah had made fresh coffee, chosen a venue as far away from the chaos of Margaret's kitchen as she could manage and had neatly organized all the things she felt they might need for a successful council of war. In spite of her preparation Sarah had to take another deep breath before they started, to stifle the fact that she felt weary of her mother's negative attitude. Someone had once told Sarah that people could be divided into three main categories: the pessimist, the optimist and the realist. For the optimist, the glass was always half full; for the pessimist the glass was always half empty. The realist concerned themselves with neither state and merely regarded the glass as another bloody piece of washing up. Sarah could not make up her mind whether her mother was the pessimist or the realist, but either way, she seemed to take very little pleasure in anything these days.

Her mother continued to tut about the accounts and the state of the business finances but Sarah refused to be drawn on the subject. Instead, she steered the conversation firmly onto Christmas Day.

"Right," she said, "I think we've firmed up the guest list at nineteen. That includes Isabella and Connor, but not Tom and Gerry since we aren't expecting them until the afternoon."

"Nineteen? That's worse than I thought. How did we end up with nineteen?"

"Apart from family we only have three extras. Edwina Johnson, Uncle David's current flower, and of course Michael."

Margaret looked up at Sarah. "Of course," she said with a knowing grin.

Sarah tried to stop herself from going red. "I'm thinking we don't really need to cater for either Isabella or Connor, so that brings us back to the original seventeen that we thought of."

"Thank God. Yes, no point counting either of the kids. Isabella practically eats nothing real and will probably gorge herself silly on sweets or potato chips without either of her parents batting an eyelid. As for Connor, I'm sure Joanna will bring whatever he requires, some mushed up baby food and his bottles. With a bit of luck he'll spend half the time upstairs asleep."

Sarah raised her eyebrows. "So much for the excitement of his first Christmas."

Margaret waved a hand. "Most kids haven't a clue what's going on until they're three. From then on it's full on commercialism and a lifelong addiction to the accumulation of new stuff."

"Hmm. Anyway, so I counted the plates, knives, forks, glasses, et cetera, and between us and Nan and Michael we've got enough for all of us."

"Michael doesn't mind lending us some of his stuff?"

"Not at all. He's pleased to have been invited."

"And his parents? They don't mind too much?"

"It didn't sound like it. He's going to see them first thing, for some sort of Christmas morning tea. Ever since Michael's brother died the wind's gone from their yuletide sail."

"Sad," Margaret said.

"I know."

"As it is, we'll be battling against sadness here too, what with Rosa having gone. I suspect Uncle Ernest will be rather maudlin."

"We'll have to try to cheer him up," Sarah said.

"Good luck. I don't like your chances. You saw what he was like at the funeral. And you know how he never notices or takes into account other people's feelings. It's bad enough that Mum feels upset, let alone him spoiling her big day by depressing us all even further."

"I suppose he can't help being sad. After all, according to Uncle Charles, he'd wanted to marry her. If he felt that deeply for her, you can hardly expect him to get over it in an instant."

"I suppose not."

"Anyway, we'll just have to manage the situation as best we can. Perhaps I'll talk to Uncle Charles, see what he thinks. He might have a suggestion of how to handle things. He might even volunteer to look after Uncle Ernest himself."

"I wish he would," Margaret said.

"Another thing that might help the situation would be to have a seating plan for the meal. I've been thinking about this a bit, looking at the dining room. I think, at a pinch, we could probably get everybody seated."

"Around the dining room table? You must be joking."

Sarah momentarily clenched her teeth. "I thought we could completely empty the room of extra furniture, push the table almost right to one end, then slide the kitchen table in to join on to it, or use Michael's plus the fold down table at right angles to that. Again, we beg, borrow and steal chairs from Nan and Michael, and if needs be ask Auntie Sheila to bring one or two of hers."

"I can imagine she'd be thrilled about that idea."

"You never know. My point is, I think it is manageable. And it might help us enormously with keeping things harmonious."

"I don't see how."

"Like I said, we draw up a seating plan. I can make some name cards for each place setting to make sure we get a good balance."

"Really? Have you got the time?"

Sarah lied and said, "Of course." She'd just have to make the time. After all, sleep was vastly overrated as a pastime, wasn't it?

"Okay, then. What about food?"

"Three enormous frozen chickens are in the freezer. We'll cook two in our oven and one in Michael's. Roast veggies are bought and will be cooked in Nan's oven. Peas, beans and carrots to be cooked on the stovetop. Gravy a la packet, and nobody will ever know. Chickens to be prepared the night before. Selection of desserts courtesy of that shop on Carterton Road - which Uncle David generously agreed to finance - are due to be picked up on Christmas Eve, together with the eightieth birthday cake we've ordered.

"Auntie Sheila and Uncle John are supplying the bulk of the drink, although I thought we might make some punch for before the meal. Michael is bringing a couple of extra bottles of wine and some crackers and potato chips for the afternoon if anyone is still hungry. Uncle Charles agreed to give the speech, the progress of which I will ask him about when I call him up to ask him about the Uncle Ernest problem."

"Goodness. You do sound organized."

Sarah shrugged. "There are one or two things to go."

"Such as?"

"The house needs decorating. I sort of thought I might ask Todd if he'd be willing to help with that."

"I guess that would be fine if you don't care about how things look when he's finished."

"Oh," said Sarah, "I feel quite sure I can persuade him to do a more than adequate job. I thought I might even suggest he ask Tom and Gerry to help. From what I can see, they're all hanging around at a loose end already."

Margaret gave Sarah a philosophical look. "Well if you can arrange it you're a bigger miracle worker than I thought. What else?"

"Just the photo board. Unfortunately, with Rosa's death we had a bit of a setback with getting it organized. But we've got everything we need now, so it's just a matter of putting everything together."

"It all sounds too much if you ask me."

"It's all in hand, Mum," Sarah said. "From what we've discussed this morning, between now and Christmas, you won't have to do a thing."

"You right there, love?" the taxi driver asked Pearl as she tried to ease herself out of his cab.

"Thank you, yes," Pearl replied. Her feet found their purchase and she stood up, flattened down her skirt and rearranged her handbag as she got her bearings. She bent down to talk to the driver. "Now you're quite sure you are able to come and collect me at two o'clock?"

The driver, a large unshaven gentleman with a cheeky grin, looked at his watch. "Two o'clock?" he said vaguely, as though it was the first he'd heard of the arrangement. He pointed at the dial, tracing the numbers with his enormous fingers and he mumbled something that Pearl could not quite catch. Then, when Pearl was about to give up hope that the poor man had any clue of how much time would elapse between now - eleven o'clock - and when he was due back, his face cracked into a smile. "I reckon that should work out fine. I've got a fare in Rosemont at one fifteen so as long as the traffic is okay, I should be back for you at two. A nice lady like you wouldn't worry about a little five minute wait, would you now?"

Pearl frowned. "I suppose not, but please do try to be on time."

"Will do."

"Do I pay you now, or later for both trips?"

"Better pay us now," he said. "Just in case."

He told her how much. Pearl reluctantly handed over what seemed like a very exorbitant sum.

"Thanks, love," he said, mysteriously pocketing the dollar change without so much as a by your leave. "Bye, then. See you at two."

She felt sure that had he worn a hat he would have doffed it at her. She closed the door and waved good-bye as he motored off. In reality if he was late it didn't really matter since Pearl wasn't in any hurry, but one didn't like to be taken advantage of. Five minutes was neither here nor there. The real miracle would be if he came back at all.

Pearl turned to face the commanding entrance to Lambton Park. Everything looked neat and orderly, a veritable haven for the elderly. Everything looked the same as the time she had come to visit with Ernest. It was just such a pity that, underneath it all, things were not the same. Even now Pearl found it hard to believe that Rosa no longer lived and breathed and made up a part of this community.

Pearl expelled a breath. No good could be gained from standing out here on the footpath getting melancholy. She had come here to help and help she would. There wasn't any way she could be an effective assistant if she had a face like a wet weekend in summer. She set off along the pathway that wound its way beside the main drive, then, hoping her memory served her correctly, she veered off onto a side path toward what she hoped would turn out to be Ernest's unit.

She paused before walking up to the front door, looking twice as if searching for confirmation she'd arrived at the right place. It seemed right, but then so many of the units looked the same that there didn't seem to be any way of being exactly sure.

"Only one way to find out," Pearl said to herself.

She walked forward with as much confidence as she could muster, then knocked firmly on the front door. She could hear small scrabbling noises inside, and before long Ernest opened the door.

It appeared, Pearl thought, as though he had shrunk since she'd last seen him. Whatever used to be inside him that kept him perpetually puffed up and full of arrogant swagger had disappeared. Pearl wondered if he'd lost weight too. He regarded her with a lackluster expression, giving her serious concerns about his health.

"You made it then," Ernest said in such a bland manner that he might not have minded either way if she hadn't made the effort at all. And it had been an effort. It wasn't every day Pearl set off from home in a taxi after all. She'd been feeling quite proud of her initiative until now.

"Yes," she said brightly. "I made it. And by the look of you, not a moment too soon."

"Eh?"

"Well, look at you. Did you concentrate at all when you got dressed this morning? You've done some of your buttons up unevenly. And have you shaved? No, I didn't think so. What will people say if you let yourself go to rack and ruin?"

"Who bloody cares what they think?" he grumbled.

"I do," she replied, "and so should you. What do you think Rosa would say if she could see you carrying on in this manner?"

He shrugged.

"I bet she'd say this wasn't any way to act. Life, to her, was to be lived and enjoyed, not endured and lamented over."

A look of anger crossed Ernest's features. "What would you know about what Rosa would say or wouldn't say? You only met her the once."

Pearl suppressed a smile, glad her plan seemed to be working. "Enough to know that she would not have approved of this...this...wallowing in self pity you seem to currently be indulging yourself in."

"Me? Bloody hell, woman, as if you haven't been doing the exact same thing for year upon year. And now, here you are, lecturing me in my own home about feeling sorry that the lady I loved went and died on me last week.

If that doesn't take the cake, I don't know what does."

"Maybe you're right," Pearl said, "but at least I've seen the error of my ways. Perhaps if I'd been lucky enough to know Rosa earlier, I might have saved myself a bit of time. You, on the other hand, have no such excuse. Oh, I'm not saying you can't be sad or feel grief, but you need to keep it in proportion. I know you loved her, but that's hardly the same thing as having been married to her for umpteen years. You ought to feel proud to have known her, glad for the time you were able to spend with her. You ought to hold your head up high as a person whom she'd counted as a friend. Be sorry for her loss but don't let that loss diminish you as a person, whatever you do. Life's too short for that, especially at our age."

Ernest stood there looking mutinous, staring at her as though she'd gone crazy. At length a new expression flitted across his face. Pearl suspected she'd seen the merest hint of a smile.

"You always were the most bossy baggage that ever lived, weren't you?" he said.

"And don't you forget it," Pearl said with a grin. "Now for goodness sake, go and get dressed properly and have that shave. Then, with your head held high, let's go over to Rosa's unit and look at sorting out some of her stuff, just like you wanted."

"Okay," he said meekly.

"And hurry up about it," she called after him. "My carriage returns to bear me home at two o'clock sharp."

The telephone rang. Todd ran to snatch it up. If only it could be for him he'd seriously consider being better behaved for maybe even a week. It might be someone like Jason or Daniel, calling up to rescue him from this hell he'd found himself in, inviting him to a once in a lifetime, never-to be-missed event. In his wildest dreams it would be Beth, phoning to say that she wanted to take a swim and there wasn't anyone home to rub suntan lotion on her back so would Todd mind popping over to oblige? Right now, he thought, kicking the plastic bag of Christmas decorations he'd been given to put up, he'd probably even settle for hearing from Tom and Gerry.

"Hello?"

A male voice said, "I wondered if I could speak to Sarah Bell?"

Todd eyed the Christmas decorations with malice and thought about

Sarah, his wicked sister who had perpetrated this cruel and unusual punishment on him. He felt overwhelmed with the temptation to lie but for the fact that she seemed to have a knack for finding him out. Right now, with plenty other heinous jobs requiring attention between now and Christmas Day, he'd better not risk it. Otherwise, on the day, knowing his luck, she'd probably end up having him dressed in some hideous elven costume and get him pouring drinks for the olds, instead of opening his presents and stuffing himself stupid like usual.

"I'll just see if I can find her," he replied. He then placed the receiver on the bench, leaned down as close to it as he could manage, and at the top of his lungs, yelled, "Sarah! Phone for you!"

He heard her open her bedroom door, heard her first footfalls on the uppermost steps, then turned and fled.

"Hello?" Sarah said.

"Sarah, it's Rob Furness here. You came last week for a job interview?"

Sarah's heart skipped a beat. "That's right. Hi, Rob. How are you?"

"Great. Interviewing is over and we've found the successful candidate."

Oh, God, she thought, here he goes. He's about to say, "Unfortunately, it's not you."

"I see," she said cautiously.

"Indeed. Anyway, the long and the short of it is that Greg and I wondered if you'd be interested in coming to work for us?"

"Me?"

"Yes, that's the general idea. We were both very impressed with your ideas, your work ethic and your enthusiasm. If you haven't got a better offer and can bear the thought of working with the two of us, then the job's yours."

Sarah felt stunned. In her eyes the interview had gone terribly. She'd starkly felt the contrast between funeral and job interview and could not seem to readily change gears from one to the other. Her eyes were red from having cried at the funeral. She'd felt about as enthusiastic as a doomed passenger on the Titanic.

"Really?"

"Really. You are interested?"

"Of course," she said. "Thanks very much."

"Don't thank us yet. You haven't actually had to put up with either of us for a working day yet."

Sarah laughed. She thought of her mother and her middle-aged angst, of Todd and his surly outlook, of her father chiseling unhappily away at life's tasks. Compared to the three of them, how bad could Rob and Greg possibly be?

"I'm sure I'll manage," she said with true sincerity.

At the close of the conversation, as she put down the receiver, she felt a huge sense of elation. Maybe things were about to come together for her after all.

"Are you sure you don't want a cup of tea before we go over to Rosa's?" Ernest asked.

Pearl shook her head. "We need to get on. Besides, if we're really that thirsty I'm sure Rosa's estate wouldn't begrudge a couple of old friends a tea bag or two from her kitchen."

"Right," he said, shifting uncomfortably from one foot to the other.

"Are you sure you're up to this?" Pearl asked. "After all, perhaps it's better leaving it for the family to sort out her stuff."

"That lot? Never darkened her doorstep from one year to the next, the miserable gits. Things might be different if there were valuables for them to lay their filthy hands on but it's not as though her stuff was worth a lot of money. Doubtless, in the fullness of time they will be called in to decide what to do with the bulk of her possessions. After all, some decision will have to be made about her unit and what's to be done with it.

"No, it's more that we had a conversation a while back about some of her things, objects she'd treasured, some of which she wanted other people to have. I must admit I didn't pay a lot of attention at the time because I never figured she would die. Or at least not so soon. However, I feel obliged to try to make things right, to do my best according to her wishes. I just didn't want to have to face going back into her unit by myself, that's all."

"Quite understandable, under the circumstances. Have you a key?"

"Course," he said, fishing it out of his pocket. He held it up proudly for her to see.

"And you're quite sure no one will object to you being in Rosa's unit?"

He shook his head. "Besides, we aren't actually going to give anything away. All I intend to do is make a list as best as I can recall, with the object and the person she'd mentioned she'd like to have it. I'll then give the list to whoever's in charge of sorting out the estate."

"As long as you're sure, let's get going."

Ernest opened his front door and ushered Pearl out with a face like a condemned man. Pearl just had to be glad that she'd at least managed to get him to be a presentable condemned man if nothing else.

Pearl followed her brother along the same path they had walked not full three weeks ago, passed pristine units with their neat gardens, the sun shining down as it had that day, the air full of the sounds of life, including the drift of a concerto on the breeze. As they neared Rosa's unit Pearl suddenly found herself catapulting into Ernest who, for some unknown reason had stopped in his tracks. Pearl looked up.

There, the scene that they beheld wasn't one of Rosa's little unit sitting sleepily as it waited for them to arrive. Instead, a hive of activity greeted them with the front door opened wide and every window tossed open to let in the air. Before the house sat a squat removal van, between which two men in overalls carted Rosa's stuff with casual disdain.

"What the blazes is going on?" Ernest demanded.

Pearl could see his fury by the way the veins stood out from his neck.

"I don't know," she said. "Perhaps we should go over and find out."

"Damn right," he said, striding off with renewed purpose.

As they reached the front door they could hear other voices. Pearl glimpsed the sight of both Marcus and Patricia as they walked from the lounge to the bedroom, in sharp debate with one another over some contentious issue.

Ernest strode into the house without invitation.

"What the hell's going on?" he said loudly.

Marcus and Patricia turned and regarded Ernest with a look that suggested he was something they might have had the misfortune to step on in the park.

"Pardon?" Marcus said.

"I want to know," Ernest bellowed, "just what, precisely, do you think you are doing?"

Patricia raised a patronizing eyebrow. "I fail to see what it has to do with you what we choose to do with our mother's possessions."

"I thought we made it quite clear at the funeral," said Marcus, "that you have no place in our mother's life - not then and certainly not now."

"No place? How dare you! She was going to marry me."

Patricia laughed coldly. "Really? How interesting. And just what, pray tell, gave you that idea?"

Ernest stammered for words. Pearl knew he could hardly lie further. In truth he'd only hoped she would marry him. They would never know for sure.

"I loved her," he said, "more than either of you two ever did, you ungrateful wretches. Never had a thing to do with her for years, you didn't, and here you are now going over everything like a bloody plague of locusts. You make me sick, the pair of you."

Marcus regarded Ernest with fresh animosity. "Then I suggest you leave," he said. "Now. Before we're obliged to call the police."

Ernest's eyes widened with shock.

"Come on, Ernest," Pearl said. "I think we'd better go."

He looked at her wildly. "But what about her things? What's going to happen to all her precious things?"

Pearl looked quizzically at Marcus and Patricia.

"It's going into a jumble sale," said Marcus. "None of it is any good to us."

"And her unit?" Pearl asked. "What will happen to that?"

Patricia said, "It's going on the market. It, like that rest of her things, is absolutely no use to us whatsoever."

Ernest took a step backward as though he had been physically struck. Pearl used that step as momentum to lead him the rest of the way home. She took his keys from him and fumbled with them in the lock.

Ernest tripped into the lounge and sank down on the closest chair, a defeated man.

"Those bloody ingrates," he said sadly.

"Try not to dwell on it," Pearl said. "There's nothing you can do. We might not like or agree with what they're doing but at the end of the day it is their right. For better or worse they are her children. They are the legal beneficiaries of her property."

He shook his head sadly. "It makes you wonder what the world is coming to. The younger generation is nothing but a pack of greedy, selfish wastrels. It makes me think that maybe Rosa's better off dead. I mean if this is how the next generation behave, I hate to think what will become of the things I value, when the time comes."

Pearl, thinking of her own children, and her children's children, for the most part couldn't help thinking Ernest had a point. The things their generation valued seemed far from the things people prized today. Then she thought of Sarah, and of Michael, and the qualities they both possessed.

"They're not all bad," she said. "You have to have a bit of faith."

"Are you sure you don't mind helping me out with this?" Sarah asked as Michael relieved her of some of her burden. She'd come loaded down with old photograph albums, card, scissors, glue, colored cardboard and a sheaf of plain white paper, from which to finally finish the photo board.

"Of course. I'm delighted to be able to help."

"I don't want to intrude on your spare time."

As Michael ushered her into the hallway he said, "I wish, for once, you could come here without being so apologetic about wasting my time. I can't think of anything I'd rather do this evening than spend time with you doing something to help toward the party."

"Really?"

"Really. If it makes you feel any better, you're doing me a favor. By helping with this I can justify my appearance at the party, can't I?"

Sarah entered the lounge and dumped the rest of her clutter onto the couch. Straightening, she said, "There's no need for any kind of justification. Everyone's pleased you're going to be there."

"Except, perhaps, the rest of the family who've never met me before?"

Sarah grinned. "Yes, well, perhaps except for them. Where are we going to work?"

He shrugged. "I hadn't thought about it too much. Do you fancy working at the dining room table? It might just be big enough. Otherwise, I could move the coffee table and we can spread everything out on the floor?"

"Let's do that."

"All right."

Sarah removed the collection of magazines off the top of the table, and Michael whisked it away. She gathered her things off the couch and began sorting everything out.

"I hear congratulations are in order," Michael said.

Sarah looked up. "Boy, news travels fast. Who told you?"

"Todd. I saw him lurking in the bushes this afternoon. He seemed to be lurking with an air of anticipation."

"I think that if they made lurking an officially recognized school subject Todd might finally get an A. I wonder what he was doing."

"Looked to me as though he was waiting for someone."

Sarah shook her head. "It's more likely he was hiding because someone wanted him to do some real work for a change. That boy. There's trouble brewing there somewhere."

"I gather you're pleased about the job?"

She smiled. "Delighted. Both the guys I'll be working for seem really nice. It's a great environment and they seem to get a lot of interesting work. Working with reputable people always helps."

"Sounds fantastic. When do you start?"

"About the seventh or eighth of January. They're closing down for a couple of weeks so they both can have a holiday. How's your holiday progressing?"

"Fine. Let's see what you've done with this photo board so far. Wow, it's looking quite impressive already. What do you want me to do?"

"Well, if it's not too girlie, I wondered if you could help me make a border for around the outside. I've brought along this colored cardboard. I sort of thought we could cut it into little squares and glue it on in a mosaic effect."

"I don't mind doing that. In fact, I've probably got some other card that might work in well. Some gold and silver."

"That'd be good."

"We teachers, we're all incorrigible bower birds. You find yourself keeping all kinds of stuff because you never know when something is going to come in handy."

While Michael went to search for the cardboard, Sarah started working on carefully sticking the last of the photographs onto the large cardboard sheet, using a special adhesive she'd bought which promised to be removable. She had no wish to damage any of the old sepia prints, most of which were irreplaceable.

"Here it is," Michael said, returning with a small stack of card.

They worked for a while without talking then Sarah said, "How about your writing? Had any opportunity to do any?"

"Quite a bit this week," Michael said. "I thought about it and decided I'd put off decorating until after New Year, to concentrate on writing first. I kind of figure that if I get into a routine of writing now I can fit painting around it. If I try and do it the other way around, I'll never get started."

"And how's it coming on?"

He shrugged. "Hard to say."

"Can you sense a best seller looming?"

He laughed. "Best selling replacement toilet paper, perhaps."

"I hope you're joking."

He grinned. "Course."

"So tell me," Sarah said, "when you are published, will you use your own name, or a pseudonym?"

His green eyes observed her with amusement. "Can't say I've ever thought about it before."

"Pity you're not a woman."

"Why?"

"You could write your thriller and call yourself something apt, like Paige Turner."

"Oh, ha ha. Any other great ideas?"

"What about a diet book, and be known as Hugh Jars?"

He groaned. "Any more?"

She grinned. "Hundreds, probably. You could write a self-help book about being more assertive. It could be entitled, 'The Doormat Syndrome', by Sheila Blige."

Michael cringed. "No more. You want my advice? Don't give up your day job."

"But I don't have a day job. Yet."

"I think the world might owe a debt of gratitude to your new employers for being brave enough to take you on. Please tell me you didn't try to tell any jokes at the interview."

"None that I can recall."

"Make sure that you ease them into it, when the time comes, won't you?"

Sarah picked up a cushion and threw it at him but he successfully dodged it.

"At least you haven't got the dubious honor of having the name Bell," she told him.

"Why? What's wrong with Bell?"

"You wouldn't need to ask if you'd had years of people saying dumb stuff like, 'Bell? Now, that name rings a Bell', or saying, 'Give me a bell,' and then sniggering. Then there was my personal favorite, a guy at school who had a crush on me who used to rave on about my voice being as clear as a bell. Yuk. Have you ever noticed that cornier the joke it, the louder the person telling the joke laughs at it?"

"Practically every day. You've got no idea how hysterically funny the average fifteen-year-old boy thinks he is. It's enough to give you a headache. Hey, what's this photo here? Is that you?"

Sarah bent over to have a look. "Yes that's me, and that's Joanna, trying to sit on Granddad's knee even though she'd got too big."

"How old were you then?"

Sarah looked down at the photo again, trying to recall. It had been taken on a family picnic for some occasion or other. She'd remembered Reuben being there, just a tiny baby in his carrycot. She remembered that Joanna had stuck sand in her hair, that they'd all been driven mad by mosquitoes.

"I guess I must have been about six or seven. Probably seven if Reuben was there. And Joanna would have been ten or eleven. She put sand in my hair, that much I do remember."

"Poor didums."

Sarah screwed up her nose. "I don't need to tell you what a pain older siblings can be."

"No." Michael looked thoughtful. "Ironically, though, you do miss them when they're gone. That's why old photos and mementos can be so important. Not to the extent that my parents have taken it - like turning their house into a mausoleum - but so that there are things to look back on to help us recall our memories. Otherwise it's scary how much you forget about what's gone before."

"I know. Now that I'm back home I wished I'd taken more photos while I was overseas. At the time everything seems larger than life. You're sure you'll remember every detail of every single thing. The truth is, the moment you turn your back on whatever it is you've been looking at, like an old church, or a famous painting in an art gallery, or a quaint English village, the image already begins to fade."

"Perhaps what we really get left with isn't images at all," Michael said. "Maybe it's more impressions. The feeling you got standing in the shadow of that old church in the late afternoon, the emotion the painting evoked in you, or something as banal as the cream bun you stealthily ate in that cute little village. Or the way you felt when your big sister put sand in your hair at a picnic when you were seven."

Sarah found herself mesmerized by the imagery he created in her mind. She might not have ever stealthily eaten the cream bun but she did remember having a cone of hot chips in one village. The smell of them came to her more readily than the image of the village itself.

"I know what you mean. But photos can help conjure up some of the things you can't easily recall. And when I think of it that's something we've not considered for Christmas Day. Being that it's such an important day, someone will need to be responsible for taking some photos."

Michael smiled. "Good idea. Preserve some more memories."

She looked at him, and their eyes met. She held his gaze, not being able to recall a time when she felt more comfortable and relaxed in the presence of another person.

"I'm really looking forward to Christmas now," she said.

The merest of smiles crossed his lips. "Me too," he replied. And with that he leaned over and kissed her.

The last thing Jim expected to see when he emerged dusty and dirty from the four-bedroom palace he was tiling was to see Margaret waiting nervously on the edge of the building site, clearly waiting to catch a glimpse of him.

She stood very still. She wasn't like a hunter waiting for a clear shot of his prey but like a rare bird balanced on an exposed branch of a tall tree, whose tenuous position on earth could at any time be compromised by a fatal error on her part. She had about her a fragility and vulnerability, as though to move before the right moment might be a costly mistake.

A soft wind blew, a zephyr. It gently pressed the folds of her dress against her frame, accentuating her thinness. He could not help thinking that her warmth and wit and intelligence had all undergone the exact same shrink- age, leaving in its wake a person who could only be described as a shadow of her former self.

The gulf that separated them had become far wider than the couple of yards distance from which they stood apart now. Jim, if he was honest, had become fed up to the back teeth with her moods and mismanagement of even the simplest tasks. But what truly irked him was that these depressions and disasters never actually seemed to be either of Margaret's own making, or indeed in any way her fault. On the contrary, she often seemed to attribute these difficulties to having a root cause that began firmly at Jim's doorstep. It did not seem to matter how far removed he was from whatever situation had arisen to cause distress. Somehow - in thinking that was completely beyond his comprehension - Margaret had developed the ability to twist things around to make him the most likely perpetrator. Lately, in the midst of everything, Jim realized he'd begun to lose the ability to care about any of it any more.

But now seeing her standing there looking so intensely lost, and perhaps more than a little sorry, his heart moved afresh with compassion and with the desire to try to make things right. To bridge the gulf. To grout over the gaps. To work toward restoration.

She slowly raised one hand to give him a small wave, and a hesitant, uncertain smile flitted across her features. He knew it required him to make the first move.

"Hi," he said, as he approached.

"Hi."

"Is everything all right?"

She looked momentarily confused, as if wondering to what he specifically referred.

"I brought you lunch," she said, lifting up her other hand which contained a white plastic bag from the store that he'd not noticed before.

"Why?"

She shrugged. "Because it's Saturday and I didn't know if you'd made you own or not. Because I thought we should talk."

"So you can blame me for some more things?"

Margaret's gaze dropped and she chewed her bottom lip gently, perhaps to stop it from trembling.

"I'm sorry."

"Are you? For what?"

"For everything. For being so hopeless and pathetic. Can't we talk about it? Sit and have lunch?"

He glanced around him, looking at the mounds of barren soil, the builder's detritus and the layers of dust. "Hardly the ideal spot for a picnic."

"We could go for a drive. To the park down the road."

"I haven't got a lot of time, Margaret. I'm working against the clock here. Why else do you think I'm working today and tomorrow when Christmas is only three days away?"

"I know. But you need to eat. Can't you spare even half an hour?"

He looked at her, a part of him wanting to make her hurt just like she'd hurt him. But then another part of him softened by the moment.

"All right," he conceded. "Just let me wash my hands."

"I thought," Margaret said, in between bites of ham sandwich, "about the idea of going to see someone."

Jim kept his focus firmly on a group of mothers and toddlers picnicking and enjoying the park. He chewed thoughtfully then said, "Like a psychiatrist?"

"No," Margaret said hastily, "not a shrink. More like a career advisor."

"What for?"

"I suppose I've been thinking some more about what you said before, about deciding on a new direction in my life. About maybe getting a part time job."

"Oh. And?"

"I suppose what I've realized is that it's time to work out what I want to do with the rest of my life. It's only a matter of half a dozen years or so before Todd is old enough - and hopefully reliable enough - to look after himself, and then what? It's not as though I'll have another little one to take care of like I did when the girls became independent. As for Sarah, now she's got a job herself it'll only be a matter of time before she flies the coop herself.

"But I really don't have the faintest clue what I want to do or even what I'd be good at. My skills are rusty, my qualifications - such as they are - aren't worth the paper they're written on. I'm technologically inept. Hardly a glowing list of qualities to offer prospective employers, is it?"

"So you think a career advisor might help?"

Margaret reached into her purse and handed him a business card.

He squinted. "Cynthia Reed. Who the hell is she when she's at home?"

"Her girls and ours were at school together. I met her quite by chance in the store a couple of weeks ago. She mentioned she's a personnel consultant and gave me that card. She said they give career advice, too."

"And you want to go to see her?"

"I thought I might start there. She's not exactly an old friend, she's not exactly solely a career advisor, but she is of my generation and I do know her. I think I'd feel more comfortable approaching her than I would being grilled by some jumped up young floozy scarcely older than Todd."

"Fair enough. Can I ask what brought this on?"

"I don't know. Lots of things really. But I suppose Rosa's funeral made me think. Death is so final. I got the sense that Rosa never wasted a moment of her life. I feel as though I've wasted whole tracts of mine."

"I don't know that's a fair assessment. Even now you lead a productive life. It's just that the things you work at don't seem to give you any pleasure."

Margaret looked thoughtful. "The younger generation seem to have got this part of their lives so much more together than we have, don't you think? These days there simply isn't the expectation on young people to get a sensible career and to become wedded to it for the next forty years of their working life. They get encouraged to pursue their interests, go with their strengths and find a career that matches those things."

"The world's definitely changed, that's for sure. The question is, can we change with it?"

Margaret caught Jim's gaze. "So you think I should do it?"

"I think," Jim said, "it sounds like one of the most sensible decisions you've made in a long time."

CHAPTER TWELVE

For the first time in Sarah's life in her parent's house, she woke up on Christmas morning not to the soft sound of carols floating on the breeze, nor to the smell of pancakes and bacon cooking, nor with the anticipation of seeing what Santa had brought, but to the jarring sound of her alarm clock. This wasn't about to be a Christmas of idling her way through the day as she had in the past. On the other hand she felt determined that it would not be a day characterized by stress and disaster. The only way she could be sure of a degree of success for the day lay in not leaving anything to chance.

She forced her eyes open, reached over and silenced the offending alarm, swung her legs over the edge of the bed. This then was the point at which the rubber hit the road. Instead of dreading it, Sarah found her heart full of anticipation. She looked forward to seeing what the day might bring.

Pearl woke up to the sound of the birds singing in the trees and the realization that she had been on her life's journey for eighty whole years. Eighty years! She lay beneath the covers, treasured the tranquility and thought about that journey. She certainly had much to be grateful for. Strangely, for the first time in a while, she did not feel the weight of solitude as she lay there. Instead she felt a sense of contentment growing within her. She had done much soul searching over the past few weeks. Rather than feeling regretful about the passing of years and the stark reality of reaching such a momentous milestone, she simply felt a sense of anticipation about all that might yet come to pass. Maybe, she thought with a smile, there was a bit of life in the old girl yet.

When consciousness came to Sheila, it came with some discomfort. Her back hurt as she lay there, as it did most mornings. She felt fresh regret about the way she had let her body go. Her stomach groaned. It felt like an over-stretched Christmas stocking. Slowly, day by day, Sheila knew her body was grinding to a halt due to over indulgence and under utilization. The previous evening - at the dinner they had attended with most of the couples in their social circle - that level of indulgence had gone up a notch. Sheila wasn't proud of herself, nor of the fact that she had done it as much as anything to rile John up. Annoyingly, he'd remained oblivious to her attempts to gain his attention.

He lay now, sleeping beside her, his hair tousled, his face boy-like with relaxation. He appeared to have not a care in the world. Or, thought Sheila, much care for her either. Well, today was another day, wasn't it? And if she could not get his attention, and a bit of affection out of him today of all days, she'd have to seriously question the point really.

Charles had woken far earlier than he had intended, before the first rays of sun had even slipped above the horizon. He experienced his daily dose of disorientation as his mind searched for reality. It did not take him long to grasp it. It was Christmas Day, and it was Pearl's birthday. He wondered if she lay awake, and if so, what she thought. How would turning eighty make her feel? Would it be an occasion tinged with sadness? Could a person truly be pleased with having accumulated so many birthdays?

His thoughts turned to his own family. To Rosemary on her animal sanctuary, up to her eyeballs in dung and hay, eating some organic nut roast with a sprig of holly poking out of the top for Christmas dinner, accompanied by a glass of vile nettle wine. To Peter waking up in silk pajamas and opening an exquisitely wrapped present containing this season's Rolex and another with the keys to a new golf buggy, then sitting back and waiting for the chef to prepare the twenty pound turkey with all the trimmings.

He thought, as he did every single day, of Mary. Mary had loved Christmas, had always made it such a special time for them as a family. Charles still missed his wife every time there a special occasion rolled around. It seemed only fitting that, today of all days, he should feel his grief anew. He wondered what the day would bring, and then he remembered. The speech. It wasn't yet finished. Why, oh why, had he ever agreed to make that speech?

Michael stood in the hallway momentarily as he went to leave the house. He collected his thoughts, wondering if he had remembered everything. He'd been up for a while, had showered and dressed, and although he was supposed to be having a sort of pseudo-breakfast with his parents, he'd ended up eating a chocolate bar one of his pupils had given him as an end of year present, to stave off his hunger. Now the idea of eating anything else at all seemed less than appealing. Michael wasn't altogether sure he could entirely blame the chocolate bar.

He cast his mind about. Was he ready? He'd closed all the windows, had left the place in a reasonable order, had is wallet and car keys. The chicken was on and roasting. He had two plastic bags of presents organized, the smaller of the two containing a gift each for his parents. He'd struggled with what to buy them but had not quite run out of imagination enough to settle for buying them a sampler box of biscuits and be done with it. So he had wasted valuable time combing the shops for something appropriate. In the end he'd decided on a thick, manly silver pen for his father and a book about the castles of England for his mother. He couldn't rule out the possibility that they would most likely be happier with getting a copy of the latest TV Guide, but figured it probably didn't matter what he bought them since it wouldn't make them any happier.

Being convinced that he had forgotten nothing, Michael was ready to go. On his return all he needed to do was call in briefly to collect the larger bag of presents which were destined for next door and to get over there as fast as his legs would carry him. For the first time in years he felt an unexpected anticipation about Christmas. He could not wait to be free of his duty and be right where he wanted to be.

Jim stood in the garage looking at the doll's house. It annoyed him that his carpentry skills were so inept. Sure, on the face of it the house seemed almost perfect. It had two storeys, a chimney, a little staircase from one floor to the other, doors that opened and closed and two large doors on the front that you opened to get into the house, and closed again to tidy it away at night. Only last evening he had put the finishing touches on the house, had hung up the little curtains in the windows that Margaret had finally got around to making at the last minute.

He supposed that what annoyed him most in the process of constructing the house was that it had not come as easily to him as he thought it should. In many ways this seemed metaphoric of his everyday life. He thought with envy about people he knew whose skills and abilities came without effort, for whom the idea of something as mundane as practice was positively laughable.

Still, he thought, as he ran his hand over the smooth finish of the roof, there was definitely something to be said for the satisfaction gained from having worked at a task that did not come naturally. He had not been beaten by it. Perhaps, in the end, that was the secret to life. To be resolute, to be tenacious, to have the right attitude. And perhaps, if Jim was determined enough, he just may well be able to apply those same principles to his marriage and make something out of it, too.

Ernest stabbed at his boiled egg with his piece of toast but could not get up enough inspiration sufficient to actually eat the blessed thing. He had decided, in a rare fit of sentimentality, to make the egg for breakfast in order to cheer himself up. He remembered vividly that his mother would always make a soft boiled egg with little soldiers of toast for any of her three children if they were out of sorts - whether through sickness or a fit of temper. Ernest could see her in the kitchen, straight backed, her eagle eyes trained on the little three-minute egg timer. She would scoop the egg out of the boiling pot of water the second the last grain of sand slipped silently from the top to the bottom and sit it immediately in one of the delft blue eggcups she always used for the children.

They'd had chickens in those days. Before Charles had reached an age deemed old enough for the responsibility it had been Ernest's job to feed them. He had not liked them much with their sharp strutting feet, their pecking beaks and a profusion of unseemly droppings. But he had liked those comforting boiled eggs and the feeling of being maternally cared for.

Of course it was ridiculous that a man of seventy-five should suddenly feel like he wanted his mummy - especially one who had been dead the best part of forty years - but in the wake of his recent loss Ernest found himself craving the concept of someone being able to make everything all right with something as simple as a boiled egg and a few strips of toast.

But, as Pearl was fond of telling him, he needed to keep his strength up. And come hell or high water he would eat his egg and do as he was told. Then, he would sit back and wait for his children to call to wish him a Merry Christmas before getting ready for Pearl's little party. He might feel like a part of him had shriveled and died but he would not let that stop him from being there at the celebrations. His determination was absolute. Come what may, he would not rain on her parade.

The advantage, Joanna had quickly realized, in conceding that she and Brett and the children would attend Pearl's birthday lunch after all, could be found in the opportunity to avoid being overwhelmed by the Lucas family. It had been important, of course, for Joanna to make her point. But at the end of the day maybe it might just prove to be a win-win situation. Not only would her family pay her more respect and consideration from now on, she would also be released from the agonies of a protracted day at the Lucas's. Brett, the youngest of the tribe, seemed so unlike his parents and his siblings, to the point where it did not seem credible that they could indeed be related at all. Being obligated to go somewhere else in the middle of the day meant visiting his parents now - without all the rest of the family - for a quiet and dignified present opening session, where her children could be the center of attention.

Underneath it all, Joanna supposed there wasn't anything particularly objectionable about Jacob and Pam Lucas. They came from a similar socio-economic group to her own parents, owned their own home, kept it pretty neat and tidy, had raised their children to mind their manners and be in paid employment. Perhaps they could not be held entirely to blame for the fact that they were as boring as the wallpaper hanging in the lounge in which they now all sat. After all, they were a product of their generation. They'd been raised by people who had endured the hardships and rigors of two world wars; raised to crave normalcy, security and stability. One could excuse the fact that they chose to live the social life of a pair of hermits, worried endlessly about the state of the economy and panicked over the merest whiff of change. These were hardly criminal offences. It would all just be so much easier to bear if it didn't make for the dullest conversation topics in the history of conversation topics.

For people who had raised five children - and who now had a total of fifteen grandchildren - they also seemed strangely inept and unprepared to deal with those fifteen grandchildren. Connor, who busily sucked his pacifier as though it was life's elixir, couldn't have cared less about his current location and as such presented no problem to his grandparents. But Isabella - who regarded life as being purely for her pleasure and interest - perplexed the two of them to the extent that they did not seem to even know how to talk to her. The living room, stuffed to the rafters with more breakable objects than a China shop, sat like a minefield to an energetic and irrepressible three year old. Joanna found herself periodically closing her eyes and waiting for the sound of splintering glass.

To top it all off, Pam Lucas's ideas of Christmas gifts for her grandchildren were tantamount to being hideous. They offered not the slightest distraction to Isabella. Connor's gift was a knitted wooly hat that, by the time the weather turned cold again, would be too small for him. Isabella had received a knitted cardigan, made by Pam's own fair hand out of the most lurid candy pink wool imaginable. Joanna practically came down with a migraine every time she glanced at it. Why her mother-in-law could not have simply asked her what the children might like she did not know. The shops were crammed with beautiful presents the children would adore, all superbly tailored and crafted with quality. Why, oh why, could grandparents not see that the charm of homemade gifts was strictly limited, and as such should be strictly forbidden?

Margaret wondered where on earth Jim had got to. Time had marched on and they still had not made time to open their presents. They had decided to spend some time together with one another and give their own Christmas wishes and gifts and try to play happy families before the rest of the horde arrived.

Todd's impatience grew with waiting. He lurked in the lounge, hanging about by the tree, his inquisitive fingers straying now and then to investigate the likely contents of one package or another. Margaret feared there wouldn't be any surprise left by the time Jim showed up.

Sarah worked away in the kitchen. Margaret could hear her humming. She'd drawn up a frighteningly organized timetable that seemed to have provision for practically every eventuality and disaster but so far everything appeared to be going according to plan. The aroma of roasting chickens already filled the house and a gargantuan mountain of vegetables had been peeled and readied. The dining room furniture had been rearranged last night. The tables were already festooned with crisp white tablecloths, with Margaret currently engaged in the task of laying out the cutlery, the glassware and the silver name place cards Sarah had made. Margaret could only hope that Isabella was not tempted to yank at the corner of one of the tablecloths and send the whole lot crashing onto the floor.

Margaret had just entered the kitchen to tell Sarah that she'd finished and to say she would go and look for Jim when the kitchen door flew open. Jim strode in, weighted down by the finished doll's house, flicking the door closed with his foot.

"I was just coming to look for you," Margaret said. "Where have you been?"

Jim rolled his eyes. "I couldn't work out how to wrap the damn thing up."

"Silly man. Bring it into the lounge and I'll help you. It's present time now, anyway."

Sarah said, "I'll go and get Nan."

When at last they were gathered, Margaret, Jim, Todd, Sarah and Pearl, it seemed more like old times. Past cross words and recriminations vanished before the Christmas tree. Familial camaraderie hung in the air. Jim presided over the distribution of presents, enjoying his fatherly role. Pearl wore an expression of peaceful contentment. Todd, knowing there was benefit to be gained from being there and being happy, did his utmost to act like he wanted to be with them all instead of off somewhere vastly more interesting. Even Margaret's smiles were genuine and she looked relaxed.

Sarah watched them all as though not entirely part of the scene. She laughed when wrappers came off and gifts were revealed, she took part in the conversation, enjoyed receiving her presents but all the while she felt removed.

Her thoughts strayed to Cassie, whose Christmas Day had not yet begun, and who at this very moment probably slept off an unhealthy dose of Scottish hospitality. She thought of the last Christmas they had spent together, drinking wine, giggling and watching The Sound of Music. It had been freezing that day. Something had gone wrong with the heating in their flat. They'd sat, huddled under their duvets, waiting interminably for their turkey to cook, laughing at Cassie's dumb jokes. It seemed, now, like another lifetime ago.

Her thoughts then went to Michael. He would be at his parents' house of course, perhaps even now looking at the clock and trying to devise excuses to leave. She hoped it wasn't going too badly for him. Somehow, in the short time she'd been home, he had come to mean a great deal to her. In the same way that last Christmas seemed so long ago, so too did the day when she had first met Michael. The incident - calling him Nan's boyfriend - made her smile now, all prior embarrassment forgotten. If anyone had told her before she'd come home that she'd end up interested in a boyfriend of her grand-mother's, she would have told them they were crazy.

Only now, she was the crazy one.

Pearl sat in the most comfortable armchair in the lounge and found herself staying there much longer than she'd intended. As the lunch guests arrived in dribs and drabs, people kept coming to the lounge to see her so that she got cornered by every new person that arrived. She began to gain, quite strangely, a new appreciation for the Queen and what she must have to endure when similarly cornered by those who had come specifically for her benefit. Her face, unaccustomed to such a vigorous workout from smiling so much, had begun to feel tight. She hoped there would be a timely lull in the proceedings since her bladder had started to feel as constricted as her face.

At first, when only one or two people had arrived, there seemed to be a bit of confusion over whether people should be wishing her a Merry Christmas or saying, "Happy Birthday," and which order was most appropriate. After a while, when more of the family arrived, people seemed to simply reserve their Christmas wishes for each other and leave the birthday sentiments entirely to Pearl.

She couldn't help thinking that everyone had been so kind, bringing her little gifts and treating her like a cross between royalty and Dresden china. It appeared that by ushering in a new decade Pearl also now some-how commanded a higher degree of care and felicitation. She'd become like old piece of furniture that required more attention than something modern. Perhaps, Pearl thought, she wasn't an item of Dresden china at all, but a rare Chippendale chair. Ironically, she knew a Chippendale chair would fetch considerably more at auction that she would.

She'd received books and photo frames, a pot plant and some chocolates. She'd been given a bookmark, some quilted coat hangers and a set of coasters with scenic photos on them. Charles had bought her a delicate blue glass vase and Sarah a beautiful embroidered cushion, reminiscent of those Rosa had made. Edwina came with a framed print of a photograph taken of Pearl at

Edwina's own twenty-first, a photo Pearl never recalled having seen before. Michael came with a watercolor painting depicting Anne Hathaway's cottage in Stratford-upon-Avon, which would ever after remind her simultaneously of Shakespeare and of Michael. Ernest arrived with a sorry expression and the regret that, what with everything, he'd neglected to buy her a thing.

So the guests arrived until the lounge seemed bursting with people and noise, all the people in her life she treasured the most, and some of whom she tolerated because that was part of what being a family was all about. It reminded Pearl of the old adage about being able to choose your friends but not your relatives. Then, in the midst of the noise, Pearl suddenly thought of Jack, the essence of him coming to her with such clarity and unusual intensity that her earlier sense of equilibrium got momentarily thrown. She could not help but simply wish he could be there.

Michael found Sarah in the kitchen. To his surprise she was on her own. Earlier, when he had arrived, she had been surrounded by people and had greeted him with a shy smile and a demure, "Merry Christmas." He'd wondered whether there would be any time during the day when they would have the opportunity to speak privately. From his vantage point at the doorway he watched her for a moment or two as she arranged some decadent looking desserts onto serving platters. She'd pulled her hair severely back to keep it out of the way and he could see her cheeks were pink with exertion. She looked infinitely more attractive than any of the sweets she now manhandled.

"How's it going?" he asked with a grin.

She stopped working momentarily, looked up at him. She grinned back.

"Murder. I feel like somebody stole Christmas and transported me to a slave labor camp."

He crossed the room, approached her from behind, and slid his arms around her.

"Poor baby."

"How did things go this morning?"

He shrugged. "Not too bad. Mum and Dad pretended to be a bit put out because I wasn't staying for the traditional lunch. Underneath it all they were as relieved as I thought they'd be."

"I suppose it's selfish to want you here," she said. "Perhaps...I don't know. Perhaps they really did want you there."

"I doubt it. Christmas is only one day out of the year. We can catch up any time we want, only we never actually seem to."

"Maybe they simply feel like they need an excuse to see you. It's surprising how things as simple as tradition can provide the impetus for people to bridge gaps."

"Maybe," he said, reaching his hand out around her to scoop up a stray shard of chocolate. "Still, at the end of the day I wouldn't want to miss Pearl's birthday. Turning eighty is a once in a lifetime occasion. Besides, there'll be other Christmases. How are things going with you?"

"Good. Apart from the fact that I haven't had a moment's peace all day, things have gone very smoothly. Maybe once lunch is over I'll be able to relax."

"I hope so. You're a saint. Do you want some help?"

"Yes, please," she said, turning in his arms to look up at him, her eyes sparkling. "We'll need the chicken from your house, and then I don't suppose you could pop over to Nan's and bring over all the roast vegetables, could you? Now that I've finished with these desserts I'm just about to take the chickens out of the oven, so we'll have room to put everything in one place."

Michael saluted her. "Yes, ma'am. Right away, ma'am."

She scraped a bit of cream off the cake slice she'd been using and blobbed it on his nose.

"Enough cheek from you," she said, "or you won't get your Christmas present."

"Then I'll have to steal it from you now," he said, bending over to kiss her, and at the same time transfer the cream from his nose to hers.

She slapped him playfully on the arm. "No more," she said. "If I don't stay focused, none of us will get Christmas dinner. Off you go now."

Michael saluted again.

"Oh," she called, as he neared the door, "you couldn't do me another favor and find Todd, could you? I want to get the gravy underway. As stirrers go, I'd say he rates pretty highly."

"Will do," he said, before disappearing on his mission.

Eventually, with as many people avoiding work as there were those who were happy to help, the meal was ready. In the end they had decided to try to keep as many people seated for as long as possible rather than having a buffet that required everyone to jump up and down all the time. They simply did not have the space to accommodate a stampede. Instead an eclectic collection of serving bowls and spoons from the three households - from the Bells, from Pearl's and from Michael's - had been gathered together so that the meal could be roughly divided between the different areas of seated guests. That way, a bit of everything should be within easy reach of everyone.

These serving bowls were interspersed with condiments and bottles of wine. Once everyone had helped themselves and their glasses had been filled, Margaret nudged Jim into proposing a toast.

"Well," he said, looking around at everyone with a bemused expression on his face, as though confused either by what they were all doing there or amazed by the fact that so many people had been crammed into his dining room, "Merry Christmas, everyone. Glad you could all make it to help celebrate this Christmas Day, and of course Pearl's birthday too. Charles is going to say a few words about that matter after our lunch, but first, a big thank you to Margaret and Sarah for organizing today. So, before we tuck in to this fine looking meal, let's have a toast. To Christmas."

Everyone raised their glasses. "Merry Christmas," they all said to one another, with varying degrees of warmth. Some party guests looked rather more reluctant than others. For now, at least, everyone seemed on their best behavior.

"Good job," Margaret said to Jim as he sat down. "Now all we can hope is that everyone gets along."

Todd found himself sitting next to Uncle Ernest. He thought he'd have to pay Sarah back for inflicting yet more punishment on him later. Admittedly, on his other side he had Jason for company. But at this precise moment in time Jason talked with Uncle Charles - who was seated opposite - talked, Todd thought, like they were old friends.

"Good of you to come to the funeral, sonny," Ernest said in his ear.

Todd could smell the old man's breath, the mustiness of his ancient clothes. He tried desperately not to sneer. "That's okay," he replied. He would like to have added that he'd come only under complete duress and that only his ulterior motives had ultimately allowed him to give in and go.

Ernest stirred his gravy around with his fork, his appetite clearly lacking.

"I miss her like hell," he said, as though Todd had asked. "It seems like every month that goes by I end up with one friend less, with people popping their clogs left, right and centre. Never in a million years did I think Rosa would be one of them."

"Sorry," Todd mumbled around a mouthful of chicken. "Bummer."

Uncle Ernest looked at Todd as though he was the only person in the entire world who fully appreciated his situation.

"Yes," he said. "Bummer indeed."

Todd took a swig of his glass of wine. He was supposed to be having grape juice – had been given strict instructions to have only grape juice - but the champagne had been sitting so handily, and through the glass you couldn't tell one from the other anyway. He did not particularly like the taste of the champagne. On the other hand he hoped it might just make the presence of Uncle Ernest more tolerable, especially if he could down enough of it before he got caught.

"Jason," he said, elbowing his cousin.

Jason swung around. He looked a bit put out by the interruption.

"Hey, Todd," he said.

"What did you get for Christmas?"

Jason smirked. "Cool stuff. I got two hundred dollars worth of CD vouchers, a Blu-ray player for my room and a new set of skis. Of course I won't be able to test out the skis until winter, but I can wait. There's plenty to keep me busy in the meantime. What'd you get?"

Todd thought of his own poxy collection of Christmas presents. He'd received one solitary twenty-dollar music voucher, a new set of underpants, a t-shirt, and a miniscule box of chocolates.

"This and that," he said, turning his attention back to his meal.

Jason, freed from Todd's attention, said to Uncle Charles, "So you must have gone ballistic when you found out you didn't have to re-sit your driving test after all?"

Uncle Charles looked over at his brother who shoveled his Christmas dinner around his plate but nowhere near his mouth. He noticed Todd looked equally glum. Together they looked like a couple of extremely miserable bookends.

"I will admit to a momentary spurt of anger," Charles said evenly, "but at the end of the day no knowledge is truly wasted, is it? Besides, there's nothing wrong with even experienced drivers brushing up on their road safety."

"S'pose."

From this Charles divined that young Jason had no intention whatsoever of ever looking at the Road Code for the rest of his life once he'd passed his test.

"Would you like me to quiz you?" he offered. "After the lunch and before my little speech?"

"Would you? That would be awesome."

Charles thought that, at the very least, it would take his mind off the forthcoming speech that loomed like a leviathan in the deep.

Jason turned back to speak to Todd, leaving Charles momentarily stranded for conversation. On his right Edwina was in the middle of a deep discussion with Pearl. This gave Charles the opportunity to introduce himself to the young woman he'd discovered sitting on his left. She was, he gathered, some particular friend of David's. David busily talked across the table and seemed oblivious to his guest.

"Hello," he said. "I'm Charles. Charles Ferguson. I'm David's uncle."

The woman swiveled in her chair to get a better look at him giving Charles the chance to do exactly the same thing in return. She smiled shyly at him, as though meeting new people was an entirely new experience for her. Looking, Charles saw that she had a strangely homogeneous face, as though it had been purposely constructed by someone with immense skill and little imagination. Upon this face she wore an expression of dreamlike bewilderment. By contrast her hair, which fell with the appearance of feathers, had been dyed a startling burnished copper. Her eyes were the color of cinnamon. The overall effect, the contrast of one on the other, made determining her age next to impossible. Charles supposed she would have to be close to forty.

"Hello," she said quietly. "I'm Daphne."

"Pleased to meet you."

She smiled that same shy smile, but said nothing about reciprocating such a sentiment.

"You're a friend of David's then, I take it?"

She nodded, then in that same small voice which made Charles lean closer to her in order to hear, confessed, "Actually, we haven't known one another too long. A few weeks. He's befriended me, taken me under his wing."

"Has he just? That's good of him," Charles said lamely. He could not imagine a situation in which a person might need to derive that amount of assistance from a person such as he perceived David to be.

"I haven't been in the country long," Daphne said, as if this explained everything.

"Really? Where are you from?"

"Australia. Perth, to be exact."

"Perth? You are a long way from home, then. What's brought you our way? If you don't mind me asking?"

Her smile gained confidence. "Not at all. No, I'm a potter, and six months ago I came over here on holiday, to look around and see what sort of work is being done here. There's something about this country, the diversity of the scenery, the people, the fusion of cultures, which I liked immensely. When I got home and looked around at my work it seemed hollow and lacking in the sort of inspiration I could sense when I was here. So I packed up my troubles and made the move."

"How brave. I wonder though, how an Australian potter would come to know David? As far as I am aware he wouldn't know one end of a potter's wheel from another?"

She laughed, showing a collection of delicate teeth. "Through mutual friends. We met at a dinner party they put on. We just sort of hit it off."

"Really?" Charles said with a smile he hoped didn't betray his incredulity. "How nice."

Her gaze drifted away from his. "I wasn't sure I should accept his invitation for today to be honest. Being that it's such an important family day, I would hate to think I'd intruded."

Charles leaned over and patted her hand. "Nonsense," he said. "Any friend of David's is welcome, and it would be a crying shame for you to have spent Christmas all alone."

"Thank you," she said.

David stuck his nose into the conversation. "How are you Uncle Charles?" he said, his voice filled with its trademark swagger.

"Well thanks, David. Yourself?"

David grinned. "Fabulous. Couldn't be better. How are Peter and Rosemary?"

"Good I think. I haven't heard from either of them today, but then, with the time difference, it's early yet. I expect that later, after I'm back home, they'll both call."

"It's years since I've seen either of them. Maybe even twenty years."

Charles thought, with a pang of regret that he hadn't seen them in a dozen years himself.

"Time flies, doesn't it?" Daphne said, looking at him with a sympathetic gaze, as though she'd known Peter and Rosemary all her life.

David turned and called to Sheila across the table. "When was the last time you saw Peter and Rosemary?"

Sheila patted her mouth with a napkin. "I don't know. I guess we must have seen Peter about ten years ago, when we went on that trip to America with the boys. As for Rosemary, well, I can't rightly recall. Of course we've been to England, but never to where she lives. It's right in the depths of the countryside somewhere. It's not," Sheila said, as she reached for more chicken, "exactly on the beaten track."

The sound of a cell phone pierced the air, playing the theme tune to *The Simpsons*. Reuben, sitting sullenly beside Sheila, sprang into life. The sound of the phone jolted him out of some sort of stasis and back to life.

"How's it?" he said as he answered.

"Reuben? It's Danielle. Am I interrupting anything?"

Reuben looked down at his rapidly congealing meal, then around at the relatives with whom he sat in close proximity, the median age of which probably came in at about forty-three.

"Doubt it," he said.

He scraped back his chair, and went to take the call outside. As he reached the door he heard his father say in a loud voice, "Bloody kids. What's the world coming to?" To Brett, John said, "Now if it was a business call I could understand the need for the interruption but I'd give a penny to a pound that it's some girl or another."

Brett practically sniggered. "Well, we were all young once, I suppose," he philosophized, as though he neared John's age, or perhaps even Methuselah's.

John looked at him with suspicion. "So, how's business?"

Brett gave an elaborate shrug. "Personally, it couldn't be better. There's plenty happening and I've got some fish frying. There is a rumor, though, that the business might be sold out from under us. Some bloody overseas interest or another."

"Oh?" said John, his eyebrows shooting up. "That doesn't sound too great. Different mind set, these foreign bods. Like to do things in ways we just don't understand."

"I know. As it is, the place could probably do with a shake-up. Some of the management practices leave a bit to be desired if you ask me. They're just not progressive enough. Everything is *reactive* rather than *proactive*. What the place needs isn't new owners, but better management."

"So what are you going to do about it? Just sit back and let it all happen?"

"Hardly," Brett said, taking a fortifying swig of champagne. It hit the back of his throat like velvet. He smiled inwardly, thinking how clever he had been to engineer the best bottle down their end of the table. It helped him avoid thinking about the looming crisis at work.

"You should consider leaving all that car selling nonsense behind," John said. He waved a hand to silence Brett's impending protest. "Oh, I'm not saying you're not good at it. Of course you are. It's just that a talent like yours is wasted on something so mediocre. You ought to be setting your sights a bit higher."

Brett's eyes narrowed even further. "It sounds to me like you have something in mind."

"I might just have," John said cryptically. He glanced from side to side like a spy hiding a secret of the utmost magnitude. "We should talk more. After lunch."

Brett studied John's face. "Right," he said, drawing the word out as if to underscore his comprehension of the situation.

"John, could you pass those beans?" Sheila asked across the table.

John looked at the bloated face of his wife and felt momentarily tempted to say something.

"Please," she said, her tone firm.

He reached for the bowl, a hideous rose covered creation that made him cringe almost as much as his wife's overeating.

"Thank you," Sheila said. She turned her attention back to Joanna. "As I was saying, she's having the most fabulous dress sale at the moment. Admittedly it is last season's fashions, but she is such a good designer, such classic styles, that I don't see it matters a jot."

"I should go and check it out. I guess I'll have to try to find some time when I can go without the children. Trouble is, over the holidays there isn't any kindy. By the time that starts up again, the sale will be well and truly over."

"Get your mother to baby-sit," Sheila suggested. "It's just the sort of thing a grandmother should be doing for her grandchildren."

Joanna's mouth went into a line. "You'd have better luck persuading the average politician to change parties."

"Oh, I don't know, dear. Recently, that's all they ever seem to do. Where is Connor, by the way?"

"Upstairs. Hopefully still asleep in Mum and Dad's bedroom. I assume we'll hear him if he wakes up. He's got lungs the size of bellows. And of course Isabella's sitting down by Nan. How she managed to wangle that privilege, I don't quite know. I suppose I should check she's behaving herself."

"I'll ask, shall I?" Sheila suggested. She leaned across the empty space to which Reuben had yet to return. "Jason? Can you ask down the table how Isabella is?"

Jason, who looked like he'd been asked to run to the bottom of the South Island with the message, turned nonetheless to Todd. "We need to find out what Isabella's up to. For Joanna."

Todd, his cheeks pink and his eyes beginning to look glazed over said, "Right-o." He swiveled to speak to Ernest, who seemed to have slumped in his chair and gave every appearance of being ready to fall dead asleep.

Todd elbowed him for good measure. "Uncle Ernest, can you ask down your end of the table if Isabella is okay?"

"What? What? Isabella? Isabella who? Oh, *Isabella*. Of course."

Ernest leaned over the table toward Pearl. "How's the youngster doing?"

Pearl smiled at him, gently, as though she knew exactly what he'd just been thinking and feeling.

"She seems to be doing fine. Model behavior, in fact." Pearl turned to Isabella. "You're being a very good girl, aren't you?

Isabella nodded wordlessly. Glancing down, Pearl couldn't help notice with a smile that Isabella had accumulated a smattering of garish green peas in her lap. They sat on the fabric of her pink dress like incongruous spots of chicken pox. She also wore on her face an expression of almost adult-like solemnity, as though afraid she might make some terrible *faux pas*.

"Are you all right, sweetie?"

Isabella looked up at Pearl, her eyes pools of innocence flecked with insistence.

"I need to go to the toilet," she said. "Quick!"

Dessert had been a serve-yourself affair with the sweet selection having been laid out on the unusually cleared kitchen bench. On its surface chocolate logs competed for space with fruit salad, cheesecake, chocolate eclairs, pavlova and, for the traditionalists, the Christmas pudding. Sarah had managed to find time to make one, richly concocted with mixed fruit and brandy.

Most guests were already groaning at the seams from their first course. Yet after a small lull, during which plates were whisked away, people seemed ready enough to investigate the desserts. They duly descended like a plague of locusts to pretty much demolish the lot.

Sarah decided to spend the time while people jockeyed for position to help themselves by making some sense of the kitchen. Michael volunteered to help. Together they scraped plates, rinsed bowls, and fed dishes and cutlery into the dishwasher. Wine glasses and the more delicate serving dishes had been left aside to be washed in the sink later. By the time they were finished they'd filled the dishwasher and the crowd around the kitchen table had thinned. Sarah filled the dishwasher dispenser with its caustic powder and flicked the machine on before joining Michael to select a variety of the slim pickings that remained.

Jim had directed guests that they take yet more dirty dishes out to the kitchen after dessert then make their way through to the lounge. In the fullness of time celebrations would continue with a few words for Pearl. Todd, with any luck, would have remembered his directive to set up the photo board that Sarah and Michael had made so that, while they waited, guests could reflect on the life and times of Pearl Hamilton.

Being one of the last to sit down with their dessert meant that Sarah and Michael were also one of the last to join the crowd in the lounge. They arrived to find standing room only, so they threaded their way across the room, to perch themselves on the wide window sills behind the chairs. A buzz of conversation filled the air and for a few moments Sarah and Michael sat shoulder to shoulder, watching everyone as though they weren't somehow part of the scene themselves.

On the far side of the room Margaret, David and Sheila stood together peering at the photo board. Seeing fragments of the past - and perhaps recalling better times - seemed to momentarily allow the siblings to put aside their current differences. They looked and pointed and even laughed as they remembered times gone by. Behind David, Daphne stood, holding her body as if she wasn't entirely sure where to put it. Every so often David would turn and try to include her in their conversation but her nervously darting gaze suggested she did not feel entirely comfortable in this situation.

Pearl sat on the sofa, flanked on either side by Edwina and Ernest. Ernest wore a glazed expression, as though some time during the last couple of hours his mind had simply drifted off somewhere else. Edwina and Pearl were talking away as though the years through which they had lost touch had never occurred.

Jim sat in one of the chairs, with Isabella on his knee. She had fallen in love with her doll's house and now considered her grandfather to be almost her most favorite person. She busily tried to slot her fingers through the gaps between the buttons on his shirt so that she could tickle his chest and make him laugh. He in turn wiggled his fingers into her sides which made her laugh.

Closer to Sarah and Michael, Charles sat in a huddle with Jason, busily feeding him question after question about the Road Code. Charles, it seemed, had done a much more competent job in learning all the detail than Jason had. This realization seemed to make Jason grow paler by the second.

Behind them stood Reuben. His face suggested that he was undergoing some sort of awful torture, and made it more than clear he would rather be anywhere else right at this moment in time. He seemed unable to find anyone of interest to talk to whatsoever. His hand kept straying to his pocket containing his cell phone as though willing it to ring.

By the door, Todd lurked. Sometime during the last half hour Tom and Gerry had arrived. They were vainly trying to engage Todd in conversation but Todd seemed strangely out of it. His gaze kept sidling off, over to Jason, and he did not seem to be able to think of anything to say to his old friends.

Brett and John stood beside Sarah and Michael. They were deep in conversation. Joanna had vanished. Sarah could only assume she'd gone off to tend to Connor somewhere upstairs. Left to their own devices, the men reverted to their favorite topic of conversation - namely money.

"It's a great scheme," John was saying. "I've thoroughly researched it. There doesn't seem to be a loophole in sight. I've had my lawyer crawl all over it and he can't find anything wrong with it either. You should take a look. Get in on the ground floor while the going is good. If my estimates are even half as promising as they seem, you'd be able to double your money in next to no time."

Michael turned to Sarah and whispered, "There's something about those two that reminds me of my brother. Do you know the very best way to double your money?"

Sarah shook her head.

He grinned. "Fold it in half and put it straight back in your pocket."

At length Charles stood up in front of everyone. He began to cough politely. A trail of "Shh, shh," snaked around the room and within moments everyone had quietened. Sarah saw Joanna appear at the door, with Connor balanced on her hip. Jim had remembered he'd been charged with recording the day's events for posterity's sake and stood by her side with the camera at the ready.

"Well," Charles said, clearing his throat, "unaccustomed as I am to public speaking, the honor of saying a few words about my dear sister Pearl has fallen to me. Luckily, because I'm not used to giving speeches, this one will be mercifully short."

"Here, here," David bellowed.

Sheila elbowed him in the ribs. He winced theatrically.

"As I was saying," Charles said, sending his nephew a reproachful glance, "I am honored to be asked to make this little speech, honored because I feel I have been a very blessed soul by having Pearl as my sister, honored because there seems a certain privilege in the fact that Ernest and Pearl and I can be together to share her special day.

"So, what can a person say to mark the occasion of someone turning eighty? What a grand old age? What an achievement? Simply, 'Happy Birthday'? Well, of course we all can and do say 'Happy Birthday' to you, Pearl, but when it comes to considering the amount of years, it occurred to me that perhaps the number of those years does not matter as much as the *quality* of those years. We none of us get to choose how long we live, nor in most cases the manner in which we die. So it falls to us then, to concentrate on how we live our lives.

"When I think of Pearl, and the way she has lived her life, there seems to me to be plenty to celebrate. I looked earlier at that beautifully prepared montage of photos and mementoes from Pearl's eighty years. They have been years filled with many happy times. Pearl has raised her family, supported a husband, been a true and loyal sister, and to others, simply a good friend. She has worked diligently at those tasks that befell her, and has contributed to the richness of the lives of her family and friends. She has a decent heart, a caring heart, a loving heart.

"Now, far be it from me to make this speech seem too funereal, as though by looking back we are summing up the life of someone who is no longer with us. It just seems to me that by recognizing the past - and Pearl's contribution to it - we can better celebrate and appreciate the person Pearl is. And perhaps, in some small way, we can determine that we too will continue to live our lives in a manner that helps rather than hinders those with whom we walk this earthly path.

"So, Pearl, congratulations from the bottom of my heart, for this day, your birthday, and for a life well lived. Well," he said with a smile, "at least so far, anyway."

Everyone applauded, before Charles led the way in singing a round of "Happy Birthday". Pearl sat in her chair and beamed. Margaret dashed out of the room and came back carrying a small coffee table on which lay Pearl's magnificent birthday cake, and a knife for her to cut it with. As Pearl picked up the knife and ran it cleanly from the cake's centre to its circumference, people cheered.

"Thank you everyone," Pearl said.

"Speech, speech," David called out.

Pearl climbed to her feet and stepped around the coffee table.

"Well, you know, I think I might just make one," she said. "It hadn't really occurred to me to say a few words, but now, I think I might. After all, it's not every day a person turns eighty, and has their family around them." She drew a breath. "Firstly, of course, there are certain people to thank. Charles, naturally for his lovely speech, all lies, but lovely anyway. To Sarah and Margaret for putting on today's party, and also to Sarah and Michael for constructing this lovely photo board for us all to enjoy. And to you all for sweet gifts, which I will treasure. Thank you all, and thank you above all for coming to share my special day.

"It's always been somewhat interesting to have a birthday on Christmas Day. I know there are others who share the same day, who do not like it. It is not their special day alone. There's the problem of whether to give one gift or two, and everyone else gets to enjoy themselves as much as you do, sometimes more. But this has never bothered me unduly. Indeed it is something of a privilege to share my birthday with the Savior, even though these days they seem to think he was probably born in about April." She laughed. "Everything changes, even Jesus' birthday, and my, have I seen some changes in my lifetime. Not just the obvious technological ones, most of which I have not kept up with anyway, but moral and ethical ones too. What was unacceptable in my day often is more than acceptable today. And while I'm not always sure these changes are entirely for the better, there's little doubt that nothing stays the same.

"My life went from daughter to sister, to wife, to mother, to grandmother, to widow, a gradual, sometimes happy, sometimes sad transition over the course of my eighty years. People have come and gone from my life, most significantly my dear husband Jack, without whom the day is not as complete. I miss him still, but in spite of this have had to learn to adapt without him. But, as Charles very relievingly pointed out, my life is not quite spent yet, and neither am I immune from change.

"I have considered of late that more change is required. The way I live my life at the moment is not entirely where I want to be. Ernest's dear friend

Rosa helped me see that old age doesn't have to mean an old attitude. So I am pleased to be able to tell you all about the next phase of my life, while you are all here together.

"I have decided to move out." In spite of the odd gasp, Pearl continued quickly to say, "Jim and Margaret have been very kind in having me to stay, but I have found myself, how would you say, new digs? In spite of my earlier protestations I have discovered that communal living for the elderly need not be as dire as I had pictured. And to this end I have purchased a unit at Lambton Park, and am to move there in the New Year. It's Rosa's unit, by the way, Ernest. I hope you don't mind. I sort of figured you'd rather have me there than some stranger. For me, I will be content to live in the same space as someone who I knew but briefly, but who helped me to make a change.

"So that's it," Pearl said. "Thank you for coming. I love you all."

The day wore on and the temperature in the room began to steadily increase. Todd had had to dive off to relieve the contents of his stomach after having secretly imbibed too much champagne. Joanna and Brett had gone home and others were beginning to make moves to leave. Michael suggested he and Sarah escape for a while. They went outside to sit on the park bench in the garden.

It was a beautiful day and the late afternoon sun slanted across the garden. The tree beside the park bench cast a friendly and welcoming shadow across where they sat.

"Interesting day," Michael said.

"I'll say. I still can't get over the fact that Nan is moving away."

"Good on her, though, don't you think?"

Sarah nodded. "I knew she wasn't entirely happy with the way things were. I only hope this new move will be all she wants it to be."

"I'd say there's every chance it will be. Your grandmother is not the sort of person to make decisions lightly."

Sarah gazed out over the garden. "I suppose it goes to show that there's always hope, somehow. That life, while you live it, is never over. There's always another bend in the road if you have the courage to see what's around it."

"True. It's funny though, looking at your family today, about how similar some of the issues are that we deal with."

"Oh?"

"I was thinking it's a bit like a bell curve, if you'll pardon the pun. If the top of the bell curve is half way through your life, a median age of perhaps forty-one or two, then those on either side of it would be, say, Brett and John. Look at the pair of them, driven by money and the desire to succeed. That's all there is to them at this point in their lives. But what happens when you move out from the middle of life a notch?"

Sarah shrugged. "I'm not altogether sure."

"Well, look at David and your cousin. Reuben, is it? One is twenty, the other sixty, and yet each of them is as obsessed with women as the other. David with all his collection of girlfriends, and Reuben, from what you told me, exactly the same way. How many furtive phone calls did you see him take over the course of the day?"

"Five, maybe six?"

"Yup. And it seemed obvious he wasn't talking to any guys. Not by his body language anyway."

"So, who's next?"

"Your Uncle Charles and your other cousin Jason. Both worrying about their driver's licenses; one on getting his, the other on keeping it. Of course, Charles did find out that his worrying was premature, that the rules have been changed so that he doesn't have to concern himself with that issue as early as you used to, but it's still coming."

Sarah looked at him with curiosity. "You're right. I hadn't thought about that before. Who's next?"

Michael considered this. "What about Todd and Ernest?"

"Todd and Uncle Ernest? I can't think of anything they'd have in common."

"What about friends? Poor old Ernest can't seem to keep his friends for love nor money, what with them dying one by one. As for Todd, his problem is that he doesn't seem to like the friends he's got. I've seen him at school, you know, trying to wheedle his way into the 'in' group and strenuously trying to distance himself from poor old Tom and Gerry."

Sarah laughed. "I didn't think I'd hear you being charitable about Tom."

He shrugged. "It's just a phase she's going though. And I can't help it if I'm so irresistibly attractive, can I?"

Sarah made a face, and nudged him. "I think I should have got you a big hat for Christmas. Something large enough to fit your big head. Who else? Who else can you think of to fit on your bell curve?"

He thought. "I don't know. I suppose if you really thought about it you could find similarities even between people as separated by age as Pearl and little Isabella, but to be honest I don't know what they would be."

Sarah pictured poor Nan and all her washing and Isabella and her wet pants. "I can," she said. "So, if you're so smart, then, what's the point to all this theorizing?"

"I'm not sure. I'm not that smart. I suppose it's a bit like Charles's words about the quality of life. Perhaps it's as simple - and as complex - as trying to be content in all circumstances, no matter what your stage of life. The thing about life is, it's all about what happens on the way. That's not to say you should never consider your destination, but your destination in not something that is part of life, it's part of death."

"That seems a bit morbid."

"Not really. It's like Pearl said. It all comes down to attitude. Maybe you need to have the right attitude about both life and death, to know what you think about both."

"Maybe. In fact, probably. I suppose what I'd been thinking about when Nan said she'd be moving lay more along the lines of how that would affect everybody else. Especially Mum. Maybe if she's got one less thing to think about - one less person to worry about - she'll become freer to deal with her own situation."

"You might be right. I hope you are."

"She's already talking about the idea of going back into the workforce, or at least perhaps training toward some new career. That's got to be a good thing, don't you think?"

"Absolutely."

Sarah studied her feet. "I have been worried about them, as you know. Not just Mum, but Dad too, and the state of their marriage. I can only hope that a change of circumstances for them, and particularly for Mum, might help them to become closer again."

"Tricky thing, marriage. It doesn't come naturally. It's something that has to be worked at. It seems to me like a balancing act, having to find both middle ground and common ground to get through." Michael picked up her hand. "Do you think you'd consider getting married?"

Sarah laughed. "Are you offering?"

He smiled. "Maybe."

Sarah rolled her eyes and glanced quickly away. "Think of the wedding. Think of the hassle. Organizing a wedding would be more difficult than Columbus discovering the New World."

Michael's smile turned into a grin. "Or harder than Neil Armstrong reaching the moon."

"Or Hillary making it to the summit of Everest."

Michael said, "Don't forget Sherpa Tenzing. He made it, too."

Sarah laughed again. "No, good old Sherpa Tenzing. Can't forget him."

They fell silent for a moment then Michael said, "So you wouldn't consider it? Marriage, I mean?"

Sarah looked up at him. "You mean with you?"

He nodded almost imperceptibly.

"You know," she said, "I just very well might."

THE BELL CURVE

At age 4	success is ....not wetting your pants
At age 12	success is ....having friends
At age 16	success is ....having a driver's license
At age 20	success is ....having sex
At age 35	success is ....having money
At age 50	success is ....having money
At age 60	success is ....having sex
At age 70	success is ....having a driver's license
At age 75	success is ....having friends
At age 80	success is ....not wetting your pants

Want to find out more about The Bell Curve?
Sign up for Keitha's newsletter and receive exclusive
Behind the Scenes bonus content

www.keithasmith.co.nz

And, if you have enjoyed this book,
please consider leaving a review at Amazon.com
It would be most appreciated.